December 2023

To Lily, with all best wishes,

Michael

GW00771365

The Copyists

Charleston, SC
www.PalmettoPublishing.com

The Copyists
Copyright © 2023 by Michael Pratt

First Edition

Hardcover ISBN: 979-8-8229-1363-9
Paperback ISBN: 979-8-8229-1364-6
eBook ISBN: 979-8-8229-1365-3

The Copyists

MICHAEL PRATT

Table of Contents

Acknowledgements

I must borrow a phrase that has acquired a new meaning to me in the two and a half years of the crafting of this tale: it takes a village, in my case maybe a full-sized town. Many friends, relatives and acquaintances have spent time reading and sharing thoughts about the manuscript, and they all have given feedback that was put to work. They are: Scott Burnham, Gabriel Crouch, Wendy Heller, Sarah Ellison, Allison Spann, Wendy Young, Jack Hill, Terry Desser, David Madole and Arnie and Peggy Cohen.

My developmental editor William Boggess took me patiently through the advice needed by a rookie novelist.

My daughter Emily's feedback was always to the very point, and always trustworthy.

Finally to my wife Marty—I could fill pages on the topic of what I owe her in the writing of this book and the writing of life itself. Through the ups and downs she has been there, with love, with cheers, and sometimes tears over memories that I tapped for Lisa and Stefan. She kept my train on the rails and moving forward up the steep climbs. My gratitude is boundless to the love of my life.

FOR *Marty* AND *Emily*

Foreword

In the weaving of this tale of...historical fiction? fictional history?... I've endeavored to place enough real people and real events in the right places and times so that those familiar with the details of Mozart's life will be in a familiar landscape. I did my best to report actual historical events (with maybe a little fleshing out), I filled in some gaps in possible historical events (like the premiere of the last three symphonies), and I plain made up numerous other events and people.

The one truth that I hope is always present is that of the miracle of Mozart's music and how it parallels the miracle of human love. The two are the same for me, and that is something I have always sought to share, through performing and teaching. And now with The Copyists.

"Time runs from present to past"
—Zen Master Dogen (1200-1253)

Overture — Prodigies

October 1762
Vienna

HIS FEET DANGLED from the stool while his tiny fingers flew over the keyboard with unbelievable speed and accuracy, never once glancing down because a handkerchief covered his eyes. Wolfgang Amadeus Mozart, age six.

His audience, stunned into silence by the tiny boy, was no less than the royal family of the Austrian empire and their invited guests at this command performance in the Mirrors Room of Schönbrunn Palace. When Wolfgang finished with an even more virtuosic work by his father, the audience roared in approval.

Anna Maria, or Nannerl, Wolfgang's older sister, had begun the afternoon concert, performing on the clavier with grace and poise far beyond her ten years. But when the little boy appeared, first showing his polished command of the violin while accompanied by their father then switching to the dazzling solos on the clavier, it was clear that Papa Leopold saw his male child as the main course of the family act.

At the conclusion of the concert, Empress Maria Therese let her children mingle with the musical siblings. During the happy melee that followed, little Wolfgang proposed marriage to the seven-year-old Grand

Duchess Marie Antoinette, then surprised all by hopping onto the lap of the empress herself to give her a kiss.

Among the guests was a child with no interest in joining the fun. She had eyes only for the magical-sounding clavier. During the performance, perched on her father's lap, she was totally enthralled with the music of the Mozarts. At four years of age, she had rich auburn tresses framing her face and wore a white satin bow in her hair to match her lacy dress. Her father looked prosperous; her mother, significantly younger than her father, also with lustrous chestnut hair, was just visibly pregnant.

After the royals glided from the room, the family rose to leave. As they made their way to the middle aisle, their child veered off, running to the clavier. With a single finger, she began to pick out the tune she had just heard little Wolfgang play, note perfect and in time. Alarmed by the sound, her father walked briskly to the girl and firmly led her away. He barked at her, "Elisabetta, that was very naughty to play the royal instrument!"

Her face fell, and she seemed about to cry. Then her lower lip poked out, and she replied with trembling voice, "But that little boy did!"

"That's different," the father said with some exasperation. "He was invited."

"Why can't I be invited?" the child persisted.

"Little countesses just don't do that," he pronounced firmly.

Her mother was watching. "Karl," she said, "she just played a complete melody from the concert. After hearing it once."

The father stopped abruptly and responded with surprise, "Indeed."

Chapter 1 — Changes of Fortune

October 2017
Vienna

THE FRAGMENTS OF music began to murmur softly in the fearful darkness. The shards slowly coalesced into patterns, then he recognized the familiar sound of violins, a sad and lovely throbbing. Other than that, he was in an empty, blank medium, floating in what could have been liquid, except he was aware of taking breaths of air.

He then remembered that the music he was hearing was an aria by Handel—a lament sung by a character, Ariodante, who has been betrayed by his beloved. He was conducting the opera from the harpsichord, and it was the last thing he heard before he fell. The piercing beauty of Handel's setting of the mournful text had stabbed him in his heart, as had his own wife's betrayal and desire for a divorce, revealed only a few days ago. Then the heart pain became literal; he stopped playing, clutching at the iron vise around his chest. He heard the chaotic clatter of the harpsichord keys as he pitched forward, but he slipped into blackness before he hit the floor.

Stefan heard a door open and pushed his eyelids up. A thin, balding-but-youngish man in a white smock was reading a chart. Stefan became aware of the number of tubes entering his body at various points, along with the beep of the cardiac monitor. His first coherent thought formed, *I'm in the hospital, so I didn't die.*

The young surgeon spoke briskly. "Good to see you awake, Maestro Radowitz. Yes, I have had the pleasure of hearing some of your Vienna performances. Please, you need not try to speak. To anticipate your questions, you are in Vienna Central Hospital, in the cardiac care section. You had a heart attack while you were performing at the Theater an der Wien. You had open heart surgery to repair two arteries and spent a few hours on the heart-lung machine. You were brought in a day and a half ago." He smiled ruefully. "It was a close thing. The emergency service saved you. But I think you will be fine."

Stefan closed his eyes once more, trying to comprehend. For all the impact the words had on the stunned and foggy patient, the surgeon may have been reading a recipe. But an urgent thought came, a name which he tried to mouth. "Ka…trina…"

"Yes, your daughter knows and arrived in Vienna from London a few hours ago. She has not left your side, except she just excused herself for the WC. Ah, she's here."

Katrina was almost as tall as her father at six feet and had his wheat-colored hair down her back and his fair complexion. Her eyes were red and puffy from crying, but joy was on her face upon seeing her father awake. He reached for her but was restrained by the several tubes that were attached to him. "Oh, Daddy," she squeaked, almost leaping across the room to take his face in her hands. "I thought I had lost you," she whispered, planting a lingering kiss on his forehead.

"Kat," he croaked, finding a shred of voice, managing to lift his hand enough to graze her arm.

The surgeon said, "Maestro, you now have a stent in one artery and a bit of an artery from your leg in another location. The operation was long but fairly routine, and your recovery should be as well. You'll be here probably four to five days, but the staff will have you on your feet tomorrow. It's important that you begin to move."

He put a reassuring hand on Stefan's arm. "Your incision will have to heal first, but you can probably resume performing in maybe three months. Until then, no lifting or anything strenuous."

"What about going home?" said Katrina.

"Let's get some rehab done. Plan on staying in Vienna for about a month, then we'll take stock. Maybe a nice train ride to London when you're ready. I'm afraid flying must wait, around six months."

———

The fog from the anesthesia lifted the next day, and Stefan found some of his voice. Kat arrived midmorning and found him sitting in a chair. His first words were, "Does your mom know?"

"Well, of course she does."

He raised his eyebrows, *Well?*

Katrina drew a breath and released it. "She's devastated. She said it was her fault. She also said that she would come to Vienna if you want but would understand if you don't."

Stefan looked at the ceiling and said nothing. There was no possibility that he could cope with the pain of seeing Hannah.

Katrina then asked gently, "Do you blame her?"

After a moment he said, "She didn't plug up my arteries with plaque. But finding out about the affair with James...didn't help. Then having to conduct an opera that's about betrayal... didn't help. The text of the aria we were in... 'Enjoy yourself in the arms of your beloved'...with the violins sobbing..." His eyes closed tightly for a moment, and Katrina put her hand lightly on his bandaged chest.

"I talked to my professors and told them they won't be seeing me much anytime soon. You won't go through this solo."

Stefan looked at her with moistening eyes. He had begun to wonder how he was to manage what lay ahead without Hannah, and he was flooded with gratitude to hear this from his only other family member.

On his release, Stefan moved to a hotel and Katrina booked herself next door, and a month passed with Kat present at every physical therapy session and much time in between. Stefan reveled in her extended company; he had often been an absentee father and husband over the years with his concert and opera appearances on the continent. This was a factor in his and Hannah's drifting apart, he knew. Kat's presence helped to ease his heartache and anger.

There was a torrent of communications from well-wishers from the European musical world, from his conducting students at the Royal College of Music to musicians in Vienna. Some even followed up with a second message, but by the end of a month things were quiet, and he was cleared by his surgeon to return home via train, first to Brussels then London.

On the train Katrina asked him, "I've not wanted to bother you about this, but don't you have some upcoming gigs to deal with?"

"Sure, but my manager has been in touch with them all, and things look at least hopeful."

"Hey, they must actually like you!"

"Everybody except the Vienna State Opera and the new *Marriage of Figaro* production. All quiet on that front."

"A new *Figaro* production for an international debut. Plenty of motivation for physical therapy!"

"Well, the contract isn't signed yet, and I haven't heard from them. Just slow, I hope, not reluctant."

The day after they both got settled in London (Hannah had moved in with her lover), they were having lunch at Stefan's when the doorbell rang. It was a delivery of a massive and gaudy flower display.

"Do I have you to thank for this, Kat?"

"Wish I could say yes. There's a card."

Opening the small envelope, Stefan read, "From the General Director of the Vienna State Opera, with all best wishes for a rapid recovery."

"That's some get well card," said Katrina drily.

"A touch of overkill, I'd say. Not a good sign."

An hour later Stefan's mobile rang, displaying his agent's number. With a sinking feeling he answered. Katrina heard one half of the conversation. "Hi...yes...yes..." A long pause, then in a darker tone "Really...yes...Well that would explain the flowers they sent me. More like something you'd expect at a gangster's funeral."

After he hung up, Kat said softly, "Dad?"

"The State Opera. In consideration of my health and need for recuperation time, they have made another guest appointment for the *Figaro* in the autumn. Said they would keep me in mind for future projects."

"Oh, Daddy…"

"The flowers meant 'goodbye and good luck with everything.'" His head hung low. "All the lit on bypasses says I should be back in full by autumn. But…risk-management rules these days. Wow, they timed everything perfectly. Waited for me to get home, to the second."

Katrina wore a steely expression. "Daddy?"

Stefan looked at her. Katrina pronounced, "Fuck 'em. You'll get well in your own time and return to Vienna on your terms."

He felt his smile muscles. She could always do that.

With a fierce Katrina standing watch, and his own fierce desire to conduct again, Stefan threw himself into physical therapy. His agent reported that most signs were positive. Nevertheless Stefan felt the loss of the *Figaro* production keenly; conducting at the great Staatsoper had been a dream of many years. That and the still-burning crush of Hannah's departure made for some dark days. He was grateful to have the PT sessions to give him something other than his losses to focus on.

Within six weeks he resumed a light teaching load at the Royal College of Music. One day Katrina arrived at his flat to discover a new worktable set up and her father whittling away with a small, obviously sharp knife at the tip of a long feather. There was what looked to be a stack of thick parchment lined with music staves and two bottles of black ink. Next to them was a shaker with holes in the top. There were facsimiles of some of the many manuscript scores from the Royal College library, and on the top was a Mozart piano concerto.

"You know they have computer programs that can do really nice copies of anything," she said, teasing.

"Where's the art in that?" Stefan shot back. "I was just looking at this Mozart facsimile and thinking how incredibly fast he must have been able to copy with quill and ink, and yet it's still readable. I started poking around and there's a string-instrument shop off Oxford Street that said on their website they had all this stuff. My plan is to make a copy of this score and try to make it look like Mozart's hand. Then if I ever get to play it, I can say I'm playing off Mozart's manuscript, once removed."

"Well, you always said you felt you'd have been happier in the eighteenth century."

"Did I say that?" He paused. "Yeah, I guess it's true. I still find it easy to picture him in Vienna. Don't know if I ever told you this, but I have a strange ritual of always visiting his burial site at St. Marx park when I'm there."

Katrina's eyes widened. "Really? Do you talk to him?"

"Well...yes."

"Does he ever talk back?"

"Wiseass. But...when I perform his music, I do sometimes think I can feel a presence there, an almost tangible connection. I probably share that fantasy with many other musicians. But, no, he's yet to say anything."

Stefan went back to sharpening his quill.

Chapter 2 — Vienna, Again and Again

AFTER SIX MONTHS Stefan performed a concert at the Royal College that had been arranged as a welcome back, and his Beethoven's First Piano Concerto performance was warmly received by the familiar audience. His energy had greatly improved, though he still had to nurse himself daily with protein and carbohydrate snacks along with his cholesterol medications.

He took a call from his agent, who had been successfully rebuilding Stefan's diary. The call today was particularly welcome news.

"Ready to go back to Vienna?"

"You know the answer to that, Colin!" Stefan said, elated. Even though his last visit had been traumatic, he loved Vienna above all the musical centers of Europe. Home of Beethoven, Schubert, Brahms, Bruckner, Mahler, and, most importantly to Stefan, Mozart.

"Please tell me it's Mozart."

"OK. It's Mozart, Stefan. It's even at Schönbrunn Palace, in the Great Hall of mirrors. Thirty-first of October 2018"

Stefan was speechless. This was the very room in which the six-year-old Mozart played for Empress Maria Therese and her family.

"It's some kind of high-roller benefit. Your friend Julya Moeck got the gig for you. She told me not to give you any of the details; said she wanted to tell you herself."

Julya was a distinguished violinist, the first woman to be invited to play in the Vienna Philharmonic. She and Stefan had worked together many times and had each other on speed dial.

He quickly called. "Julya, I understand you've been hatching plots around me."

"Anything to get you back to Vienna, my love."

Stefan's throat caught at this. "So, my agent said there was something about the concert that you wanted to tell me. Aside from it being at Schönbrunn."

"It's a costume ball, to benefit education for children of immigrants."

"That's months before ball season!"

"There's more. The theme is superheroes…Superman, Wonder Woman…That and its being on Hallowe'en are in keeping with the children's aid mission."

He laughed hard for the first time in weeks. "I claim Iron Man. And you'd make a great Black Widow."

"I think of you more as Spider-Man, but no such luck. We'll be in the livery of eighteenth-century court musicians."

Stefan snorted. "So, like the costumed bands playing for summer tourists?"

"Well, the costumes will come from the State Opera, so they should be decent."

The State Opera was still a sore subject. "Great, so I'll finally get backstage at the fucking barn. Repertory?"

"Don't be bitter, and D Minor Piano Concerto."

"So, for a benefit for children, some idiot chose one of Mozart's darkest pieces?"

"Probably the favorite of a board member."

He paused, and Julya continued briskly, "Your agent said you're medically cleared. You want to wear the costume and do the gig or not?"

"I'd take it if we had to perform naked."

———

Stefan's first post-surgery flight was fairly comfortable, although he was happy that he only had to get to Vienna, not Tokyo. Julya was waiting for him at his hotel, and they embraced long.

"It's so good to see you, Stefan."

"Jules, it's good to be seen." He smiled ruefully.

The next morning was a perfect brisk October day, and they had breakfast at the hotel, full English for Julya, cereal, yogurt and fruit for Stefan.

"How virtuous you've become!" Julya said.

"Virtue has nothing to do with it. Survival is the game," said Stefan.

After a productive and smooth orchestra rehearsal at a church, they headed over for fittings at the State Opera costume shop. They were buoyant from a fine lunch, a bottle of excellent Austrian white, and the pleasure of musician friends talking shop. "Jules, I feel better than I have in…a long time. Almost normal."

But as they approached the front of the massive building, Stefan stopped in his tracks. There, taunting him, hung a large poster of the *Figaro* production that he should have been conducting, had his faulty heart not given out on him. He read the name of his replacement aloud, then continued walking, his mouth grim.

Once inside they walked through the stage door, down two flights of stairs, then they encountered a series of twists and turns to the double doors of the spacious, almost warehouse-like costume shop. They both stood speechless at the long rows of costumes from dozens of opera plots.

The assistant had already laid out their garments, for Stefan a long jacket, waistcoat, loose linen shirt, breeches, stockings, cravat, and of course a powdered wig. Julya tried on a festive copper gown (although she declined the corset). All the materials were quite fine. Stefan gave a low whistle. "These aren't chintzy costumes. They seem more like real eighteenth-century garments."

Even with his gangly frame, Stefan needed no alterations. The waist-coat and jacket were a little full, but extra room to play was useful. He was struck by how heavy the long jacket was, made with a woolen layer under the satin. With the clothes in a suit bag, he headed back to his hotel, where he took the garments out to hang. As he was patting the jacket down, he noticed a small but heavy bulge embedded in the lining on the right side.

How had he missed this, even within the weight of the coat? Perhaps because it was placed toward the back, he wondered. Stefan's curiosity piqued, he methodically examined the lining, finding the nearly invisible slit, too small for his hand to pass through. With two fingers, he managed to extract a leather drawstring pouch. A vigorous shake revealed it to be filled with coins, tightly packed. Stefan poured them out on the coffee table and stared in wonder. Many of the coins showed the Habsburg double eagle on the backs, while the fronts carried a portrait of Maria Theresa, the great eighteenth-century empress, mother of two emperors and two queens. Stefan was mystified. Did some chorus member at the State Opera also collect coins? Did he carry these onstage to feel more authentic in, what, *The Marriage of Figaro? Così fan tutte? Der Rosenkavalier?* How could he have forgotten them when returning the costume? After wondering about the coins' provenance, Stefan carefully restored them to their hiding place, figuring he would show them to the shop when returning the garments.

———

The next evening the small orchestra met at the palace for a sound check before the guests arrived. The luxurious surroundings should have been overwhelming: lavishly decorated gilded walls and mirrors, cavernous hallways, and endless ceiling frescos. But Julya and Stefan couldn't stop giggling at their costumes. "Mine even came with a bribe to get me to wear it," Stefan exclaimed, showing Julya the secret pouch and opening the bag to show her the treasure.

Her eyes widened. "Stefan, these look like real eighteenth-century coins, and that's several months good wages in old Vienna, as any decent student of Austrian imperial history could tell you. How did they land there?"

"Not the foggiest. Left behind by a chorus member? I'll give them back when I return the coat tomorrow."

"Your virtue is commendable."

———

The patrons were sipping after-dinner coffee when the small orchestra entered, greeted immediately by well-lubricated cheers. The performers sat and then tuned quickly. Stefan waited for total silence before conducting the start of the D minor concerto's agitated, syncopated heartbeat motive in the violins and funerary downbeats in the basses. The troubled movement unfolded further, rose a bit, fell back, then exploded in high passion and drama.

As he conducted and played the solo Stefan felt barriers dropping away—between himself and the orchestra, himself and the music, the entire ensemble, and Mozart. In the midst of this absurd situation, with wealthy Viennese citizens dressed as Batman, Superman, and other superheroes, and the bewigged musicians appearing as if they were in a scene from the movie *Amadeus*, a powerful energy emanated from the orchestra and piano. Stefan felt in turn elated, heartbroken, downcast in despair, pulled into the pink clouds of the ceiling fresco—all propelled by the ever-changing music.

Playing this work in this space, known by Mozart himself, with his field of vision encompassing only what appeared to be an eighteenth-century orchestra, Stefan started to accept what he saw as real. His back was to the patrons, but he had a notion that if he turned and looked, they would all be dressed in lavish gowns and suits from the 1780s. And perhaps he would glimpse a small man with a pointed nose, sporting a bright red coat, watching and listening. The sense of displacement was strong. Stefan accepted the magic; he would happily remain in that century, playing Mozart's music.

The finale cast off all the first movement's shadows, and the music swirled to triumph. The audience members exploded like a champagne cork and shouted as they rose. The spell broke, jarring Stefan back to the present to acknowledge the cheers from the D.C. and Marvel universes. He was used to Viennese audiences being blasé, but whatever unifying magic that had descended on the musicians also enveloped their listeners. The ovation lasted several minutes.

Afterward as a DJ took over for the dancing, Julya confronted Stefan, her eyes shining. "Stefan…that was amazing. I'm not sure what was happening. Where did that come from? We were blown away!"

Stefan replied almost breathlessly, "As was I." He paused, then said in a hushed tone, "I felt like we were…here, but *then*, in 1784. And with Mozart watching."

"There was something extra in the room, no doubt," she said, nodding.

Stefan then said under his breath "Jules, I felt I was where I belonged. 1784. I didn't want to come back."

Julya took him by each arm. "Stefan, I know things have been bad, but you belong here. *Now.* The hell with the fucking Staatsoper. You speak to these musicians in a language they understand. You will come back. And there is much music to make in Vienna other than the Opera."

Stefan was moved and embraced his friend tightly before turning to leave.

"Where are you off to?" she asked.

"To visit someone I haven't seen in a while."

She looked at him quizzically.

"Mozart," he said, a little sheepish.

"Aaahhhh, you're going to St. Marx Cemetery! When's the last time you went?"

"It's been a couple of years. But I need to spill my guts to him like I used to. He's my shrink. And I need to thank him for tonight."

"Hey, let's hit the bar first. You don't want to face him cold sober. He wouldn't approve, from what I've read."

Before heading for refreshment, Stefan reported the success of the event to his daughter in London. "I'm having a drink with Julya, then one more stop before bed, then I'll see you tomorrow."

"One more stop?" Katrina asked. Then she laughed. "Ahhh. Going to see Mozart, yes? Give him my regards."

———

About an hour and a half later, Stefan, still wearing his eighteenth-century garb, was sitting on his knees, feet tucked under, at Mozart's memorial in the old St. Marx Cemetery Park. The modest marker was of a sad little angel leaning on a column. The inscription was just as modest:

W.A.

Mozart

1756-1791

The seclusion, and his bottomless love for Mozart's music, made the cemetery a refuge he often sought when in Vienna. It didn't matter that no one knew the exact location of Mozart's remains; he had been buried, as was the custom of the day, in a common grave, not a pauper's grave as was said so often.

Here, in solitude, Stefan let his thoughts flow freely, sometimes speaking directly to Mozart. For him, it was the safest place in the world. There was nothing that the great sage of human passion, anguish, and foolishness, Mozart, would not understand.

Now he turned inside to his deep unhappiness and allowed it to come front and center. He poured out memories of Hannah to the sad little angel—of their initial meeting, she a sculptor, he a musician; their fast-burgeoning passion; of the initial shock, then joy of Hannah's pregnancy; of their marriage.

"But then came that terrible day that I don't talk about; Katrina doesn't even know. When Katrina was two, Hannah became pregnant again. We were thrilled that Katrina would have a sibling, something she still wishes she had. Then one night about four months into her pregnancy,

Hannah woke with the bedsheets bloody. We were at the hospital in minutes, but it was too late. The miscarriage was done.

"After that…things changed; exactly why, I still don't know. I stayed away longer on the road, and she became more immersed in her sculpting. We drifted apart. Then…the affair…and my heart broke. Literally." A couple of muffled sobs broke from Stefan.

He looked at his phone to check the time. "Act four of *Figaro* is about halfway done at the State Opera. If things had gone differently, that's where I'd be right now." He rose and walked about to ease the stiffness in his legs. About to leave, he turned, suddenly wanting to offer his thanks to the composer who was almost everything to him. As he was dressed as a musician of Mozart's time, he threw off the reminders of his own century by placing his wallet and mobile on the other side of the memorial.

Facing the angel, he spoke again. "Thank you, Wolfgang Amadeus Mozart. Your music is probably the only thing that fills this hole in me." Stefan then started mentally replaying the evening's D minor concerto and felt its sorrow and triumph again. He focused on it with all his concentration. God, he yearned to be there when such music was new, the latest thing! Before music making became industrialized and more about technique than soul.

Something shifted. First the air lightened as if some pollution had been cleansed. Then a stronger change—a slightly pungent whiff of ozone, as if heralding a thunderstorm.

Stefan looked into the sky. Perfectly clear. Then his eyes were drawn to a sudden anomaly; against the dark outline of bushes near the memorial marker, there was a slightly *less* black spot, a graying splotch getting gradually lighter as he watched. The splotch began to take form, human form. It was a figure, someone of not great stature. Vague wisps of detail appeared, including the long line of a gentleman's red coat with its many buttons and braids.

The face remained a blur, but by now the impossible had started to become "maybe" in Stefan's mind.

Mozart?

Or a hallucination brought on by being *in extremis* emotionally for a year? Stefan stood, ready to stride to the phenomenon, when there was a movement within the pool of light-form—a hand raised then beckoned to Stefan to come nearer.

Jesus, I am fucking losing it!

Stefan advanced, extending his hand to touch the shoulder. He fully expected it to be insubstantial like a hologram. But he laid his fingertips on cloth that he could feel, something completely corporeal. He felt a sensation in his chest—not the dreaded tightness, but a mild effervescence followed by a painful whole-body electric spasm. Then he fell, and seemed to keep falling, much farther than the distance to the ground. Before he met anything to stop his fall, he passed out, as he had with his heart attack.

When morning light awakened him, his first thought was of his heart. But, on getting up on all fours, he felt no chest discomfort. In fact his breathing seemed somehow easier, with the air lighter, even sweet. Then he noticed the quiet; there was none of the nearby A23's usual traffic hum. He sat back on his heels, turned his head to the left, and experienced one the greatest shocks of his life.

The Mozart memorial with its sad little angel leaning on the column had disappeared, as had many of the old headstones he remembered. The messy, crumbling St . Marx that he knew was gone; this looked to be a fairly new cemetery.

Chapter 3 — Stepping Out of Bounds

31 March 1784

THE COUNTESS ELISABETTA Rheinhardt Grünewald stood before the full-length mirror in the hallway outside a box at Vienna's Burgtheater, making a last-minute inspection. Her violet velvet dress covered her shoulders and chest modestly. Her luxuriant auburn hair was twisted and coiled up on her head with mother-of-pearl combs, four tendrils descending to frame her face. Her neck was long and delicate. Her brow was high and fell into a gracefully thin and slightly pointed nose. Her cheeks and jaw were classically structured, but there was a softness in the curvatures of her face. Her light green eyes were transparent, open to what was within her, yet could be pointed and heated. Lisa, as she called herself, was twenty-six and a widow.

She questioned her reflection, *Am I really going to do this?* She imagined the hail of fury that was waiting for her inside the theater. She tensed her jaw muscles then relaxed them and opened the door. She slipped into the golden and lushly ornate hall, flickering with the light of a thousand candles and filled with a rainbow spread of lavish dresses, and took her seat. Following her directly was Georg, the large man who was her longtime house servant. It took a few moments for the reaction that she had expected to set in, but slowly the preperformance chatter subsided, and dozens of pairs of eyes turned toward the young woman. Cutting through the silence, whispered comments began, little of which she could make out. One, a little louder and more incensed than the others, did get through. "She has come out of mourning *now?*" It knifed through a mix of murmurs and even a couple of hisses. There were also younger voices giggling.

Trying to be oblivious to the demonstration, the countess closely studied the playbill of the performance about to be given by the great Mozart, a new piano concerto in D Minor. She had anticipated a noisy attempt to drive her away. But instead of being cowed, she felt her fury rising. Many of the individuals directing venomous looks at her had been close friends of her family. But a day came when her father saw his finances collapse. He had turned to some of these very families—several of them important bankers—for loans, and all of them made the cold-eyed calculation that Lord Rheinhardt's situation was not recoverable and that their money would vanish. Not a single florin were they willing to loan.

Rescue seemed to arrive with a handsome suitor Charles Grünewald, himself a count and the beneficiary of a family fortune, seemingly smitten with Elisabetta. He was charming to all. He was also willing to accept the family house as dowry and to pledge in the prenuptial negotiations a significant portion of his fortune to his future wife upon his death. But what appeared to be a heaven-sent solution had catastrophic results for Elisabetta and her family. Her peers started noticing bruises and abrasions on her arms, and on one occasion, she seemed to have difficulty walking. Her father tried to address the shocking situation legally but was turned away; the law recognized no rights for women in this predicament. She strongly believed all this contributed to her father's death, and she blamed the very people who were hissing at her for putting her family in the position of needing a savior like Charles.

She felt her face flush, her pulse sped up, and a fire-breathing scream of fury began to surge up from her viscera. Since her husband's death, she had had explosions of anger that she did not understand, as if there were an always-present hot reservoir of angry magma in her that sometimes overflowed. This time it had an understandable cause. But a quick look into her eyes from Georg and his massive hand on hers said it plainly. *Don't.* He had been a steadying influence on her since she was small and still knew when and how to step in and cool her down.

Of course there was another issue in the mix—the matter of her rejecting the earlier advances, before the collapse of the family finances, of a number of young men who pursued her when she came of age. Some of them came from the very families whose members now were making this ugly demonstration. Lisa was sometimes spoken of as the most beautiful woman in Vienna; that and her father's fortune made her the catch of several seasons. The attractive young men walked through the door with pride, not a little arrogance and supreme confidence in their manliness and marriageability. They excelled at hunting, drinking, feasting, with an occasional dalliance at establishments whose specialty was teaching young men the ways of the flesh.

Lisa, growing up surrounded by books and especially music was— unusual for high-born ladies—highly educated. She was appalled at these swaggering creatures who would take her as wife. Indulged since child- hood in her tendency to speak her mind, she dismissed them, sometimes ungently, and they left, enraged to be thus addressed by a woman who should have been grateful for their attention. Their families took great umbrage. They also took their opportunity to levy a pound of flesh with satisfaction by refusing to aid her father in need. To Lisa, they had thus helped make her an orphan, this highborn class of hissing serpents.

Her hunger for music was one of several factors that brought her to the Burgtheater on this date. One, it was a performance by Mozart, whom she admired above all other of the day's composers, even the great Haydn. Today also was the sixth-month anniversary of the death of her husband. Six months was the standard mourning period for men, as opposed to two years for women. This seemed to her grossly disproportionate, especially when the widow had been terrified of her husband and viewed his death from a heart ailment as a great moment of liberation. For all these reasons, she had resolved to quit mourning when a man would and to take what she needed for her soul: Mozart's music. This was Elisabetta's first concert in over a year and a half. Her husband had feigned an interest in music during their courtship, only to reveal eventually his contempt for what he regarded as a useless frill. This lack in her life she planned to correct starting now. As she sat in the venerable theater, she felt she was both hurling defiance at past terrifying memories and also feeling release from them. She was breaking out from being imprisoned in her house and moving toward a future that again included what she loved most, music.

The hum of disapproval directed to the box died quickly as the orchestra filed onto the stage to mild applause. Finally the maestro entered to clapping and cheers. Lisa had always marveled at how such a supremely brilliant being could be so young and modest physically. He was short, maybe five feet four, with a head slightly too big for the body and eyes slightly too big for the head. A pointed nose extended over a slight chin. Lisa had met him once, two years ago at a salon performance, and had noted the pockmarks on his cheeks, likely from childhood smallpox.

Yet in this setting—surrounded by musicians, a pianoforte within his reach, and an enthusiastic audience greeting him as their own—he was radiant. He extended his arms in a gesture of embrace, and his smile lit the room brighter than the candles ever could. This was all set against the extraordinarily red coat he wore, as red as that of a British general.

Mozart sat at the keyboard, from where he would also conduct, and waited until the audience chatter had completely subsided. Then from the quiet emerged the subdued but deeply troubled opening of simple syncopations that developed into a sudden dramatic blast from the orchestra, and the music became a full-on tragic drama. Before the piano entered, the orchestra ended the first section with a sorrow-filled lament from the violins.

Then Mozart began his matchless playing. A magical tone arose effortlessly from the pianoforte. Every note had bell-like clarity, perfectly measured, and moved to the next note with natural inevitability, forming beautiful shapes out of delicate points of sound. Then, out of nowhere, the whole instrument rang heroically, and the entire hall responded as if part of the instrument.

Mozart's sorrowful music seized Lisa and held her tight to the end as the movement finished in a sad whisper. *He knows me, my anguish*, she thought. *But this slight man then turns the pain into radiant beauty.* Only music could do this. *At least to me*, she thought. *Does music affect others like this?* she wondered. The second movement was a serene respite, and Lisa welcomed its comfort. The finale exploded into drama again but gradually worked its way to a blazing, trumpet-led triumph at the end.

I need to sit at the keyboard again with Mozart's music in front of me. I'll visit the Artaria music shop tomorrow! The serene middle movement had made her itch to write her own such movement and more. It had been three and a half years since she had sunk her hands into blank music paper and ink. *By the Gods, I will create again.*

She exploded out of her chair to applaud. She then swept from her box; she had no wish to hear anything else. She found that her anger at the demonstrators had subsided. Her heart had, for the first time, turned away from the three-year darkness of her father's financial collapse, the nightmare of a marriage that crushed her body and spirit, and her father's death. The coming day finally seemed as if it would be brighter than the current one.

"Tomorrow there will be *music* in the house again," she said firmly to Georg.

1 7 8 5

Chapter 4—Time and Again

STEFAN SAW NOTHING but neatly manicured grass where the Mozart memorial had stood for so long. There was no sign that anything had ever been there. Looking to his right, he saw a trimmed lawn with a few grave markers, not the packed and overgrown ancient grounds that he knew. There was no head-high brick wall at the perimeter.

He stood upright and walked to where the brick wall had been and looked into a lush forest and a farm, not noisy highways and buildings. He turned and looked for the Leberstrasse that led to the park from Vienna. There was only a single, well-used packed-dirt wagon track with grass in the middle. The big roadway, the A23, was gone.

For a long while, Stefan kept turning and looking, hoping that he could stare down this impossibility and make it return to normal. He screamed inside at his own mind, which had taken him somewhere that did not exist. What he saw appeared to be an earlier time, many decades past, even centuries. Had his hurt and emptiness done far more damage to his psyche that he had thought? Was this a psychotic episode, a complete breakdown? His mind was running amok in a new reality.

Then a fearful thought, *What if I've had another heart attack and am lying in a bed in the ICU, hallucinating all this while in a coma?* Would this all dissolve into the proverbial bright light of the afterlife? Or would he wake up with his body perforated by tubes? Terror took him, and all he could do was lock himself still and await awakening, either in a hospital bed or to the knowledge that he was dead. He held this attitude for what seemed like hours. He thought in anguish of Katrina.

When after a while the reality did not change, he calmed a bit. He had no choice but to move and interact with what was presented to him. Slowly pushing back against the panic, he finally formed an intention that would lead to action. *Whatever my mind has constructed, it seems very real,* Stefan thought. He would have to proceed within this reality, going along with his mind, and hope to snap back. He would get into Vienna and…do what? *See what my mind had created and try to find my way through it—and back.*

He made his way down the path to the dirt road, turned left, and began trudging the three miles to Vienna. Not far along there was a rise that gave him a view of the city. He topped it and caught his breath sharply. At some distance beyond was a mighty stone and brick wall that extended in both directions, encircling the city. Fronted by a wide swath of upward-sloping open grass, it was a tall brick barrier with parapets and jutting towers. He had seen illustrations of it and knew a little of its history; it was built to hold back the Turks, finally breached by Bonaparte around 1808, torn down by Emperor Franz Joseph, then replaced by the Ringstrasse and the many imperial-looking buildings that were situated on it, like the Royal Opera, now the State Opera. *My mind must have created this image from those illustrations. When were the illustrations from? 1780 or 1790? What's the year in this hallucination?*

He trudged on, wishing that every second would be the last before waking up. He neared the city and was amazed at the extraordinary detail: people, animals, wagons, the roadway, all as if he were on the set of some brilliantly designed period film. How was it possible he knew so much?

There were pedestrian entrances to the city accessible by stairways under each of the bastion towers. Stefan joined a light stream of people (few dressed as nicely as he was) and ascended the stairs. At the top he saw with dismay that all who passed by the impressively uniformed sentries were presenting papers. Well, no choice but to try and fake his way through. He worked fast to prepare a scenario that would make sense in this fantasy.

"What is your business in Vienna?"

"I'm a musician, and I have a concert."

Stefan's modern Viennese-dialect German was, of course, excellent, but he found some difficulty in penetrating the sentry's dialect.

"You're dressed rather well for a musician," said the sentry, looking Stefan up and down suspiciously.

Stefan just nodded.

"Identity papers, *Herr Muziker.*"

"I'm afraid I left them in my inn in the city. I wanted to take the fresh air outside the walls."

Scowling and disbelieving, the sentry purred with exaggerated courtesy, "Then you must send a note to the inn and ask the innkeeper to retrieve the necessary papers, *Herr Muziker.*"

Stefan thought desperately and found a desperate solution. Feeling in his pocket, he touched the coins from the costume shop. He pulled one out, not knowing its value, and tried not to be obvious in offering it.

"Will this help my cause, *Herr Offizier?*"

The sentry's eyes grew wide—apparently the coin's value was considerable—and he burst out, howling in outrage. Stefan could not grasp all that he shouted, but he picked up enough key words to get the gist: "…bribe…Majesty Joseph II…crime…arrest…!"

He then called for another soldier of lower rank and commanded him, "Take him to Central."

The soldier took him by the arm. He was a larger man than Stefan, so any struggle would be useless. Where would he go if he got away? They headed west, toward the complex behind the main city gate. Then came a parade ground with barracks around and a large stone building of three stories, which Stefan guessed was administrative headquarters. They entered.

A squat man was sitting behind an elevated desk, shuffling sheets of paper rather like the many modern precinct stations on police shows.

"Name?"

Stefan saw no advantage in dissembling. "Stefan Radowitz, musician."

"Purpose of visit?"

"A concert with Herr Mozart." Might as well try to drop a name, but it meant nothing to the man.

"Charge?" he asked the escort.

"Attempted bribery and public scandal."

"Take him to Schmidt's level to await the magistrate."

"How long will that take?" Stefan asked as respectfully as he could.

With a mean smile, the desk jockey sneered, "Oh, the magistrate is a very busy man."

Schmidt's level was two flights down into an increasingly dank, moist complex, which stank more and more of human waste as they descended. They turned down a torchlit corridor, past a few empty cells, and were confronted by a more modestly sized man. He unlocked a cell door, out of which burst yet an even stronger stench. Stefan fortunately had a handkerchief and covered his nose.

"The magistrate will send for him, Schmidt" said the policeman, waddling away.

"Name?"

The fat officer turned and said, "Oh…I forget. What does it matter?"

There was little light, but Schmidt looked Stefan up and down, not unkindly.

"What's a gentleman doing here?" he asked, not without sympathy. The proper clothes had already done some good.

"I tried to enter the city without papers, then tried to bribe the sentry."

"Ahh," exclaimed Schmidt, eyes rolling. "Some of the sentries were caught accepting bribes last year and were drummed out. Otherwise, your coin would have worked.

"You may be here awhile," Schmidt continued. "The magistrate is a drunken sluggard." After a pause, the kindly man offered, "See here, you're a gentleman and must have acquaintances in the city. Can you send for someone who is known, to come and vouch for you?"

Here was a possible opening, and only a desperate gambit would suffice. Time again to test his improvising skills.

"Do you know of the composer, Herr Mozart?"

"I have heard of him, yes. And who should I say needs him?"

Stefan wracked his knowledge of history. Thankfully his escort had not revealed his name. Guessing he was now in Mozart's lifetime, he thought of Süssmayr, who finished Mozart's last work, the *Requiem. No, that wasn't until 1791, the year Mozart died. Too narrow a target. Schickaneder, librettist of the Magic Flute? Also too soon....No, wait, Mozart had met Schickaneder in Salzburg much earlier when his touring troupe came through! Better target.*

"Please tell him Herr Emanuel Schickaneder has found himself in a pickle barrel and requires some assistance. And Herr Schmidt...one question more before you leave."

Schmidt turned and looked. "Yes?"

"My mind has taken a bit of a turn but...can you tell me the date?"

"November first, Herr Schickaneder. All-Saints Day."

"And the year?"

Eyebrows raised, Schmidt said slowly, "The year of our Lord seventeen hundred and eighty-five."

Schmidt disappeared into the semidarkness. Stefan made a monumental effort not to scream. Then he remembered that 1785 was the year Mozart began *The Marriage of Figaro.*

Chapter 5—False ID

AN HOUR, OR two or three, went by. The darkness was not total, but only a wall torch around the corner gave any illumination to the cell. And as he trembled in the dank and stinking gloom, a new and terrifying thought took him. What if his senses were not lying, and he had, impossibly, *traveled through time* to the Vienna of Mozart? What would he do? How would he live? For starters, how would he get out of this prison?

He felt that he was ready to start shrieking in the silence when he heard a door open and close, followed by brisk footsteps in the hall. More light spilled into the cell, and Stefan could see Schmidt leading the way for a smaller man. Stefan was on his feet, and as the two approached, he could see details. Round eyes, pointed nose, tapered chin. Elegant dress with an exquisitely fitted wig. And a tenor voice that exploded with considerable power.

"Damn your eyes, Schickaneder; is this one of your fucking pranks? How dare you rouse me in the morning, you prick! Why are you in Vienna anyway?" His voice was a bit raspy, either from not enough sleep or too much drink, or both.

Wolfgang Amadeus Mozart.

He was approaching the cell, winding up for another outburst, when his eyes met Stefan's, and he stopped instantly, his face full of shock. His mouth was wide open, as were his bloodshot eyes. He froze and stayed frozen, only his mouth working. Stefan was also in shock—was the psychotic episode deepening? *Mozart!*

Schmidt, with a concerned look on his face, finally said, "Are you quite well, Herr Mozart?"

Mozart slowly extended a hand toward Stefan, and he finally said, with low intensity,

"You!"

Stefan had seen the instant of recognition, and he was as staggered as the man staring at him. Finally he managed a whisper.

"Yes, it is me."

After a long pause, Mozart recovered and said in clipped tones to Schmidt, "Yes, Herr Schickaneder is known to me. I vouch for him. Please release him under my care and return his belongings."

Schmidt bowed his head slightly and took Stefan's purse with its coins from a desk drawer. Handing it to Stefan, he muttered "My apologies, sir. I will see you both out."

Mozart stepped briskly into the street from the compound, keeping a step ahead of Stefan. As they passed an alley, Mozart turned into it then wheeled on Stefan, his finger in his face and his voice filled with fury.

"Damn you, sir; I dreamed of you last night! Now you summon me to the city jail. Who in hell's blazes are you?"

Stefan had yet to think of how he would answer such an inevitable inquiry. He settled again on his real name and wildly tried to think of a plausible birthplace. His real home of London was a little too widely known, and he could not answer questions about the city in the eighteenth century. All he could think of was Beethoven's hometown.

"Stefan Radowitz, Maestro, your most humble servant. I am from Bonn and came to Vienna to learn from you."

With a look of disbelief, Mozart replied, "You heard of me in Bonn? I have traveled widely but never close to Bonn."

Stefan drew a breath, then said truthfully, "I know as much about you and your music as any man alive, Maestro Mozart. I saw you too. You beckoned to me."

"Yes, in my dream you were too distant to see."

"But you recognized me just now."

Mozart raised both hands, gave a big shoulder shrug, and sighed. "Herr Radowitz, you are a man of mystery." He paused. "Where are you lodged?"

Stefan had not the slightest idea of where an inn might be, so he revealed that this was actually his first moment in the city.

Mozart took this in, then said, "I have an extra room in my apartment. Stay with me for a bit. I need to talk to the man who knows as much about me as any man alive. And about whom I dream."

Chapter 6—Over the Threshold

MOZART SET A brisk pace, and Stefan was surprised at how much he had to exert himself to keep up with the smaller man. They made their way toward the city center and to the main landmark of Vienna for many decades, the dominating St. Stephen's Cathedral. Wolfgang Amadeus Mozart and Constanze Weber Mozart had been married there and lived not five minutes' walk away.

The two men entered the plaza of the cathedral, and Stefan was quite surprised to see how much cleaner the stones of the structure were than he remembered. *Well, of course, no auto fumes.* The tradeoff was that one had to mind carefully the horse shit as one traversed the cobbles. But the odor of the droppings and sewage, along with rarely washed humanity, could not be stepped around.

The morning sun had given way to a windblown cold drizzle. Stefan was grateful for the wool lining in his long coat. Mozart wore no cloak, and his jacket seemed of lighter fabric, but he did not seem to notice the weather. He charged on with agitated determination, and Stefan had to work to keep up.

Stefan had been in the two-story house at Schulerstrasse 6 (Schuler Street) twice before. On his first trip to Vienna in the early 1990s, it was simply a preserved historical site. Several rooms had authentic-looking furniture, including Mozart's study with the large table at which he worked and a pianoforte. All a little dusty, but you could smell the history. In

2006 for the Mozart 250th anniversary, the Vienna Museum had heavily renovated the building. It was now an interactive museum, with some displays of interest but much pure kitsch. One could buy Mozart golf balls and Mozart mobile-phone cases. *Disneyworld Mozart*, Stefan had thought as he left.

Wolfgang and Constanze had moved there in 1784, the beginning of the most successful era of Mozart's life. The original house had multiple levels wrapped around a central staircase—suitable for a conquering young composer and pianist who was glowingly received by the emperor himself.

As they turned down Schulerstrasse, Stefan recognized the house, even surrounded by different structures than he remembered. Mozart stepped up to the corniced doorway, pulled out a large key, unlocked the door with a snap, and stepped briskly inside, almost without breaking stride. Stefan followed tentatively, and after crossing the threshold, stepped fully into the entry hall.

He had an overwhelming sense of finally stepping through the looking glass into an impossibility—entering the home of this small man who here created some of the loftiest artistic achievements of humankind, in any era. Still...dream? Psychosis? The reality being presented to him was not made of shards of mental pictures improbably pieced together. It was full, consistent, and, in every detail, utterly tangible. Part of him began to accept it, from fatigue if nothing else.

He also felt an odd sensation, a gentle but insistent physical pull from somewhere deep behind his ribs. He somehow knew that the pull was coming from Mozart. It strengthened, and Stefan went faint for a second and slumped against the wall.

Mozart whirled, anxious concern on his face. "Is anything wrong?"

Stefan recovered quickly and waved it off. "Nothing, Maestro. It has just been a trying day. I've never been in jail before."

Mozart smiled wryly. "No, I suppose not. I've never been in one either."

Removing and hanging his coat, Mozart invited Stefan to do the same. "Come to my study. We have good Turkish coffee."

Stefan could see into parts of four large rooms on the first floor and realized why he was not being received in a sitting room. There were empty and half-full wine glasses scattered among mostly empty bottles. Plates with crumbs of cheese and olive pits lay here and there. A young serving girl was just getting started with cleanup. He could also see the fabled billiards table at which Mozart had crushed opposition from around the continent and taken their money.

Mozart noticed Stefan taking in the conditions and said, a little abashed, "We were playing string quartets for friends, and later we danced. Do follow me."

To the servant girl, he said courteously, "Ani, may we have coffee in my study?"

"Of course, Herr Mozart," she said, curtsying.

The upstairs study was large and exquisitely neat. An expansive table was at the center, and on it were tidily squared stacks of manuscript paper. Near the main chair was a collection of manuscript piles that were not as orderly. Next to what seemed clearly like a working space was, to Stefan, a familiar collection of writing tools: several quills in a little well, two inkpots, two sharpening knives, blotting paper, and two shakers of sand for drying.

Stefan almost grew faint again with the realization of what he was looking at. Each stack was likely one composition in progress. He remembered that Mozart could work on multiple projects simultaneously, much as a chess grandmaster could play dozens of games at one time.

And what was the immediate project spread out? *The Marriage of Figaro?*

Mozart gestured toward a smaller table, around which were four chairs. Stefan took a seat, and Mozart sat across from him. The two men looked at each other for the first time in stillness and clear light, and Stefan was newly startled. That Mozart died an early and tragic death was known to all who knew anything about him. But Stefan now saw up close how extraordinarily young he was. He was twenty-nine but looked younger than some of Stefan's college students in London. Yet he had already composed works that would live for as long as humans listened to music.

After a silence which Stefan dared not break, Mozart said quietly, "It is a remarkable thing that two men should appear in each other's dreams at the same time. I won't even try to account for it. Can you?"

Stefan chose his words carefully. "Maestro, I have closely followed your career. I have made a study of your travels when you were a child and have come to know much of the music you composed. You are the greatest composer I know. Your music is in my mind most days. So, that I have connected with you in dreams is not impossible. In a way I have knocked at the door of your mind, and you answered. Perhaps people sometimes have unseen and unexplainable connections." This was all pretty much true, as far as it went.

Mozart seemed moved by this and slightly bowed his head in acknowledgement.

After another silence and another direct look, Mozart added, "I suppose we must leave it there, as something beyond our full understanding. However, I think there is more to this than you are saying…You said you wanted to learn from me, though you appear old enough to be an experienced teacher yourself. Do you wish to study the pianoforte? Or composition?"

"Maestro, I have no gift for composition, but I do play the pianoforte passably."

"Very well. May I hear you play?" He gestured to the beautiful instrument across the room.

Play for Mozart?

Stefan whirled mentally through his repertoire to make sure that the work he picked was already in existence.

"I have a particular fondness for your Sonata in F major. I believe you wrote it while still in Salzburg. May I play it?"

Mozart smiled slightly and nodded.

"Fondness" was putting it mildly for what Stefan felt about this sonata. He considered it one of Mozart's great middle-period works. Starting with exquisite, serenade-like lyricism, it then bursts into D minor, one of the keys that always meant drama in Mozart. Pivoting back and forth between violently opposed characters, tender and fierce, then building enormous tension in the middle section, it finally melts with sudden ease back to the lyrical opening.

Stefan played the first movement. His modern technique was informed by music far more demanding technically than Mozart's, music that called for physical power. When he played the first loud passage, he used the strength that he would use on a modern piano, overloading the smaller eighteenth-century instrument and making it ring harshly. Stefan felt Mozart wince. But he quickly adjusted and found the measure of the instrument. His later *fortes* and accents settled down from harshness to fullness. When done, he looked at the great composer, terrified of what he might say.

Mozart had a finger on his chin, listening intently. Then he stepped forward, and, smiling, stroked the shell of the instrument delicately with his fingers. "I wonder, Herr Radowitz, do you love your wife with the same force you use to play?"

Stefan blushed fiercely, remembering from the letters Mozart's penchant for the ribald.

"You play with great strength, too much at times. But you have a sense of line that is rare. You make it flow, like oil." He smiled, then looked at Stefan with narrow eyes. "You are considerably older than my other students, and I think you probably can play much more difficult music than my sonata."

Stefan said, "I am more interested in playing music that is beautiful than music which is just difficult."

Mozart's smile broadened. "Just so, Herr Radowitz. Spoken like the man of experience you seem to be." Stefan wondered if this was an acknowledgement that he was older.

Ani arrived with coffee.

Mozart kept quizzing Stefan about his origins, with whom he had studied the pianoforte, and where he had performed. Stefan applied the lash to his memory, then to his imagination. He kept up the Bonn-as-hometown lie, since he had played in Bonn and knew its history a little. As for his instruction, he gave Mozart the real name of his old teacher in conservatory.

"I know many fine clavierists around Europe but not this name. How could a man with a student like you go unnoticed?"

"He…had a small studio and did not seek attention."

"But your technique is so powerful! An unknown teacher gave you this? Pupils should be flocking to his door."

"Well…he preferred a quiet life."

Mozart would not give up. "What were his teaching methods? Can you demonstrate?"

Stefan was starting to sweat under his arms a little. Then he thought that Mozart would not know the nineteenth-century technical studies that he had been brought up on. Maybe if he played a conservative one, then Mozart would accept that it was from his teacher and back down.

So he picked one of the early studies that he knew, one within eighteenth-century technical demands, and played it. Yet it still had hints of the early nineteenth century, and at a couple of these moments, Mozart raised an eyebrow.

Stefan finished. "That was by my teacher."

Mozart squinted suspiciously. "Once again you bring mystery to my door. I believe that there is more to say and that for some reason you hide something. But there will come a day when I will learn all," he said, playfully wagging his finger.

Yes, and have me locked up when you hear the truth, thought Stefan. But his relief was considerable now that the interrogation seemed over. Mozart flashed an amused and charming smile.

They sipped their thick Turkish coffee mostly in silence; the brew had a punch that Stefan welcomed. Mozart seemed relaxed and savored his coffee. Stefan knew from letters that the composer very much savored the pleasures of life: good food, wine, and elegant clothes. The house seemed simply but tastefully furnished, nothing extravagant, except perhaps the beautiful billiard table.

Footfalls and voices could be heard coming down the steps from the upper floors. Mozart rose, and Stefan leapt up as a slight woman with black curly hair and round dark eyes entered the room with a small child on her hip. Constanze Weber Mozart had a bubbling energy that made her eyes sparkle, and her entrance lit her husband up.

She dipped a small curtsey to Stefan, who, remembering from an opera director how to do the formal bow of the time, responded appropriately.

"My dear wife, may I present Herr Stefan Radowitz of Bonn, a most interesting musician," Mozart said with an ironic tinge on the last two words.

"Your most humble servant, Frau Mozart."

"I thought I heard playing by someone other than my husband," she said gayly but with obvious curiosity. "This is our son Karl," she said, indicating the child who seemed about a year old.

"A most handsome young man. He resembles both of you," Stefan said with all the charm he could summon. Both parents were pleased at the compliment.

"It's time for Karl's nap," Constanze said, handing him off to the busy Ani.

Constanze sat, and the two men joined her.

"Herr Radowitz has journeyed from Bonn to study with me. I've invited him to stay in our loft bedroom temporarily."

Constanze took interest in this and asked sweetly, "How long do you plan to stay in Vienna, Herr Radowitz?" Stefan remembered that Constanze had revealed herself as an astute businesswoman after Mozart's death, and while he was alive, had tried to keep his extravagant tastes in check. The lady wanted to know how long they would have an extra mouth to feed.

"Frau Mozart, your husband is most generous with his offer. I can afford an inn, however, and would not wish to be a burden." After a pause, Stefan saw a disappointed look in her eye...had he offended her? Wait, of course! He was welcome to stay with them but doubly welcome if he could make a contribution toward running the household.

Time for a roll of the dice. Stefan fished for the leather purse and coins. "I exchanged some Prussian currency for Austrian, but I honestly don't know how far this will go." He took some of the coins out and lay them on the table. In trying to close the stiff purse, he dropped it, and the entire contents of the purse emptied.

Two sets of eyes widened on taking in the sight. "Herr Radowitz," said Mozart, "this is enough money to stay in Vienna comfortably for some time."

Again Stefan was dumbfounded. At some point he would learn how much money he actually had, but for now he said, "I would be honored to use whatever of this you think appropriate to defray the expense of my staying with you."

Quickly Constanze replied, "What a very kind offer, dear sir! We are honored to accept." Mozart gave a quick head nod and smile in affirmation.

Holy shit, thought Stefan. *I am moving in with the Mozart family.*

—

Stefan thought the couple must have found it strange for him to have no trunk, although they did not ask. He knew his exhaustion must be plain. Constanze directed him to the loft bedroom, several flights up, then showed him the privy. The room was small with a garret window; a simple wooden-frame bed and coverlet; a small vanity with a mirror, washbasin, towel, and pitcher; and a chamber pot for middle-of-the-night needs. *Yes, I can deal with this*, he told himself. He took all his clothes off except his shirt and underwear (wondering if people had started wearing undergarments yet). He got under the coverlet and was asleep quickly.

Stefan awoke from what did not feel like a long sleep. It was dark in the room, except for the candle burning on the vanity. He could not remember where he was for several moments. Then he remembered, but…*maybe I'm back. Maybe it's over,* he thought in desperation.

He sat up, but his heart sank as he found himself in the garret room. And for the first time, he admitted the possibility that what was in front of him was real. The thought bored out from the center of his mind, *How will I get back?* His old fantasies about being in this century with Mozart had never dwelled on the return journey; a round-trip ticket was always assumed. Now he looked into his mind, in vain, for the return stub. His old life, until the divorce and despite professional frustration, was exactly how he wanted it: work, leisure, artistic satisfaction, and family, at least Katrina. Now, all gone. The thought of never seeing Katrina again was catastrophic. And what would she think when communication from him stopped? He would be just another missing person. A search would be made, then the case eventually closed, leaving her in a pit of loss and despair.

The rich smell of roast pork drifted up the stairway, and the sudden connection with his long-empty stomach provided a strong distraction. Stefan then became conscious of the lit taper and the fact that someone had put it there for his convenience. Doubtless Ani. He dressed, took the candle in hand, and carefully descended the steep, narrow stairs.

He followed his ear and nose to the dining room, where Mozart was about to cut into the roast. On the table was also smoked herring, a fragrant pot of boiled cabbage, a plate of red grapes, another with a wedge of pungent cheese, and a dish of olives. A bottle of Italian red wine was yet to be poured. That and the olives reminded Stefan that Vienna at this time was the center of an empire in which dozens of languages were spoken and as many different cuisines were enjoyed.

Mozart beamed broadly when Stefan entered. "Welcome, good sir! Please join us." Mozart was at the head, Constanze to his right, and a place setting for Stefan on his left.

"Frau Mozart, Maestro, I humbly thank you for your gracious invitation." Stefan sat.

The dinner conversation was halting at first, but Stefan did his best to engage. He felt that the transition to 1785 had unsettled his whole system, both neurologically and possibly digestively as well. Plus, despite the nap, he was soul-crushingly tired, as if he had run a marathon. Mozart, however, began cheerily asking questions, wanting to know about Bonn. He seemed especially curious about how a musician of Stefan's level and age could be completely unknown. Stefan improvised a self-portrait of a man who had been happily tucked away from the world. Thankfully for Stefan, he had been to Bonn several times for concerts at the Beethoven House, so what he had to say about the city had a ring of truth. He had an amused chuckle with himself when he thought of a most outstanding thing about Bonn—right now a fifteen-year-old boy named Beethoven lived there, who would change the world.

Mozart's apparent high spirits buoyed Stefan's energy. It was Stefan who unwittingly dampened things when he asked his host, "I have never been to your hometown of Salzburg. Tell me of your memories there."

The couple went silent and glanced quickly at each other. Mozart recovered and started to answer tentatively, "Well…"

Constanze rescued him with a pleasant but firm tone, "My husband's memories of his home are many, but not all of them are pleasant. Especially not in recent years."

Stefan wanted to kick his own shin. *Idiot!* He had let his small talk become thoughtless. Mozart's father and sister approved of almost nothing he did, especially leaving Salzburg for Vienna and getting married. He had abandoned working for the upkeep of the family at home in order to become a world-famous composer with his own family. How could he have forgotten that?

"I humbly ask your pardon for bringing up an awkward subject. I meant no disrespect."

Mozart familiarly patted Stefan's forearm. "No disrespect taken, sir."

The table was cleared by another servant. Dessert was a lovely Tokay served with roasted almonds and dates. Stefan sipped at the wine but felt himself slipping into a hole.

Constanze accomplished her second rescue of the night. "Dear Herr Radowitz, I think we need to get you into bed. You will find warm water in your room to refresh your face." Mozart started to speak, but she held up a finger. "Tomorrow's plans can wait for tomorrow, my sweet Wolfi." And she planted a soft kiss on his mouth.

Stefan rose, bowed, took the candle, and made his careful way to the garret. He disrobed, washed his face, got into bed, and blew out the candle. In the darkness he started mulling over just what in hell had happened to him and fell suddenly and profoundly asleep.

Chapter 7—Employment

ON AWAKENING THE next day, Stefan found that he was still in the wrong century. His fruitless struggle with this new reality was wearing, and he stopped resisting as hard. He recalled wondering of late if he were better suited for an earlier time in music history than his own century. *Well, you're about to find out,* he thought grimly. He felt better physically but still weak in a peculiar way. Clearly the jump through two-plus centuries cost him something. He pulled himself out of bed, needing badly to pee, and remembered the chamber pot. He left the pot, guessing that that was a servant's job.

He started making a mental list of things in his own century that he would have to find compensations for. Hygiene was one. People did not know about bacteria and rarely washed their hands. He would simply have to find opportunities to do so without calling attention to himself. Then his spine went icy when he remembered something far more serious—his heart medication. He reached inside his shirt and ran his finger down his scar, something he often did. Without the protection of a daily statin, the eighteenth-century cuisine of fat and more fat would likely kill him. He remembered the research he had done on natural remedies for cholesterol: flax seed, garlic, fish oil, and oatmeal. One of his first stops would be an apothecary.

Making his way to the kitchen, Stefan was delighted to accept a bowl of warm oatmeal with nuts. The house was quiet, and he walked, as silently as he could, toward the study. He slowly looked inside the sanctum. Mozart was at the table, intently working with quill at a sheet of lined paper. He had a fierce concentration about him that Stefan dared not break. Both a cup of coffee and a small glass of wine were at hand. It was exactly the way he would have imagined Mozart working.

Who is this? Stefan asked himself, still not sure of his reality. *He seems to be a perfectly cordial and generous person, almost too good.* But history had revealed other less palatable sides to Mozart.

Stefan backed up, intending to leave unnoticed, but a floorboard made a loud squeak. Mozart looked up abruptly, and just as abruptly, a smile lit his face.

He enthusiastically boomed, "Ah, good morning, Herr Radowitz! I trust you passed a good night?"

"I slept without moving, Maestro, thank you."

"Delightful!" He indicated the seemingly disorganized manuscript in front of him. "You have caught me *in opera flagrante*."

Stefan sat. He knew the answer to what he was going to ask. "Opera?"

The smile never leaving his face, Mozart started chatting rapidly. "Yes, an Italian comedy taken from a very scandalous French play, *Le mariage de Figaro*, by a brilliant Parisian, Pierre Augustin Beaumarchais. It has been banned in France because of its anti-aristocratic tone, and the emperor wanted to do the same here. But da Ponte, my librettist, and I took all the political tone out of it, leaving the hero Figaro to rail against unfaithful women rather than aristocratic tyrants. After that change it was deemed suitable. Why would I speak against aristocrats? They are my sources of income! The opera is now about love. The emperor recently employed several wonderful singers to take residence here and form an Italian opera company. They will be the cast. My opera was chosen over two others, including one by Salieri. He is a fine composer but is no match for me." This last pronouncement was not said as a boast but simple fact.

At this mention of Salieri, Stefan recalled the handful of Mozart biographies that made it clear that the animus between the two composers as presented in popular media and literature, going back to Chekhov, was largely fiction. Rivals, yes, and as such there was jousting between them in Vienna's competitive opera world. But clearly comments from Mozart such as he had just heard could stir resentment among his colleagues like Salieri.

"At what point in the opera are you now, Maestro?"

"I've just started the finale to act two. It will be like nothing anyone has seen. Starting with two people, then adding others one by one until finally there are seven onstage singing a *prestissimo*. It will take almost twenty-five minutes but will slowly build and build to a thrilling climax." He paused, then said softly, "No one else has done this, and no one else can."

He is right about that, for all time, thought Stefan.

"But there are always distractions. Two of my Masonic lodge brothers have died, and there is a service for them on the seventeenth. My brothers want music from me. I've written the music, but now I must copy the parts since my main copyist is no longer in Vienna. It takes time."

Stefan took a deep breath, then offered, "I can help Maestro. I have a good music hand," he said, thinking of his hobby with quill and ink.

"Indeed?" Mozart thought for a moment, then quickly got up. He took up one of the neat manuscript piles from another part of the table and put it in front of Stefan.

"This is my Masonic Funeral Music. Let me see what you can do with the first violin part."

In Stefan's time he would have scanned the score into the right software, selected the first violin part, pressed a button, and had it all in minutes. In the eighteenth century, the job was to copy each single part out of the full score by hand so the players would only have to read a single line. Every member of the orchestra would need their own individual part. It was labor intensive and slow. Quickness for a copyist was an asset, but accuracy was essential. It was a special skill.

Stefan began to set down the violin part with quick and delicate strokes. The piece itself was not long, and Stefan was done in a few minutes. He handed the single sheet to Mozart, who, after examining it, showed a look of happy surprise. "Excellent, very clear. Your hand even looks somewhat like mine!" *Hours of practice at that very thing*, thought Stefan.

"You could make some decent money as a copyist in Vienna," Mozart observed. Then an idea lit up his face. "If you will copy for me, we can compensate by reducing what you pay for room and board."

Stefan was dazzled by how fast this all was moving and just nodded.

"Ah, the other composers will all be so jealous when they learn I have a resident copyist," Mozart exclaimed with wicked glee. "There is more manuscript paper," he said, pointing, "and you can work from that very spot. Three first violins, two seconds, two violas, two celli, and one contrabasso."

Thus Stefan Radowitz found himself working at a table across from Wolfgang Amadeus Mozart as he composed an opera for the ages. That night, his second in the Mozart house, he lay in bed and started to consider that maybe this, after all, wasn't a hallucination. Maybe a hole had opened up in the fabric of space-time, between him and Mozart, and he had fallen through it.

There was much in his own time he could easily drop and consider it fair exchange, at least musically, for what he had fallen into. His life had become terribly frustrating in the twenty-first century. Yet, as far as he could tell, he was in 1785 with no clear path back, and he needed to find the same door again. There was one part of his modern life that was irreplaceable, Katrina. The thought of never seeing her again…

And what about Doc Brown's *Back to the Future* conundrum—the integrity of the historical timeline? What if he inadvertently changed something that then had terrible repercussions in the future? Alternatively, what if his time travel was already baked into the timeline and all was as it should be? But what if he inadvertently let slip some impossible piece of knowledge that he should not know? Was witchcraft an issue in the Age of Enlightenment? He would need to guard his speech constantly.

Chapter 8 — A Salon

THE DAY AFTER hearing Mozart play his piano concerto, Lisa left the Artaria music shop with Georg in tow, and he carried a thick stack of scores of piano music in two large canvas bags with handles. Much of it was Mozart, but also J. S. Bach, C. P. E. Bach, Haydn, and one piece by Antonio Salieri. She had been cut off from the treasure that Georg was carrying; it was water for the desert of her soul. Mozart's concerto still rang in her mind, and she mentally replayed much of it, even singing its melodies in the carriage. Her excitement brought a broad smile from the older man.

Lisa took fresh joy this day looking out the carriage window, riding down the street on which she grew up. Her house at twelve Nightingale Street was grand and spacious, though not so much as the great estate houses further out in the countryside near to the Vienna Woods. The whole estate was perhaps twenty acres by modern measure and had an exquisite and expansive garden that took up a sizable fraction of the total space. Lisa knew every tree and shrub on the property and had spent much happy time alone when she was little, exploring the garden and surrounding woodlands. She especially loved the brook that bubbled through the far back and often returned soaking wet and streaked with mud from her solo explorations and crayfish hunting.

The carriage turned into the short, curved driveway and the iron rims of the wheels and horses' hooves made their noisy clatter on the cobblestones. Lisa's impulse as a child was always to open the carriage door from within and hop to the ground without using the step, not waiting for the footman to help her. Today she almost forgot again but remembered at the last moment to take the proffered gloved hand. Georg brought the bags of music into the parlor and placed them by the pianoforte. She was right behind him with the joy of a child at Christmas. She did not notice when he took her light shawl from her shoulders as she dug her hands into the treasure.

Since the day she had mimicked the child Mozart at Schönbrunn Palace when she was three, Lisa had been drawn to the keyboard like a bee to clover. Even through the trauma of her mother's death by miscarriage not long after that afternoon at the imperial castle, not a day went by when she was not at the pianoforte, making up melodies and even supplying underlying harmony. Her father brought in a teacher whose specialty was young children, but after only a few months, he reported, "I have nothing else to teach her."

She showed astonishing brilliance in everything she undertook, such as mastering both French and English in a year spent in London and Paris when she was thirteen. She began to play private concerts *en salon* for family and close friends before her feet could reach the floor, and she also started to read the books in her father's library, which she would eventually devour. Her father indulged her, bringing tutors of various subjects to the house, all of whom shook their heads in amazement at the lightning mind in the beautiful young girl.

Today, after a period of almost three years in which all these joys were suppressed, she took out the music of a Mozart sonata in A minor that was composed just a few years back, while he still lived in Salzburg. She stared at the page before playing, taking it in as a whole, focusing on what seemed to be more complex passages, and noting the tempo indication: *Allegro maestoso.*

"Lively, majestic," she said out loud. "Majestic. So, lively but a little slower?" She started the movement with what she thought might be a tempo that satisfied the marking, thought it too slow, started again a bit quicker, played two lines, and knew she had found the right character. It was solemn and yet urgent. "That's it," she announced to herself. The three movements unfolded before her, every note in exactly the right place, carrying the perfect amount of weight, or lightness, that it should. *One miracle after another*, she thought.

Lisa had wondered about how her playing ranked with the famous male pianists of her time, like Muzio Clementi. She would not dare compare herself to her idol, Mozart, but when she heard Clementi, she came away thinking that there was nothing that she had just heard that she herself could not do. Her adult teacher had been one of the finest in Austria, Joseph Anton Steffan, the teacher of two queens, Marie Antoinette and Maria Carolina of Naples. She had had counterpoint lessons—the study of the proper moving relationships between notes in music—with the renown Johann Joseph Fux. They had each been wonderful, but even though the men both told her that she was possibly their finest student ever, neither ever mentioned a word about her performing in public, or composing. Lisa knew that there were indeed female performers and composers, but they faced steep odds in being heard, and she did not know of any who came from her class. "Just not the thing for a Lady" she had heard more than once whenever she mentioned that playing in public would be something she would aspire to.

But that was not on her mind at the moment. She gorged herself with music the rest of the day and into the night. And into the days that followed, fueled by coffee and pastries. She never hurried. She would pick individual phrases and puzzle over how they should be shaped, asking questions like a lawyer in a cross-examination. She loved all the composers, but Mozart was beyond…She had ached for this; the scorn of her peers for attending a concert too soon was a small price to pay. And she felt new urges to put on paper the sounds that were starting to flower inside her. Sometimes they strongly resembled those of her idol, Mozart, but would often take their own twists. It seemed that there was always more music waiting for her at the edge of her imagination, and it beckoned to her to find it.

After a number of hours at the keyboard, Lisa said, "Georg, please bring the gig around. It's a beautiful day, and I need to get out."

"Yes, My Lady!" She had been almost a shut-in for many months. In the days following, Lisa began to reclaim the greater world around her, going for carriage rides in the beautiful Austrian countryside or just taking long walks. It was an early spring after a stern, bitter winter, and the magnolias and cherry trees sent forth their blossoms at almost the same time. At home she changed the plot of the garden and added some plants that would yield flowers later in the season. She even donned some old clothes and explored some of the secret woodland places of her childhood, getting delightfully filthy. She felt free for the first time in years, and the unexplained angry outbursts had abated.

———

Over the next two months, Lisa's social isolation began to thaw, and she received a few invitations to tea at the homes of peers. At one of these teas, Lisa encountered an old friend of the family, the Countess von Thun, highly respected among the Viennese nobility and a supporter of Mozart's.

"Dearest Lisa, I am so pleased to see you, and to see you being seen," she said knowingly.

"Maria, the most surprising thing to me about receiving these invitations is the fact that I have actually accepted some of them; I still believe Christ was right about forgiving those who persecute us, although that can seem impossible. But when I learned that you would be here today, I came gladly and forgave freely," she said, looking about the room.

"Lisa, attitudes have started to change. People are beginning to put two and two together about Charles," she said in a low voice. "Your bruises, the time when you walked with a cane, and those excuses about being clumsy…No one who remembers you climbing trees like a sprite when you were growing up could believe that…at least when it was pointed out to them. There is more sympathy now with your defying the traditional mourning period."

Lisa thought over that surprising news and wondered whom it was that might have done the pointing out. The answer came to her quickly, in the person of the lady with whom she was talking, the Countess Maria Wilhelmine von Thun und Hohenstein, probably the only lady in Vienna with the stature to change the often-miniscule minds of the nobility.

Moved, Lisa bowed her head formally to her older friend. "Thank you, My Lady."

"Nonsense, I did nothing," she said, her voice the lightness of a sparrow song. "As a matter of fact, I am giving a salon in two weeks to introduce a promising young pianist from Hungary who is in Vienna studying with Salieri. Do come! I would value your opinion."

———

Two weeks later, in the Countess von Thun's palatial house, Lisa sat politely along the back wall of the salon and listened the young Hungarian. The young man was dashing and glamorous and had dazzling finger technique. Lisa was impressed by that but thought his musical expression was flat. He then switched to some of his own compositions, and they were obviously written to showcase what he thought was his greatest asset, a lightning right hand. Lisa was appalled, however; it was all derived from other music, with not a speck of originality. It was a frustrating experience, and she could not keep still.

Later, speaking quietly to Lady Thun, Lisa allowed her frustration to give itself expression. "Never have I found virtuosity so boring." Then she said, "I'm sorry, that was out of place."

"No, my dear, I find your words apt. I actually wanted you to hear him for that very reason."

Taken aback, Lisa stammered, "I'm not...sure what you mean."

"Didn't he make you want to stand up, push him off the bench, and just take over playing?"

Lisa's cheeks reddened, then she dissolved in a good laugh. "Am I that transparent?"

"To one who has known and admired your gifts as long as I have, yes. Lisa, I know you are practicing again, and composing. Oh, don't look surprised…servants talk. My dear, more women are stepping up. At my next salon, I want to present you."

Lisa was speechless.

"You need not speak. Just nod your assent."

Lisa's head moved slowly on the vertical axis, her mouth still agape.

———

The date was set six weeks hence, near midsummer. But Lisa insisted that the invitations not go out until a few days before the event. Lady Thun was perplexed at the request.

"Lisa, darling, people need more time than that to plan their engagements. You'll get a smaller crowd." The countess tilted her head with its dark coiffure to one side and narrowed her eyes. "You already know this. Is that what you want to happen? To keep your visibility low?"

Lisa shrugged. "I guess a smaller crowd would not be the worst thing. But it is more to give me time to change my mind."

The older countess nodded with understanding. "You must be ready for it to be a sought-after invitation. Those of my generation remember hearing you play ten or fifteen years ago. You were adorable!"

Lisa responded rather sharply. "Adorable is the last thing I feel like now." She took a breath. "So much has happened since then, and the only thing that's the same for me is my love for the music."

"Then share that love with old friends!" the countess pleaded. "That's all this is, my dear."

Lisa smiled slightly. "I'll try to keep that in mind."

———

Over the next weeks, Lisa went through many pages of music to make her program. She planned on keeping it short, under an hour. Along with her beloved Mozart and almost-as-beloved Haydn, she had found an Italian composer whose difficult music fascinated her, Domenico Scarlatti. To end the program, she had composed a sonata modeled along the lines of Scarlatti's single movement sonatas. But she knew it was no mere imitation; she had unusual harmonic twists that would surprise.

Yet this decision to play her own music came with a dark cloud, almost a dread that she could not define. There was some menacing memory that resisted being brought to light. She knew full well that her playing of other composers' music was at a dazzling level and that her listeners would be bowled over. But to play her own music was like opening some door inside her, behind which was something highly personal, maybe frightening, and to invite the world to take a look.

The day came, and the Countess von Thun's vast salon was laid out with delicacies from the far corners of the empire. The late sending of the invitations seemed to have done little to suppress the outcome, although there were faces missing that could be counted among the leaders of the demonstration against Lisa at the Burgtheater concert. Lady Thun shrugged. "Still angry that you did not want to marry their imbecilic sons."

The attendees were welcoming and supportive, and once she started the program, she was not nervous at all; rather, she was in a state of delight to be sharing that which she loved so. Expressions of admiration were sometimes sounded as she played, and she felt as if she were conversing with her audience.

As she was nearing the end of the penultimate work, her thoughts drifted to her own music about to be premiered, and she felt a stab of unease. An old and familiar cloud developed in her viscera and mind. When the moment came to start her sonata, she suddenly asked for a glass of water and a pause. The unease was building rapidly into severe anxiety. She suddenly was flooded with fragments of memory: of being seated at a keyboard, of trying to play despite bursts of derisive laughter surrounding her, of shame flooding her and a flight to her own bedroom, of her husband's angry red face screaming at her, of sharp pain on her, then in her.

Lisa, terribly confused, could not tell which was reality—the vivid and terrifying images in her mind's eye or the friendly but puzzled and concerned faces around her. She became frozen in the clutch of fear, time stopping. Her heart seemed to want to pound through her chest; she could not catch her breath and became dizzy. She thought she might die. Dream state and reality coalesced. Lisa burst into hot tears and finally was able to flee from the salon.

———

Two days later Lisa was seated in the small gazebo in her garden with Lady Thun. Roses and rhododendrons wrapped the grounds in a lush color palette, and the carefully tended honeysuckle vines on the gazebo supports enveloped them with fragrance that seemed edible. Maria was listening to Lisa's attempt to describe her panic-driven departure. "So, it was like a waking dream?" she asked gently.

Lisa was still partially in the grip of the shame and anger, and words came haltingly. She feared to make a complete recounting of the incident lest she bring it back again fully. "Not a dream, My Lady. Parts of a terrifying memory I had forgotten…it seemed so real." She paused, then said more quietly, "Charles's anger…how he hurt me…oh, how he hurt me!" she exclaimed as her face fell into her hands, her rage and fear starting to rise once more.

Maria reached for her younger friend's hands with both of hers and clasped them tightly. Lisa leaned her head forward toward her companion, and the older woman then moved and wrapped her arms around her young friend, laying a hand on Lisa's head. The compassionate warmth of a tangible body finally calmed Lisa.

Sitting up she asked, "I wonder what he did that I don't recall."

"It wasn't difficult to see the evidence of his treatment of you, Lisa. And I had the feeling that there was much that was not observable."

Lisa shook her head slowly, her lower lip trembling.

"I am your confidante if you ever wish to unburden yourself. You are safe with me."

Lisa mouthed, "Thank you." Looking up into the bright sky, Lisa shielded her eyes and asked, "How badly did I frighten everyone?"

"Well, all were certainly concerned but assumed that you had taken suddenly ill. Which, I think, is by and large the truth." She then added emphatically, "You played brilliantly. That is what people will mostly remember. You'll have a willing audience anytime you want, my dear Lisa."

"I wonder if they will ever hear my own music," Lisa responded, dejected.

"They would welcome your music if they could hear it. I know." Maria sighed. "My father was a young man in the war with Turkey in 1718, and when he grew old, he would speak of how war damaged his mind…at the sound of a loud noise, or anything even mildly surprising, he would imagine himself back in battle, and it seemed real to him for a moment. After much time went by, it faded but…" She looked into Lisa's eyes and said, "You were in your own war. I hope the day comes when the noise of battle ceases for you."

Chapter 9 — Foul Mouth

OVER THE NEXT days, Mozart was able to take advantage of the time Stefan's copy work bought him and brought act two of the great opera to a close. Two more acts to go. "I'll put Signor Figaro to rest for a while," Mozart said to Stefan. "I have other children to tend, and the *Figaro* premiere is not until the end of April. Herr Radowitz, you can start copying the parts for the opera," he said brightly. Most mornings and parts of afternoons passed with the two at the study table.

Stefan had a close look at Mozart's working methods. He did not compose a long and complex work completely in his head as many had thought, but neither did he make extensive sketches. He used pieces of manuscript paper to work out counterpoint or try different melodic gestures, but it was clear he carried the framework and much of the detail in his head. He then just copied what he had constructed in his mind.

Mozart was highly disciplined in his work habits but loved nothing more than a good party, and the Mozarts both entertained at home and were entertained at numerous gala events and costume balls. The floors of the bottom level rooms supported many a contra-dance melee. Stefan did his best and took part when there was a partner who was patient with him. He adored watching Mozart play billiards at these events, who easily took his opponents' money; with only three balls, the number of angles and shot possibilities were infinite, and it involved both making good shots and preventing your opponent from doing the same. The ability came from the same region of that extraordinary brain as did the music.

Once or twice a week, Mozart would take Stefan to dine with him at one of his two favorite inns, and after dinner there always was a card game, which Mozart joined. Stefan would sip wine while watching, and it became clear to him that Mozart was good at this as well. A favorite game was whist, a forerunner of hearts, and money was definitely involved. Stefan had read modern scholarly musing on the possibility that Mozart's money troubles toward the end of the decade were due in part to gambling. As far as Stefan could tell, the games that he saw were low-stakes affairs, which Mozart usually won. The losses and gains were negligible in these games, but he was an enthusiastic player, and his ability to keep track of cards must have been phenomenal. Stefan was always left choking by the cigar and pipe smoke—he definitely preferred his own century's smoking restrictions—but was willing to endure secondary smoke to watch this man do most anything, even at play. After each game Mozart would happily stagger home, Stefan supporting him.

It was at one of the frequent parties at Mozart's home that Stefan saw the side of his idol that he had read and wondered about. The dancing had not yet started when Mozart, already deep in his cups, insisted on passing out sheets of music for some kind of group singing event. Stefan looked at the familiar hand on the staff paper, and his hair stood on end. He was about to witness the first performance of what was possibly Mozart's most infamous work—a six-part canon whose text started with the line, *"Leck mich in Arse."* ("Lick my ass.") Stefan knew about the obscene ditty but had never heard it. Now he was about to witness its premiere and the public's first reaction to this side of the great genius.

And the opening response as guests perused the sheets in their hands was silent shock, which was surely what Mozart intended as he began guffawing at his guests' astonishment. Three or four of them came forward, shaking their heads, trying to hand Mozart his sheets back, saying, "No, no, no, Wolfgang," or just "What's the meaning of this?"

That only elicited more roaring laugher from Wolfgang as he put his hands behind his back. "This is one of my most brilliant works! The door is locked and will remain so until you all do your duty!"

His laughing insistence and will were so strong that the protestors shrugged their shoulders in acquiescence. *He is amazing, in more ways than one*, thought Stefan as Mozart conquered then divided the guests to cover the parts.

The first line was actually the only bawdy part of the text; the rest went on to praise merriment over glumness. And the counterpoint was astonishing—six interdependent lines that fit together like a great time-piece, meshing perfectly. *In just a few years he will write the Jupiter Symphony with its five-part counterpoint. Did that impulse start at a drunken house party?* thought Stefan as he sang. *No*, he thought, *he always had a potty mouth in his letters.*

The singing guests started losing their places from laughing as they sang more; the juxtaposition of the sublime and obscene were masterfully blended. The group effort almost disintegrated before the last measure was reached, and Mozart had tears running down his face, nearly falling down from hysteria. It was infectious, and the guests crumpled into balls of merriment as they held their sides in roaring laughter.

The robust dancing afterward lasted long. *Never was there such an ice-breaker for a party*, Stefan thought.

Chapter 10—A Premiere During Intermission

December 1785

"MAESTRO, I DON'T quite understand. Your E-flat concerto will be premiered in the middle of an oratorio by Ditters von Dittersdorf? First his, then yours, then his again? How will that work?"

"Simple. They perform part one, they leave, I perform my concerto, we leave, then Dittersdorf finishes. You seem surprised. Is the practice different in Bonn?"

Stefan had seen that programming practices were indeed different in Mozart's time. Here was another example of a major work being split apart. He had seen it done with symphonies, but seeing an oratorio torn like this was still a surprise.

Stefan mumbled a nonresponse which thankfully Mozart did not answer.

"So, there's copying to be done. I've found another copyist to help, but since it's in a week, it will still take both of us."

"How will three of us work off a single manuscript?"

"Only two will. I have my own copy," Mozart said, smiling and tapping the side of his head.

Stefan thumbed through the just finished work. "Where's the solo part?"

Again, a tap on the head and that wry smile.

The day of the concert, the twenty-second arrived, and Mozart and Stefan were there an hour before the rehearsal at the Burgtheater in order to distribute the parts to the proper music stands. A number of the musicians were already there to take an advanced look at the music. Stefan became librarian for Mozart and placed the parts on their proper stands.

Stefan knew that working musicians in this era were regarded as common servants, and that even Mozart himself had been on occasion mistaken for a servant. A similar affront would lead to an explosion from Beethoven twenty years later. But Mozart had simply bowed politely. He did not address the musicians as servants but as colleagues. "Gentlemen, I hope you are all well this morning and that you will enjoy playing my new work," he said with a gracious smile. This was answered by bows being tapped on stands, as was still the custom in Stefan's time. The respect and admiration the orchestra members held for him was clear at a glance.

Stefan took an observation seat behind the first violins, and he was quivering with excitement. Mozart had told him that his plan was always to play the work through without stopping, then go back and attend to what needed work, which was exactly Stefan's approach to first rehearsals.

Mozart put his hands to the keys, looked around to make sure he had all eyes, then gave a vigorous upbeat with head and body, and the jubilant E-flat chords exploded into life. Stefan's breath left his body; he was not prepared for the fullness and power that Mozart's music, and Mozart himself, drew from the musicians.

As one who had performed many Mozart concertos as soloist and conductor simultaneously, Stefan had always wondered how much actual conducting Mozart did when not playing. He quickly saw the answer— very little. Mozart would play the solo passages while looking directly at the particular instruments that were playing with him. At the big orchestral entrances, he would give a strong hand gesture and often joined the whole orchestra on the pianoforte.

But Stefan saw it was not Mozart's hands or head. His playing was compelling enough, but like almost all great conductors, his eyes spoke stronger than anything else. He was in constant eye contact with the players. With his facial expressions, he affected their volume, their quality of sound, the way they shaped the music. It was a deep connection and marvelous to behold. By the end of the rehearsal time, the concerto seemed ready to present, and at a high level. Stefan was seeing the greatest performer he had ever witnessed playing music of unsurpassable beauty and brilliance.

At the end of the rehearsal, Mozart did a quick checklist of what the players needed to review before the performance. He bade them good day and received applause and bravos, which he courteously acknowledged.

As the two exited the stage door, Stefan struggled for words. "That was marvelous, Maestro," was the best he could do.

"It's a good group of lads," Mozart responded modestly.

"They were motivated by the music," Stefan said.

Mozart threw modesty aside. "Yes!" he said brightly. "It's the best concerto ever written!"

Wow, what a braggart! But it's true and will be…until the next one, thought Stefan.

———

While walking to the theater that night with Wolfgang and Constanze, Stefan asked who was conducting *Esther,* Dittersdorf's cantata.

"Salieri," said Constanze tersely.

Annoyance? thought Stefan. *But that stuff about him in* Amadeus *was all crap.* Gathering himself, he tried to say knowingly, "Ah yes, Salieri."

"Not a welcome name in the Mozart household," said Constanze.

"Well, he took a prominent pupil whom I thought was prepared to study with me," Mozart patiently explained.

Stefan probed, "So, things are bad between you now?"

"The unpleasantness was a few years back," added Mozart. "We'll probably always pursue the same prizes. He is not a bad man. But you can't extend an arm in Vienna without touching him. He's the rooster in the henyard, the Royal Court Composer."

They arrived at the theater and presented their performer passes, then Constanze and Stefan made their way to the first row while Mozart took a side door to the stage area. The chorus, orchestra, and soloists took their places. Salieri strode confidently on stage. He had dark hair lying in bangs on his forehead, was serious and distinguished of demeanor, and, like Mozart, was not a big man. He was greeted warmly by the audience and musicians. His stern look lightened a bit while acknowledging the applause with two formal bows, then he turned, raised his hands, and began with an authoritative upbeat. Salieri was a fine conductor, although without the benefit of modern technique; he simply beat the patterns without much variation, and with both hands. But he had total mastery of the score, with sharp rhythm and snappy energy.

Stefan was pleasantly surprised by the quality of Dittersdorf's music. It was well-made, sturdy music and pleasing without being moving. Vienna's air and water at this moment in history was nourishing handfuls of gifted composers, but almost all were forgotten except for the trio, none of them native to Vienna, of Haydn, Mozart, and Beethoven. Was there another giant somewhere who had gotten squeezed out because history has only so much room?

Then came the concerto, taut, thrilling, sensual, dramatic. The performance done, the audience response was warm but not what Stefan thought was deserved for something he regarded as a miracle. He clambered from his first-row seat directly onto the stage, not waiting for Mozart in the wings. Completely dumbstruck as he took Mozart's hand, he finally blurted out, "That was the greatest performance I ever heard!"

Without dropping a beat, Mozart casually replied, "Yes, you're right."

Chapter 11—In the Audience

22 December 1785

LISA WAS PRESENT at much of Vienna's concert life and came to know the work of a number of the city's composers. She especially was eager for a concert in late December, on the twenty-second. The main attraction that night was an oratorio by Dittersdorf on the Old Testament tale of Queen Esther. It was in two big parts, and the concert format followed the practice of the day in presenting such works with a separate piece to fill the gap between the two parts. In this case it was the new Piano Concerto in E-flat by Mozart. For her, this was the main attraction. She was there with her Aunt Catherine, the Dowager Baroness Hohenberg, who had taken up the duties of looking after Lisa as best she could in the aftermath of Lisa's father's death and the travails of her disastrous marriage.

They sat through the first half of the big Dittersdorf choral work, conducted by Salieri, attentively. "It's impressive, but I'm not as inspired as I think I'm meant to be," commented Lisa wryly.

"I'm not inspired at all," grumbled her elderly companion.

The break in the performance was only as long as it took for the stage to be reset for the concerto. Wearing a blazing red jacket, Mozart's step was quick onto the stage, with the applause strong. Unlike the formal Salieri, Mozart looked into the seats, raised his arms in acknowledgement, and smiled broadly. He sat and began briskly. He was energized by the audience, and from the first beat, he was a channel for that energy from the house seats to the performers. The concerto opened triumphantly with majestic chords played by the full orchestra, including brilliant trumpets and drums. Then Mozart played. Every phrase seemed like a new character had stepped onto the stage as in an opera. The middle slower movement was serious in contrast to the joyous opening, sometimes bending toward tragedy. It seemed that a serene respite was not in the offing.

But Mozart was setting the audience up; for out of nowhere in the merry hunting-tune finale, there appeared another, and as-yet unheard, leisurely *andantino*. It was a gentle woodwind quartet in dialogue with the piano and strings—four lovers pleading their cases to each other and answered by a velvet string choir—over which Mozart at the keyboard improvised a lightly dancing butterfly, an angel offering blessing.

"He casts a spell!" Lisa exclaimed, overcome.

"And such inspired pianoforte playing! Almost as good as you!" Aunt Catherine added.

Lisa waved her aunt off, then said, "His music just gets better with each new work, even though the previous one was perfection." Lisa longed with all her heart to plunge her hands into that score. And dreamed of playing with an orchestra!

There was a short break after the concerto, and the two women decided that they had had enough Dittersdorf. As they rose Lisa took note of a light-haired taller man who was sitting in the front row almost directly behind Mozart. She pointed him out to her aunt. "He was engaged during the music as if he were performing, making movements with his head as if he already knew the work. He climbed up onto the stage to greet the Maestro, who obviously knew him. How did he know a work so well that's just now being premiered?"

As the carriage bore them home, her mind was happily filling up with music, both that which she just had heard and the new music in her that was forming in response. But the memory of the man who seemed to know the concerto ahead of time stayed with her.

Chapter 12 — Slip of the Tongue

AT DINNER ONE night in late February at Schulerstrasse, the conversation took a turn toward Franz Joseph Haydn, at that time the most famous composer in Europe.

"Papa Haydn is the one composer who can match me. I have learned much from him, especially his string quartets, which we often have played together. I studied them closely."

"He is still in service to Prince Esterházy?" Stefan already knew the answer to this.

"Yes, forty-eight kilometers distant, in the middle of nowhere but with the enormous resources of a wealthy court. But there are rumors of his leaving his post in Hungary to tour more. He would be welcome anywhere in Europe."

Constanze nudged her husband, saying, "Tell Herr Radowitz about the quartets you dedicated to Haydn and what happened."

Stefan knew this tale as well but was utterly thrilled to hear it from the horse's mouth. And Mozart welcomed the opportunity to relate the story. "Well, as you know, Haydn has more or less invented the string quartet. So in gratitude I sent six quartets to him with a dedication letter."

"Such a beautiful letter," Constanze said, "about a father sending his sons to a beloved friend."

"And earlier this year, we gathered here on two occasions and read them through. Haydn played first violin, Dittersdorf second, Johannes Vanhal the cello, and I played viola."

"I would have given anything to be there," said Stefan with absolute truth. He had often thought of this rare gathering of genius.

Constanze eagerly said, "And Wolfgang's papa was there! Tell Herr Radowitz what Haydn said to him. No, let me tell him!"

This was a famous quote, relayed to Mozart's sister by his father, and it had come down through history. Constanze intoned, "Haydn said, 'I tell you before God and as an honest man, your son is the greatest composer known to me either personally or by reputation. He has taste, and what is more, the most profound...'"

"'...knowledge of composition,'" Stefan said *sotto voce*, before realizing what he'd done. He'd had too much wine and was feeling close to the family. A little too much so.

Wolfgang and Constanze both looked at him in astonishment. In a soft voice at his lowest pitch, Mozart asked, "Where did you hear that?"

"Perhaps...I overheard it in a conversation...," he said in hopeless reply.

"No one but my family and Haydn know of those words. My father put them in a letter to my sister, who put them in a letter to me."

Stefan had two choices: try to spin this lie into plausibility, or to tell the truth, which may get him thrown out.

"I'm fairly certain I heard of it from a colleague in Bonn. Someone else at the occasion must have heard the remark and passed it on."

Mozart was open-mouthed, and Stefan started sweating, a rivulet running down his back.

Constanze came to the rescue. "Wolfgang, you were not in the room when Haydn spoke to Papa. Several people probably heard the remark. Besides, how else could Herr Radowitz have known?"

Mozart and Stefan both relaxed, and Constanze guided the conversation to fashion, a topic that always caught Mozart's attention.

Later Stefan lay in bed, trembling. He put down the copy of the German translation of *Gulliver's Travels* that he had purchased to read himself to sleep; it was not working tonight. It was both the close call, which must have deepened Mozart's suspicions about him, and the scare of being revealed that awoke Stefan's feelings of deep loss.

His thoughts, as so often, were of returning to Katrina. Even if a way back existed, would his heart fail him before he could find it? His visit to a highly regarded apothecary appalled him. It was as if the man did not even know the location of the heart in the body, let alone what cholesterol was. The last straw was when the man recommended a physician who was particularly skilled at bleeding "which can release the pressure and allow the heart to beat more freely." Stefan realized that his own poor knowledge of treatment—eating foods that lowered cholesterol and exercising—was superior to anything in 1785.

Being with Mozart—*Mozart!*—was like a powerful and addicting drug that blotted out everything. Yet his anguish of being torn from his old life was breaking through the drug's ecstatic grip. Stefan carried within himself both wrenching loss and constant thrill.

He then took a healthy step. For the first time, he admitted to himself that he felt helpless, and wept. He cried himself to sleep and had dreams of both worlds.

In the morning he resolved anew to get back to his time. But how? He had gotten here from the future. Surely it wasn't a one-way track. Time's flowing only forward was an illusion, he had read in Buddhist texts. That made new sense. *I have to find the right train, on the right track, going the right direction.* He belonged in his time, with Kat.

———

Stefan gained more of a complete picture of Mozart the man as time went by. Sometimes on entering the study, he found him sitting quietly, gazing out the window, but seeming not to be looking at anything. Other times he found him at the keyboard, his arms folded, looking blankly at the keys, distress on his face, as if he were trying to break through some barrier to access the music within him.

In those times he also overheard, from his garret room, fierce arguments between the couple. The topic he could not discern, but the dynamic was usually an accusation from Constanze, then a fierce rejoinder from Mozart, a pushback from Constanze, and finally an eruption from Mozart that silenced things. There was no physical violence but enough frustration and anger to yield plenty of verbal violence.

Stefan was no psychologist but knew that there was an unmistakable sadness—or, as it was called at that time, melancholia—that was not far beneath the gay surface of the genius. Some sore and aching wound. Of course all in Stefan's time who loved Mozart's music knew that there were often dark chromatic clouds of suffering beneath the beautiful surface.

Stefan had always felt that Mozart's intent of the effect of his music never quite seemed as personal as it did with Beethoven's, where the sense was always of a man in your face, pressing you against the wall, demanding that you "LISTEN to this!" Mozart's music itself was sorrowful, or merry, or however this supernaturally gifted human being had found it in nature. And its passions, no matter the color, were always enclosed in a bubble of unsurpassed beauty. "Mozart ist die Sonne," stated Antonin Dvorak. ("Mozart is the Sun.")

1 7 8 6

Chapter 13 — Soprano

FIGARO REHEARSALS WERE in rooms at the royal resi-
dence at the Hofburg Palace. The first set of rehearsals for an opera was
always musical one-on-one sessions between the composer and individual cast members. Then it progressed to ensemble sessions with multiple
singers.

Stefan was about to meet and hear the legendary singer who created
the role of Susanna, the English soprano Nancy Storace. She was the
highest-paid singer in Europe and had come to Vienna from Italy in
1782 as part of the emperor's desire to have an Italian-language opera
company. She had married, while in Vienna, a bass player who immediately started abusing her. When the emperor heard of this treatment of
one of his prize artists, he banished the man from Austria. Nancy had
a child by him who did not survive and, after that, a vocal breakdown.
Figaro marked her comeback.

Mozart asked Stefan to help notate any changes in the music that
might come out of the rehearsal process. The room was a spacious
salon. The furniture had been moved aside to make room. The res-
onance from the parquet floor was offset by the muffling of heavy
drapes, which went from the top of the tall windows almost to the

floor. The acoustic condition was thus fairly well balanced—resonant but still clear.

Mozart was at the pianoforte when Storace entered, wearing a brilliant blue flower-print dress. Her hat was like a flower wagon, massive, and charmingly tilted, much like one in the images of her that came down through history. She was slightly darker in skin tone and hair than in those portraits and miniatures; she was, after all, half Italian. Her eyes were dark but nevertheless lit the room like children's sparklers, and she bestowed a dazzling smile on Mozart. "Maestro," she said with warmth as she curtsied in response to his bow. "Signorina," he replied, as if she were still single. He seemed completely starstruck.

She turned to Stefan with a querying look that asked, *"And who are you?"*

Mozart introduced Stefan as a dear friend who had proven invaluable and was here to keep track of any changes she might request. Stefan, trying to break the ice, said in English, "It would be my honor to assist two great artists."

Nancy laughed with delight as she broke into English herself. "A fellow countryman! How delightful to hear my mother tongue!" she said, in her definitely non-aristocratic tones. "Were you born in England?"

"No, but I have spent most of my life there."

"And were well educated there, I think, from your speech."

Mozart, whose English was rather behind his other three languages, nevertheless added, "Then we are all well met," which elicited another sparkling burst of laughter from Nancy. Charm poured from her in waves.

For rehearsals, each singer had been given their solo part with only the vocal and bass lines, not a full score with all parts. Mozart filled in the rest as they rehearsed. The purpose of these one on ones with the composer was to focus on the arias.

They began with one of the arias Stefan most loved, from act four. Figaro thinks Susanna is about to betray him to the Count. Susanna knows he thinks that and is determined to teach him a lesson. With him listening, she sings a serenade, pleading for her lover (Figaro thinks she sings of the Count) to *"Deh vieni, non tardar!"* (*"Come, don't be late!"*) In her heart, of course, she is singing this showstopper to Figaro. It was Stefan's favorite moment in all of Mozart's…no, make that all of opera. And to hear the soprano who created the role actually sing it…

Stefan's secret hope was to see evidence of the long-rumored powerful attraction between the two, but what he saw instead was a business-like session between composer and performer on what they still considered to be a work in progress.

"The end doesn't work for me," Nancy said bluntly. "It's too extended, and you have me go so low here (pointing) that I won't be set up for the high note here (again pointing)."

Mozart received the request to change his music calmly. He put his hand on his chin thoughtfully. "Well, I liked the idea of making the moonlight last a little longer." She smiled at this. "But I suppose I do need to remember how much singing you've been doing over the whole evening." He took a sheet of paper and quickly sketched some fragments of melody. "This…" He sketched again directly under the first one. "Or maybe this."

Stefan looked and saw that Mozart had, with remarkable speed, created two different treatments of the end of the aria.

"Try these," Mozart said, showing them to the soprano. He demonstrated at the keyboard as Nancy hummed along. She shook her head. "I'm still worried about the length."

"Then let's just make a cut," he said decisively, and he did so on her score. Stefan looked, and suddenly, there was the sublime version of the aria that had come down through history. Stefan was again astonished. Mozart had listened to his performer's need and incorporated it seamlessly, on the spot. The result was perfection.

They then went through it without stopping. Such a beguiling invitation to lovemaking in a moonlit garden had never before been penned, nor ever would be again. It recalled to Stefan's mind the times Hannah and he made love outdoors, and he bowed his head sadly.

For the rehearsals of ensembles, Stefan was an observer. Mozart's attitude toward what he had written outside of the arias was different. The score, as it had been written down, was not to be changed. However Luisa Laschi, singing the role of the Countess, expressed concern about the upper range in the Act two trio.

"I can take her part, and she mine," Nancy boldly suggested. Mozart agreed, but after that, Laschi and Storace became rather frosty with each other.

Stefan chuckled taking all this in. *Some things never change*, he thought. The soprano with the top line complained that it was too high; instead of adjusting the writing, the composer simply assigned the top line to another singer, relegating singer number one to the—humiliating!—middle line. It didn't matter which century. *A soprano is always a soprano and wants to be on top*, he thought.

The chorus was scheduled to come to one of the final-week rehearsals. Before they came, Stefan approached Mozart with a suggestion.

"Maestro, will the chorus rehearse together?"

"Oh, they'll gather and sing through the parts a few times."

As I figured, Stefan thought. "If you would allow me some time with them, I think I can improve their performance for you. I can make them sound better vocally and have better ensemble. Maybe even we could understand their words."

Mozart raised his eyebrows at this but then said with a shrug, "Please, as you wish."

Stefan found the assembly room for the chorus, got their attention, and said, "My name is Radowitz. Maestro Mozart asked me to work with you for a few minutes before you go on in act one." Stefan did some basic diction and voice placement work with them, and the small choir suddenly heard that they could actually sound markedly better. Pleased looks circulated in the room.

Toward the end of act one, Figaro brings in the villagers to sing to the count. The choir sang, and Mozart almost stopped conducting in surprise. The rest of the cast could not help but turn and look. It sounded like a brand-new choir; it was so good it became a distraction for a few moments. Mozart grinned broadly.

In the interval after act one, Mozart found Stefan and said in his best Italian accent, "*Stefano! Il coro é bellisimo!*" ("*The chorus is beautiful!*")

"*Grazie, Maestro,*" Stefan responded, bowing low.

After that, Mozart never called him anything but Stefano.

———

The production picked up steam in the whole rehearsal process pretty much in the manner to which Stefan was accustomed. Bigger and bigger pieces of scenery, costumes, props began to appear, and the orchestra appeared in the last week. Stefan saw famous historical anecdotes unfold before him almost exactly as they had come down through history. It made him wonder again if this all wasn't his own mental projection of what he already knew. But he had no choice but to continue in the extraordinary reality.

Chapter 14—View from Backstage

1 May 1786

THE MARRIAGE OF *Figaro* premiere was received with decent praise, although Stefan thought the applause a bit tepid. The orchestra was slightly shaky in parts—it was a complex work—but he knew that these moments would correct themselves with more performances.

He also knew that its success would be respectable but not the hit that *The Magic Flute* would be in 1791. Mozart was right in thinking there was a cabal at that time in Vienna that tried to hinder him. Much of it had to do with the rivalry between the German versus the Italian company, but much was also pure jealously of Mozart's gifts.

Mozart conducted the first two performances and turned the rest over to the music director of the orchestra. Stefan was there for Mozart's performances but was not allowed a seat in the house since he was not a paying customer. So he watched from the wings. He had a partial view of both the stage and some of the boxes in the house.

He had a sight line into the lowest box on house right, and in it sat a startlingly beautiful woman with auburn hair, which hung about her shoulders, eschewing the current fashion of constructing an elaborate sculpture on the head. Her gown was maroon with a jeweled front piece, over which rose her décolletage. Her face was open, clear, with penetrating eyes that never left the stage. It was that which first caught Stefan's attention. Some of her splendidly bedecked neighbors seemed half involved at best, gossiping, giggling and pointing, but the lady was locked onto every moment. She laughed heartily during the sextet at the revelation that old Bartolo and Marcellina had had a love child, who turned out to be Figaro, and at Susanna's furious misunderstanding of Figaro embracing his new-found mother.

But her reaction at the end was unexpected. When the Count takes a knee in front the Countess, asking her forgiveness, Stefan had always found that a tearful but warm, feel-good moment. The lady in the box reacted not with gentle tears but with suppressed and pain-induced sobs. Her older companion put her hand on the lady's arm.

She was there again at the next performance, on the third of May. The same thing happened at the end, although she seemed more prepared. Her head dropped to her chest, and she choked back a couple of sobs. But with her vigorous applause at the end, she showed how she felt about the opera as a whole.

Stefan found himself haunted by her, and even though she did not attend the next performance, she filled his thoughts in the coming days. What, in this scene of forgiveness, had brought on a reaction that seemed so painful? Yet, given that Stefan always felt that there was sadness at the depths of Mozart's greatest music that many did not hear, who was this woman who did indeed hear the sorrow? She was deeply moved by music that moved him, and it branded her into his thoughts.

Seven more performances were scheduled, but after the spring, only once a month through to December. The opera always sold decently. So well that it was hard to understand the paucity of performances. But Mozart thought he knew.

"The fucking German opera company," he said bitterly. "Working behind the scenes with that scoundrel Rosenberg to limit the performances!" Count Rosenberg was in charge of opera at the court.

Stefan tapped into his historical knowledge to reassure Mozart that an opera such as *Figaro* could not be suppressed forever and that (in his opinion) Vienna had not seen the last of this work.

Mozart shrugged. But the fate of future productions of even an opera such as this were the last thing on Stefan's mind. Who was the tragic beauty? How could he, a nobody assistant musician, find out?

Did her aristocratic station make trying to find out a pointless exercise? It was unthinkable to approach her after an opera performance with no introduction. He felt like a schoolboy with a crush on an actress. He knew that Mozart may have known her identity, but he felt foolish, and he feared mockery.

Chapter 15— Premiere

1 May 1786

LISA EAGERLY AWAITED the premiere of Mozart's new comic opera *The Marriage of Figaro* in the Burgtheater. All knew of the scandal that the French play on which it was based had caused in Paris. It had been banned there because of its anti-aristocratic sentiments. The French Queen, Marie Antoinette, had advised her brother, Joseph II of Austria, to do the same, which he did.

Lisa followed the scandal and even procured a copy of the original French play by Pierre-Augustin Beaumarchais. It was sparkling, naughty, delicious, and quite heated in revolutionary fervor. Lisa had seen enough of aristocrats behaving badly to be on the side of the servants. She had wondered how Mozart and his librettist, Lorenzo da Ponte, were going to clean it up to get it through the local censors, but apparently all the political content was successfully watered down. It was approved for production even though it was still a story in which a lecherous nobleman is put in his place.

The first of May came, and she and Aunt Catherine arrived at the Burgtheater for the seven o'clock curtain. They entered and turned up the house-right stairway and then down the hallway, past the mirrors, and into their accustomed place on the first level of boxes. Lisa had been here a few times since the eruption of hisses against her two years ago, but still felt uneasiness as she opened the door and entered the glittering auditorium. The orchestra was already tuning.

"Why do they always saw away like that before beginning?" the dowager baroness asked.

"You would hear why if they neglected to," answered her niece sweetly.

Cheers erupted for Mozart. He stood before the pianoforte and did not wait for the crowd noise to completely subside before beginning the whispered, presto opening of the brilliant three-minute overture. The curtain then flew open to start the events of one day, one on which the loyal, resourceful manservant Figaro is to be married to the adorable, quick-witted lady's maid Susanna. And in that same day, the lust-driven Count Almaviva intends to invoke the hated old custom *droit du seigneur* (right of the lord) and take Susanna into his bed, under the very nose of his long-suffering and beautiful wife Rosina.

Lisa did her best to explain to her aunt the complicated plot so loved by the French, in which the delicious subplots weave in and out of each other: characters hiding behind chairs and doors, secret messages sent (all of them deceptive), a hormonal teenager who would bed the Countess Almaviva, a parentage revealed, disguises backfiring, and finally the lascivious count unmasked before all.

Lisa and Catherine both cheered lustily with everyone demanding a repeat of Figaro's brilliant act one-ending aria, in which he torments the lusty page boy Cherubino about his upcoming life in the military. The twenty-minute act two finale started with two singers on stage and ended in a tumult of triumph and consternation with seven singing.

At the interval following act two, Lisa fanned herself with swift strokes. "I can hardly breathe after that!"

Aunt Catherine said, "Goodness, I can't quite follow it all...the part with Figaro's debt...the seal on the commission..."

Lisa started to jump in with explanation, as she knew the details from the original play, but Catherine smiled and raised her hand. "It hardly matters. I can follow enough of it, and the music is so exquisite. Besides, we can come again!"

Lisa beamed.

Act three, with a phony agreement to an assignation and more secret and false notes, yielded a simple duet between Susanna and the Countess that made Lisa think she might faint from an excess of sheer beauty. Figaro and Susanna are finally married, but act four remained—in the garden, all at night, and misidentification abounding. All of the strands finally coalesced, and the Count is caught by one and all as he tries to seduce whom he thinks to be Susanna but is actually his wife Rosina disguised as Susanna.

How are you going to get out of this, you pig? Lisa thought triumphantly. But he does not try to get out of it. He takes a knee before his wife. The text was utterly simple. Da Ponte had given just enough words, on which Mozart would drape some of the most beautiful music he had written:

"Countess, forgive me. Forgive me, forgive me."

Rosina pauses, then says simply, *"I am kinder. I will say yes."*

The rest of the characters who were assembled onstage took up her tune in rich harmony, *"Then let us all be happy."* It was a prayer for love to prevail in life. Then the cast went silent, and the orchestra whispered a benediction over the company, topped by two serene high oboe notes, like hovering spirits. The spell suddenly broke, and there began a final two-minute party, exploding with fireworks of joy.

Lisa knew from reading the play that a plea of forgiveness was coming. But wrapped in such heartbreaking music, it opened her inner gates out of which flowed never-fulfilled wishes of having her husband ask for forgiveness, to tell her it was all a bad dream. *If only.* She would have replied to Charles exactly as Mozart's countess had and gently said yes. The desire for a reconciliation that had never happened was a deep wound, and sorrow swept through her. She bent forward, trying to stop her wracking sobs. The music was painfully beautiful, yet she wished that it would never stop.

Aunt Catherine, quite alarmed, put an arm around her and held her as well as the clumsy chairs would allow. At the conclusion Lisa rose quickly. She had recovered somewhat by the time they settled in the carriage.

"My darling, what is it?" Lisa's aunt pleaded.

"Charles," she said softly. "Maybe if I could have gotten him to listen to Mozart…"

The old woman said, "I don't think even the miracle of Mozart could bring about that kind of change. At least Mozart's count realized at the end that he really did love his wife."

"It hurts to have private places in my heart touched, but it makes me feel less alone," said Lisa. "I want to come back."

Chapter 16—New Music

IT WAS APPROACHING midsummer but was still cool in Vienna. Stefan awoke one morning to a silent and seemingly empty house. Perhaps Mozart had gone for a horseback ride; owning a horse was one of the extravagances he treated himself to. He went riding twice a week and left early. Stefan dressed, went downstairs, and helped himself to the oat porridge in the pot. There was no coffee…very well, he would have coffee at a café and read the newspaper.

A sudden thought seized him, a forbidden desire that had long sought release and now saw its chance. He crept back up the stairs to Mozart's study. The door was half open. He had never been in there alone. He pushed his way in and saw the neatly organized table with three stacks of ongoing projects.

Why was he there? Stefan would never dare touch a manuscript without permission. But his gaze rested on Mozart's pianoforte. He had already played it, his first day in Vienna, with Mozart's permission, so he did not see the harm of another visit. He sat and began playing one of his favorite Mozart sonatas, the A minor. He began, and soon the room was filled with sound.

He paused at the end of the first movement and put his hands in his lap. Now a truly rogue and utterly forbidden thought shaped itself into a desire.

What would Chopin sound like on a pianoforte?

Stefan simultaneously was pulled and horrified by the desire. Playing music written in the 1830s in 1786…Would this not cause a catastrophic break in the space-time continuum, causing a rip in the fabric of reality into which the universe fell?

He had seen too many time-travel movies. Stefan clenched his fists against his eyes, took his hands down, and sounded the C octave of the opening of Chopin's G minor ballade. He then lifted his hands after playing the octave.

He looked around, listening. So far, so good. No rips in the universe. Another note?

He started again, added two notes, stopped again, checked again, and then let the music continue, completing the heavy opening arpeggio that introduced the melancholy little waltz tune, which he also played.

Still all at peace.

He continued into the first burst of rapid passagework that packed many quick notes into one measure, then settled into the deep song of the *meno mosso*. It felt like the ultimate forbidden pleasure, a vice unspeakable that he had yearned for deeply. *Music of the nineteenth century, thank you, dear Lord!* A deep hunger that he had not been aware of was being sated. He surged into the *fortissimo*.

He heard the loud creak of a floorboard behind him. He started violently, then turned and saw Mozart standing in the doorway, wonder and incredulity in his every particle.

After several thunderous but silent moments, Mozart walked into the room and stood over Stefan.

"Who composed this music? And don't think about telling me that it is your old teacher in Bonn."

Stefan knew there was no way through except the truth, or some part of it. And pray he didn't end up in an asylum.

"The composer's name is Frédéric Chopin. Polish."

"Polish?" A thoughtful pause followed. "I have never met any composers from Poland. Are they all such radicals?"

Stefan did not answer. Mozart motioned for him to move off the bench. Stefan rose and Mozart took his place.

Mozart sounded the opening C octave. Stefan had been astonished many times in his presence, but none so much as now, as Mozart played perfectly the ballade he had heard but once. He had to slow down at the measure with the rapid passage work, but even at half speed, the fact that he could remember the sequence of the notes was beyond belief.

He then went back to several places that he found to be odd and repeated them, then repeated again. "I can see there is a strange logic to this, but the phrase structure is so distended. Some of the harmonic moves jar me, like this, and this. And to have a cadenza but a few minutes in is so odd. Where you stopped…so many notes in each chord, it's not attractive. I can't really hear the musical point of view. Still there is ingenuity, and beauty."

When he finished he turned to Stefan.

"When was it composed?"

The moment was now. After a deep breath, Stefan said simply, "It has not yet been composed, Maestro."

Silence, then a short burst of a laugh from Mozart.

"And this Chopin has not yet been born?"

Stefan was unable to continue.

"I know you're not deranged, and yet you're serious about this, aren't you, Stefano?"

Stefan nodded.

"When was Chopin born, please," he asked, speaking slowly.

"The year eightteen hundred and ten."

"And the year this work was composed?"

"Eighteen thirty-one."

Mozart looked at the keys, his hand characteristically resting on his chin in thought.

"Then you're telling me that this composer traveled back through the currents of time and left his music some place where you found it."

"No, Maestro, Chopin did not travel back in time." Stefan took a deep breath and said, "I will never understand it, but the day we met, the date for me was the first of November, two thousand and eighteen. I came back through time two hundred and thirty-four years. I was born in the year nineteen hundred and seventy-six."

Mozart had been holding his breath, then exhaled. "Madness." After another pause though, his facial lines turned upward, and he started chuckling. "Bravo, Stefano, you had me hooked for a bit. This is good, better than I could ever do. I love a good joke, and this one was admirable. Polish composer, ha!"

Stefan sat still. A pause of a full minute ensued.

"Now stop," Mozart pleaded.

Stefan remained silent, and Mozart waited but clearly was losing patience.

"Stop!"

"I don't know if it's true or not, Maestro, I may be dreaming. But I swear to you, I believe it to be real. Judge for yourself after having known me these months as to whether or not I am mad."

Mozart's jaw was tight, his lips pursed, his fingers clenched on his chin. He spoke slowly and deliberately. "You are staying with this, aren't you?"

"I'm speaking what I know to be the truth."

Suddenly Mozart broke into a broad smile. "What I accept is that you are a marvelous prankster. Almost my equal! Holding on so long to the story after discovery is always a wonderful touch. And that piece! That must have taken some real dreaming. Well done!" A manly slap on the shoulder followed.

Stefan saw the uselessness of pushing any farther. He was indeed relieved. He had dodged the Chopin bullet, although unwittingly. But yet he admitted to nothing, for he did not know if another slip might come, and he wanted the truth to still be in the air. He shrugged his shoulders as neutrally as he could. But Stefan thought that Mozart's jolly dismissal was a little too pat. He wondered if Mozart, despite his blustery cheeriness, was not completely settled about this strange new friend. If he did not accept Stefan's time-travel account, there was still the Chopin, the Haydn quote, the way he played, his ease with Mozart's music…all this added up to a picture that was still unclear.

"Come Stefano, or should I say Master Chopin? Let's go get some coffee and cake."

Chapter 17—A Name, an Assignment

IT WAS THE beginning of August, and the summer heat had settled in. Stefan was starting to be in demand, both as copyist and voice teacher. The latter came about as a result of his few minutes with the chorus at the *Marriage of Figaro* rehearsal—word had gotten around that he knew something about teaching singing. He was at a disadvantage though, not having his own apartment, and he needed to talk to Mozart about that.

A note arrived from Michael Kelly, the Irish tenor who had played the roles of Basilio and Curzio in *Figaro*. He was a favorite of all in the company, personable and funny, and Stefan liked him enormously. As the Irish said, he had good *craic*.

The invitation was to dinner at a *heuriger*, an inn that made its own young white wine. Also attending would be Nancy's brother Stephen, a composer who took lessons with Mozart. It was thus to be an all-male gathering for what Kelly said was the best schnitzel in Vienna.

Mozart and Stefan arrived at the inn and saw Kelly and Storace waiting outside. They found a table and got to the business of sampling the new wine. Stefan had met Kelly several times outside of rehearsals, usually at an inn or at Mozart's house. He came there to drink and to challenge Mozart at billiards. He was unsuccessful, every time. At table, with wine, he was a wonderful raconteur. The stories he told about Italian exploits with the Storaces—Nancy at fifteen was already a *prima donna*—were sidesplitting to Mozart and Stefan, especially the nefarious deeds done under their mother's eye. Now they were all assembled in Vienna with a genius whom they loved at the nexus of their social circle.

The conversation took a turn toward the *Figaro* production, and Stefan asked how it was going. Since the opening, the weeping countess was still constantly on his mind.

"Well, we miss our Maestro," Michael said, pointing to Mozart. "It was a shock when he wasn't there. The assistant is competent, but I did not envy him. We learned that we would just have to work harder to reach the audience."

"The cuts I made may have helped the singers' stamina," said Mozart.

"*Cuts?*" Stefan said, horrified.

"Yes…look it's Vienna. The audience consider themselves the most sophisticated in the world, but many of them have the ears and brains of ducks," said Mozart with a little edge in his voice.

Stefan at this moment decided to finally ask the question that he was sure would earn him mockery but that had been burning in him since the premiere. "The first two nights, there was a very attractive lady with beautiful chestnut hair in the first box on house right. She wept both nights at the end, when the Count asks for forgiveness."

"She's been at most of the performances," said Kelly, "and she always lowers her head sadly at that point."

"*Every* performance?"

"Almost."

Mozart said, "Her name is Lady Elisabetta Grünewald, a countess. Very wealthy widow. I understand she plays the pianoforte quite well. Better than most men." Stefan wondered why he had not asked Mozart in the first place.

"Widow?" said Michael, raising an eyebrow.

"You may put foolish thoughts out of your drunken Irish head," said Mozart. "She is a *countess*. A little above the social level of itinerant musicians like the four of us."

They laughed, as more of the yellow sweet wine appeared at their places.

Stefan was not ready to let it go despite Mozart's cold splash of reality. "How long has she been a widow?"

From Mozart, "Around two years." He swirled his wine around in his glass, then decided to keep talking. "Her family had fallen on hard times, although they still lived in a beautiful garden house. Her mother died when Elisabetta was a little girl. Her husband was a count. She had remained unmarried into her twenties. She was apparently very studious, with, as I said, skills at the pianoforte. Elisabetta finally married for the good of her family. Around a year later her father died."

He paused, considering. Stefan pressed, "And…"

"There were rumors of her husband's cruelty. Once she was seen with a bad bruise around her eye; another day she was walking with a cane. It was said that the servants of the house were protective of her, but usually there was little they could offer but comfort. So when he died suddenly of a heart ailment, there were few tears shed. The family's situation was saved, as the fortune was said to be immense. And Elisabetta was saved."

"What a bloody bastard," Stefan growled. "He should have been jailed."

"The law says that since a wife is the husband's property, he can do as he wishes," ventured Michael.

Stefan grew quickly heated. "Any man who strikes a woman is a fucking coward!" Stephen Storace, who had seen the toll taken on his sister by a wife beater, nodded grimly in agreement.

Stefan's angry voice had raised its level considerably, and other patrons looked up. He was somewhat under the influence, and his red face reflected both that and his fury. His friends shushed him, and he finally calmed enough to express his regret at the display.

"That's all right," they all said. "Point taken."

Stefan said, "Now I understand her tears at the end. Maestro's countess gets what Elisabetta never did—a heartfelt apology from her husband." More wine arrived.

—

At another meal a week later, the whole Storace clan dined with the Mozarts and Stefan. The last performance of *Figaro* would be in December, and all were lamenting both the end of the run and that there had not been more performances. Mozart waited until what he judged was the right moment and said dramatically, "*A propos* of the last performance, today I was told the director of the theater orchestra has asked to be excused from the last night. Stefano, might you be available that evening to take charge of things?"

Stefan blurted out like a little boy, "Me?"

"I have several concerts during Advent, or I'd do it myself," Mozart said. "You're the logical choice."

Stefan could not speak. He thought of the wound of losing the *Figaro* at the Vienna State Opera in his time. How trivial that suddenly seemed! To conduct the first *Figaro* cast ever assembled, taught by Mozart himself, and, to him, the finest he had ever heard, was the true gold ring. "Thank you…I hardly know what to say," he said, on the verge of tears.

Stefan had often weighed the differences between his time and this time as a working conductor. The stunning virtuosity of modern ensembles would overwhelm their eighteenth-century counterparts, but to Mozart's orchestra, his music was the newest, most revolutionary work there was. And it showed in the rugged intensity of expression that modern orchestras often lacked. And now he would interact with that dynamic. He was indeed in the eighteenth century and would conduct the greatest "new" music that he had ever known.

He then suddenly realized with a small thrill that he might also see the tragic countess again.

Chapter 18—A Letter

THE INTOXICATION OF proximity to an immortal sometimes distracted Stefan from his grief about Katrina, but a conversation with the Storaces about their upcoming travel to London brought it back. Katrina would be in London in 230 years. She would be wild with worry about him. If only he could leave word that he was well where she would be sure to get it. But how, where? What was in London in 1786 that would still be there in 2018? And how would she know where to look?

An idea came to him on thinking, once again, of the *Back to the Future* movies. In one, Doc Brown had left word in the past for Marty McFly at a Western Union office to be delivered to him on a specific date, one hundred years in the future. What was the equivalent in London of an institution that would accept a charge of holding on to something? A museum?

He quizzed Stephen Storace. "Is there a museum in London called the British Museum?"

"Yes, it's the finest museum we have! Its collection has objects from around the world."

"Might you know the name of the head of the museum?"

"I not only know his name, I know the man quite well. Nancy and I have performed concerts at the museum several times. His name is William Collins. Very witty gentleman."

"Do you have an address?"

"Why, my dear Stefan?"

Stefan hesitated but answered simply, "I want to write to him."

Stephen half raised an eyebrow but was enough of a gentleman not to probe farther.

—

That night, working in Mozart's study, Stefan penned a note to Mr. William Collins. He had used the quill pen often but only for music notation. In the twenty-first century, with email, hand-written notes had become a rare practice. In Mozart's time good penmanship was taken for granted, as having a laptop had been for Stefan. He couldn't even remember what his own cursive handwriting looked like. It was trial and error, mostly the latter, and he wasted several sheets of then-expensive paper.

Stephen had suggested that he, Stephen, write an accompanying letter of introduction. Now, working by candlelight, Stefan finally got a few crab-handed lines down:

Schulerstrasse 6

Vienna

12 August 1786

My dear Mr. Collins,

My good friend and colleague Stephen Storace has kindly offered to provide the enclosed introduction, and I am grateful to him.

I come to you to ask a favor that, while relatively simple, is also somewhat odd. The source of its oddness I am afraid I am not at liberty to reveal, but I assure you that it is nothing nefarious or in the least harmful.

If you will agree, you will receive from Mr. Storace a sealed letter that will be contained in a simple wooden box with a key. On the box there will be, firmly attached, a label that will say:

"Please do not open until the first of November 2019

If you could keep charge of the box and ask your successors to do the same, down through the years and decades to come, so that it falls to your professional descendant in 2019 when the time comes, you would have my undying gratitude. I have little to offer you except perhaps the pleasure of a mystery in your midst that you know will, one day, be solved.

With thanks and with great respect, awaiting your response,

Your most humble and obedient servant,
Stefan Radowitz

—

Stefan posted the letter with many mixed feelings, ranging from desperation to contact his daughter to feeling utterly hopeless about such a roll of the dice.

—

The Mozarts were expecting another child, and Constanze's mother planned on moving in to help. Stefan moved out of the house on Schulerstrasse on October first. His new apartment was farther from the center, at eight Morgenweg (Morning Way). Four rooms and an indoor privy, for which he was grateful even if he knew it emptied more or less directly into the Danube.

He bought some very simple furniture to meet basic needs: bed, bedside table, washstand, large table to work at, three chairs for guests, several simple candle holders, a few plates, and a little cutlery. He also procured a stock of paper, quills, ink, and sand spreader. Most importantly he acquired a used but serviceable pianoforte.

He had no kitchen and didn't think he would be very successful without modern appliances anyway, so all his food was prepared elsewhere. He found an inn to deliver him a simple breakfast with coffee five days a week, which was a boost.

He soon had a fairly steady stream of pupils, both keyboard and voice, who found him by word of mouth. The talent level of his studio was modest, but he was grateful to be independent. His income covered his living costs, though barely. The coins that he had brought from his time were becoming depleted.

But he did miss the warmth of the Mozart household and the daily companionship of his hero, now friend. Being in a home with meals presented in front of him and access to social life was a great comfort. And Constanze appreciated his willingness to spend time with little Karl. Stefan had loved taking care of Katrina when she was a baby. He had wished fervently for a son as well, but it was not to be; the pain of Hannah's miscarriage still haunted him. So he considered time with Karl as being like borrowing a son, just for a bit, and took great joy from the bright little boy.

Chapter 19 — Revealed in Grief

CONSTANZE GAVE BIRTH to a son, Johann Thomas Leopold, on the eighteenth of October 1786. He was, by the midwife's accounting, two to three weeks early and was quite small. His color was definitely on the pale side. Constanze and Wolfgang were filled with anxiety; they had already lost a child several years ago.

Then in mid-November, the baby became quite feverish and could not rest. A doctor thought his ear seemed inflamed and recommended an herbal infusion, which the infant would not tolerate. The infection became systemic, and on the fifteenth, the little boy died.

Stefan had known from history that this would happen and had winced in pain upon learning of Constanze's doomed pregnancy. The grief at the loss of his and Hannah's child roared back to life. He also remembered sadly how a dose or two of a pink, sweet amoxicillin solution from a medicine dropper would chase Katrina's ear infections away inside of twenty-four hours.

Condolences poured in for the devastated parents—from the *Figaro* cast, composers Salieri, Sarti, Paisiello, Haydn, and many working musicians in Vienna. Constanze and Wolfgang stayed isolated for several days, although Stefan was received for a short visit. They were seated in the kitchen with tea, disheveled and with red eyes. They began to rise when he entered but he bade them to stay seated.

"My beloved friends, I grieve with you," he said, his own eyes welling. He stretched his arms and rested a hand on both their shoulders, bowing his head. "I am at your service, for anything. Getting food, taking care of Karl…anything."

"There is nothing for now, dear Stefan," said Constanze. "Mama is here, so we are in good hands." Stefan had met Cäcelia Weber and knew from history something of her story. Mozart had boarded with her when he had first moved to Vienna. Cäcelia remained close to and was trusted by both daughter and son-in-law.

"If she then needs anything, send for me. I am a few minutes' walk away, and with my teaching and copying, I'm home most days. Maestro, I know you have a full December. You will please tell me how I can help."

Mozart asked, "Stefano, perhaps we could meet for lunch tomorrow?"

"With pleasure." To Constanze he said, "Tell your mama I will come by tomorrow to say hello."

The next day Stefan stopped by their regular inn early to reserve the table they both preferred—it was around a corner from the rest of the room. On cold days it lacked warmth from the heat of the fire, but it was isolated. The day was warm for November, sunny with a vaulting blue sky. But it was for the two men a dark day, sitting in their dark corner.

They sat in silence after the waiter took their order. Finally Mozart spoke in a weak voice.

"It's the second child we lost." Stefan knew this.

"What was the first child's name?" He knew this too.

Speaking deliberately Mozart said, "Raimund Leopold. Born in June three years ago. A healthy boy. We were so thrilled. Then in August we went to Salzburg to try and make peace with my father and sister. We left Raimund with Constanze's mother. It was a difficult visit. Papa never accepted Constanze. I don't think he would have accepted anyone; he wanted to stay at the center of my life and was angry that someone should take his place. Then the terrible letter came from Constanze's mother. Little Raimund had taken a fever and cough and had died."

Stefan saw that this first tragedy was still raw. Knowing of the family's losses in advance, he had wondered if the high mortality rate for newborns in that time made the loss of one child a little less heavy. He had now the answer before him—it was not one whit less crushing.

Mozart was pulsing with sobs, softly. Stefan, knowing all too well his friend's pain, slid his chair to be next to Mozart and wrapped his arm about the slight shoulders. Mozart leaned into him slightly.

Stefan had thought long after the Chopin Ballade incident about what to do if another opening came for him to reveal his secret. Part of him desperately needed to share it, but more of him was terrified of the possible historical consequences. Had he already crossed the line when Mozart heard the music of Chopin? Would Mozart's music change from what Stefan knew was established historical fact? What else might that butterfly change in history? His mind began to conjure catastrophes— maybe no Brahms, no Mahler, no Debussy?

But his own annihilating experience of losing a child now spoke over everything. If there was comfort to be offered to his stricken friend and idol, he had no choice but to try.

"Maestro…please believe me when I tell you that you will have more children."

Mozart raised his head and wiped tears away. Stefan nodded, but Mozart's look hardened. "Are you really raising that old joke again at this moment?" He sat up and anger started to flare in his eyes. "This is unbelievable that you would toy with me now about knowing the future. Why?"

Stefan spoke. He was walking through plate glass, leaving destruction behind and in front of him. "All right, I know you don't believe me. Then how do I know that you are working now on a piano concerto in C and a symphony in D, yes?"

"Yes, damn you! So what?"

"The symphony will have only three movements, not four."

Mozart started to retort, then stopped. "How…how do you know that?"

After exhaling Stefan said, "The motive that begins the slow introduction is this," and Stefan sang the first several measures. "The slow movement, andante six-eighth, begins with this." He sang the shapely melody. "And the finale two-four like this." Harder to sing because of its speed, but Stefan managed to make it intelligible.

"And you know this…how?"

"Because I have conducted it."

A long, tense silence followed. Finally Mozart whispered, "Then you know…"

"Far more than I wish I did," Stefan said.

"And you say we will have more children."

"Yes."

"Can you tell me how many?"

Stefan hesitated. "No, don't," said Mozart, putting up a hand. "I don't wish to know my future."

More stunned silence, then Mozart said haltingly, "I almost believed you when you tried to tell me, though I didn't want to. But several things… you knew what Haydn said to my father…the way you play…even the way you walk. And I know *you* did not compose the Chopin. It adds up."

Stefan then told Mozart the tale of the spectral vision on All Hallow's Eve, about the shock when he touched Mozart, and his awakening to an earlier Vienna.

Mozart asked, "Were you at my grave?"

"Yes."

"And you know when I will die."

"Ask me no more."

"I will not, I swear. And you must swear to me to divulge nothing, to anyone, about what you know. It is dangerous knowledge."

"You have my oath on it."

The waiter, whom Stefan had waved off before, looked around the corner quizzically, and Stefan motioned that he could come now. Steaming plates of potato dumplings, sausage, and cabbage were set down with a pitcher of red wine. Mozart picked up his cutlery and placed his napkin at his throat.

"I finally feel a little hungry," he said. "Thank you for sharing some good news. You should not have, but I am grateful."

———

They began to talk of the two works Stefan had just identified, for they were scheduled to be performed in three weeks. Mozart proceeded to converse as if nothing unusual had passed between them and made no reference to Stefan's knowledge. Talking shop provided a welcome distraction from tragedy and staggering revelation.

"A symphony and a concerto, quite a package," observed Stefan. "Performance in three weeks? How far along are you?"

Mozart said, "Oh, the usual for the concerto. Outer parts done, structure fixed, that's always the hardest part. Filling in the inner parts is easy but time consuming.

"The symphony is a different matter. I want to do something new with counterpoint, use it in and of itself as an element in drama. And I do want this one to have real drama, like an opera. Not just entertaining, but a finish with real power. I think I have it now," he said, tapping his head. "Both works are triumphant and heroic. It is so odd how my composer self can be disconnected from real life around me. I feel nothing now like what these works sound like. But other times when I am joyful, the music that speaks through me is filled with sorrow."

Stefan said, "That your music and your own life's emotions don't line up simultaneously doesn't mean that anything is wrong. The overall balance is there."

Mozart mused on this and shrugged. "It will always be a mystery. Maybe I will solve it someday. And it doesn't really matter if I don't. The music is always there."

He continued, saying, "There'll be much last-minute copying. There are more decent copyists here than there were, but…"

"You know I will be there."

"Thank you, I know you will." Pausing, he asked softly, "Stefano, do you feel that there is some kind of connection between us? Not kinship…I can't put my finger on it. Almost an invisible physical bond. A…cord."

Stefan did not hesitate. "Yes, I do feel it, since I first walked into your home. It's stronger now. I believe that that's what brought me back. Some connection across time and space between us. I don't pretend to understand it."

"Then with this intimacy in mind, you should address me as Wolfgang, don't you think?"

Chapter 20 — View from the Pit

18 December 1786.

STEFAN'S PERFORMANCE OF *Figaro* had arrived. The previous performance had been fifteenth of November—a long break in any era, but such was the helter-skelter operation of the Viennese theaters, which were under heavy demand. Pickup rehearsals were always needed to review an opera as long and complex as this one; that had not changed in modern times.

It was still the original cast at the Burgtheater. They had been contracted through to the end of the year, but this was the final performance of this production. However stories had been circulating of a new production of *Figaro* that had opened in Prague and was being enthusiastically received. On the eighteenth, a Prague newspaper printed a scoop that Mozart himself would be present in Prague come January. *Figaro* was not about to disappear.

Stefan had meetings with each member of the cast to go over their parts. These usually went quickly, but there was a lot of ground to cover. Drinks and meals with Storace and Kelly after rehearsals were merry gatherings.

—

The *Figaro* performance night came, Stefan was relaxed and happy…no, more than happy. He felt blessed. It was like a dream come true, beyond any dream he had ever had. There was one thought, though, that intruded persistently, and that was the sad countess.

Will she be in her seat? Of course why should she miss this performance after attending so many others? He stepped into the house. *Don't look, don't look!* He kept his head down as he walked to the keyboard. If he could get past a brief acknowledgement of the applause, just look straight ahead, sit down, start the overture…

He shot a sideways glance to the box. Empty.

Good! He did not want to feel like a schoolboy trying to impress a pretty girl with his athleticism. He was leading maybe the greatest opera ever written, with the cast that Mozart had tailored it for. Clear the mind.

But there still was sore disappointment.

———

Stefan started act one and could feel that his presence was energizing, so much so that he momentarily forgot about who was behind him. The table-setting act of the opera done, he hurried from the pit to the house left wings.

Intermissions were long, and Stefan was both excited and disappointed. Well, too bad she wasn't there. He was making a tiny bit of history. He stepped into the house for act two on his way to the pit, glanced up, and momentarily broke his quick stride, coming dangerously close to tripping,

Lady Grünewald, the sad countess, sat in her box with the elderly companion he had seen before. Her gown was a delicate yellow, and it seemed illuminated from within. She fanned herself lightly; even in winter weather the old theaters could become stifling. She turned and met his glance long enough to see him having to regain his balance after a faltering step.

When had she arrived? Pay attention!

His stride recovered, he took his place and began the sorrowful aria in which Countess Almaviva laments the loss of her husband's love. Stefan wondered about the effect on *his* countess.

The pace of act two was quick, and Stefan was suddenly at the finale. The entire ensemble, cast, and orchestra, were so locked into the rhythms and gestures that Stefan almost stopped conducting at places, gently guiding the pace often with just a lift of his eyebrows.

The orchestra was used to lesser conductors more or less beating the time, with little variation for any musical events. Here was a conductor who knew how to concentrate on the important events, not just an unchanging bare beat. The art of conducting in the eighteenth century was not yet fully developed, and Stefan's physical sophistication and deep musicality brought out a beauty of tone and commitment of expression that had not been heard since Mozart's performances.

Curtain. Stefan left without looking around, but on coming out for act three, he looked up to the box, and his eyes and the countess's met and held for longer than just a glance. She was aglow, eyes sparkling, and applauding with gusto. Heat blossomed in Stefan's chest and face.

Act three—Susanna dangerously toying with the count, two arias, the trap for the count set, the actual marriage ceremony and dance, and quickly over.

Out for act four to warm applause, he signaled for the orchestra to stand. They got out of their seats; Stefan acknowledged them, and there was a roar. His and the countess's eyes met again, and his heart was beating almost too fast to execute Barbarina's sad little opening lament. The tying up of the different strings of the plot began, climaxing with the final unmasking of the Count's nefarious scheme in front of all.

And the plea for forgiveness from Almaviva to Rosina. Stefan wondered how Elisabetta Grünewald was responding. Presto, finish!

Stefan stayed in the pit to acknowledge the performers, then turned himself to greet the cheers.

She was there for one more instant, her smile radiant on him, then she turned and left while the applause was still strong.

———

It was late and all in the company were too exhausted to go out after the performance. By the time he got to his flat, Stefan was wrung out completely, and he hoped his exhaustion would guarantee at least some sleep. It was not to be. He closed his eyes, and he heard melodies from *Figaro* tumbling over in his mind. But he saw the face of Elisabetta Grünewald, warming him like the May sun, looking into him.

What is wrong with me? he thought. *I have not even spoken to this woman!* Superficial crush. That's all this was, right?

It was more than her being blindingly beautiful, more than her tragic history that moved him to want to protect her; it was a mutual understanding of the deepest currents in the music of Mozart, one of the most precious things in his life, which he knew they shared.

So the night passed, turbulently filled with music. *"Non so più cosa son, cosa faccio,"* sang the hormonal teenager Cherubino breathlessly. *("I don't know what I am, what I'm doing.")*

Chapter 21—View from the Balcony

18 December 1786

TRUE TO HER word, the Countess Grünewald came back to *Figaro* repeatedly. Subsequent performances were a disappointment, as Mozart was no longer conducting. Yet the great cast still was intact, and they picked up the slack. Their love for the work was in their every note and movement.

The performances were stretched over the rest of the year, sometimes a month apart. Lisa missed a couple, but when the last one on December eighteenth was announced, she purchased her ticket. She and her aunt were late and missed the overture. She paid no attention to the conductor, whose back was turned. Yet things sounded livelier, and when he entered for the second act, she was startled to see his face, for he was quite familiar…yes, the concert a year ago with the piano concerto, the man who leaned into the phrases while listening as if he had foreknowledge of this new piece.

What was even more startling was that his eyes went directly to her as he was walking out for act two, and when their eyes met, his step skipped a little, as if he had been startled. He then averted his eyes and went to his station. Coming out for the third act, he sought her eyes again, and she was waiting for him.

Lisa said to Aunt Catherine before act three started, "I have seen this man, a year ago at a concert. What is strange is that he seems to recognize me."

"Well," said Catherine, "indeed odd. In your opinion, is his conducting good?"

"Yes! He shapes the music as if he were…kneading dough. Sometimes he almost lets his hands drop, yet he still radiates authority. And everything sounds so much more alive and just…right, somehow."

Lisa had searched her playbill for his name but no conductor was listed. Perhaps a last-minute replacement. When he came out for the fourth act, he indicated for the orchestra to stand for a bow. The unknown conductor looked again directly at Lisa, and she fixed her eyes on him. Not just for an instant but a full moment. She was startled to feel this connection with someone she had never met but who had communicated with her musically.

The two women stayed for one more bow at the end and, from Lisa, one more quick glance, stage to house and back again. Once they were in the carriage, Aunt Catherine commented neutrally, "That was an interesting evening."

Lisa did not even hear her. She said decisively, "I'll come back to the theater tomorrow and find out his name." Then she said more thoughtfully, "His eyes went right to me. How did he know where to look?"

Chapter 22 — Substitution

TWO DAYS LATER Stefan was sharing a late lunch with Mozart.

"I am told that you are as good a conductor as anyone has seen lately," he said, raising his eyebrows.

"Present company excepted, of course."

"No, truly," Mozart said. "Kelly was full of praise. He said you sometimes almost stopped conducting, and the effect was marvelous on the company. All were forced to listen to each other!"

"Well, if they didn't know it by then, there was nothing that I could do to help them," Stefan said truthfully. "Are the rumors about your going to Prague true?"

"Yes, and I think you may know that already."

Stefan was resolved to meet such comments with a stone face, neither confirming nor denying.

Mozart added, "I hear that Prague is mad for *Figaro*. People sing the arias on the street and in cafes!"

"Will you perform there?" Stefan actually did not know the answer to this.

"Yes, I'll play and conduct my new symphony. Possibly a *Figaro* performance as well. I haven't received a reply to my last letter to the theater management." He added after a sip of wine, "This will be good for Constanze."

"It will be good for both of you. It's such a beautiful city, and from what it sounds like, they listen to your music with their hearts open. God, Vienna is so cynical, many of the Viennese think it's beneath them to be enthusiastic. Your musically literate enthusiastic followers are the exception, but there are not enough of those."

Stefan was surprised to hear this criticism come from his own mouth about what had been his ideal time and place—Vienna in the time of Mozart and later Beethoven. He had the same criticism for the Vienna of his time. He had been moved to tears at performances at the State Opera, applauding lustily, while those around him just clapped politely. Had they heard what he had? Maybe they were actually touched, but it just would not do to show their passion. And now he witnessed the same thing in this century. Yet every city would seem to have its own DNA that binds the years. For decades in Vienna, from the late eighteenth to early twentieth century, one brilliant composer after another had made a mark here.

"I often think I am in the wrong city for just that reason," Mozart said. "But where else would I be? Paris? Lully and Rameau were gifted but are not my cup of tea, and I would not wish to compete with them. The Storaces and Kelly keep talking about bringing me to London, and they sing the praises of the theaters there. I'm considering it, even though my English is only good for dirty verses."

Stefan knew that Storace and Kelly in a few years would find the money to offer Mozart a commission for a new opera, but death would take him before it could be transacted. Mozart would not see London. Of all the terrible events that he knew were to come, such as wars, knowing how little time Mozart had—scarcely more than five years at this point— grieved him most deeply.

"But for now, it's Vienna for us. And Prague. It will be nice to get…" Mozart didn't finish, but Stefan knew he meant "some damned appreciation."

—

Three nights later was one of Mozart's Advent concerts in Johann Trattner's casino, at which he would perform his new C major concerto and D major symphony. They were both complex masterpieces, but receiving their usual scant one rehearsal. No modern professional ensemble would ever mount a Mozart program on one rehearsal. And yet the premiere performances were good enough to make powerful first impressions, especially with the ultracharismatic composer leading. The Vienna musicians were comfortable with the musical language of the day, the only one they knew, and that was enough. Some in the audience were puzzled by the challenges Mozart set before them, but almost as many were enthusiastic.

Concert over, music collected, stands and chairs pushed back for the gaming tables, the two friends were walking to their inn when Mozart said suddenly, "I almost forgot! Yesterday I was offered a salon next month by a dear friend, the Countess von Thun. The guest list is quite elite. We have been together many times, and she helped me get my *Abduction from the Seraglio* mounted in Vienna. But I'll be in Prague on the date she requested. Stefano, you know my music as well as any in Vienna and play it better than anyone except me. Would you substitute? She is a dear friend and a rare, truly great lady."

Once again, Stefan's response was to say stupidly, "Me?" Mozart smiled and nodded.

"But they have been expecting you and now will be told they'll get someone they have never heard of. Who would come to hear me?"

"Nonsense! I'll speak to the countess of you, and she will get the word out about you."

"Well…could you write me a letter of introduction that I could present? I feel that I need as much verification as I can get."

"Yes, yes, of course. Agreed then?"

Stefan swallowed hard. "OK. Agreed."

"Good!" Then Mozart asked a question. "What does this 'OK' mean? You keep using it. An expression you brought with you from the future?"

"Ah!" Stefan chuckled. "It's an affirmation of what was just said by another person."

"That makes zero sense but…O…K!" said Mozart with definition.

1 7 8 7

Chapter 23—In the Parlor

STEFAN, THE MOZARTS, and a number of other well-known Vienna performers celebrated New Year's Day 1787 with wine, Constanze's punch, smoked fish, venison, sausage, red cabbage, four different cheeses, fresh bread, various pastries, and an evening of dancing at the Mozarts' that went very late. Mozart and Constanze seemed to have revived after the tragedy of losing a child, and there was general optimism in the air. From Stefan's perspective things in Vienna were stable and prosperous. He knew vaguely that war with Turkey was approaching, but he could not remember when, and of course he could not look it up. But for now Joseph II still seemed to be vitally interested in Enlightenment reforms, and the city and empire seemed full of music.

Stefan knew from history the kind of greeting that awaited Mozart in Prague and also what he would come away with—a commission for a new opera. The couple themselves seemed to sense good things were about to happen. Mozart certainly was happy about being away from Vienna for a month or so. Stefan promised to look in on Karl and his grandmother a few times each week, a task he happily anticipated.

Stefan prepared for the salon at the Countess von Thun's as thoroughly as he had for any performance of his life. He found out that the expectation at these private, invitation-only concerts was simple: musical entertainment. A charming oral presentation was not expected, but the format was up to the performer. Stefan brought three Mozart sonatas and two sets of variations. Likely too much, but Mozart had advised him to rely on the Countess von Thun's sense of the temperature of the room as the afternoon went by. He also brought some Scarlatti and C. P. E. Bach in case she felt some variety was needed.

The house was outside of town, toward Heilingenstadt, where wealthy Viennese, aristocracy and otherwise, had built magnificent chateaus. Stefan used the intimidating knocker, and a liveried servant answered.

"Herr Radowitz? This way please." And Stefan was escorted through the large and ornate front hall. The salon itself was filled with plates of pastries, delicious smelling coffee, wine, and distinguished lords and ladies. At the center was the Countess von Thun, as erect and stately as a ship under full sail. She saw Stefan and immediately broke away to bestow a grand welcome.

"I am so happy you could come today! It's wonderful that our Wolfgang has been called away to as lovely a destination as Prague, and he has sung your praises!"

Stefan did the most proper bow he could, then reached into his pocket for the introduction letter from Mozart.

"Your Ladyship, I should show you this letter…," he said, fumbling in an inner pocket.

"Oh, don't be daft!" she laughed gaily. "Wolfgang said you had insisted on a letter, but it is totally unnecessary. Your conducting of the last *Figaro* performance has been the talk of the town! Everyone, your attention please!" she chirped, and the room went silent quickly. "Please welcome our guest today, Herr Stefan Radowitz, Maestro Mozart's close friend and associate."

Polite applause echoed as Stefan bowed. His eyes swept the room and landed on the countess he had exchanged glances with, Lady Elisabetta

Grünewald, who smiled warmly at him. He froze and, for a moment, could see nothing but the blue garland of flowers in her glowing auburn hair.

———

Stefan ended up playing better than he thought he would. As he initially sat at the keyboard, his mouth dried and his throat clamped shut. She was not across a large space this time. She was here, in this room, a few feet away, listening with what he knew already was a high degree of receptivity. And they would undoubtedly meet.

All this he carried as he played the music of Mozart, Scarlatti, and the younger Bach. The virtuosic Scarlatti sonata made a major impression. Stefan, calling on his experience as a lecturer at conservatory and at his own concerts, chatted between works about the music itself, a modern concert feature which apparently was unheard of then. But his audience was delighted at this novelty.

He strove with all his might not to look up at Lady Grünewald, feeling he might get caught out by the rest of the room. However, he did not have to make any decisions about what to do when the event was over, for she made a beeline for him.

A curtsy, then she spoke her name in a melodious mezzo soprano. "Elisabetta Grünewald, Herr Radowitz."

Stefan responded with slightly too deep a bow. "Stefan Radowitz, at your service, My Lady." *Could my heart beat any louder?* "I am so pleased to meet you."

"Well, in a way we met at your *Figaro* performance. That was a marvelous night. Do you remember me? I was in the first box on your left."

Stefan kept it simple. "Of course, I do, My Lady."

"You play…unlike anyone else in Vienna that I've heard. You made the Scarlatti sound simple, and it is anything but."

"I take it you play, My Lady?" The answer Stefan of course knew from Mozart.

A little pause, then she answered softly, "Yes." A brief silence, then she said briskly, "I must be off. I do trust we shall meet again, Herr Radowitz."

Pushing back against the crushing letdown, he said with his most confident, manly tone, "I know that we will, My Lady," and bowed. She paused then for a heart-stopping moment, smiling at him. It was the first time he had seen her up close and still. Her face was of classic Austrian simplicity: high cheek bones, a delicate jaw and chin, and a wide, full mouth, above which perched a slender and pointed nose. Unfashionably for the period, she allowed her hair to fall naturally onto her bare shoulders. Her green eyes were large and possessed an inviting openness. But it was the animation of her features that was captivating—they were not a perfect and static still life but constantly in motion, responding to an agile and abundant mind.

Then in a swirl of light blue flower print, she was gone.

———

After the last *Figaro* performance, Lisa had had no trouble finding out from the Burgtheater management the name of the conductor who did such a marvelous and knowing performance. Stefan Radowitz, said to be from Bonn, had appeared rather suddenly about a year ago and had become an assistant to Maestro Mozart. She still did not have any notion as to why he sought her out with his eyes on his way to the orchestra pit. But he did, and when he found her, he was so surprised he almost tripped. Then it happened again, and yet again. He was not looking at a random, attractive audience member; he was looking at *her*. It was pleasantly stimulating to think about, even though she knew the chances of their meeting again were nil.

Until it happened in January. She was hungrily looking forward to hearing Mozart at the Countess von Thun's salon. Her disappointment was considerable when the announcement was made that, owing to a pressing emergency, Maestro Mozart was not available. But when the replacement, Maestro Mozart's close assistant Herr Stefan Radowitz was introduced, her letdown disappeared in a swirl of excitement. The mystery man to be unmasked!

His playing at the salon was unlike anything she had heard. He pulled new sounds from the depths of the instrument. His technique was dazzling, and some of the most difficult works, such as the Scarlatti sonata, sounded tossed off like child's play, as if he were able to play music far more difficult, unimaginably so. She yearned to get home to her instrument and see if she could push her tone and fingers to these depths.

Upon introducing herself she found his clumsy formality and stiffness somehow endearing. There was no swagger at all from this accomplished artist. And the way he looked at her was just as he had that night in the theater—with an unhidden intensity that said, "*I am touched by you,*" rather than the dozens of looks from men over the years who simply were sizing her up as a prize.

She took one day to think about whether or not she wanted more of his company. Herr Radowitz was not what most women would have thought to be an Adonis. He was tall, light, and a little gangly, with sandy hair and kind eyes set in a slightly uneven face. His simple looks indeed put her a little more at ease. Yet there was something mysterious about him, and she was drawn by that.

The next day she woke and penned the note.

Nightingale Street 12
15 January 1787

Dear Herr Radowitz,

If you are available, would you do me the honor of calling on me at my home on Thursday the eighteenth at two o'clock? I would like to discuss the possibility of my becoming your pupil on the pianoforte."

Yours most sincerely,
Elisabetta Grünewald

Chapter 24—First Lesson

THERE WAS NEITHER time or the money for Stefan to buy a new outfit before January eighteenth; his initial bag of coins had been mostly depleted because his income had taken a while to rise to make him self-supporting. So he asked for assistance from the Mozarts' knowledgeable servant Ani to clean his suit. The countess will have seen it before, as he had conducted *Figaro* in it, so it was important that it be presentable.

Ani also gave him a hair trim. Stefan usually gave little thought to his hair, but Ani pointed out that if he was not wearing a wig, then his hair should be at least trimmed respectably around his ears. It was now long enough to gather and pull back into a ponytail, to his surprise.

Nightingale Street lay not far outside of the inner city, to the north-west toward the Vienna Woods. The houses were large but not on the scale of the estate houses further out. But one thing most of them had was a spacious rear garden and were referred to as garden houses.

It was not a short walk for Stefan. January weather can be miserable in Vienna, but he lucked out on that Thursday with the sky partially cloudy, the temperature mild, and no bitter wind out of the north.

As he walked he felt calm. He would start discovering whom she really was, not obsessing over a romantic figure whom he thought he might somehow save from her sorrow. He would first hear her playing level and then teach her as well as he could. Maybe she would respond, maybe not.

It might all lead to nothing. If his balloon of fantasy was punctured, then so be it. He was the one dealing with a real-life crisis, after all.

As he walked up the cobbled driveway to the gracefully set front door, it struck him that this was someone who did not look as if she needed saving. He tapped with the knocker, and in a few moments, the door was opened by a big and rugged looking man wearing a pleasant expression.

"Stefan Radowitz is my name. I have an appointment for a pianoforte lesson with the countess."

"My Lady is expecting you, Herr Radowitz. Do come in," he said in a Hungarian lilt. The servant, noting that Stefan did not own an outer wrap, paused briefly, then gestured toward the parlor. "This way please."

The entryway and the parlor to the left were simply decorated, unlike the Countess von Thun's house in which the ornate decorations were themselves ornately decorated. The room off to the right of the entranceway held shelves upon shelves of books. Just at a glance, they seemed to be possessed by a reader, not a collector, as they showed frayed, uneven edges, not rows of perfectly matched bindings. They had been read and loved.

Stefan stepped into the parlor and the countess was waiting for him. She wore a rose print dress, open from the waist to a gold petticoat. A broad garland of lace wrapped around her shoulders and met crossing her chest. Her green eyes penetrated his from across the room. He started the mechanics for his best bow, but she glided effortlessly into his field with her hand extended, not offering it to be kissed with the palm down, but to shake hands, palm to the side.

"Herr Radowitz, I'm so pleased to see you again."

Stefan took her hand and noticed quickly that it was large like his, and the grip was firm. Shaking hands seemed more informal and intimate than the distanced bowing, and his heart raced at her touch. He hoped she did not notice.

"My Lady, your request does me honor." He also hoped his smile was not stupidly going through the ceiling.

"What an utterly pleasant day it is for January!" she offered. "So nice to be able to dispense with outerwear." She had noticed apparently that he had entered without a cloak.

"Yes, the walk was most refreshing!"

"Can we sit and chat?" she said, offering him one of two chairs next to a small serving table sprinkled with delicate Viennese pastries and coffee. The last thing his taut nerves needed was caffeine, but the heavy Turkish brew was irresistible, and a slight female servant poured for them.

Stefan was profoundly tongue-tied, so he waited for her to speak. He braced himself for mostly small talk, which he had always found difficult. But she effortlessly took him through questions about his phony hometown of Bonn, Viennese cuisine, and Emperor Joseph II's reforms (of which they both approved). She seemed genuinely to enjoy the light chat, and her smile was always present but never forced. *Charm is putting it mildly*, thought Stefan.

"Well," she exclaimed with a nervous exhalation of air, "should I play for you?"

"I would be happy to hear you. What will you play?"

"A sonata by Mozart in A minor."

Stefan knew the sonata; it was one of Mozart's greatest from his time in Salzburg.

Her pianoforte was from a maker about whom Stefan had learned from Mozart, Anton Walter; he was regarded as the finest in Vienna. She sat at the keys, and he moved his chair to a place from where he could see her hands. She cupped her hands, blew her breath on her fingers, lowered them slowly to the keyboard, and began suddenly.

From the first sound, developing into a measure, then a phrase, Stefan knew he was hearing no wealthy hobbyist. Her tone had a bell-like ring, and she played into the keys without forcing. Mozart's tempo marking for the first movement was *allegro maestoso*, both a tempo and a character instruction. So many pianists started with a statelier tempo for one measure, then plowed ahead impatiently, losing any sustained sense of majesty.

The countess, however, played with tempo restraint and deliberation throughout, but with inner shaping and articulation that kept it moving in a reserved but inevitable manner, like the tide coming in. There were extreme contrasts in the middle section; Mozart rarely used dynamic markings such as *fortissimo* (very loud) or *pianissimo* (very soft), but he did here in the middle section. She got a rich, orchestral sonority in the former and a delicate whisper in the latter; the contrast was electrifying. The closing approached inexorably, and the last big chords signaled the end of a great structure that had been beautifully revealed.

Stefan had been stunned many times in Mozart's circle, but not often like this. Lady Grünewald was a major artist by any measure. He had not heard or imagined this movement played so. What could he say in response?

In measured tones he said, "This is a beautiful instrument, and you bring a beautiful sound from it. Few in Vienna play like this."

"I've been practicing hard since the Countess von Thun's salon. I had never heard anyone in Vienna play like you, with your sound, and I've been trying to replicate it. I hope I have succeeded to an extent."

"My lady, I'm afraid I must respond that you have not succeeded in replicating me. You have you own unique sound. If my playing helped you to find that, I'm pleased."

"Have you any comments?"

"If you know the other movements, I'd hear them before I respond."

She nodded and played the songful, upward-reaching melody that began the slow movement. It was serenity itself, with delicate decorative ornaments laid on top, until, using the same material, it became stern and dramatic in the middle section. There the countess found a new sound, like a different character in an opera, before returning to the original tranquility.

The fleet, troubled finale flew by, but not skittishly; every note was pronounced, nothing was lost to the urgent tempo.

She finished and looked up with a hopeful smile.

He could not just say, *"You play it better than anyone I've heard across three centuries."* He racked his brain, then made a few minor suggestions of where to put a breath, and why, and where to accent a little more with one hand or the other. Finally he gave up.

"My Lady, you play this sonata as well as anyone in Vienna, save Mozart himself. You…," he searched for the right phrase. "You understand what it is saying at a deep level. You play the music *behind* the music."

"Thank you for your kind words." She smiled happily then her face became serious. "I think it speaks of grief, but in a highly formal and measured setting. I wonder what may have happened in his life to call this forth." He marveled at how malleable her facial expressions could be.

"Sometimes he writes tragic music when he is feeling frolicsome, sometimes the opposite. But I do know that this was composed after the death of his mother." He thought a moment and added, "I'm sure he would enjoy hearing you play his music."

"He would hear a woman?"

"Oh, he has had women students. He once told me that in general he prefers women players to men. He feels they have more passion and refinement." Stefan could not reveal that this was something he had read in a volume of letters in his time.

Now it was her turn to be astonished. "What a remarkable thing to say!" Then drawing back, she said "You flatter me, sir."

"Not in the least," he said deliberately. "I could arrange for it this week, except that he is in Prague."

She weighed the idea, then shrugged quickly. "We'll see." He wondered why she would hesitate.

Stefan then considered asking why she did not play in public. This lady was a countess, could sponsor her own concert and suffer no ill consequences. He decided that the first meeting was not the time for that conversation. He hoped with all his heart that there would be a second meeting, although he knew there was little that he could teach her, at least about the music of 1787.

It seemed that the lesson was over, and Stefan was starting to shift his weight forward to stand when she asked, as if in answer to his thought, "Can you come again?"

He felt a strong tide swelling inside his chest, then said as evenly as he could, "It would be my pleasure."

"Are you free Saturday after next, the twenty-seventh at two o'clock? Ten days hence."

"If I have anything scheduled, I will move it." She smiled at this. "What music would you like to explore? More Mozart? Another composer? Perhaps music you're not now familiar with?"

"I do have some unopened volumes of Bach."

"J. S. Bach?" His sons were very much alive, and one had to check which Bach was being discussed.

"Yes. One in particular looks most interesting. A volume of preludes and fugues, all in different keys."

"*The Well-Tempered Clavier!* You've not studied it?" Stefan could not believe this good fortune.

"That's it! No, I haven't studied it, but I need to correct that. Oh, I so look forward to exploring it with you!"

"With great pleasure! You are in for a treat!" He was exuberant, unable to restrain his glowing spirits. She laughed and did a quick twirl of happiness with her hands clasped, as if she were a child being offered chocolate.

They bade farewell, and the elegant older servant opened the door.

—

There had never been such a January day. The clouds had given way to clear skies. The temperature had dropped, but he had not noticed. His only bodily sensations were a delightful tingling on his skin and a racing and happy heart. Everything his eyes fell on glowed. Every person he met was a delight. He stumbled, got his shoes muddy and did not care.

Never had he dreamed he could be affected so strongly in such a short time by another human being. Her poise, brilliance, and beauty all combined in eyes whose green light pierced him through.

After he re-entered the city, he stopped, tried to calm his inner winds, and take stock of what had just happened. He stood ready to jump into a wave of youthful euphoria. Then he realized with a shock that, for the first time, he was half imagining a permanent future for himself in the eighteenth century. A tangible reason for *staying*. Heretofore his fantasy regarding her had been…what? A chivalrous and romantic chapter in a book in which he eventually, in some hazy way, found his path home.

Now after one meeting and a powerful musical connection, it all felt real, and the haze had cleared. A sea of potential rapture lapped at his feet. If he allowed himself to be pulled by this current, he might never see his daughter again. They would live their lives separated by centuries.

No. He could not allow himself to surrender to this. His daughter, Katrina, born of his essence, still was his emotional and psychological center, and he could not yet admit to the possibility that a return to the twenty-first century might be impossible. He should cleanly end his meetings with the countess.

But he could no more do that than he could command his blood to stop flowing.

A cutting breeze kicked up as he continued back to his flat. His heart carried equal measures of thrill and dread.

Chapter 25—Return Post

THREE DAYS LATER Stefan received a letter from London.

London
23 November 1786

Dear Mr. Radowitz,

I have received your letter of the twelfth of August, along with that of my good friend Mr. Storace.

I completely agree that your proposal is one that will leave the British Museum with a true mystery for some time. A museum's usual mission is the keeping of old things so that they can remain new for present-day viewers. Your proposal is that we take something new and keep it until it is old, for the sake of future viewers.

I, for one, find that an intriguing variation on our usual mission, and I accept. I will try to cover the box and its contents with spells and curses that will ward off the ill designs any future directors may hold on it. I assure you of their potency.

In all seriousness, I look forward to receiving your box and its enclosed mystery from Mr. Storace's own hands in the near future.

I am, yours faithfully,

Charles Collins
Director, The British Museum

His letter to London, with Stephen's introduction, had slipped to a corner of his mind since the lesson with the countess. Reading the letter powerfully reinforced the conflict he faced. And another element—did he want to leave Mozart? He knew the huge historical events he would soon witness. If he found a way to go back now, would he? But he also knew how this would end, with the great composer dying in agony, and that would be too terrible to witness.

Over the past two days, he had worked hard getting his rational mind to reassert itself. The strong chemistry with the countess might have been pure illusion, constructed by a lonely mind. Surely it was a common enough trap people made for themselves, especially when they were displaced, as he.

Stefan decided that the purpose of the letter was to tell Katrina where he was and that he was well. No more. The next day he assembled his writing materials.

Morgenweg 8
Vienna
22 January 1787

Dearest Kat,

I can only imagine the shock you must be feeling at this moment after having read the date above. An explanation is coming, but first let me tell you that, as I write these words on the date listed, I am alive and well, living as a professional musician in Vienna. I can tell you only what I remember of what happened. I can no more give you a scientific explanation than I can lecture on the topography of the moon. Unless I am in a coma in a modern hospital and just dreaming all this, this is very real. So here is Doc Brown writing a letter to Marty McFly, hoping the Western Union guys will follow the instructions.

In a gush and tumble of words, Stefan related the basics of the story: St. Marx Cemetery, jail, Mozart, being taken in, and very quickly starting to make himself useful to Mozart as an assistant. He spun the extraordinary events of *The Marriage of Figaro* premiere, and the numerous other premieres of canonic works he had witnessed. He tried to be patient and write slowly, but it was hard to hold back the flood of extraordinary memories. He made no mention of the Countess Grünewald. It was a swirl of Mozart—the good boy / bad boy reputation, the incomprehensible genius, and the emotional scars from his family that caused him to hurt others.

Even though I pinch myself every day when I witness these miracles, I intend to find a way to return. It's a very simple deduction. I time-traveled here, so I can time-travel back. But that's as far as I am. I know that what happened has to do with a strange, almost physical connection to Mozart, which he says he feels as well. Maybe I can get him involved in some exotic ritual that the Freemasons might know about. One has heard about old Freemasonry as an umbrella organization that included mystical practices.

Yes, Mozart knows my origin. I was forced to reveal it when he heard me playing Chopin when I thought I was alone. I still had to prove it to him by knowledge of pieces that he was working on but had not finished.

It is terribly difficult knowing what is in store for Mozart. His earthly life will be so brief. Every time I set eyes on him it hurts me. He has wisely told me to keep my mouth shut. It tears me apart to think about saying goodbye. I do love him so.

On the other side of the ledger, there is much I don't miss, but more which I do, like antibiotics, hot showers, and of course, hugely, immeasurably, you. It's a giant hole that aches all the time. And it drives me to keep hope. In my heart of hearts, I don't think you've seen the last of your old man.

How is all this possible? Am I an accident in time? Do I have to be exceedingly careful that I don't cause some kind of butterfly effect, i.e., kick the wrong stone while walking and cause the moon to crash into the earth in ten thousand years? Or am I already baked into the books? Doing exactly what history intended; in which case I will see you again, because I don't think I ever encountered my own grave from two hundred-plus years before. Seems like somebody would have brought it to my attention.

That's as good a summation as I can muster, and my hand is starting to cramp using this fucking quill; it's so thin and dainty. I miss big plastic ballpoints.

I'm not saying goodbye. If I can get to London, I'll write more. God bless the British Museum.

I love you, tankards and tankards.

Au revoir, beloved Kat.

Your Pop

Chapter 26—Second Lesson

THE DAYS UNTIL his next meeting with the countess on January twenty-seventh were full—voice and piano lessons, copying for Sarti and Salieri, and looking for a copy of Bach's *Well-Tempered Clavier* in the Vienna music shops. He found none, although one shopkeeper informed him that the last copy had been sold the previous day. Very well, he would just look over her shoulder.

Saturday afternoon arrived, and before he knocked, Stefan stooped and flexed his entire body, then relaxed and took the knocker. The same genial servant, Georg, greeted him, and waved him in. Once again, he wore no cloak and it was much colder that day. The countess, waiting, took note of his shivering but tactfully refrained from making a comment. She advanced, and this time he was ready, after blowing on his fingers, for her extended hand.

"Lovely to see you, Herr Radowitz!" The voice was so melodious.

"And you as well, My Lady." Her warmth washed irresistibly around him.

He looked frozen from the inside, and finally she offered, "Can I get you something hot to drink?"

"Very kind of you, My Lady, but I'm fine." She then beckoned him into the parlor.

He drew a sharp breath at what he saw. Not one pianoforte but two side by side, the second from a different maker but still a quality instrument.

He turned an amazed look at her and was delighted by her child-like pleasure at the unveiling.

"I've always wanted a second instrument but had no reason until we met. When I was a girl, my lessons with my teacher were in a studio with two instruments, and it's so much easier with two…Do you not agree?"

"My Lady, I wholeheartedly agree. Forgive me, but I'm a little speechless!"

He saw a volume of music with a hard cover on the music desk of the new instrument. He picked it up and opened it to find it was another copy of volume one of *The Well-Tempered Clavier.* With a chuckle he thought, *It was she who got the last copy!*

"What's amusing?" she asked as he flipped through the pages.

"Oh…just that I know where you bought this and when, because I was there the next day."

She brought her hands together and said, laughing, "I've inconvenienced you, and I'm sorry."

"The important thing is that it's now here."

"When the pianoforte maker, Mr. Stein, came, he saw this copy on the desk. He said that they were technical exercises that demonstrated a new system of tuning. But I've played through some of them, and they are anything but technical demonstrations."

"No," he said. "Each is an expression of a part of our humanity."

"Shall we begin exploring temperaments?" she said lightly. Her voice contained musical colors.

The countess then produced her original copy. She sat at the Walter instrument, Stefan at the Stein. He suggested that they proceed with her playing a prelude or a fugue all the way through, then he would comment, demonstrating from his keyboard.

This time he had much more to say, as her understanding of Baroque style, phrase structure, and tempo was much less thorough than her understanding of the Classical era in which she had grown up—even though only thirty-three years had passed since Bach's death. She quickly grasped though, in the fugues, the differences of touch that each voice required and the importance of underlining arrival points. The preludes used a much less straightforward phrase structure, and unlike in the classicism of Mozart and Haydn, one could not always feel where the landing point was coming.

After they played the C-sharp minor prelude she said, "This is haunting! Can we go from the beginning again? There are so many shades of sorrow in it."

They did not move quickly. Stefan had the advantage of having known the repertory for years. Yet he was struck by her ideas and responses to the music. Her outlook was untrammeled by knowledge of a 250-year-old performance tradition. Stefan found himself freshly reconsidering some passages as a result of her insights.

The time went well beyond the usual lesson length, as they had both become absorbed. She finally broke it off, saying, "I'm spent! Let's save some for next time. Oh, and it's getting dark." It wasn't that late, but the sun waned quickly in Vienna in January. A female servant was just entering the room with a taper to light the candles. Lisa's remark, "Eva, thank you," was met with a smiling, "Yes, Your Ladyship." Eva met Stefan's eyes, and he briefly smiled at her. She returned it, and he was struck by how few smiles he saw on servants' faces in the great houses in Vienna he had attended with Mozart.

"Well, My Lady, we have only made it to E major, so it will take a while to reach the end."

She thumbed ahead in her volume. "Bach. It flows out of him…richly complex, but nothing is without meaning." She seemed to lose herself for a moment in contemplating the pages.

Then she asked, "This says volume one on the front, but it goes through all the keys. Is there a volume two?"

"Oh yes!" replied Stefan brightly. "He wrote this volume as a young man when he was at the court in Köthen, then two decades later he did another entire set when he was cantor of St. Thomas Church in Leipzig."

The countess gave him a surprised look. *Woops!* he thought, *few here know this much.*

"You seem to know a lot about him."

He drew a breath, the time of the intake being the amount of time he had to form an answer. "Well...he's better known in Germany than in the Austrian Empire." Which happened to be true to a point.

She made a little noise in her throat, the meaning of which he could not decipher. Then her look changed.

"Herr Radowitz, you left last time without collecting a lesson fee. I insist you must be compensated."

He knew she was right. Teaching her *gratis* would have been improper. She was the aristocrat, he the servant.

Yet he was reluctant to name a price. She would have paid anything that he asked, no matter how high; he knew that. But for that reason, he didn't want to come near the impression that he was taking advantage of her status and wealth.

"My Lady, I thank you. I will accept whatever fee you feel is fair."

She was a little surprised, then smiled and said, "That will be fine. Let me consider it, and you may expect to hear from me in two or three days.

"Meanwhile," she added, "may we plan on more Bach, on say, the eighth of the month?"

—

As he walked in the now-harsh chill, he marveled at how quickly she had grasped Bach's essence. After seeing the mournful C-sharp minor prelude for only a few moments, she had played it and brought tears to his eyes. What else was she capable of? Being in her presence removed every other thought or volition. Stefan stopped walking and looked up into the partly cloudy sky that promised a lovely sunset. As the pink sky became fiery, it lit him from within, and his resolve collapsed. Gazing into the frosty, brilliant evening glow, he trembled, only partly from the cold. He allowed his mind to say it, *God help me. I am in love.*

—

Three days later a fairly substantial package arrived at his door, wrapped in very nice paper and tied with string. He unwrapped it to find a heavy woolen cloak of good quality. Inside was a note:

> Shall we say this will cover the cost for as many lessons as it takes
> to get through the cold weather?
>
> Yours, E.G.

Chapter 27—Fee

27 January 1787

LISA WAS LYING on the plush couch in the library after her second lesson with Stefan. This had always been her sanctuary. Years ago she had finished reading its volumes, and many of them had been reread. The worn bindings showed the stains of being held many times by loving hands. They were her close friends, and this was the safest place she knew.

Both lessons with Herr Radowitz had been revelatory for Lisa. At the first lesson, his comments on her playing of Mozart's A minor sonata were not so much instruction as they were a sharing of his musical insight and the emotional meaning of something that was precious to him.

She was on new ground with Bach, but he had encouraged her budding insights into the older style. He welcomed her wish to go back and experiment, and often seemed happily surprised by her ideas. He was a fellow explorer as much as he was a mentor. And she took great fulfillment in sharing with someone who loved music as she did.

Then after he left, she had done something that maybe had crossed a line in appropriate behavior. He had come without a topcoat of any kind on a raw day. She was appalled but had had the presence of mind not to comment and perhaps cause him embarrassment.

"Georg," she said as the sound of Stefan's footsteps faded, "I want you to go tomorrow to the tailor on Kärntnerstrasse and see if he has a gentleman's topcoat or cloak of some kind that is ready for delivery. I want it delivered to Herr Radowitz. He lives on Morning Way," she instructed as she quickly wrote a note to accompany the parcel.

———

Georg raised his expressive eyebrows, started to speak, then noted the look on her face and bowed.

Now she was nestled on the couch. A mistake? She could still stop Georg. She looked around her and asked aloud to all the authors she loved, "What am I doing?"

Some of her peers might view such a gift to a commoner as inappropriate. She hoped her act would not make him feel awkward, but as for what others said…Truly, after what she had been through, she no longer cared. All they could do was talk and not invite her for tea. This man was not going to take ill merely because he was coming to her house to engage with her on music and could not afford to dress for the cold.

She had never met anyone like him. What he said about music made her hungry for more. His thoughts on music seemed as if he had considered them for a hundred years. He was also odd in so many ways: how he held himself, how he addressed people, the cadence of his German.

But any ideas about a relationship beyond teacher and student, she chopped off as soon as they peeked up. She had barely survived her marriage. It had been a living nightmare in ways that she had never divulged to anyone, not even her Aunt Catherine. She was done with that.

Yet she eagerly looked forward to again hearing his steps on the cobblestones.

Chapter 28—Third Lesson

ON THE EIGHTH of February, the Countess Grünewald was at the entry to the parlor and enjoyed watching Georg take the heavy cloak from Stefan. He took two steps toward her, his hands spread in a gesture of gratitude.

"Your Ladyship, there are not enough thanks…"

She was ready. Briskly she said, "None needed. I will keep you from freezing when you come so you can execute your duties once here properly." All spoken with a pleasant but slightly neutral smile.

Stefan saw her determination, then bowed, saying "Your most humble servant, My Lady."

They both sat down to the aromatic coffee. The countess, as usual, effortlessly led the conversation. Stefan turned the talk to his upcoming schedule.

"Wolfg…the Maestro returns from Prague next week, and I'm not quite sure what new projects he will have in the pot. Sometimes he needs me at short notice, and I have more or less pledged to him that I will be there when needed."

"Of course, I understand. What is it you do for him?"

"Coming up to a project, I mostly copy orchestral parts. You never know when some request will come in for a work only three weeks hence. He is so fast, and I have to be ready."

She thought for a second, then said, "I have a good music hand. Perhaps I could help."

He paused, causing her to wonder if this was an inappropriate offer coming from her.

"Later, I can show you a sample of my hand."

He smiled and said, "Of course. I'll tell him of your offer."

The lesson, like the previous two, was more an exchange of ideas. Lisa had internalized and made her own much of what they had gone over in Bach interpretation the previous time. "You're starting to find your own voice in Bach," Stefan said. They even had a couple of disagreements, and in these she held her own. Again her lack of experience with any Baroque performance tradition (other than what Stefan offered) was freeing for her creative mind. This man kept opening Bach's doors for her, inviting her to go through, and once through she was faced with a wealth of choices, all of which, when assembled, formed yet another door.

—

They both slowed down when the light started to fail, and once again Eva slipped in with a long taper to do the rounds. The room became bright enough for work, but they both realized that they were drained from the intense engagement. Eva, ever attentive, brought in fresh coffee, of which Stefan took but a sip, saying something about staying ahead of the dark on the unlit streets outside the wall.

"Oh yes," said the countess, remembering what she had promised. She opened a nearby desk and took out a folder that contained music manuscripts. She opened it for Stefan. "Legible enough for Mozart?" Her hand was highly legible, and professional performers would have been satisfied with it.

"Completely, very clean," Stefan said as he started to explore the music itself in the manuscripts, thumbing through the pages. It was a work for piano and seemed to contain some complexity. "What work is this?" he asked.

"It...it is my composition," said the countess, suddenly tense and nervous. She had not planned for the music itself to be examined.

"How wonderful that you compose!" Stefan exclaimed, full of delight. But she waved him off, making it clear that she did not want to discuss her music, and he raised his eyebrows. Her unnamed anxiety surged up like stomach bile. Stefan said gently, "I would be delighted to hear you play your own music."

This was the worst thing he could have said. In a blinding flash the memory came roaring back to her in disjointed images; her playing, being subjected to mocking laughter, leering faces, flight, pain, violence, fear, anger.

She froze, stiff and locked, then looked at Stefan with her face full of panic, until his gentle touch at her elbow brought her back. She unfroze, recovered, and said softly, "I'm afraid I cannot. I have unpleasant associations with doing so."

"My Lady, I am so sorry, and regret that I have caused bad memories to arise." He boldly took one of her hands in his and squeezed it in reassurance. "Wolfgang will be delighted to have your help."

"I so look forward to seeing him again," she said, recovering further.

"Can we set our next meeting tentatively ten days hence, the eighteenth? I'll contact you if I must reschedule."

"That will be lovely," she said, trying desperately to shake the webs of the horrible memory. Had she scared him? Why was he saying *tentatively*? Damn these monsters in her mind!

———

Stefan harshly berated himself in the coming days for calling up some trauma the countess carried. Was it really related to playing her own music? Doubtless it was something her bastard of a husband had inflicted. What kind of monster had she been trapped with? She clearly had triggers of which he was unaware, and he would have his antennae on high alert.

But meanwhile Mozart was returning from Prague soon, and he had to be ready for whatever might demand immediate attention.

Stefan, as usual, knocked, then let himself in. He shook the snow from his garments before stepping inside. Mozart greeted him.

"Stefano!" Then noticing the new cloak, he said, "Your station has come up in the last month! I'm pleased!" Stefan hoped fiercely that he would not be quizzed further on the item.

The table was set with simple fare: roast mutton, sauerkraut, cheese, fresh bread, butter, jam, and wine. No matter how simple, home cooking was heavenly to Stefan.

Stefan beamed happily, "I have heard rumors that you were the monarch of Bohemia. Vienna needs to learn a thing or two from Prague."

Wolfgang was in an electric state and rattled out his speech. "I wish I could bring a caravan of the Praguers back to Vienna. I have never been received like that. All anyone wanted was *Figaro, Figaro, Figaro*. On the streets, in the cafes, dancing—many arrangements of Figaro's arias especially. The wily servant who gets the goat of the aristocrat. All love Figaro and his music."

"Is anyone performing any music other than yours?" Stefan asked, laughing.

"Well, there was a performance of an opera by Paisiello that I attended called *The Competition of Generosity*. I can't tell you much about it because I was being rude and talked for much of it. A few nights later was *Figaro*, and I was much quieter." With a devilish smile, he then said, "Take from that what you will about Paisiello's opera."

Constanze, with little Karl in her lap, said, "Tell Stefan about your performances." She was glowing from her husband's triumph.

Mozart said, "Well, I played my E-flat piano quartet, conducted my new D major symphony, and improvised, all at the Nostitz Theater—that's the opera house as well. My God, they were so much more appreciative than the audiences at that fucking casino. And finally I conducted a performance of *Figaro* at the Nostitz, by popular demand!"

"The key to the city!" bubbled Constanze.

Some of these details were not in the history books, and Stefan was thrilled at hearing them. Eagerly he asked, "How were the cast and orchestra?"

"Oh, well, the cast was not like what we just had, but still quite strong. The Count was sung by an excellent baritone, Luigi Bassi. Figaro was no Benucci, but who is? Women not quite up to the men, but a very funny Marcellina."

"And the orchestra?"

"Ah, quite good. Strings not as virtuosic as Viennese players, but very musical with a good tone and sense of ensemble. Real pride. But the winds were outstanding. There's a strong tradition of wind-playing in Bohemia."

Stefan asked as innocently as he could, "Are there any possibilities of a return to Prague?"

Mozart shot him a quick look that Stefan knew meant, *You damn well know the answer to that already, don't you?*

Taking first a gulp of wine, he said "Well, there have been discussions. There may be a commission for an opera in the fall. Libretto not chosen, but I told them to do nothing until I talk to da Ponte."

Constanze was alight with the possibility of good fortune coming their way. Stefan tried to smile noncommittally. He always dreaded the possibility of confirming something unintentionally.

"Stefan, you will join us tomorrow, yes? Many friends will be here. Jacquin, Stadler, Puchberg," Constanze said, naming first an important patron, then the first great clarinetist in history and finally a lodge brother.

Mozart said, "We'll start around three thirty, and end…who knows? Do say you will come!"

Stefan hesitated, prompting Mozart to exclaim, "I'm not taking no for an answer!"

Stefan said, "Well, I do have a lesson at two o'clock."

"Plenty of time; you're just around the corner!"

"Well, the lesson is on Nightingale Street. And sometimes we go over the usual time."

Mozart raised a delicate eyebrow. "And who is the other half of *we?*"

"The Countess Grünewald."

Significant silence ensued, with four raised eyebrows.

"How did you meet?" asked Constanze, breaking the silence.

"She was at the salon that I covered for you, Wolfgang. She introduced herself, and a couple of days later I received a note from her asking me to her home to discuss lessons. I have seen her three times."

A silence of surprise took the room. Stefan rushed to fill it. "She's a superb player. She played your A minor sonata for me, very powerfully. I think she's the best keyboardist in Vienna, present company excepted. She also is a good copyist and would be glad to assist you if needed."

Mozart took a sideways look at his wife, then looked intently at Stefan.

"Stefano, my friend, you have spoken of her before. She is very beautiful, and you know something of her troubled history. Be careful. She is an aristocrat and doesn't need you to rescue her. Guard your heart. That's something I rarely say, for I believe in love. But I say it to you in this case. The aristocracy are as beautiful as the stupidest of swans, but they are also a den of savage lions, ready to slay. I knew of a fine young violinist who had a dalliance with a duchess. They were found out. At her family's insistence he was banished by the emperor; she received a scolding. They amuse themselves with us, that's all."

This was not the response he had expected. Lisa was neither a stupid swan nor a savage lion, and he could not accept Wolfgang's bleak pronouncement about the miraculous flowering he was experiencing. Angry resistance boiled up, and his face darkened.

The couple saw the unhappy look in their friend's eyes. "Enjoy giving your lesson, then come be with friends, where you are truly loved," said Mozart.

Chapter 29—Fourth Lesson

"WELCOME ONCE MORE," Lisa said, offering her hand and strong grip. The angle of the sun coming through a nearby window illuminated the copper highlights in her hair.

"Thank you, My Lady," he said, giving a restrained smile.

They proceeded to the parlor; Eva poured coffee and left. The countess gestured for Stefan to sit, and they took up their cups for a first sip. Afterward her face became serious.

"Herr Radowitz, I feel that I owe you an apology for my behavior at the end of our last meeting," she said, her voice not quite steady.

"It's truly not necessary, My Lady. You were distressed, and I didn't respond well. The apology should be mine to offer."

"That's very kind, but in truth, I feel you are owed an explanation for my reaction."

"You owe me nothing, but I stand ready to listen should you need me to."

She took a sip, then put down her cup. Placing her hands in her lap, her eyes focused on them, she took a deep breath and spoke. "There was a party of my husband's friends. Mostly merchants and tradespeople, but all very well to do. A few of noble rank. Suddenly Charles told me I should play for everyone. 'Something we can dance to!' he said. I only knew a couple of dance pieces, and I played them. I told everyone that was all I knew.

"Then he said loudly, 'Play something else, then!' He was quite drunk by then. 'You're supposed to be a composer!' What could I do, he was my husband? So I played my music, which is not dance music, and they began to titter, then laugh out loud, mockingly. I ran out of the room, shamed, up to the bedroom. Eva undressed me and I got under the covers. It was when the party noise finally died down that the worst happened. Charles burst through the door, berating me at the top of his lungs. Why couldn't I play more polkas? I had embarrassed him. I was his wife; I belonged to him and would always obey him. He mocked my composing, saying such a silly pastime should be made useful."

She stopped. She had never been able to relate fully the rest of the incident out loud, and when she had tried, she had gone into a full panic. But something in Stefan's quiet demeanor…she could sense him deeply listening and sharing, and it softened her mounting fear. She found herself feeling safe enough to say it briefly, softly. "He struck me hard. He was… brutal."

Looking up, she saw a still face, mouth grimly drawn, but his eyes were welling.

She started to grow uneasy from his silence, but finally he spoke. "For a husband to…unforgiveable," he said in a low, tight voice, trying to find the right word. His tone then softened. "The memory must be a terrible thing to carry."

"When I recall it, I feel…ashamed…" This word burst out, as if it had inadvertently escaped. She seemed to be revisiting the nightmare, and her face grew crimson.

Stefan bent forward closer to her and took one hand. He said decisively, "No fault lies with you, My Lady, no shame is on you. You did nothing wrong."

She softened and relaxed, dabbing at her face with a handkerchief from her bodice. "Thank you for that."

Stefan released her hand, then said with deliberate care, "May I say, My Lady, that it might release the infection of this wound if you were to play your music in an environment in which you feel it is safe to do so.

The last time you played your music, it may as well have been for a flock of geese. All they know how to do is make noise and relieve themselves. I am a musician and have heard the music of many new composers with an open mind and heart. If you wish to avail yourself of my service in this, I am yours to command."

She smiled at the geese metaphor and kept her gaze on him. She looked down, then up at him and said, "I cannot thank you enough, Herr Radowitz. Let me give it some thought."

A settling pause, then Stefan said, "We near the end of volume one of the Bach. I brought a four-hands work of Mozart's, if we have time."

She brightened considerably at this. "Oh?"

Stefan had picked a duet and brought two copies. It was a joyful, uncomplicated work in D major, with particularly lush sonorities. The four-hand works were meant to be played at one keyboard, but Stefan decorously sat at the second keyboard, thus creating more space between them.

They made their way through, and soon their better spirits reasserted themselves. "There are more of these, you know," Stefan said when they reached the end.

"Oh, *do* bring them!"

"And I must tell you that Mozart is back with concerts coming up. I have a feeling I will be busy."

"And what are they?"

"On the twenty-third, a farewell concert for Nancy Storace, with music by Wolfgang and several other composers."

"I'm sad she is leaving."

He suggested, "You might want to consider attending that one. Mozart has written an aria for the two of them to perform together. Then another concert a few days later. He will need me, but I could be free on Saturday the twenty-fourth." The date was set, farewells were said, and she could hear his steps receding down the driveway.

Lisa retreated again to the well-worn library couch. She dropped onto one end of it, slouching at an angle. She closed her eyes and listened to her heart gradually slow down. She was sure the decision to apologize had been the right one, but it was not meant to have gone like that. It should have been perfunctory, business like, fewer…details. She had thought some explanation was needed and that she could tell the story of that awful evening objectively. *That was foolish*, she thought.

But her resolution had been softened by something in his presence. He had not judged or even reacted at all while she spoke. He'd just listened, very closely, as he did when she played. When she'd looked up at his face, she saw the anger set in his mouth. But his eyes were fully open and moist, filled with compassion. Then came his surprising offer; never had it occurred to her that anyone would again actually ask to listen to her music.

After that, playing Bach and Mozart…At first she wondered why he'd sat at a separate keyboard for the four-hands work, but then she guessed it—the gentleman respecting her boundaries. Many men had a gentlemanly shell they put on. But his was no costume. He even treated her servants with respect; it seemed just a part of his nature.

And now she sorely wished he hadn't left.

Georg's head appeared at the doorway. "Some port or sherry, My Lady?"

"God, some port and a few of those nutty crackers would save me, thank you so much, Georg!" He disappeared.

With this revelation of a dark secret, had she stepped into misguided intimacy? There was no future in a relationship with this fascinating commoner that was the tiniest bit beyond where they were now.

She had ventured over a line of familiarity today and could not do so again. But she was resolute about keeping the relationship they had. She had many acquaintances among her peers, a few of whose company she actually enjoyed. But there were none who had made the music in her start to flow again. And the truth of it was that she was deeply lonely—except during his visits.

Georg came in with the port and crackers. "May I get you anything else, My Lady Lisa?"

"No, I won't need you any more today, Georg. Ask Eva if I may have dinner a little early, in the kitchen."

Georg bowed, cast a lingering and knowing smile on her, and left.

After her simple dinner in the kitchen—sometimes Eva dined with her, something that was never divulged outside the house—Lisa went back into the parlor with a candle to the desk near the keyboards. She took out the folder that contained her composition manuscripts, opened it, and by candlelight silently looked through her piano piece that Stefan had seen, beginning to end. She then sat and began to play.

———

Stefan was once again walking toward the city after leaving another encounter with the countess, his mind again churning. Once more he was amazed at her ability, this time in sight-reading. She was so quick and had a powerful intuition for what lay ahead, even on first encounter. She was the best keyboardist he had ever played side-by-side with; her playing elevated his. At each meeting she surprised him with yet another gift. As he was marching furiously, he measured the advice he had received from his younger but worldly friend Wolfgang against what his heart was saying.

"Don't get involved," Mozart had said. "They don't welcome outsiders."

Stefan knew from history that Mozart was right. He had to think no further than Beethoven's affair with a beautiful young aristocratic widow during his second decade in Vienna, the Countess Josephine von Deym. His passionate letters to her had survived. But her family crushed the relationship, threatening her with the loss of her children if she married a commoner. Not even a personality with the force of Beethoven's could break the convention.

But when Stefan saw the countess starting to melt down just now, whatever grip he had on Mozart's advice melted as well. He needed to hold her protectively as he needed his next breath. His daughter, Katrina, would have roasted him for being chauvinistic: "Who ever said women need protecting?" At least in the twenty-first century…

But he was hardwired, and every step took him farther from where he wanted to be—next to her, making her feel safe. Nothing could turn that instinct off.

Nevertheless he had to think about her greater welfare and not do anything that would jeopardize her other relationships, her family. She had only referenced one relative, an aunt named Catherine—what about her view? Stefan guessed that Aunt Catherine was someone who carried a lot of weight, especially in such matters.

He would be glad to get to Mozart's and blot some of this out with Constanze's punch. And he hoped Mozart had piles of work for him.

Chapter 30 — Love Letter

STEFAN GOT BOTH wishes, punch and work. The party at Mozart's lasted between nine and ten hours. The dancing became more and more uncoordinated with the rise in punch consumption, and Stefan saw some distinguished citizens of the community literally falling down, feet in the air, choking with laughter. Mozart was a small man, but his tolerance for alcohol was beyond that of most. He ruthlessly parted several guests from their pocket change, and more, at the billiards table. Stefan was relieved at the absence of scatological canons.

The next day brought the work for the Storace concert. Arias from four different operas by different composers, which Nancy had sung in Vienna, made up the core of the program, plus some instrumental interludes in the form of overtures from those operas. Mozart was the only composer to provide an original work, and there was nothing else of his on the program.

Nevertheless, the assembling of all the disparate parts from different sources for the instrumentalists fell to Stefan, and it was a massive puzzle. There was to be one run-through on the morning of the performance, and all music had to be organized neatly on the music stands in the right order.

The performance was at the Kärntnertor Theater. The rehearsal was an easy one and Nancy seemed happy and relaxed. Stefan was an extra pair of ears out in the hall, making sure that Nancy's light voice was not covered over by the instruments. Concert time was seven o'clock, and Stefan arrived thirty minutes early to cast an eye over everything, something he always did for his own concerts.

The audience was filtering in as Stefan gave one more critical glance to the stage. He felt a tap on his shoulder and turned to see one of the liveried hall ushers. The man pointed to the boxes where he said a young woman was trying to get Stefan's attention. He looked where the man pointed and saw the Countess Grünewald, gaily waving. His heart leapt as far as his chest wall would allow, and he waved back broadly. She then gestured for him to come up to the box. He noticed her companion, the same elderly woman who had accompanied her to the *Figaro* performances.

Stefan took the stairs two at a time, almost jogging down the hallway. He gave a knock at the door and cracked it open to see her smile beckon him in. She and her companion were occupying two of four chairs, and she invited him to sit next to her. Before doing so he bowed to the companion, an aged woman with the sharp eyes of a hawk looking over a field, waiting for a tell-tale blade of grass to move. The corners of her mouth rose slightly as the countess spoke, but nothing else in her face moved.

"Aunt Catherine, this is Herr Stefan Radowitz. Herr Radowitz, this is my great aunt, the Dowager Baroness Hohenberg."

"I am honored to meet you, Lady Hohenberg," he said, coming up from his formal bow.

"It is nice to make your acquaintance, Herr Radowitz." Still, the face did not move.

"Will you join us for the performance?" asked the countess. This got a slightly raised eyebrow from the baroness.

"I think my duties of the day are fulfilled, and I'm no longer needed near the stage. I accept." The countess beamed warmly, not noticing her aunt's building scowl. Stefan saw it, though.

But he and Lisa fell into easy conversation, mostly about what they were to hear, Storace's time in Vienna, speculation about why she was leaving, and her rumored closeness to Mozart.

The performance began, and the musicians on the stage were all attention. The emotion in the hall was high; Storace had been adored in Vienna and the affection from the audience was palpable.

The countess had seen all the operas from which Storace sang, and occasionally she sang along very softly. At one lovely passage in a work of Salieri's, she joined in, and Stefan saw the baroness turn to smile very tenderly at her niece.

The intermission started, and Lisa asked Stefan about Mozart's aria that he had written for Storace.

"The text is from *Idomeneo*, Mozart's opera seria from 1781. 'Ch'io mi scordi di te?' 'You ask that I should leave you?'," he replied "It's purely a concert piece, not meant to be in the opera. But the text is so important. It's about sacrifice and saying farewell."

"Oh...apt," she said.

"The piano embellishes the vocal line like...with..." He struggled to express himself tastefully. "...great intimacy. The piano will play a sighing motive, and the soprano will ask *Are you sighing?* There are places where the piano and voice are so...intertwined. Holding each other, so to speak."

"Goodness," she responded, much intrigued.

The baroness had been listening intently. "You speak so well of music, Herr Radowitz. What do you do?"

"I am a musician, Lady Hohenberg."

"A *musician?*" she said, in the same tone as if he had said, "*I am a pickpocket.*"

"Herr Radowitz is my pianoforte instructor. He comes to me every week to ten days or so."

"I see," said the hawk, beginning to glower.

There was applause, and this exchange came to a sudden stop. Stefan could feel tension on various levels next to him as the concert began anew.

Mozart's aria was last, and the applause for the entrance of Storace and Mozart together was enormous. Here was the pair at the center of an opera that was still on everyone's lips.

The strings set up the soprano's first searching question: *"You ask that I forget you?"* The instruments and voice hurled angry defiance at this terrible fate, and readiness for death. *"Come death!"* Then a change as the six wind instruments enter consolingly, followed by a melody of simple sweetness from the pianoforte. The soprano then responded tenderly with the same tune: *"Fear nothing my beloved."*

Lisa put her hand to her mouth as the intimate dialogue began. It was an extraordinary exchange between two souls, one voiced by the piano, the other by the soprano. They caressed each other, intertwined, separated, returned, and repeatedly found new ways of touching.

The text raged against the cruel, pitiless stars, then asked *"Can a faithful heart endure such torment?"* The words spoke of despair, but the music was filled with sunlit hope as the piano caressed and consoled the voice that expressed the torment, a calm hand placed over an anxious heart. The work ended in a triumphant finish, and the hall erupted.

Stefan looked to Lisa, who seemed struck as if by a revelation. She leaned in closely to Stefan and said, "My God, Mozart just told the world that he loves Nancy. A love letter."

Stefan did not speak, but, leaning in himself, nodded in affirmation. They were closer physically than they ever had been, their faces coming perilously close to touching.

As the applause died down, the spell broke. Lisa sat up and said brightly to Stefan, "Until tomorrow, with Mozart!"

"I look forward to it."

The baroness visibly started at this. As they rose and began to open the door, she said tightly, "Herr Radowitz, may I have a moment with my niece?"

Taken aback, he said, "Of course," and went through the thin door. Through it he heard agitated conversation, though both parties were trying to keep their voices low. He heard one clear line, Lisa's voice, with a desperate tinge, "But you misunderstand!" It went on for a few moments, then the door opened. Lisa came through, quite pale.

"Herr Radowitz, I ask your forgiveness, but I cannot keep our appointment tomorrow. My aunt reminds me of…cousins visiting tomorrow from Linz. I had completely forgotten…" Her voice trailed away. She finished weakly, "I will be in touch with you about rescheduling."

It was simple enough to see what was happening, and Stefan felt himself grow pale. "But…of course. I will await word from you."

The baroness fairly hustled Lisa along, turned to Stefan, who was going to walk them to the door, and said curtly, "We'll see ourselves out."

Watching them around the corner, Stefan felt as if a glacier had descended quickly on him. Nothing but horrible cold and crushing weight.

—

Two days later —— the British Isles contingent took the morning carriage to Salzburg, where Mozart's father would meet them for a tour of the small city. From there to Munich, Paris, Calais, Dover, and finally London. Stefan had met Stephen Storace the previous day to give him the mysterious box containing the letter to Katrina, destined for the British Museum. "I'll post a letter to you on the same day as I deliver it to the director," Stephen promised him.

Vienna's most celebrated composers were there at the station to bid farewell. Mozart held back, not wishing to be in the front crush, and Stefan was beside him. The crowd of well-wishers finally thinned. Stefan went first, to make room for Wolfgang. Wolfgang shook hands with Stephen, and by the time he got to Michael, both men were openly weeping. A long embrace, followed by an even longer embrace with Nancy, who was in pieces by now, then the group held each other fiercely. Just before boarding the carriage, Michael turned back and said to Wolfgang in a commanding voice, "By God, Mozart, we will see you in London!" then disappeared. The door closed, the whip cracked, and the carriage rode into history.

Stefan walked back to his flat glumly. It was always devastating to know what plans would never materialize. He then saw the letter waiting on the inside table, and he trembled, recognizing the countess's hand. He opened and read.

24 February 1787

Dear Herr Radowitz,

I am beside myself with embarrassment and deep regret. It seems invariably when we are together that I am the cause of some terribly upsetting situation.

My Aunt Catherine took an impression of our association that is totally erroneous, but she refuses to be dissuaded. She insists that we not be together under any circumstance. For now, I must accede to her wishes.

Lest you take a false impression yourself, let me assure you that she holds no legal or financial sway over me. But she is all the family I have left, and I do not wish to confront or defy her in a way that may bring on a shock-induced illness to one so elderly.

I hope that, with the passage of a little time, she might soften and listen to reason. I will work in that direction. I beg of you, please be patient. The thought that I might lose your friendship kindles deep grief within me.

Elisabetta Grünewald
Lisa

Stefan was crushed lower and lower as he read, although nothing she said was surprising. They had indeed talked very closely and intimately in the box, a poor idea in a public theater, even if not being watched by a hawk.

When he read the tiny second signature at the bottom of the page, he wanted to shout for joy. It was only an intimate afterthought, but that little intimacy spoke powerfully.

———

What Stefan hoped would be days turned into a week, then weeks, then a month, then more. At times he felt serene in his faith that Lisa would carry the day with her aunt. At other times, he was in a black pit overlooked by the baroness, who had transformed from hawk to harpy.

He continued his routines. The flow of pupils was fairly steady, and copy work was up and down. But grief was exhausting, and some days were excruciating. From time to time he would take her letter from its drawer and reread it aloud. That gave some comfort, but less and less as the weeks stumbled by.

Chapter 31 — da Ponte

THE MOZARTS MOVED again in April to the suburb of Landstrasse. Stefan knew the opinion of historians that this move was due to a dip in the family's financial prospects, but he could detect no sign of this being the state of affairs. The Vienna *Figaro* had not done terribly well, with its performances curtailed, but the Prague production was brilliantly received, and the promise of a new opera there held great hope. All Mozart told Stefan was that he thought the air in the suburbs was better—fewer people, fewer horses. It turned out that Constanze was also pregnant, so all felt the move was a good one.

With Landstrasse being further from the center, Stefan had a hefty walk from his flat on Morgenweg. His first trip there in mid-May was for an early dinner.

He knocked, and a familiar face appeared from an unknown space. "Just in time!" sparkled Constanze, with a warm hug that yielded a smell of fresh bread and roast meat. Stefan had always felt compassion for her, both from what he knew to begin with and what he observed. Living with Mozart was not easy; when he was depressed, he could be cruel and hurtful. Once Stefan had made a late-night copying error, and Mozart had erupted at him. "Idiot! Do something useful! Go find some sad countess to fuck!" Wolfgang apologized the next day, but the shock of the explosion dissipated only slowly.

"Wolfgang and Lorenzo have just finished working," said Constanze.

Lorenzo da Ponte's being here meant that *Don Giovanni* was in the works for the Prague premiere! Reminding himself yet again to be on guard against citing facts that he shouldn't know, especially in the presence of the observant da Ponte, he entered the study.

"Stefano! You remember my great friend Lorenzo!" His spirits were high.

"A pleasure once again, sir," Stefan said. He looked to Mozart, "Is this the Don Juan opera I heard you mention?" he asked, using the Spanish version of the central character's name.

"Italiano, per favore! *Don Giovanni!*" exclaimed da Ponte, half singing. "We will send the rascal to the fires of hell!"

"Let's drink to the fires of hell!" proclaimed Mozart.

"'Questo è il fin di chi fa mal!'" da Ponte declaimed the text at the end of the opera. *This is the end which befalls evildoers!* Mozart and Stefan recited the verse in Italian immediately after him, which earned Stefan a quizzical look from Da Ponte that said, *"How do you know that line, I just wrote it?"*

"Your poetry stays in the mind effortlessly after one hearing, Signor!" responded Stefan to the look. Which earned him a fast side-long glance from Mozart. *Careful!*

Dinner continued in an ebullient mood. Schedules, cast, theater, orchestra, all were discussed thoroughly. The target opening date was October fourteenth, to celebrate the marriage of Emperor Joseph II's niece. Truly a brilliant occasion!

Turning to Stefan, Wolfgang said simply, "I could use you. Can you come to Prague?"

"You could not stop me," said Stefan.

"I have several works to finish before I can begin the opera, some songs that various publishers want. Also a four-hands sonata." The mention of a four-hands sonata brought thoughts of Lisa flooding to Stefan's mind, and a cloud covered his heart.

"And Stefano, I have finished two string quintets recently, in C major and G minor. I want to distribute them to some good string players for performance, but I don't have a publisher yet. Until I do, I need to have a set of manuscript copies. If you can do it, you may just take my originals home with you rather than commuting here."

Stefan had usually done his copy work at Mozart's home, so it took his breath to think about handling the priceless manuscripts of two towering masterpieces of the chamber music literature. That he would lay hands on them was humbling. He wondered, if he ever got back to the twenty-first century, if someone may have found these copies in his hand. Which led him to wonder again, was his presence changing history, or was it already baked into history? If he went back to his present and looked hard enough, would he find evidence of himself?

Chapter 32—Death in the Family

STEFAN HEARD FROM another composer for whom he was copying that Mozart's father had died on May twenty-eighth. Mozart did not attend the funeral, and the next day he began work on *Don Giovanni*.

Two weeks later, with not much progress on the opera, Wolfgang met Stefan in their usual isolation booth at their favorite inn.

Wolfgang did not seem grief-stricken but was nevertheless listless. "How are you?" he asked Stefan briskly, with a bit of a forced smile.

"Oh, well enough."

"I have heard that you no longer meet with the Countess Grünewald."

"And you know that how?"

"Vienna is rather a small town."

"The unfortunate circumstances have arisen from a misunderstanding, but yes, that is true."

Wolfgang looked at him kindly and said, "I did warn you."

"That you did."

"I am sorry, my friend."

"Thank you." He paused. "And how are you holding up, considering your family news?"

Mozart took a long breath. "Stefano, how much do you know about my papa?"

Stefan thought, *I might know a lot more than you would care for me to, as I've read very personal letters to your father that you never dreamed would be published.*

"Well, I know a lot about your childhood, the tours with your family, how you charmed the crown heads, including the current queen of France."

"And other royalty," Wolfgang interjected quickly.

"Yes, of course. And I have a general sense that the more you tried to establish yourself individually, the more strain there was with your father."

"Correct," Wolfgang sighed. "Up to a certain age, he was the sun and moon to me. But past that, I could never please him." He paused, gathering himself. "You know that quote from Haydn to Papa about me? Being the finest composer whom he knew or knew of?"

"Yes…"

"What you don't know is that it was in answer to a question. Papa asked Haydn how truly talented he thought I was! In the presence of my playing my wonderful string quartets that Haydn adored! It seems Papa still wasn't sure!" Mozart grew angry. "I heard later that he told others of how marvelous he thought *Figaro* was. I had sent him the score. But he never mentioned it to me, ever."

Stefan looked down and slowly shook his head. "That must be painful. It's as if he felt that if he spoke approvingly of what you did, it would mean he approved of your pulling away from him."

"Ah," Wolfgang snorted, with a dismissive wave of his hand, not responding to Stefan's observation. "The best thing about Papa's death is that I will receive a thousand florins from the estate, as per agreement with my sister. Paltry. Still, it comes at a good time."

"Well, times like this are never good."

"Bah!" Mozart almost spat. "I should have fought for more, but the less I have to do with Nannerl, the better."

"Wolfgang, I've never heard you speak of your sister. Where is she in all this?"

"By my father's side, loyally, as she always has been. She followed him slavishly. I can't understand it. He crushed her when she was young."

"How so?" Stefan was unaware of this chapter in the story.

Wolfgang looked at him directly. "You do know that she was a part of the traveling Mozart family show when we were children, yes?"

"Yes, I knew that."

Wolfgang spoke in an intense whisper and drew close. "When she reached a certain age, Papa began featuring me, and began leaving her out. *But her gift was the equal of mine!* Papa thought it was cute at first, brother and sister, but as she matured, became less of a little girl, he began to suppress her. She was forbidden to compose. He thought it unseemly for a young woman, and even worse, a distraction from the son. Her job was to marry well. I became very angry. God, I loved her!" He paused and said more sadly, "I made it clear to Papa how much I missed her. No matter. Somehow, she came to blame me and took Papa's side. She rarely writes now."

He lowered his voice even more. "Stefano, all those tales about what I could do as a child, those seemingly magical powers—there was *nothing* I could do that she could not also do!!"

This was a profound shock to Stefan. Modern scholarship had established her great talent when she was young, but Leopold had withdrawn her from all appearances as she approached marriage age. *Could there have been two equal Mozarts, one male, one female?* After a moment Stefan said, "So she remained in Salzburg. And now finally has control as executor of his estate."

"Ah yes, the money. My father kept so much of our—*our*—earnings from the tours. Money and gifts, like gold-inlaid snuff boxes. Yet he could not bear it when I wanted to stand on my own, with my own family."

Stefan shook his head in sad disbelief. "A heavy and sad burden for you. Yet you must mourn him…"

"YES, I mourn him!!" he said, giving the table a single blow. He paused, then tears started to spurt, "And I am so angry. He could not bring himself to tell me he loved me. Sometimes it seemed he hated me, there was such anger. And he said…God, he blamed *me* for my mother's death! I was on tour in Paris. Mama came, but Papa stayed at home. She took seriously ill and died very quickly. And it became my fault."

Stefan shook his head, afraid to speak at this new shock.

"But I *never* failed to tell him of my love. I opened every letter with 'Dearest Papa' and told him at length how much I loved him. Every time. *Every time.*"

Stefan said, "And it was never returned."

Mozart abruptly shook his head.

His eyes were tightly closed, and his hand was balled into a trembling fist. After a few moments he relaxed into a dejected slump.

"Stefano, how can I hold love and hate in my heart at the same time for the same man?"

Stefan laid his long arm across his friend's shoulders. "I don't know how that is possible, just that it is possible. Do you not have deep love with great anger and hurt, side by side, in your music?"

Wolfgang sighed deeply. "Yes. You know, sometimes I don't even think about it. That's just how it comes out. *I'm* not expressing anything. It's just…the expression expressing. Love and sorrow, both.

"As if you're taking dictation."

"Well, yes."

"But it is you, without doubt."

"I hope I never have to prove who it is." A touch of the wry smile stole back in.

They ate in silence for a while, then Wolfgang said, "You listen well. Some only hear, but you listen."

Stefan said, "Sometimes I need to listen better to my own common sense."

"It's hard to hear through the crashing waves of love."

Stefan just nodded.

"Stefano, I'll be going home now. I think I feel like composing."

Stefan nodded. They rose, had a back-clapping embrace, and Wolfgang was gone.

Well, here's a reason to smile, thought Stefan.

Chapter 33—An Advocate

LISA WAS DETERMINED not to be crippled by losing Stefan's company and guidance. She knew in her bones that this was not a permanent break. In the short term, she would keep fanning the flame he had inspired in her. She practiced the pianoforte with discipline, energy, and sometimes even a little anger. She was in a defiant frame of mind. Maybe she would pay for her own concert. She was a countess; who could stop her? She had attended a concert by a female former student of Mozart's, Josepha Auernhammer, at the Kärntnertor Theater, which had included Mozart's D minor concerto. There had been sparse attendance, and some social grumbling, but appreciable applause at the end for a good performance. There had been others as well, from different teachers.

But maintaining defiance was difficult with an aching pit in one's middle. She would start a practice session feeling full of positive energy, but inevitably she would wonder what he would advise for the phrasing or coloring of this passage or that. She wanted him there beside her. She thought a social faux pas like sitting too close to each other at a concert did not warrant banishment. She would forgo further public mixing with him, fine, but there was nothing scandalous about daytime music lessons surrounded by servants. Her desire for his company was completely innocent.

When she was very young, she had brought her little girlish dilemmas to Georg, not too long on the job at that time. He had always listened to her as if she were the only person in the world. As she matured, and especially after suitors materialized, she revealed less and less to him. But they had become closer again in the wake of her marriage and widowhood, and he had unerring radar for her states of mind.

The two sat in the little garden gazebo on a sultry afternoon in late August. Georg did not need to be told the topic at hand, although she had explained nothing to him.

"I take it the baroness has insisted you end the association with Herr Radowitz."

"You always are a step ahead. Yes, she thinks we were behaving improperly at the concert and clearly headed toward scandal. She thinks that he is interested only in my money. But as you know, we have done nothing but gather at the keyboard." She hesitated, then confessed, "The problem is, she does see into my heart. I am drawn to him. Musically, of course."

"Ah yes. I do understand how her suspicions have arisen, but she does not know Herr Radowitz as we do. So we must be able to reassure the baroness of his honorable intentions. And tell her that if he does attempt anything that makes you uncomfortable, he will suffer unpleasant consequences."

Lisa was puzzled. "And what would those be?"

Georg shrugged and said lightly, "An encounter with me." He gestured with his large muscular hands.

She opened her mouth in shock and started to speak, but he cut her off, "Of course I will do nothing of the kind. This is a show for the baroness's benefit. My Lady Lisa, no one can tell you how to feel toward Herr Radowitz. All you must do is be discreet and not associate in public, at least not without a third person present. As far as she is concerned, I can reassure her that only musical discussion takes place between the two of you and that I will remain watchful. Ready to intercede."

Tentatively she replied, "All right then. I will bring this proposal to her…perhaps you should accompany me. Your presence could be persuasive."

"Of course, My Lady Lisa."

Chapter 34—Dark Resolution

OVER THE SUMMER Mozart worked on *Don Giovanni*, and Stefan did copy work as it materialized. Things were moving slowly it seemed to Stefan, but history told him it would all get done. In the midst of this titanic project, Mozart also composed two works at extreme opposite ends of the sublime-to-ridiculous scale. At one end was a stand-alone orchestral slapstick act in music, *A Musical Joke*, featuring the breaking of every rule of sound composition technique, with phrases that never end, phrases that end far too soon, wrong notes, and pointless trills from nowhere.

At the other end was a work of effortless perfection, the title famously reused by Stephen Sondheim: *Eine Kleine Nachtmusik—A Little Night Music*. It had been one of Stefan's principal awakening-to-Mozart works in college years. Now he held the finished manuscript. Mozart had started and finished it in that staggering mind and copied down his vision, as if the universe itself had yielded this moment of sublime grace from nowhere, and Mozart simply found it.

To normal observation, these two works were a mad distraction from the task at hand, the opera. Stefan, of course, was no ordinary observer, but was again wondering if his being there was part of history and that his role was to keep Mozart on track for the premiere.

The departure date for Prague was October second. With good weather, four nights in the carriage should be plenty.

On September twenty-eighth, in the late morning, there was knock on Stefan's door. A messenger handed a letter to him and said that he was to await an answer.

28 September 1787

Dear Herr Radowitz,

I am Head Servant to the Countess Grünewald, and it was my pleasure to meet you at her residence. I trust you remember me.

Would it be possible for us to meet two days hence, Sunday the thirtieth, at your residence at one o'clock?

The messenger bearing this note will bring your answer. I look forward to hearing from you.

Georg Rákóckzi

"Tell the gentleman that I will await his visit on Saturday."

Stefan's knees were a little weak after he closed the door. What news did he bring? Reconciliation? A final and forever I'll-never-see-you-again? The next two days would be very long.

—

Georg was prompt. Stefan opened the door and offered his hand, which was taken.

"Georg, welcome."

"Herr Radowitz."

"We are both working men. Please call me Stefan."

Georg paused in mild surprise at this, then bowed.

Stefan motioned him in, gesturing for him to sit. Georg sat, back erect, legs straight. "I know my note must have been a surprise, perhaps not a pleasant one. First let me tell you that I am not the bearer of bad news."

The knot in Stefan's gut relaxed a bit.

Georg continued, "This must have been a difficult period for you. Let me say that it has been the same for the countess as well."

Stefan sighed and ran his hand through his lengthening hair. He nodded awkwardly in understanding.

"Please...Stefan. Tell me what you know about Lady Grünewald's marriage."

By this point he actually knew quite a lot about the marriage, from Mozart and from the countess herself. He related it all: the potential financial ruin of the family, the seeming rescue by a count with a fortune, his turn from charm to brutality, her father's death from heartbreak as a result, and the salvation of her husband's demise.

"Yes, all correct."

"A terrible thing to happen to anyone."

Georg met Stefan's eye and said, "It was more terrible than you know. At first he could not do enough for Her Ladyship. But then one evening, not too long after they married, she said something to him teasingly, pretending to mock him. I was there, it could not have been more innocent. He rose with the swiftness of a panther and struck her across the face with an open hand. She fell, in pain and shock. He just stood over her and said in a savage voice, 'Never mock me again.' I went to protect her, and he held a finger in my face. 'Lay a hand on me and your family loses all they have, including you.'

"It was quiet for a while after that, and we began to think all would be well. Then came the incident when he forced her to play for his friends, only to send her from the room with derision, and worse following. I believe she spoke to you of the incident.

"The next day he brought her a beautiful necklace. 'I am sorry we argued' he said with sweetness and real sorrow. I think he may even have believed it. That was the pattern—an act of violence followed by an expensive bauble. As if he were paying her to allow him to beat her.

"He would strike her for the most trivial of reasons, such as if he did not like her choice of dress. He usually struck her on her body or legs so that his work would not be revealed to the world. He would drive his fist into her thigh and leave her limping for days. Sometimes this happened on mornings after coming home in the very early hours, smelling of alcohol and cheap perfume. He would strike her to relieve himself of the pain of a hangover.

"Quite early I reported this to her father, who contacted the local magistrate. The magistrate was sympathetic but said he was helpless in issues between a husband and wife. When her father saw her, he could see the toll it was taking.

"Her father, whose health was never good, soon fell deeply ill and passed away. The countess blamed herself. Her aunt, Lady Hohenberg, was now her only family, and the old lady was a rock. Charles recognized the sad event by refraining from striking her for several weeks. But he was soon back to his old ways.

"I decided I would intervene with the only solution that I thought would work. I planned to wait for his return from all-night whoring, intercept him before he entered the house, and kill him." Here Georg mimed strangulation with a cord, using his two clenched hands. "It would have been a terrible crime, but I was ready to commit it. God was merciful and intervened. At about the time he would have arrived home, I heard the sound of a wagon approaching. As it came near, I saw it was driven by a young man, with an older woman, possibly his mother, sitting beside him. I went to the driveway and met them. The boy jumped down and went around to the back of the wagon where the was a shape beneath blankets.

"The young man pulled back the top blanket and the woman said bluntly, 'Is this your master?'

It was indeed the count, eyes lifeless and glassy.

"'Yes, it is,' said I.

"She went on in the coarsest manner you could imagine. 'He went upstairs with one of my girls. Half an hour later she came down and said he was sick. I went up, and he wasn't sick, he was dead. He had identity papers. So I brought him home for you. I done my Christian duty, so please take him.'

"I was revolted, almost sick. Then I was elated. God had saved me from doing a terrible thing. He had also saved Lady Grünewald's life, although too late for her poor father.

"I gave the pair some coins, took the body up to his room, undressed him, put on his nightshirt, and put him in bed. I splashed some whisky from a decanter on him and put it on his table along with an overturned glass. I blew out the candle and said good night.

"The next day I went up as usual to wake him for breakfast and found him still quite dead, happily. I alerted the household, including the countess, and sent for the magistrate and the surgeon. They both agreed that the poor man had died in his sleep, probably due to a heart ailment exacerbated by alcohol. My lie allowed him to be given a funeral befitting an aristocrat and spared the countess embarrassment."

Finally Stefan asked with a pale voice, "Does the countess know all that you just told me?

"No."

"And the baroness?"

Georg drew a breath. "She knows more of the grim side of life than Lady Grünewald, and I think she would not be surprised by the truth. Stefan, you must understand that the baroness is fiercely protective of her niece. She had seen her taken advantage of before by a charming monster who seemed too good to be true. You seem the same to her, in addition to not being of proper rank, so she is determined not to take that chance again. I vowed to her to shield Lady Grünewald from this ever happening."

After a moment Stefan replied, "You should know that I would take the same vow." He then asked, "Has the baroness changed her position then?"

"She still disapproves of classes mixing, and to her, you are like me. But she will allow your meetings at the pianoforte to continue as long as I give her reassurances that nothing improper is taking place. For you, that just means discretion."

"Georg, you've been there for all our lessons."

"Yes, and it was on that basis that I could give the baroness my assurance regarding your character."

"I thank you for that."

"Lady Grünewald would be pleased to see you tomorrow."

Yes! Stefan almost verbalized, then remembered. "I'm leaving for Prague the day after tomorrow with Mozart for the premiere of his new opera! I'm afraid there is much for me to do; I cannot delay."

"Ah, I see. How long will you be away?"

"The performances are the twenty-nineth and thirty-first of October, then the second and third of November. It will all take just over a month. After that I will be free and at her side."

"I will relay that, Stefan."

"Georg, deepest thanks to you for this visit."

"I am pleased for the opportunity to help."

Stefan looked at him steadily. "You love her very much, don't you Georg?"

He said simply, "As if she were my own child."

Taking his hand strongly Stefan said, "Goodbye, Georg. I will see you soon."

"Goodbye, Stefan."

Stefan wanted to run up and down the streets, screaming like an eagle soaring on a thermal. But he had to get ready for Prague.

Chapter 35 — Dramma Giocoso

STEFAN, EVEN WITH his foreknowledge, was shocked by how much of the libretto was yet to be set to music when they all arrived in Prague. Mozart had not even written the principal arias for the title role, saying he needed to hear his Don Giovanni sing more! A little more than three weeks lay between the arrival of the Mozart train on October sixth and the premiere on the twenty-nineth.

The carriage arrived at the villa where Mozart would stay, Bertramka. It was a lovely house a little outside of the town center and was owned by Mozart's friend, the soprano Josepha Duschek. Stefan was not privy to the financial arrangement, but the talk was that a concert aria for the soprano was part of the fee.

Stefan took a room at a nearby inn, as he felt it was more important to be nearer to Mozart than to the theater. The Nostitz (which Stefan knew from his day as the Estates Theater) was in the center of town. He could travel independently as he had picked up enough Czech from his own concert appearances in Prague to manage on a very basic level.

But soon he was needed to take some of the rehearsals to support Mozart. Both the *secco* recitatives (those with only keyboard) and *accompagnando* recitatives (those accompanied by full orchestra) were particularly involved and tricky. Stefan already knew them in their finished form, so he could rehearse with authority. His ease at rehearsing without the score was noted, and the cast whispered about his almost magical knowledge of music just finished. The whispers reached Wolfgang. "Stefano, please, make more of an effort in rehearsal to look at the score once in a while, even if you don't need to! The cast members are whispering!"

Each whirlwind day was different, with impossible schedule conflicts to resolve, egos to sooth, different theater machines that would break, questions about rewriting vocal lines—in a word, normal opera production. But it was not just any opera. *Don Giovanni* was the most path-breaking opera to date, far more challenging than even *Figaro*.

Da Ponte arrived on the eighth, and his presence for the cast was its usual tonic. The man could talk nonstop for long stretches, and every word was fascinating. He worked beautifully with the singers on opening up the libretto's meaning and poetry.

But after a week, he was summoned back to Vienna by the emperor on behalf of Salieri, whose opera *Axur, King of Ormus*, needed some attention, even though it was not due to premiere until January. Mozart unleashed a torrent of profanity.

"Yes! I know he's the fucking court composer, and I am horse shit on his shoe, but Salieri knows how close we are cutting it! He has all the time in the fucking world!"

Da Ponte received this with equanimity. "Wolfgang, your outrage is understandable. My assistant Grosmeier will stay and help. He is very able."

"I'm sure, but this needs da Ponte! This is real human interaction and passion! Salieri's staging is simply gods and goddesses walking up and down huge stairs, looking for somebody to fuck!"

At this da Ponte bowed formally and said, "My dear friend, we will be together soon. Meanwhile, you have my best wishes." With that he was gone.

———

There were more details to attend to in this stupendous work than there were days in which to list them. But compromises were made, and some issues that Stefan was greatly worried about were rather simple to accomplish. There were, in both finales, musicians playing from the stage, strings in act one, winds in act two. The trickiest was act one—there were three different dances going on in a party, each with its own string band, and each in its own meter. Stefan expected an excruciating rehearsal, but these excellent musicians simply read the music down at sight to perfection. Stefan wanted to treat them all at the inn down the street, but there was always another task, another emergency.

Miraculously the strands began to weave together and make sense. The date of the dress rehearsal arrived, and it seemed like the task had been pulled off. Then the pit musicians, searching the sheets of music on their stands, began to ask, "Where is the overture?"

Mozart serenely looked about, held his hands up in a placating attitude, smiled, and said, "Tomorrow."

"Maestro, tomorrow is the performance," said the concertmaster, dumbfounded.

"It will be fine," Mozart replied calmly. "I'll make it easy."

Stefan thus remembered a historical detail. *Wolfgang had not even begun the overture yet!* After the dress rehearsal would be a long night.

The run-through was not without stumbles, but they were usually corrected in midstream and did not stop the overall momentum. Mozart expertly brought wayward players or singers back into the fold. There were cautionary notes afterward about those spots, which Mozart remembered in perfect detail.

Stefan knew that he would be up all night with Wolfgang, frantically copying parts as Mozart poured the score out of his mind on to the manuscript paper. As they worked Stefan moved ahead and did some of the parts independent of progress on the score. It was an opera he knew like his own heartbeat. Mozart noticed that Stefan had finished the flute parts before he had done in the score. He looked quizzically at Stefan, asking a silent but loud question. Stefan just shrugged and smiled.

Later Stefan wondered if the overture would have made it to the music stands had it not been for his journey through time and resulting foreknowledge. If he had not done this, who would have? Was he actually a part of the history that he knew? If so, why didn't he, or someone closely resembling him, appear in any of the accounts of Mozart's life?

Constanze stayed up long with them, fueling them both with cookies and coffee. The overture was finished by early afternoon, and they both collapsed in the villa for a few hours of sleep while a messenger took the overture materials to the theater. Josepha Duschek kept an eye on the time, then awoke them both and sent Stefan to his inn and Mozart to his bath. Stefan would return to the villa for the carriage to the theater with Wolfgang and Constanze.

Drawing a bath at the inn would have taken too long, not to mention being too expensive, so Stefan shaved and made himself as presentable and nonaromatic as he could with the wash basin. He put on his better suit and made the fifteen-minute walk to Bertramka to join the Mozarts in their carriage.

Once underway Wolfgang reached into his inside pocket and pulled out, enfolded in a larger piece of paper, a ticket to the performance. "We can't have you lurking around backstage," said Wolfgang. "You might get in the way of the hellfire machinery at the end and get dragged off to hell yourself."

Stefan looked at the ticket. "Wolfgang, this is in one of the boxes. I'd be happy to be downstairs."

"Wouldn't think of it. With all that you've done? You deserve a very good seat," he said with his warmest smile.

They arrived at the Nostitz Theater. Wolfgang gave Constanze her ticket, which, by the looks of it, was not in a box. He said to Stefan, "You get to go in the front door for a change. I still have to go to the servants' back entrance." Stefan saw that Mozart was genuinely excited without being nervous. His faith in his own powers was secure.

Stefan climbed the right-hand stair to the second tier, walked down the hallway, found door four, and went in. There were three empty chairs. He took one and eyed the stage and pit. He had never felt quite comfortable as an audience member; he belonged on the stage, doing, not in the audience, witnessing. The orchestra filed into the pit and eagerly sought out the single page of the overture to glance through it. The memory of last night would never leave him. They were brothers in combat under enormous pressure, gobbling cookies. *I may not be in the history books, but by God I'm here now,* thought Stefan. *We did it. Wolfgang and Stefan.*

Stefan was exhausted but not at all sleepy. His mind felt keenly taut. He jumped a little when he heard the door open behind him. He rose to make room for more access in the cramped box. He turned and found himself looking eye to eye with Georg. Next to him was Lisa, her rich smile framed by delicate tendrils of hair.

Stefan was speechless. And he did try, but the words stopped in his throat. Finally Georg said, "Hello, Stefan."

Stefan tried harder. Looking at Lisa, joy closing his throat, he finally managed, "Lis…apologies! Your Ladyship!"

"Stefan," she said simply, "we are not in Vienna."

Stefan fumblingly offered them seats, almost comic in his lack of coordination. His mind, which had felt like lightning a moment before, was now stuck in low gear. He blurted, "What…what are you doing here?"

"Well, we're going to the opera. You did give the dates to Georg, did you not?"

They sat. Stefan lowered himself to his seat slowly, barely on the edge, unsteady. No one spoke.

Stefan blurted out the truth when he realized it. "Wolfgang!" So he was involved…but how?

Lisa and Georg smiled at each other. "The information you gave Georg was most useful. First, it let me know when the next Mozart premiere was, which I would not have wanted to miss. Second, it presented an opportunity for us to socialize away from the prying eyes of Vienna. Well," she made a playful gesture to Georg, "*most* prying eyes."

"And you contacted Mozart," Stefan said.

"He could not have been more accommodating. I said I wanted to hear his new opera on its opening. I also asked after you. He replied that he would be happy to seat us together so I could ask about you directly."

Stefan looked to the floor, then started laughing, his laughter growing to be almost raucous. It was contagious, and Lisa and even Georg joined him.

The laughing fit subsided. "So how long have you been here?"

"We arrived three days ago and have stayed at Lord Thun's estate."

"And returning…?"

"Tomorrow."

"That's a lot of concentrated travel to see an opera performance."

She shrugged. "Mozart."

Lisa, turning the conversation, asked, "So is *Don Giovanni* like *Figaro?* With such a subject matter, I assume not."

"Not in the least."

"Mozart calls it a *dramma giocoso*, a merry drama. Is it really both?"

"The way it moves is like a comic opera, but the content is dark. It begins with a murder. *Figaro* is full of love. There is great passion in *Don Giovanni,* but little love, except between two peasants. Giovanni is only interested in satisfying his own desires, no matter who gets in the way."

Stefan only realized the relevance Lisa might find in this as he was saying it. Suddenly with a touch of panic, he put it together that Lisa was about to experience a dramatization, by the greatest musical dramatist the world had seen, of one of her worst moments—the death of her father at the indirect hand of her husband. Giovanni directly murders Anna's father, who dies excruciatingly, and Anna runs in to discover his lifeless body, killed by her attacker. Her abuser.

And the music to which Mozart set this is anguished, vengeful, throbbing with grief. The audiences for whom Stefan performed the opera in the 2000s had in their ears all the music written since—Mahler, Strauss, Stravinsky—music that split the language of 1787 into a thousand shards. But to those hearing Mozart's latest music for the first time in the 1780s, it was a vast and dark canvas that rent the air with its dissonances and tore at one's insides. Lisa would have no defense for this post-traumatic reenactment. She had had none for the gentle, transcendent end of

Figaro and was overwhelmed. And *Don Giovanni's* start was an avalanche of suffering.

What should he do? Advise her to leave? Rescue her from Mozart somehow?

Leaning in so he could whisper, Stefan touched her arm.

"My La...Lisa, there is something about the opening of the opera that you need to be prepared for. It depicts a terrible event."

"Yes," she said, turning as much to him as she could, "I understand the first thing that happens is a murder."

"A lady discovers the corpse of her father, who was killed by the man who...just attacked her."

"Oh my God, Stefan..." Her jaw fell open as she absorbed what he was telling her.

"And the music is brutally descriptive. Mozart at his fullest power."

She paused. "You seek to protect me from my memories."

"I want you to know what awaits you, in light of your powerful receptivity to Mozart's music."

She drew a breath, then said firmly, "Stefan, I'm touched by your concern, truly. But I will endure. I am indeed highly sensitive to Mozart, but that doesn't make me breakable."

She said this last with finality and a look that said, *"I'm staying, let's hear no more about it."*

Mozart entered the pit to a torrent of applause; he bowed, turned abruptly, and started the overture's crashing chords before the audience's noise died down. The house was abruptly silent as the second set of chords thundered in. The overture did not end, it just made a seamless transition to the action—another brilliant stroke.

Curtain, and the brutal tragedy unfolds: A masked man flees the woman he just assaulted; her elderly father appears, sword in hand, to defend his daughter and is run through mercilessly by the much younger man. The young woman returns with her fiancé only to discover her father's corpse, and she faints. When she recovers, she and her fiancé swear oaths of vengeance.

Lisa, whose hands had gone to her face at the mortal thrust, then reached for Stefan's hand on one side and Georg's on the other. She squeezed hard, and her tears flowed down her cheeks and onto her dress unabated. She lowered her head and closed her eyes, then willed herself to look again, gripping fiercely all the time. She stopped weeping, however, at the vows of vengeance, and her expression became stern, as if she were swearing an oath as well.

At the end there was some applause, but many were too stunned by the grim violence they had just seen. Stefan looked to Lisà, whose eyes were closed. He kept his gaze on her, waiting for her to come back from the horror and open her eyes.

She finally did, releasing their hands, just before the next scene began. As the pianoforte rolled in the first chords, she turned her head toward Stefan with a wan look that said, "*Well, you were right.*"

She whispered, "Is there more like that?"

"Donna Anna describes the attack to Ottavio before her next aria."

"I may need a hand again."

"It's yours, anytime you need it."

———

The opera flowed on. Soon came the only real comic number, Leporello's aria, in which he shows the abandoned Elvira the massive catalogue of Giovanni's sexual conquests. This brought to Lisa's mind a rumor she'd heard at Lord Thun's that the man who may have inspired da Ponte, the now-elderly Giacomo Casanova, might be in attendance.

Mozart's setting of Giovanni's seduction of the peasant girl Zerlina began with a feather light touch and worked its way gradually to intimate holding. The simplicity and seductiveness of the music sent Lisa's hand lightly to her chest. When it was over, she leaned to Stefan and whispered, "No wonder he has so many conquests, with Mozart's music to sing." Lisa did not need to hold a hand for Anna's account of the fateful evening to Ottavio, but she reacted with a painful clench to the excruciating chromaticism describing the writhing of bodies.

The act one finale thundered to its close, with Giovanni escaping as he mocks all, even though he is exposed as a rapist.

Lisa turned to Stefan. "This music is beautiful but filled with foreboding and darkness. What's it like to work on it day after day?"

"Like being in the midst of something dangerous and thrilling at the same time."

She took a pause, then said, "Thank you for your warning. Onstage murders are not uncommon, but with agonizing music like that…There's not the least emotional shading that he cannot make vivid."

"Had I expected your appearance…"

She leaned forward and said quietly, "Well, I wanted to surprise you. Are you not pleased to see me?"

He swallowed and replied as evenly as he could, "I am delighted to see you."

Act two did not contain the hidden emotional mines of act one, being involved with the consequences to the Don for his misdeeds. The richness of the music was greatest when Giovanni sang. There was sensuality but no love from the Don.

When the shattering chords from the overture's beginning summoned the slain commander, Anna's father, to take Giovanni to his hellish end, as the overture predicted would happen, Lisa was sitting ramrod stiff. Her fists were clenched in her lap as she watched God's judgment come down—once again—on a murderer of an old man. Mozart had conjured the sound of an angry God and the cries of the villain's torment as demons dragged him down to the Pit.

The rest of the cast came onstage and sang their coda, and the opera ended with a moral about bad people always being punished. Lisa had a sardonic smile.

They rose, and Lisa said, "The Maestro invited me back to say hello. Can you accompany us?"

"Of course, with pleasure. We'll have to go outside, then to the rear door."

They circled around to the stage entrance, made their way in, and took a flight of steps down to Mozart's room. The spaces were cramped, so Georg decided to wait on the street. On their way down the stairs, they passed, coming up, an elderly gentleman who was dressed in an older-style but beautifully tailored suit. He nodded to them pleasantly but then bestowed a suddenly dazzling smile and a deeper head bow to Lisa, which seemed to have an impact on her.

Wolfgang and Constanze were in the tiny dressing room. Stefan hugged them both warmly, ignoring Mozart's sweat-soaked jacket. He then turned and introduced Lisa, using her title. Lisa thanked him graciously for arranging for the tickets, which delighted him. Constanze dipped a curtsy to Lisa, and Mozart took Lisa's hand for a kiss.

Stefan said, "Wolfgang, I hope you were happy with that. You've unleashed an extraordinary force on the world."

Lisa added, "I've heard almost all your operas, and much other of your work as well. Tonight was…a very important evening for me. I am thrilled, and also exhausted. The emotions you evoke are powerful, and real."

"That is my hope, My Lady. I hope you can rest from your fatigue tomorrow."

"Alas, back to Vienna."

"I understand from my dear Stefano that you are quite the pianoforte player. And copyist."

She blushed deeply. "I…suppose…I am passable, Maestro."

"I hear you are that and a great deal more. I would be pleased to hear you play when we can arrange it. Perhaps in the next few weeks?"

Nonplussed, she finally responded, "It would be my honor, Herr Mozart."

"Good! Stefano can make arrangements. Oh, and by the way, you just missed Signor Giacomo Casanova. He supposedly wrote some of da Ponte's libretto, although they are both tight-lipped about it."

Stefan replied, "I believe we may have passed him. Too bad, that would have been a pleasure." Lisa laughed nervously.

"See you in two days, Wolfgang. Prague loves you, for good reason."

Mozart bowed, and Lisa and Stefan departed.

When they got outside, Stefan said, "Mozart gives the world another immortal work."

Lisa gave him a quizzical look. "Do you see so far ahead?"

"I am…making an educated guess."

"I think I would make the same guess."

Stefan then swallowed and decided to make a try. "I have the day off tomorrow. Could you not delay…"

"I'm sorry, but commitments in Vienna await," interjected Georg in a very firm tone.

Damn, damn! Stop pushing it! Stefan berated himself.

Lisa rescued his awkwardness, chiming gaily, "I expect to hear from you when you return, and to see you at my door with a Mozart duo sonata in your hands. Maybe two!"

He shook hands with Georg. Lisa offered her hand, palm to the side to shake, but Stefan brought her hand to his lips with a low bow and lightly kissed it. "Until then."

Chapter 36 — View Downriver

STEFAN COULD HAVE followed only a day behind Lisa to Vienna. His duties in the opera's preparation were over. There were three more performances through November third, but there was an assistant conductor at the ready should Mozart take ill. Stefan had done his job and was free to depart.

But he decided he would stay through the run, and not leave until the final performance was done; he would do this this in large part because he regarded each opportunity to watch Mozart perform his music as yet another priceless jewel. It was leagues, at least musically, beyond any other performance of the work he had ever experienced, including his own. Maybe in some century or another, Stefan would have another opportunity for a *Don Giovanni* production and use this newfound inspiration. But if not, just watching and hearing Mozart was enough.

Another reason to stay was that he had to think through his considerable confusion about his preference of centuries.

He could not have been more shocked when Lisa and Georg appeared in the box than if a boar had charged through the door. Right after the shock came delirious joy on seeing her face.

—

Then they sat together, witnessing the first performance of a world-changing work. It affected her powerfully in ways that he understood, and perhaps in ways he did not. He saw what an extraordinary listener she was, hearing deeply into the music, and also her vulnerability to it—exactly the kind of listener composers pray for. The combining of the experiences of the premiere, watching the effect of the music on Lisa, and just being next to her, yielded perhaps the most intense four hours of his life, save for the birth of Katrina.

Then suddenly she was gone.

Stefan was alone on the street at the theater, watching Lisa's carriage depart, reeling even without any alcohol. He decided that that was a waste of some good reeling, so he took a carriage to his inn, drank far more than he usually did, had an animated conversation with some locals (no details of which he later remembered), and stumbled to his room, barely making it up the stairs. The alcohol knocked him out for a few hours then woke him up as it metabolized. He stared at the ceiling until dawn, developing a hangover, the likes of which he had not felt since his student days. He finally rose, washed, dressed, and shaved. He could not face breakfast but knew to drink as much water as he could stand, to fight the inevitable dehydration. He then set out on foot, determined to walk the headache off. He longed with all his heart for the ibuprofen in the medicine cabinet in his own time.

———

Over the next days he walked. He visited all the places he had known and loved in the Prague of his century: the castle (or as close as he could get, as it was not then an open tourist destination), the Charles Bridge, the Old Town Square with the Astronomical Clock, the Clementinum Library, and the Jewish Quarter. Emperor Joseph II had decreed toleration for Jews in 1782, so the quarter was bustling.

He realized anew that a reason Prague was so beloved in his time was that so much of it seemed, at least at first glance, unchanged from the days of the Habsburgs, and even earlier. Standing in the Old Town Square, one could squint and come close to imagining the outlines of distant centuries.

But his favorite place for contemplation, in both centuries, was the ancient castle Vyšehrad, the mythical founding site of Prague. Downriver a bit, it had a magnificent view of the mighty Vltava River, and Stefan loved the deeply peaceful atmosphere there. In future years, some of the great Czech artists of the nineteenth and twentieth centuries would be laid to rest in its cemetery, including composers Antonin Dvorák and Bederich Smetana, whose music became the voice of nineteenth-century Bohemia.

In future years. What would those years look like for him, and in what century would they be? When he had contemplated the issue of a return journey to the 2000s—which was most every day—he had begun to feel a premonition that a moment would come when the door back might suddenly open. He had nothing to base this on except his mind and gut, but he did feel it stronger when he was with Mozart.

In the twenty-first century was the young woman he regarded as his brightest light, Katrina. There was an area of his heart that she ruled. She must have decided that he was dead by now, so if he returned, her shock would be profound. Through all the disbelief, upheaval, and also the thrill surrounding what was now his life, he thought of her achingly every day. How could he not return if a path appeared? And what was this like for her? Her father, now nothing but another "misper" police file. Had he died in the hospital, she would have had closure. But to just vanish…

But in the eighteenth century was the most remarkable and captivating human being he had ever met. He had never thought such a pull on his heart was possible. Every encounter with her yielded a new amazement. He wanted to disappear into the bottomless wells of beauty and intelligence that were in her eyes. How could he part from her, even if a path back appeared?

As he looked downriver at the Vltava from Vyšehard, he thought of the obstacles in Vienna to being with Lisa. The aristocracy was still mighty in Central Europe. To aspire to a union with a countess was the steepest of cliffs to scale.

For now he decided to respect fully these obstacles. Would she ever be moved to take the defiant step toward him? The twenty-first century had given him no preparation for this social structure, and waiting for… whatever…was at least temporarily safe.

And Katrina? He could not abandon his hope of seeing her either.

That night he dined with Mozart at Stefan's inn. The final *Don Giovanni* performance had been the previous evening, and Stefan would leave for Vienna the next day. Mozart would stay almost two weeks more.

"So tell me, friend Mozart, was keeping the countess's arrival a surprise your idea or hers?" asked Stefan.

Mozart's face crinkled with glee. "That you will never know."

They sipped the tart Bohemian wine. "Stefano, I know that I warned you about getting involved with her, but when she wrote me asking for tickets and mentioned you, it seemed that things had crossed a line. It is clear she carries feeling for you; I could tell the way she stood with you in the dressing room. You are more than an amusement for her."

After another sip, he asked, "And you? Do you love her? Express it to me!"

Stefan took a deep breath and said, "I love her like...like a rose loves the sun."

That got a boisterous slap on the shoulder from the composer. "Any less poetic answer would have gotten you a glass of wine on your head and my foot in your arse. Of course you do! The obstacles are still there. You, a poor commoner, her, a title and wealth. You cannot imagine the pressure that will come to bear on her. You'll be ignored. It all will fall on her. But after a certain point has passed, I believe in love more than anything. Besides, I think the aristocratic barriers are weakening around Europe."

"Weakening in Vienna? Truly?"

"Well, Vienna is not Paris, but if you have enough patience..." Mozart shrugged.

Stefan cut him off. "I don't know what the outcome with Lisa will be. How can I? But...my daughter...I long for her every day."

"Of course, you do, but..."

"Wolfgang, I am getting a...a premonition...about going back to my century. It's that a moment will come when I may have a choice...I feel that a door will open. I can't explain it. And somehow it is connected to you. That makes a certain amount of sense because I think it was a connection with you that brought me."

Mozart paused long after this. He speared a small sausage with a fork and chewed it thoughtfully. Then he looked Stefan in the eye.

"But, Stefano, are you sure you will have a choice? You did not choose to come here; you were brought. It may go like that. If I brought you here, then maybe when I am gone, you will be too. I think you should look to this moment, this life, and make as much a success—in music and in love—as you can."

Stefan shuddered, then nodded in agreement. But it was a night of little sleep.

—

Lisa, in her bedroom at the Thun estate after the performance, lay in a sleepless swirl of thought. She was flying high as she congratulated herself on a plan that was well conceived and executed. She had seen the great premiere and thought her surprise appearance to Stefan got the desired response.

But she had her own surprise—she became finally and fully aware of the truth of her heart. No more rationalizing. Stefan was why she was there, far more than seeing the opera. Then came the performance, and there had been a living charge between them as they communed in this blazing music. It was a moment of unguarded sharing and intimacy, and it shook her.

Although she had slept poorly, she started the multiday carriage journey back to Vienna in a gay mood. But as the day wore on, she grew more and more subdued as the exhaustion, physical and emotional, sunk in. By the time they reached the first overnight stop, she was not talking, and dinner with Georg was almost silent.

"I'm sorry I've grown glum. I'll try to do better tomorrow, Georg," she said rising.

He just smiled and said, "I wish you a good rest, My Lady Lisa."

The next morning she was in no better a mood. Through the morning she went from only silence to full glumness. Finally Georg spoke, "You have a troubled thought, My Lady Lisa?"

"No, Georg. Many thoughts. Lashing me like devils with whips. But mostly having to do with wondering why I dragged us both on this exhausting journey."

After a pause, Georg ventured, "Would you care for an opinion?"

"God, please."

"I see two simple reasons why we have made this trip."

She leaned forward.

"Mozart's music. And Stefan. You love them both."

Her face winced, she closed her eyes, and a small trickle of tears started.

"Georg, I *can't* love him!"

"Why?"

"Well, our damned different stations! Stefan is a penniless musician, as my aunt points out."

"Stefan is very strong, I think. As for your aunt…" He shrugged. "Not easy."

"And my heart has shown it can be a fool." Lisa stopped, put a closed hand to her mouth, shut her eyes, then exploded heatedly, "I have been married once, and it was a living hell."

"Is Charles the measure for all men?"

"He is all that I know!"

Georg asked more softly, "Did you ever give him your heart?"

Her tone lowered in response. "I thought I might in time, at the beginning. Then he changed."

"Then your heart was not wrong. He did not change, My Lady. He was bad from the start. He was charming to you and your family. Everyone else, he treated like annoying insects. We, the staff, all knew but said nothing…to our shame."

Lisa's tears had stopped, but her head hung low.

"And you think Stefan is different?"

"I have seen that he treats people with respect, no matter their class. I said this before; I think he is not from…here." His inflection on the word made it clear that he could not imagine where Stefan might be from.

Lisa shook her head slowly. "Yes. Not from here." She took a breath and sat up in preparation for a statement. "I did not know what to expect from this…adventure. I acted like a schoolgirl. But I think I had to come. To find out."

Georg cocked his head in question.

She went on, her voice not always holding up. "To find out if I love him. And I *do* love him. He is so kind, yet there is strength in his gentleness. And the way he hears music touches me so deeply. I think he may be the only person I've ever met who loves music as much as I do."

Georg smiled, took one of her hands, and squeezed. His touch calmed her, as it always had.

"But Georg," she said with sudden tightness, "To be…*with* him. I am so frightened…oh God…" A trickle of tears started once more.

Georg leaned forward and brought his other hand to her upper arm. "It will take time. Patience. Wait for him, then he must wait for you."

Georg released her and leaned back against the cushion. He then removed his jacket and folded it. He handed it to her and said, "Lie down, My Lady Lisa. Put your head on this and get some sleep. You did not look rested this morning."

———

This part of the road was smooth, and there was only the rocking from the coach springs. She slept for five hours. They did not speak of Stefan again and passed the remaining days on the journey mostly reading—Georg, a volume of the *Meditations* of Marcus Aurelius, and Lisa, *Don Quixote*, which she had read before in her teens. Three nights later in her own bed, she tried, after nightly wrestling with her feelings, to reach finality of how to address her conflicting goals: not causing a scandal that could send her aunt into a possibly disastrous spin, and being with this fellow soul in music. For now she decided that restraint with Stefan was best, as hard as that would be. Maybe with time.

Chapter 37—Fifth Lesson

STEFAN WAITED A couple of days after returning to Vienna and then sent a note to Nightingale Street about a meeting on Saturday, November tenth. The acceptance came within a day. He took with him a copy of a four-hands duo in F major that Mozart had finished in August of the previous year.

Georg opened the door, let Stefan in, and closed the door before taking his hand and shaking it with firm grip. "Georg." Stefan said his name with extra warmth, to which Georg bowed and motioned toward the parlor.

Eva was waiting with the usual coffee and enticing pastries. She was still shy with Stefan, not having seen him for many weeks, but beckoned him to the service table. He chose a pastry that looked like a tiny birthday cake, except covered in glaze. The layers inside revealed themselves as nougat, chocolate, and apricot jam, while the glaze was made of a rum punch. Stefan carefully bisected it with a fork, put half in his mouth, and after a couple of seconds, emitted a moan. Eva laughed and covered her mouth.

When he could speak, Stefan asked her,

"Where do you buy pastries like this?"

Very shyly she said, "Did not buy. I make. *Punschkrapfen.*"

Stefan put the plate down and said, "This is the work of a magician. Brava, Eva!"

Eva bubbled at the compliment as she thanked him.

Stefan heard a sound behind him, turned, and was filled with the glow of seeing Lisa, who apparently had observed the little scene that just played. She was smiling like a sunrise.

She held out her hand for him to shake, and he took it in both of his. "My Lady Elisabetta," he said with mock formality, wanting to sing it.

"My good Herr Radowitz," she returned, equally songful. She was dressed in a full flower-print dress with elbow-length sleeves, ready to play.

They sat for coffee first, which gave them each a chance to get over the shock of seeing each other again in Lisa's salon. They had both brought a resolve to be reserved, each for their own reasons. They would have to resist the mutual pull in each other's presence. But where was the line that defined decorum?

They spoke more of *Don Giovanni* and of the possibility of a Vienna production. Were the Viennese ready for such strong medicine? They also spoke of the unsettling news of the war between Russia and the Ottoman Empire, and the rising concern that the emperor might be drawn in. He had signed an alliance with Catherine the Great, and the word at court was that she was pressuring him to honor it.

Stefan reached into his valise and suggested, "Something more pleasant?" He pulled out the score of Mozart's four-hands duo in F.

"Yes, *yes!*"

The second pianoforte had been pulled back to a corner of the room, so they both would have to sit on the same bench rather than splitting the duo between two pianos. Stefan was surprised at the shift in furniture arrangement; he was not prepared for the proximity of sharing a pianoforte bench. They sat, Lisa in front of the upper register to play the *prima* part, and Stefan to her left to play the *seconda*.

Lisa gave him a playful smile, as if to say, *"See, we can be bench mates and stay proper!"*

—

They began the slow and mysterious introduction. They read through the entire work, stopping only at rhythmic miscues or if one of them did not think the tempo of a section was right.

When they got to the end, they spent some time discussing and dissecting the piece, then began more painstaking and detailed work from the beginning. They sought to penetrate the searching and troubled lines in the slow opening, each of which ascended to a single star of a note before descending to start again to a new star. They talked about how best to reveal the burst of sunlight at the *allegro*. Again and again they concluded that Mozart required little help from them—they only needed to allow the music to unfold naturally. It was already perfect.

Time fell away, but the end of the last page of music marked the terminus of their session. They each put their hands in their laps and looked silently ahead. Without looking at Stefan, Lisa said simply, "Well, that was so satisfying." She turned to look at him. "Thank you, Stefan. I could do this for hours."

"As could I." The feelings flowing through him included a new awe of the musician next to him. He turned to her, trying to stay composed, but he knew his eyes were open and revealing. He then stood, to escape drowning.

"Would it be acceptable if I contact you prior to our next meeting?" said Stefan. He wanted to exercise some control over how often they met. "My teaching schedule is backed up from the Prague trip. Some of my voice students have engagements coming and need my help to prepare."

"When do you think that might be?"

"Two weeks?"

In a slightly disappointed tone, Lisa said, "Perhaps you could contact me in a week's time to confirm?"

"With pleasure, My Lady," he said with an inflection that was far beyond formality. Georg had appeared holding Stefan's cloak, and he stepped into the late fall evening.

Stefan walked several paces, took an enormous breath, held it in, then expelled loudly. Never had he felt as much in over his head, but he did seem to have made his way through the lesson without anything…terrible?…amazing?…happening. When Lisa had asked about the next meeting time, his honest reply would have been *tomorrow*, but he steeled himself to carry out his resolve. And he wondered about her temperature toward him.

Stefan did not see Lisa in two weeks; Aunt Catherine had a spell of gout and needed attention. It was over a month before they met again.

He did see Mozart on December eighth, and his news was not good. Christoph Willibald Gluck had passed away on November fifteenth, and the emperor no longer had a Chief Court Composer. Mozart seemed the obvious choice but was only able to land a secondary position that paid far less. He had hoped for more from the emperor and strongly felt he had earned it.

Stefan tried to find a more positive subject and asked, "Did you compose more in Prague?"

"Ah yes," he said as the drink and company buoyed him. "I wrote a fine aria for Duschek in partial payment for staying with her at Bertramka. It's so, so difficult to sing. She and I made up a story that we tell people. She says that she locked me in a room and would not let me out until the promised aria was done, and that I said she would have to sing it at sight perfectly or I would tear it up." He found it a delightful joke and obviously loved telling it. "The thing is, she almost did sing it perfectly. Fine, fine musician." Stefan had known the tale but did not know that it was fabricated between the two conspirators.

"Stefano, how is it with Lady Elisabetta?"

Stefan was chewing some cabbage and chestnuts and finished it slowly. He raised his utensils and let his hands drop to the table in consternation. "With every step in my heart I take toward Lisa, I step away from Katrina. But I can't yet choose not to return if it turns out I can. So I'm trying to be reserved, though it may prove a useless exercise. God, how my heart burns when I see her." He took a bite from a chestnut, then added, "I'm seeing her tomorrow."

"Good! Be careful. Or not," said Mozart, giving that irresistible half smile.

"Useful advice, my friend," Stefan gave a mock frown.

1 7 8 8

Chapter 38 – Private Premiere

AT THEIR NEXT meeting, Lisa and Stefan explored yet another Mozart duo sonata, enjoyed Eva's coffee and pastries, and reveled in the musical comradeship. But there was a certain stiffness in the session, Stefan felt. How long could he keep doing this and not seize her at the keyboard? And what was she feeling? They set the next meeting for shortly after New Year's Day.

Lisa and Stefan saw each other three times in January. They were beginning to have touches of testiness on musical points, such as missing each other at cadences and arriving at different times. Stefan curtly suggested that she was rushing the tempo, and she responded tersely that, no, he was behind. Stefan, as a conductor, was not used to being contradicted and almost pushed back before catching himself.

Stefan related this episode to his good friend. "Looking at the way you are drawn together but are pushing each other away, it's understandable that you get annoyed with each other," said Mozart.

"I'm torn and also feel powerless." Stefan snorted, then said with disgust, "So I behave as if I have a billiard cue up my ass."

Mozart laughed heartily, then said "She has a reason to hold back as well."

"Oh, the voice of her aunt, reminding her how her last marriage worked out," said Stefan. "I think we are both waiting for the other to offer an invitation, like a lowering of a barrier. It never comes, so we reach out by snapping at each other. Then we apologize."

"I think neither of you is any good at courtship," observed Wolfgang.

———

Stefan next saw Mozart at a sad occasion—the German opera company in Vienna had failed, and its home, the Kärntnertor Theater, was closing. The last performance was tonight, Mozart's *The Abduction from the Seraglio*, popular throughout Europe.

"What's the cause of the closing?" Stefan asked.

"Maybe the war with Turkey," sighed Mozart. "The Austrian army has headed for the field and taxes were going up on the aristocracy. Which hurts me. Their patronage is my lifeblood."

"Are you less busy?"

"No, no, very busy. But war is a bad backdrop for art. Oh, I almost forgot, how foolish! Just yesterday I received a letter from Prince Esterházy, Haydn's patron; you know who he is. He wants a four-hands concert at his castle in Eisenstadt. Would you be hands three and four? There will be an orchestra and we can play my E-flat major concerto. He's paying a nice fee, which we can split."

Stefan lit up like a child's sparkler. Suddenly things were far brighter, and the eighteenth century more delightful than ever. "Wolfgang! That would be…a dream come true!"

"I take it you accept?" He said with a sideways smile. "April sixth."

———

Before Stefan had departed Nightingale Street after their last January meeting, Lisa had told him that she would provide the music for their next meeting on February seventh, so he arrived as instructed, empty handed. Stefan entered the parlor for the usual coffee and Eva creation, and Lisa was waiting for him, dressed casually in a slender and simple dress with no panniers or bustle. Stefan always tried to brace himself not to be freshly bowled over at the impact she had on him at the beginning of each meeting. It never worked; she always took his breath from him.

"So, My Lady, what are we playing today?"

Lisa rose, went to the pianoforte, and took a manuscript off the music desk. She turned back to Stefan and gave it to him.

She said hesitantly, "I…have revised this since you last saw it."

Stefan held his breath as he touched her manuscript. He let his breath out when he felt his heart racing. "It would be my honor to listen." He held out the music to her.

"No, that's your copy. I don't need the music."

Lisa sat before the keys; Stefan sat three meters away, his hands in his lap.

The first surprise was that the work announced itself with a single voice, playing a repetitive, moderate-in-speed, rhythmically even motive. It gradually expanded on both sides of the pitch, adding registers, speeding up slightly, but remaining very soft for a surprising time span. Stefan felt that some big event was being forecast but was being held back.

Suddenly a *fortissimo* exploded forth, one that combined the motives. The effect was of heroism and anger, and Lisa started calling sounds from the pianoforte that it strained to make.

The composer who came to Stefan's mind was Beethoven.

A sudden change, like the wind coming from a new quarter, transformed the entire scene. All pivoted on a single note that then slowly blossomed into a solitary line, until an arpeggiated chord rolling up from the bass gave it definition. The music became filled with longing. It wound down finally, sweetly tired from the expenditure of passion. The composer who came to Stefan's mind this time was Berlioz.

Lisa paused at a cadence and said, "I haven't found an end yet. I'm looking for a way to connect it to a fugue I'm writing, but I'm thinking that won't work. Maybe the fugue will just stand alone."

She was done. She put her hands in her lap and looked at Stefan, her face tense and filled with anxiety.

Stefan, as before with Lisa, found words a challenge. He had heard something original and moving. A little wild and undisciplined. But the work of a powerful imagination.

"Say something!" she pleaded.

"Lisa, I am trying to find superlatives. Your music is compelling, in ways that I have never heard."

"You're not just being kind?"

"I have never been less kind. It's the bare truth."

Lisa's eyes moistened.

"You have the gift."

"The gift?"

"The music you hear in your mind is music that will move others. You constantly surprised me, and each surprise drew me into your world farther. Your music sings and has drama also. Fury and love."

By now her elated face was starting to tear. Stefan was feeling his eyes moisten as well. What else to say?

Lisa asked, though. "Can you make any suggestions?"

Stefan was taken aback. "Oh, I have no gift for composition and would be of little help as a teacher." He thought for a moment. "I don't know to whom you would take this work. It breaks boundaries. But you could write something in a more traditional form, like a sonata movement, and show it to an experienced teacher. Salieri comes to mind."

Salieri did indeed have a good reputation as a teacher, and Stefan knew that he would go on to teach the likes of Beethoven and Schubert.

"The only thing I would say of your music is that it could use more clarity of structure, and spending some time working in a traditional way may help you focus your own original voice without stifling it."

Lisa was still, then nodded slowly. "Yes."

The tension that had gnawed at them of late vanished. Stefan was ready to kneel before a gift like hers, and his heart was ready to explode from his chest. He thought to leave before he said something better left unsaid, but the coffee tray had just appeared, and to turn on his heels right now was impossible.

The intensity of what they had shared still had them in its grip, and they had little to say as they sipped the dark, strong brew. Minutes passed by. Finally standing, he said gently, "I will never forget this. Please don't stop. Compose every day. Let me know if the Salieri idea is appealing, and I can inquire of him." He smiled. "They say he is partial to attractive ladies."

She laughed, breaking the solemnity. "Oh, be quiet!" Then she said quietly, "When I start putting notes to paper, sometimes I can't stop."

"Being a composer means to be unable not to compose."

They made their next date for mid-February. Stefan stepped into the evening, and Lisa made for her beloved library.

———

Stefan was in shock as he walked. What had he just heard? She had, as Beethoven would say of Schubert, "a spark of the divine fire." One in a billion. And neither world—eighteenth century nor twenty-first century—had any idea who she was. Could he effect a change, in either time? He had told Mozart that he felt he had come back for a reason. Stefan had always assumed that the reason had to do with Mozart.

But a deeper mission had just revealed itself—the nurturing of this blazing musical mind. He carried more than love now; he carried a responsibility to do all he could not to allow Lisa to be yet another brilliant woman talent who faded into the mists—as Nannerl Mozart had. But how to respond to that weight? And Katrina? Was he being pulled irrevocably from her? How would he live with that?

Chapter 39 — Audition

THEY MET AGAIN in February, and Stefan heard more of her fantasia. Her musical imagination was richly abundant and seemed to Stefan to be growing more so.

The next meeting was set for March eighth. The day before, Stefan received a note from Mozart to come right away.

"Aha, Stefano, I need your advice. It's about our concert in April at Esterházy's. The two-piano concerto concert. I am crushed with work and deadlines. The bedeviling thing is the Vienna revival of *Giovanni* in early May. The tenor doesn't like the original aria, it's too much passagework. The soprano singing Elvira wants an aria, and a comic duet between Leporello and Zerlina has been requested. Anyway, we'll need to find a second pianist to replace me; I just can't manage it. Any suggestions?"

Immediately Stefan said, "Lady Grünewald. She's better than I am, and the Viennese need to see good women performers."

Mozart's eyebrows were up at this. "What an idea! But may I hear her play?"

"I'm to be at her house tomorrow at two. I'll send word to expect a guest."

"Can she read at sight?"

"As well as any I've seen."

"Does she have a second instrument?"

"As a matter of fact, she does."

"Good! We'll play though the concerto."

"Fine. We have already played through most of your four-hands sonatas."

Mozart switched to a softer tone. "How are things with her?"

"We still meet at the keyboard, nothing more than that, but the time together is wonderful." He thought for a moment, then added, "Wolfgang, she composes. Music such as I've never heard."

Wolfgang made a noncommittal sound in his throat, then said, "First things first." He added with his bad boy smile, "Don't tell her it's me."

Stefan rushed home to get a note to Nightingale Street

8 March 1788

Dear Lady Grünewald,

With apologies for the sudden switch, I ask if I may bring a special guest tomorrow. I think you will be thrilled.

May we have the second pianoforte moved in to nestle with the regular one? It would also be good to have the lids removed.

Until tomorrow,

S.R.

———

Lisa was quite beside herself with anxiety and annoyance at Stefan's wicked toying with her. It did not take a genius to know who was coming and what was going to happen. With one day's bloody notice!

But maybe that's how it always was with Mozart. She took a resolute grip on the situation. She had Eva double the amount of pastry, knowing Mozart's reputation for having a sweet tooth. She had fresh flowers in abundance in the parlor. And she was at the door to greet the party. She was not missing a second of Mozart being in her house.

Mozart's dress was immaculate, with what appeared to be a new wig. He was at his ebullient best and poured out his courtly charm shamelessly.

"My *dear* Lady, so lovely to see you again!" he said, then planted the most gallant of kisses on her hand.

"Maestro, you do my house great honor!" she replied with her own velvety delivery.

Greetings done, they sat down to Eva's serving table for coffee and pastry miracles. Mozart happily did his duty as a guest, exclaiming about the rare tastes in these creations and extolling Eva, who blushed scarlet behind her smile. Lisa saw Stefan chuckling, trying to hide his amusement. She noted that when Mozart poured it on, he left quite a wake. The chatter was all of food, restaurants, new dishes, and the new spring wines.

"Maestro, I heard you play many years ago, when you were six, at Schönbrunn. I was four. It is my earliest memory."

Mozart's face lit with delight, and he laughed. "And do you remember my marriage proposal that day? Alas, I was spurned!"

Lisa now laughed. "My father had to tell me what happened later, but I do remember you climbing into the princess's lap."

The amount of food had diminished. Mozart looked at Lisa and said in a much lower pitch, "My dear Lady, shall we play? I see you are ready."

"Dear Maestro, do tell me what we shall play."

Mozart took from his valise two scores, both of which had the two parts for the Concerto for Two Pianos. "I'll play the *prima*, you can play the *seconda*. They are pretty much identical in what they play. Just not when they play."

Lisa, seemingly calm at being asked to sight-read, took the score, and turned through it, page by page. Mozart took his place and put the score in front of him. He said casually, "I wrote this for my sister, Nannerl, and me."

Lisa could tell that both parts were at an equally high level of virtu-osity; he had not written down to anyone's level at all. It seemed to her that Mozart had considered his sister an equal. And now he would play with another woman.

They started. There was no full orchestral score at hand, but no matter. Mozart played it from memory and effortlessly blended the orchestra with the solo part when necessary. All without turning the first page of the score in front of him.

Lisa felt she did not play quite flawlessly, but the slips were few. But Mozart's impulses were so strong that it was easy to know what he was about to do just before he did it, and she was there. The effervescence and youthfulness of the concerto filled the room.

They finished, and as he had done after hearing Nancy Storace sing, he clapped three times as hard as he could. His face said the rest. Lisa blushed, but her smile rang in the room like the clapper of a bell.

The next thing Mozart said was a bit of a surprise. "Do you improvise?" he asked Lisa.

She shrugged and said, "If you give me a theme, I can try."

Mozart smiled impishly, then played the first sixteen bars of Figaro's first aria, in which Figaro invites the count to "dance" as he, Figaro, plays the tune. The melody was simplicity itself, just a minuet, and when Mozart ended, Lisa picked it up without dropping a beat, adding delightful ornamentation above and below the tune. As she neared the cadence, Mozart held up his finger as if to say, *"My turn,"* and played the same sixteen bars with even more fancy elaboration on the tune. Lisa took him up, this time with the melody in the bass line and dazzling swirls in the right hand. Mozart literally squeaked in glee, and as Lisa neared the end, he called out, "Fini ensemble!" (Finish together!)

They played simultaneously, notes spraying upward like fountains, and crashed the final chords together. Wolfgang and Lisa each leapt up, circled around the instruments to meet, and threw themselves into a brief but uninhibited bear hug.

"You are beyond belief!" cried Mozart. "Why do you hide yourself? And who in God's name did you study with?"

Lisa, stunned at Mozart's reaction, finally caught her breath and answered, "His name was Joseph Anton Steffan, from Bohemia. He was at court before he went blind."

"Yes, I know him!" said Mozart. "He was the teacher of two future queens, Maria Carolina of Naples and Marie Antoinette! Did you ever meet them?"

"No, no. I only saw him in his studio. But he was a fine teacher."

"Did you study improvisation with him?"

"He considered it essential."

Mozart bent his head forward, his hand on his chin. Then looked at her. "Your Ladyship, are you occupied on April sixth?" He then related the circumstances of the concert at the Esterházy palace in Eisenstadt.

"Could you play with Stefano? The expectation is two four-hands sonatas, some improvisation, which you have just shown you excel at, and the double concerto. You have been highly recommended," Mozart said with his irresistible wry smile.

A realization dawned on Lisa's face. Looking at both men, she said with acid, "Have I just undergone an audition?"

Mozart clasped her hands and said, "Yes, My Lady, and my apologies. But the audition was over after you played two measures." He paused and said wistfully, "You remind me of my brilliant sister."

Lisa was moved by this and smiled. "Apology accepted." Then asked, "Wait a moment. Is this a public concert, or for a small invited audience?"

Stefan said, "It's public, and we hope for a full audience."

Lisa blanched. "I…I've never played for more than a few people…"

There was a silence. Stefan spoke. "Completely your choice, of course. But I hope you can share your gifts with Vienna, soon, if not now."

She looked at Mozart's kind and hopeful expression. Then she looked at Stefan and reflected that he would be there with her, and how safe she had always felt with him.

"Yes, I'll play."

Stefan reached for her hand and squeezed.

"Marvelous!"

The smell of another round of Eva's pastries preceded her into the room.

"This calls for more of Eva's treasures!" intoned Stefan with a hand flourish.

Chapter 40 — Four Hands

THE PLAN WAS that Lisa would take her carriage to the Esterházy palace at Eisenstadt outside Vienna, picking up Stefan on the way. They rehearsed with each other twice and even had the luxury of an orchestra rehearsal the day before in the Burgtheater—theaters made room in their schedules for a man like Prince Esterházy. Stefan advised Lisa that, as important as this event was, they should not over rehearse. They needed a little something still to achieve during the actual performance, to keep spontaneity.

Mozart had suggested against making a big announcement of the substitution. "Just say I'm indisposed, and that there will be a special guest keyboardist. When the countess walks out, some won't like hearing a woman, but it'll be too late for them to leave. When she starts playing, no one will think of leaving. Don't worry about Prince Esterházy; he will know."

Lisa had picked a deep crimson gown with a square neck, but without lace so the décolletage was more abundant than was usual for her, and an exquisitely embroidered front panel. She did not wear the usual side panniers as she and Stefan both needed to fit on one bench for the sonatas, and she had the gown altered to fit this adjustment. She rarely wore jewelry but had on a simple crimson garnet necklace that matched her gown.

Stefan wore his usual concert affair: a simple pin-striped coat and matching waistcoat with a cravat. He felt like a chewed dog bone next to Lisa.

The carriage arrived at the palace, and they were escorted around to a side door that served as one of the ballroom's entrances. A gentleman, probably Esterházy's majordomo, stepped to the front of the performance area and called for attention. He informed the audience that unfortunately Maestro Mozart was indisposed but that his distinguished associate, Herr Radowitz would still play as originally planned, taking Herr Mozart's parts. His playing assignments would be taken by the Countess Grünewald.

Low talking ensued, including some high-pitched, questioning voices. *"A countess?"*

Stefan took her by the hand, and said, "Let's go, before they can think about it." Striding toward the front of where the music stands awaited the orchestra, he turned behind her and said, "Best smile!"

Her stunning appearance drew some admiring gasps, and her smile, applause. They bowed, Stefan still holding her hand, then sat down to play the sonata in F, with which they were already dear friends.

An audience that is quiet but not quite fully attentive is one kind of sound; an audience rapt in close attention is another. Performers try to stoke this energy and, if achieved, are fed by it. Lisa and Stefan bathed in it, as the opening mysteries, the searching, and then the effulgent energy of the sonata unfolded.

When they finished, the applause was instantaneously full voiced, starting immediately after the last chord.

They then moved to another beloved friend of their times together on Nightingale Street, the later sonata in D major. They reveled in the proud martial clangor of the beginning. Stefan had told Lisa that whenever they'd played it, he always heard trumpets and drums in the first movement, so he had suggested they play the big moments as if in imitation of those instruments. The slow movement started as a courtly dance and soon blossomed into deeper revelations. After they finished the quick, witty dialogue of the finale with brisk final chords, once again the rapt silence exploded into cheers.

Lisa had decided on a short improvisation. Her selection of Zerlina's tender second aria to her betrothed Masetto in *Don Giovanni* as a subject for variation seemed like an odd choice to Stefan; it was not perky and rhythmic but gentle and legato. Usually improvisation involved adding garlands of fast extra notes that hung around the main tune. Lisa turned away from that, however. Each of the variations was an addition of some aspect of tenderness, either an additional song that went with the original one, in the upper range, or a quicker intensification of the melody's contours, turning tenderness into something deeper.

Stefan heard in Lisa's treatment and concept of Mozart's melody something completely original and captivating. The last measures ascended quietly into a final chord of fading sweetness. She held her hands in stillness above the keyboard after releasing the chord, commanding the silence into which the sonority faded. Then she lowered them, and the rapturous applause was there again.

There was a break during which the orchestra was set up and the second pianoforte rolled into position. Stefan could not resist; he took both of Lisa's hands, looked long into her eyes, and said, "That was it. The gift. A new kind of beauty."

Lisa's eyes got wet, then she pulled away. "God, stop, I won't be able to play if you keep that up," she said, dabbing with her handkerchief.

The concerto was the high point, and everything before this had been an upbeat. It was different from the sonatas in two ways. One, there was a full orchestra playing with them. Two, they were seated across from each other, and their eyes met and locked.

The concerto expressed the connection between two young, brilliant minds, genius siblings in a language only they shared. Much of the concerto was a call and response between the two instruments—one keyboard would play a motive, then it would be taken up but changed slightly by the second and build from there. Thus it was much more than a concerto for a double keyboard instrument; it was a dialogue, an exchange of fluid feeling between two individuals, until the two pianofortes did finally join together with the orchestra with a sunlit burst of sonority.

Lisa's and Stefan's inner states while playing were a mirror of the musical phenomena—conversing, suggesting, playing, and finally embracing each other within Mozart's rich orchestral palette. Neither felt that they were exerting any effort, but rather just hitching a ride on their partner's energy. It was as much a joining as was possible between musicians. That it was between two people who yearned for each other brought the thrill of union to a level undreamed of by most.

The joyful finale swept to a close, Lisa's and Stefan's hands were in the air having rebounded from their final chords, and this time there was a split second of electric silence before the thunder poured out of the audience as they leapt to their feet. Acknowledgements all around, conductor, orchestra, then each other, their hands joined. Stefan then suddenly dropped her hand and stood back a couple of steps, as if leaving the stage to her for a solo bow. A new burst of cheers rang out and went on for many minutes.

Chapter 41—Wounds

MEMBERS OF THEIR public wanted to meet them. *Well, they want to meet Lisa*, observed Stefan happily. One of the first was the elegant Prince Nikolaus Esterházy himself, who said, "What a wonderful surprise you have given us, Lady Grünewald! Please do not continue to hide your glorious light." He held and kissed her hand as if he were handling a Ming vase. "I do hope to hear you again, and soon." Lisa blushed brilliantly.

Most of the others offered warm congratulations with the exception of an elderly couple who wanted to let Lisa have a piece of their minds for such an inappropriate display from a young woman of the nobility.

"My goodness, they were truly upset! But of course they would accept women singers," said Lisa tartly as they donned their outerwear.

"When you break through barriers, this always happens. Amazing that they stayed and heard something of which they so strongly disapproved. Maybe they liked it more than they cared to admit."

"And the Prince seemed genuinely pleased!"

"Such an important man," Stefan said in a low voice. "No Esterházy, no Haydn. He has given him a place to create for years on his estate."

They settled into the carriage, seated across from each other, and it began to move. They both were filled with expectancy and uncertainty. Stefan sat across from Lisa, and the silence was choking them both. Lisa finally broke it.

"I'll never forget that as long as I live."

"Nor will I…It doesn't have to be the last time…"

"No, it doesn't."

She stopped, then spoke in a lower, softer tone, "Before I met you, I never played with anyone else. Always alone."

Stefan replied carefully, "I can bring some musicians to your home for chamber music."

She gave him a look that said, *"That's not the point."* Out loud she said, "Then I should have less time with you."

"It would be selfish to keep you to myself…" He paused, then continued quickly and breathlessly. "Although that is exactly what I'd rather do."

Stefan reached across, took her hands, and squeezed.

"We were like one," she said with soft intensity, squeezing back. "I still feel it."

"And I."

Stefan felt his blood rising to a flood surge, overflowing its banks. He could feel her pulse in her hands and knew it was the same for her. He got up and sat beside her. All this time each had been waiting for an invitation from the other. In the end it never came; they simply drew together, like two magnets placed in proximity. Their mouths lightly touched, each half open, hands tightly locked.

"Oh my God," whispered Lisa, still touching his lips with hers.

They wrapped their arms as far around the other as they could and pressed together with abandon.

"I've waited for this…my whole life…," Stefan breathed, amazed.

They kept their grip, with occasional flurries of kisses, wordlessly, until the carriage slowed and stopped at Lisa's threshold. The footman helped her out, and she turned and extended her hand to Stefan. "Please come in, Herr Radowitz," Lisa said formally. Turning to the carriage driver long in her employ, she nodded. He urged the team ahead after the couple had disembarked.

She took Stefan's arm to the front door. Georg, having heard the carriage drive up, gracefully greeted them. He revealed not the slightest knowing glance. He took their outer garments to be hung and disappeared without leaving any wake.

They passed quickly to the stairs, Lisa leading Stefan by the hand. Ascending the stairway hurriedly, they went the ten paces down the hallway to the double doors of the master bedroom. Lisa opened them both, gestured Stefan in, then pushed them closed.

In the next instant, they hurled themselves into a full collision, holding each other tightly again, gently kissing at first, then ravenously, as if they had been starving. They finally slowed down, as the next moment arrived. Neither spoke. Lisa stepped back, undid the pins that attached her gown to the stiff stomach panel. The gown opened with ease, and she stepped out of it. The front panel was in turn pinned to the corset, and she released those pins. She was now in a corset, layers of petticoats, and shift. At this point she would need Stefan to unlace the corset in the back.

Lisa approached him, turned, and said softly, offering her back, "I'll need some help." Then, "Please, slowly. It has been some time."

This final collapse of walls had staggered Stefan, so strongly had he been trying to hold his ground against the forces tearing him from his daughter. But the dam had cracked, and he was helpless in the flood.

But Stefan then realized that he would be bare-chested, the scar from his open-heart surgery fully exposed. It was not something that he had thought about until this moment. Wouldn't Lisa be shocked by some impossible wound that in this century could appear on no living body? He felt he needed to reveal it openly, to give her the option of absorbing it or not. Stefan said a quick and fervent prayer.

He took Lisa gently by the shoulders and turned her to face him. "Lisa, I want our lovemaking to be open, both of us fully revealed." A deep sigh, then he said, "There's a mark on my body that I must show you. You may find it frightening, and your feelings may change after you see it. I am on fire for you, but first you must see this."

Lisa's expression had grown from concern to real worry. But she did not flinch. "Then show me."

Stefan took off his long jacket and waistcoat and draped them over a chair. Then he pulled off his cravat followed by the full shirt, dropping both on the floor. He stepped forward.

He ran his finger down the long scar. It extended down the middle of his chest, the length of his sternum.

Lisa's worried expression progressed to horror. Speechless at first she finally formed a couple of questions.

"You were in a *battle?* How did you survive…a saber wound to the heart?"

Stefan spoke slowly. "Lisa, this was not inflicted in battle. A surgeon did this. My chest was spilt open to repair a fault in my heart, and it saved my life." He demonstrated on his chest with his hands closed, then opening his fingers wide. "Afterward my chest was closed with sutures…metal fasteners, and it has all healed. This was done while I was unconscious, from a medicine that was injected into my bloodstream."

Lisa's expression froze. Then, still silent, she stepped back to the corner of the bed, and sat. Her face finally released a little of the horror, but none of the astonishment.

"In what world is there a physician who can do such things?" Her tone was soft but demanding.

"I will answer that. But…" He gestured to his chest with his hand, and asked with quiet intensity, "Will you still take me to your bed?"

Stefan watched her face, so transparent. He could trace her thought in her eyes and eyebrows. It all transformed as she stood and stepped toward him. She placed her palm on the scar, and the warmth from her hand filled his entire system.

"Right now I will consider this a miracle of God and thank Him for saving you for me." Her eyes warmed him as had her hand. "Yes, Stefan, I will have you. But…slowly."

"Nothing will happen that you don't want. Just tell me."

He then gently turned her around again and touched her upper back, facing for the first time the task of loosening a corset. "What do I do?"

"Start with the tie at the top, then unlace all the way down."

He did so, marveling at the tension that eighteenth-century women put their torsos under daily. It popped apart at the back, and she inhaled in relief. The rest—two petticoats, slippers, and stockings held by ribbons—came away easily under his hands, leaving her in only a light linen shift.

She stood shyly before him, her hands slowly moving across her body as if not quite sure if they should cover anything left exposed in the sheer garment.

Stefan was stunned at this sight of all of her. His felt himself swelling, not just below but everywhere, and he felt like a giant. His need to take her was fierce, but he resolved to be deliberate and to listen to what she wanted.

Approaching her, he left the shift in place and, raising his hands to her face, began by tracing her cheekbones with his fingertips, barely touching her skin. He lingered there for a moment, then sought her jawline and slowly made his way down her throat, then outward to her shoulders via her collarbones. Then down her sides, giving each rib attention.

By now her eyes had closed and her breathing increased. "God, that feels wonderful," she whispered. Even through the shift, Stefan could feel that tiny goosebumps were rising on her skin.

He dropped to one knee, made his way down to her hips, giving a little extra attention to her rear, tracing each crease and cleft lightly with a fingertip. Down to the tops of her feet, then back up to her shins. When he encountered the shift, the tops of his hands caught the hem, and he began to raise the garment. When he got to her dark patch, he planted a slow kiss, inhaling her warm scent, then kissed his way back up her abdomen and sternum. Stefan raised the garment over her head and arms, dropping it to the floor. Kissing and tasting her deeply, his fingertips stroked the sides of her full breasts, then he cupped one, gently squeezing and lightly touching the dark tip with his thumb. He bent to take it gently to his lips. She gave a deep and sudden sigh and thrust as much of her body against his as she could.

Stopping momentarily, Stefan went to the head of the bed and pulled the embroidered coverlet off half the mattress. He then guided her to the open sheet and gently laid her down. He expected her to cover herself, but she lay in her full nakedness, looking at him. Her legs were parting, and he could see that she was already opening to him. He felt that his whole body was trembling.

Stefan slipped out of the rest of his clothes and reclined beside her, kissing her face lightly. He put his hand on her hip, then deliberately laid his cupped hand lower down. He felt her swell with the rapid change in her breathing as he remained there, gently pressing. His body drank the feeling of her pleasure, swelled in response, and his need surged. He got on his knees, kneeling between her legs, and made the gentlest initial contact he could.

But through his desire he could sense her becoming tense. She then looked down, saw him fully for the first time, and alarm took her face. It quickly intensified, then she whispered, looking at him and shaking her head, "No, I can't," Then she said it again louder. Pulling her legs back together, she rolled on one side, then began crying out in short bursts, getting out another "No!" then "STOP!" She was now caught in a wild fit of fear, arms flailing. Then as suddenly, she froze, trembling violently and crumpled into a tight ball, knees pulled tight against her chest. "No-no-no-no," she cried in a child's small voice.

Stefan was shocked into stillness for a few seconds. He backed away, lowering his head, and rapidly thought through what had just happened. She was fine until the moment he had touched her with his penis; that had called up a past trauma that could only have been from one source.

Stefan cursed himself for a fool. She was making sounds like a frightened mouse as she trembled. Would she now allow him to touch her at all? Was she even aware of him? Should he retreat?

No. She had collapsed into this state at his touch, and if she were ever to trust him, it was up to him to get her back. He pulled the coverlet over them, then said, "Lisa, I'm lying down next to you, and you'll feel me against you." He slid down beside her and drew his chest against her back. At this she began sobbing in spasms, which he thought better than a catatonic state.

Damn him to hell. Charles.

"You're safe. No one is going to hurt you," Stefan whispered quietly.

Her sobbing finally stopped. He waited for what seemed to be about thirty minutes, then gently encircled her with one arm and squeezed her lightly. She squeezed back. Good, at least that expression of confidence was there. That was where they would have to start. They finally lay calmly as their bodies relaxed. He could feel her heartbeat slowing down.

It still seemed a long time before there was a sound other than breathing. Finally, Stefan broke the silence. "You don't have to say anything. You've suffered terribly. Probably in this very bed."

"No," she said clearly. "Not this bed. That bed was thrown out and burned."

"The scene of the crime," Stefan said, grimly.

"Crime? I was his *wife!* So I was told!" she said hotly.

Stefan said firmly, "Rape is a crime, marriage or not. At least where I'm from."

Turning and looking at him, Lisa said with some force, "Then you are from somewhere other than Bonn."

She turned back and continued shakily, "I had hoped that being with you would finally drive the demons out."

He wrapped her as completely as he could. "I *will* fight these demons with you," he said firmly. Then more gently, "Can you tell me any more?"

She said bitterly, "Charles enjoyed hurting me, bruising me, even making me bleed. Any time he wished. He said all men wanted that."

Of course, her tears at the end of *Figaro.* She had witnessed a powerful dramatization of that which she had so deserved but never received: a wrongful husband kneeling before his wife, asking humbly for pardon.

Stefan bit his lip, then said with simmering anger, "And just now, I became him to you." His rage built. "Would that he were alive again so I could kill him," he said hotly.

She turned her head, and he saw that this actually brought a little smile from her. "My brave *chevalier.*" Then seriously, "It's true. I forgot that it was you. But it feels right that I told you. I haven't felt safe telling anyone before you."

Stefan said as if taking an oath, "Lisa, should anyone ever try to harm you, I will shield you with my limbs and my life."

They nestled together in silence. The night slipped by, but finally they were relaxed, even tired. "Shall we try to sleep?" he suggested.

She curled onto his chest, drawing her finger on his scar. "Yes, I think I feel safe with a man who can survive a saber cut to the heart."

Chapter 42 — Believing

THEY SLEPT RESTLESSLY but stayed in physical contact the whole night, even if just a foot touching another foot. Stefan was awakened by morning birds outside the window. He listened contentedly, then dozed a little. Lisa woke with a start, looked at Stefan, then went back to where the night had started, on his chest. He responded by wrapping her in both arms, pulling her warmth to him.

The bed clothes had trapped their scents, and these washed over them as they moved. Body moisture, the musk of arousal, the natural smell of skin. Without a word they began to kiss and press against each other in growing hunger.

Stefan pulled back slightly and said, "Lisa, what I was doing last night with my hand…Did that make you afraid?"

"Oh no, not at all! It was lovely…and I wonder how it is you know exactly where to touch me?"

"Well, I haven't been a priest. I'd be happy to continue doing that, if you like. Hands only, I promise."

Lisa kissed him then nodded.

Stefan, as before, found his way to her, and proceeded as he had the previous night. Lisa gazed in his eyes with a look that became more desperate as he increased the tempo. "Stefan, Stefan," her trembling voice rising in pitch. He watched as her chest, then face, flushed scarlet. She seized his arm, her strength powerful. Her body spasmed, and she emitted two short loud cries, the last coinciding with the sudden release of tension, and she collapsed.

He withdrew his hand, and she rolled back on his chest. Silent, except for her breathing slowing down, then she whispered, almost too soft to hear, "I love you, Stefan."

A joy new to Stefan rose from his spine and through his body. He whispered back, barely audible, "I love you, Lisa." Laying his hand in the middle of her chest, he said, "My heart." He then took her hand to his scar. "Your heart."

———

They dozed again sweetly for an hour or so. Stefan was dimly aware of a head poking into the room discreetly to check on the countess's status and disappearing after ascertaining that all was quite well.

Lisa awoke giddy, "I am ravenous!"

"You've been working hard of late; I'm not surprised! How and where do rich Viennese ladies break their fast?"

"Usually at the breakfast table, silly, but not today." She took up a small bell and rang. Inside of thirty seconds, Eva stepped in, smiling, and dropped a quick curtsy. "My Lady?"

"Breakfast on the cart, please, Eva. Eggs, toast, sausage, marmalade, and melon. With coffee."

"Very well, My Lady." Hesitating, she then asked, "For two, yes?" Still smiling, she glanced at Stefan, starting to seem a little giddy herself.

"Yes, Eva," said Lisa sweetly. She looked at Stefan, who was by now completely under the bed clothes, crimson red. Lisa giggled at his embarrassment.

"And Eva…"

"Yes, My Lady?"

"Try and keep your eyes in your head and your tongue in your mouth."

"I do my very best, My Lady," still smiling.

After she left Stefan, emerging from the bed clothes, observed, "You're on familiar terms with your staff."

"We are close, thankfully. They became protective of me during my marriage and have remained so. The first presence of a new man in this room is going to be the cause of considerable excitement."

"I'll try not to disappoint," he said with a low laugh. "I hope I've done well so far."

Lisa's expression suddenly changed, from giddiness to something more like wonderment. She seized both his hands and interlocked their fingers. "I've never felt anything like that just now."

He replied tentatively, "You've never had anything like…this physical experience?"

She gave a little shrug. "Not like what just happened. You brought out something extra in me." A wave of pleasure washed over Stefan, and he felt himself blushing, at which she laughed sweetly. Which made him blush more.

She continued. "And something very close to that happened last night in the concerto. Just now we…merged for an instant. And last night we merged playing Mozart's music, but for much more than an instant. They were very different, of course, but also very similar, like they came from the same place in my heart. No, not just my heart. All of me. The music, the love…the same."

"Like we were one," Stefan said. "Each of us present, but no separation."

"One," she echoed.

"And when you had your orgasm, I felt it in my arm, in my depths."

"Orgasm?"

"A word for what you experienced, your release. Climaxing."

"Oh…is that a word from your place of origin?" she asked, with a little asperity.

Stefan realized that the word *orgasm* might not yet exist in the eighteenth century. He also noted the tiny dig at his now obvious lie about his being a Bonn native and lay his hand on the side of her head, "We'll find our way to full physical union. Slowly, a little bit at a time. Approach the old terror gradually, in a safe setting, until it loses its grip, and your fear fades. We'll replace it with a new feeling. Meanwhile, there is always four-hand music."

Lisa laughed again. "No bleeding to release the bad humors, no leeches. I prefer your solution."

Looking about the room, Stefan suggested, "Let's cover ourselves before breakfast arrives."

Lisa swung her legs to the floor and, to Stefan's delight, hopped naked across the room through the door of a closet. She came out wearing an exquisite gray velvet dressing gown with silver ruffles. She then went through the opposite door and brought out a crimson silk dressing gown for Stefan.

"Charles never wore this, so I won't mind at all looking at you in it." Stefan put it on and was swallowed by it. *You fucking coward, beating someone half your size*, he thought in fury.

Breakfast arrived on a fancy wooden cart with plates with silver covers. Two matching, highly embroidered chairs were set across from each other next to the trolley. There were blazingly colored peacocks on the backs.

The eggs in cups were soft-boiled, the pieces of sourdough toast were perfectly browned, the sausages had just enough spice, the fig marmalade was succulent. There were also scoops of melon and orange slices. Stefan wondered where Vienna got its oranges.

They ate playfully, laughing often, feeding each other mouthfuls. A drip of marmalade on Stefan's chin was a cause for hilarity. Lisa wiped him clean with her finger and took the excess into her own mouth, giggling.

—

Stefan knew that Lisa would bring up the scar's origin again. She had said that she accepted it as a miracle "right now," but she would come back to it, for sure. What could he possibly tell her? He remembered Mozart's refusal to believe him and how it had strained their friendship until Stefan had finally put hard proof before Wolfgang: his knowledge of Mozart's as-yet uncomposed music. He had no such proof to put before Lisa, and he feared the worst—that she would think him a liar, or deranged.

They rose and shared a lingering kiss. Then Lisa said firmly, "Stefan, I'd like for us to dress and have some more coffee in the garden. I want to hear more about your scar. And how it is that you are not dead from it."

———

THEY SAT NEXT to each other in Lisa's lavish garden with its small gazebo. It was a bit warmer than usual for early April, and the sun was abundant. Early blossoms like crocus, coltsfoot, and white butterbur had appeared, encouraged by the warmth, and there was sweetness in the air. The garden was enclosed by mature maples and chestnuts that gave shelter even when they were not yet fully leafed out.

After a sip of coffee, Lisa asked her original question, deliberately. "In what world are there physicians with such medicine? Not Bonn."

"No, not Bonn," he said evenly.

"Then where?"

He took her hand and spoke slowly. "Surgeons will not be able to do what I described," indicating his chest, "for almost two hundred years."

Lisa smiled tolerantly and said, "Perhaps you could clarify."

"I know that it seems insane, wild." He gathered himself with a long pause, then said as simply as he could, "Lisa, I was born in the year nineteen hundred and seventy-six. In 2018 I fell through some kind of…I don't really know, but a hole in time and space to 1785. In my time, right now the year is 2021. I'm…," he said, shaking his head helplessly, "from the future. This world, but as it will be in over two hundred years."

Lisa went blank and did not move.

"I'm not sure how or why I arrived, but I achieved an unexplained connection with Wolfgang across two centuries. I was standing at his gravesite in Vienna. Without knowing it, I called to him over the reaches of time…and he appeared. I touched his image, felt his coat, fainted, and woke up in what was to me the distant past. But it's not distant anymore. It is my present, my *now*. Being with you here is the most wonderful *now* of my life."

Lisa's face became stern. "But…this is *not* possible."

Stefan pressed with more eagerness, almost desperate. "That's what I would have said until it happened to me. Lisa, I can't begin to explain it. But I have no reason on earth to deceive you with such a wild tale. Look at my chest. This is surgery that happens every day in the time I am from. It repairs damaged hearts. It's called open-heart surgery, and it has saved countless lives, mine among them. But that's not all. In 1788, people can die from a simple cut on the hand if it becomes…inflamed…you know, turns red and hot and drains pus. In my time there are medicines that prevent this, easily. And other things that would seem like miracles now. Amputated limbs replaced by mechanical metal ones that function almost as well as the original. Self-propelled…carriages that can get to Prague in under four hours, no horses involved. Ships that can sail the Atlantic in a week with no sails. And people can talk directly to each other from opposite sides of the world with little handheld devices." He grew even more urgent. "Everyone experiences time, but who can say what its true nature is? Is it not possible that under the right circumstances, it could reverse and flow backward for an individual?"

Lisa was speechless, trying to comprehend this avalanche of unbelievability, trying to make the impossible leap, her face pale and tight.

"Stefan…," she said, then a long, terrible pause. "I wonder what you expect me to say."

"It is difficult, I know."

Her voice took on force. "No, Stefan. It is not difficult, it is *impossible*. I have believed everything that has come from your lips and trusted you as a child would. I want to believe you. But this is ungraspable, even from a man who is everything to me." She then started to flush, and her voice grew more strained. "I've given you my heart, my soul, and my body. I've taken the same from you. But to tell me this fantastic tale *now*, after the heart's truth of what we have just shared…*Why?* I also can't believe that you would lie to me. This is madness. I don't think you are mad, though that would be the easier thing to accept." She rose. "But I must think about this all, try to make sense of these conflicts. And I must do that alone." She lowered her head and issued a single, strong sob. Her voice unsteady, she said, "Would that you had tried to spin this tale before we made love." When she finally looked up, her strong jaw was firm and her face set. She said evenly, "Stefan, I think you should go now. I will be in touch with you."

Stefan rose, numb and colorless. He knew further attempts to convince her were a lost cause. He walked through the house to the front door. Georg was not there, and he let himself out.

Chapter 43—New Aria

IN THE FOLLOWING days, Stefan sought relief as Beethoven often had, walking the forest trails around Vienna, even in driving rain, sometimes lost, but not caring. He knew that real solace was far distant, as it had been when Hannah divorced him. But this was worse. The hurt from Hannah was like a deep knife wound. This was like having his limbs torn off. He had never known love like this and thus had never felt such agony at its loss. Had he made a massive mistake in telling her the truth? Could he somehow have built a life with her, dissembling about his origin over the years? It seemed improbable.

He had no investment in any religious dogma, but he still believed that the universe was governed by a deep, orderly intelligence. On occasion he even prayed, but he was never sure what or who was the recipient of the prayer. But it was within that framework that he was sure of the feeling in his bones that his travel back had not been a random event. There was a reason. At first he'd thought it had something to do with Mozart, but on witnessing Lisa's astounding abilities, it seemed obvious what the calling was—to love her and work for her gift.

Now, in the rain, everything that had happened seemed random and pointless.

So should he just give up and look for the opportunity to return to the twenty-first century? Katrina was his beloved child, but Lisa was his soulmate, and despite what it seemed like now, he had traversed time to meet her. He had convinced Mozart with hard evidence. But what could he do to convince someone of time travel without evidence? What would evidence even look like? He searched and grasped, and his hand was empty. But the briars of the woods were merciless as he walked through them.

—

The days creaked by with no word from Lisa. Mozart finally contacted him, and they met at their usual inn for lunch. He was already there when Stefan came in. Stefan was unshaven, with dark circles under his eyes. His trousers were mud-splattered and ripped. His entire posture looked like it was under a pressure that was pushing him into the ground.

"Good God, man, there are residents of the cemetery that look fresher than you," Wolfgang said anxiously.

"Always the tactful touch, Wolfgang."

"What in blazes happened? I've been told the concert was a brilliant success, especially for your beautiful countess."

That remark elicited a sharp jab in Stefan's gut, which Mozart picked up. As he had so many times, he put a hand on Stefan's forearm. "I take it things *after* the concert could have gone better." Silence. "*Tell me*, man."

Stefan started his tale. It was almost killingly painful for him to recount out loud the events, first joyous then quickly turning disastrous, that had led to Lisa's asking him to leave her house. And there was little relief in the sharing. Mozart slowly shook his head and squeezed his friend's arm.

"Stefano, I am sorry. But you can't be that surprised. I didn't believe you at first. Then you demonstrated the impossible by knowing a symphony I had not written down. It's a shame you don't know any music that she's going to write." He pondered a moment, then said, "I do think it was right to try. You might have kept it from me but not from a woman you love."

"That was my thinking. At the time it seemed like sound reasoning."

Wolfgang sipped his wine and looked at the glass pensively. Then an idea came. "I expect time weighs hard on you now, but maybe I can help, and you can help me. Listen, I'm in the middle of the *Giovanni* Vienna premiere, and I can always use someone like you with good fingers and ears. You know how it is, opera, always a constant state of crisis and never enough hands to help. Some in the cast still need notes pounded into their ears from the pianoforte. I can't do it all."

Stefan brightened at this; music making was the one thing he could probably still do with any conviction. "Thank you, Wolfgang. Tomorrow morning? Burgtheater, yes?"

"Eleven o'clock. And God, my friend…clean yourself up. Maybe even a bath?"

Wolfgang said this with his sardonic smile, and Stefan actually laughed a bit.

———

Stefan had become at home with the protocols of late eighteenth-century opera production, and he slipped easily into the frantic and often disorganized work. He now preferred this culture to what seemed to him the rigid approach to opera production that he grew up in. This was new art, exciting and edgy, not dull repetition of a well-known work.

Mozart trusted him to listen to rehearsals, then take singers aside who seemed to need extra coaching. Mozart had composed three new pieces in *Don Giovanni* for Vienna and made cuts from the original Prague production. Stefan, of course, already knew these additional pieces from his own experience. As always the production's evolution seemed haphazard at times, and yet somehow under Mozart, things were starting to jell. Stefan's pride in again being a part of history sometimes cooled the fiery hole in his heart and gut, and sometimes not. He worked, ate, drank to excess, slept fitfully, but kept going.

Stefan was listening to an orchestra rehearsal that featured a cast member, Caterina Cavallieri, one of the best-known singers in Europe. She was singing the role of Donna Elvira, a spurned lover of Don Giovanni's who still loves and pursues him. One of the new arias was for her, a long and brilliant showpiece. It was the week of the opening, and Stefan heard something in her voice that was disturbing—tension and fatigue in her top range. At the end of the rehearsal Stefan and Mozart met to confer, and Cavallieri was asked to join them.

The experienced *prima donna* knew what the topic was without being told and cut to the chase. "Yes, I'm getting tired before the end. It's long and sits high. But it's so beautiful, I don't want any cutting. Can you alter the vocal line, Wolfgang?"

Mozart thought, his forefinger tapping the tip of his nose. "What if it was all a half step lower? In D rather than E-flat? Would that help?"

"Yes, but…you can do that?"

"Well, a bit of a job but, yes. With Stefano's help." He looked at his friend.

"We open in less than three days, Wolfi," the experienced artist said pointedly.

Mozart replied decisively, "Caterina, start practicing it in D, to get used to it."

"You knew this would happen, didn't you?" Wolfgang asked Stefan, who maintained the poker face he reserved for these questions on events about which he may have had foreknowledge. In fact he'd known of the two versions of the aria in different keys but had not known the circumstances.

"Do you have copyists lined up for a last-minute panic?"

"Well, you. There are others who can do the secondary copying once the original copies are done by someone who's trustworthy."

"And besides me?"

Wolfgang sighed. "Not in town right now."

"If you want the end product done by the dress, then I'll need help."

Wolfgang tapped his nose again, then said, "You once told me the Countess Grünewald has a good hand."

Stefan was staggered. "Are you serious? After what's happened between us?"

"It's an emergency. I know she's kindly disposed to me." Then he had an inspiration. "You said she also composes. I'll give her composition lessons in exchange."

Stefan's head was now spinning. "Look, if you want her involved, you should ask her. She may be suspicious of a note from me. But you should also tell her that I'll be there too, so she has time to get used to it. Or wants to say no."

Chapter 44—The Copyists

LISA WAS ALONE, in almost every way she could be. She had held everything of the last terrible exchange with Stefan to herself. The one person she could have shared the burden with was the person who was the source of it. To confide the details of such a thing with anyone else, even Georg, was inconceivable.

She had never trusted anyone like she had Stefan. It was incomprehensible to her that after she had lowered every wall, shared every dark place, opened herself body and soul, he would come back with such a maddening answer to a simple question: Where are you from? Why, why, *why?* That he might have deliberately betrayed her trust for some unknown, perverse reason was the notion that burned her, head to feet, inside and outside. What was the point of opening to love if this was on the other side?

She tried repeatedly to wrap her imagination around the possibility that what Stefan had said about traveling backward in time might be the truth. As was almost everyone in Austria, she was raised Catholic. But she had lost faith in church dogma after her marriage—what kind of just and loving God would bless a marriage such as she had endured? Yet her education had its tendrils deep within her values, and there was no escaping them in her beliefs about how the universe worked. And although the idea of dropping to another time had not been addressed by her tutors, instinctively she was sure it would be regarded as heresy.

It took almost two days after banishing Stefan before she felt anything other than numbness. She ate only mouthfuls at meals. She saw her servants' taut, worried expressions, but could not address them. Of course she knew that it was not unusual for servants to catch enough shreds of conversations that they knew how things in the house stood, but she was certain that hers and Stefan's last exchange had gone unheard by any other ears. Nevertheless, they seemed to be aware that some catastrophe with Herr Radowitz had transpired.

She hoped it was a good sign that she finally gave vent to her grief and started crying. But the quality of the tears was frightening—slow, heaving sobs, like giant windswept waves in a storm, more than once a day, and running on for days.

After several days she ran dry, and she hoped for the numbness to come back. She tried playing to divert herself, but that was a mistake, as it triggered the waves again. The days staggered by, wet or dry, but always empty.

Now a month later, a letter had come from Mozart. Its content was extraordinary, and as she read the request for her services as a copyist on an emergency basis at his home the next day, her heart actually lifted. To see Wolfgang! Then came the line about compensation, an unspecified number of composition lessons, as his schedule permitted. There was the signature with its characteristic flourish—then a *post scriptum*. Herr Radowitz would be in attendance as her fellow copyist. Herr Radowitz felt it was only fair that she knew this in advance.

Her heart squeezed hot. Was this a trap? No, if it was, there would have been no mention of his presence. Stefan was giving her the option of not coming. Then a slight hope shined faintly through—maybe he was going to take it all back and tell her the truth. Unlikely…but she had to grasp the chance.

Mozart was seated at the oval studio table in his Alersgrund flat when Lisa came to the door the next morning. He was putting the last touches on the manuscript of the new score for the aria. He rose to greet her, bowed formally, and said, "Your Ladyship."

She replied formally as well, "Herr Mozart, a pleasure to see you."

Mozart described briefly how the emergency had come about. "I had to stay up most of the night, although there were only minor changes for the new key. If you and Stefano can split the instruments that would be the answer to a prayer. No need to do the horns. Horn players are good at sight transposition."

"I am at your disposal, Herr Mozart. Herr Radowitz, will join us, yes?" Her stomach knotted tightly as she said his name for the first time in weeks.

"Yes," said Mozart, casually inspecting his pocket watch. "He does seem to be running a little behind time."

———

Stefan was jogging down the street, his head splitting from a hangover, an attempt to drown his anxiety the previous evening. Arriving at the address, he knocked, and the door opened right after. He came into the room and his eyes locked with Lisa's for a searing instant. Then Mozart broke the silence. "Welcome, Stefano, and thank you both for your help. Let me blot the last page, and you can start."

Lisa greeted Stefan with a curtsy, which she had never done before. "Herr Radowitz."

Stefan saw, with crumbling heart, how thin she was and knew that he presented a similar picture. He bowed. "My Lady." He tried to keep his voice even but felt that he might soon be in collapse.

They took seats on the same side of the table, leaving enough room between them for the score. There were sets of quills, ink, blotter, and manuscript paper. Mozart set the fresh score between them. He said, "There, ink barely dry. Now please pardon me while I go upstairs to get a little sleep. Constanze and Karl are at her mother's, so you will have quiet." He then turned and left.

They were both motionless, staring straight ahead. Stefan felt like one of two close and uninsulated electric currents, threatening an explosive short circuit. Lisa swallowed, then broke the vise of silence. "Let's start. I understand the parts are needed tonight," she said briskly.

"Shall we do the violins first? They are more involved."

"Agreed. You take the firsts, and I'll take the seconds." And after examining the quills, she chose one, dipped it, and started with careful strokes.

Stefan was in torment. *How can she jump right in, be so damned efficient as if nothing were wrong?* he thought as he labored to even grasp the quill. *Is this already so easy for her?* He felt anger that she might have progressed past the hellish state he was in. With difficulty he dipped his quill and started slowly, gathering a little more ease as he progressed.

Neither said a word, and the air had taken on a pre-thunderstorm feeling. Stefan then heard Lisa's breathing rate—it was rapid and shallow. He noticed his own breathing, and his was matching hers. His heart was pounding like an alarm bell.

All of Stefan's will was focused on the page in front of him as he inscribed stroke after stroke. It took all that he had to prevent him from disintegrating, sitting next to Lisa, her scent tearing at him. The first violin part was his only lifeline, and he tried to put his whole mind into every note and rest.

He was two-thirds of the way through when Lisa stopped writing and asked in a highly annoyed voice, "How did you get so far ahead of me?"

Stefan was shocked to hear her speak, especially in a tone that she had never used with him. But as he suddenly realized what she had asked and why, he put down his quill deliberately. He turned and looked in her eyes for the first time since that tense glance after he had entered. Her look was still querulous. He said softly, "I actually don't need to look at the score. I know this music from memory, having conducted it…numerous times."

Lisa rose angrily and was almost shrill. "Are you attempting some trick?" She abruptly took Stefan's copy from him and looked at his end point. She then found the corresponding place in the score, a number of pages past where it had been open. She sat down slowly. Her expression underwent a gradual transition, from anger to shock to dawning truth as she fully grasped the implication of what he had just said and what she had just seen. She put her hands over her mouth, as she often did when moved, and held them there long, as if paralyzed, then slowly lowered them and said in a tiny voice, "Then…it's *true?*"

Stefan could not make a sound, but they both turned at the squeak of a floorboard to see Mozart leaning on the doorjamb, his arms folded. He answered Lisa gently. "Yes, My Lady. What he told you about his origin is true."

Lisa seemed about to swoon, but she held on. "How do you…" She could not complete the question to Mozart.

"Because he knows music of mine that I have not yet composed. As you can see."

Lisa swayed in her chair, and Stefan took her hand to steady her. She gripped back fiercely.

Mozart said, "Stefano, I remembered what happened when you copied the *Don Giovanni* overture parts in Prague and finished them before I had finished the score. It just occurred to me that you might unwittingly do the same stunt here, and I waited." He wore a slight smile.

"*Stefan!*" she whispered intensely, gripping hard.

"*Lisa,*" he replied in the same tone.

"*Both of you!*" said Mozart in imitation. "I'm delighted for the truth to be out, but this is not why you are here. There is a rehearsal tonight that needs orchestra parts. And I do need a little sleep. Can I trust you two to work alone and accomplish the task?"

They both nodded as sheepishly as school children. Mozart retired. And slowly, as if they were recovering from a blow, the two copyists picked up their quills and resumed work.

After about five minutes, Lisa whispered, "Please come to me tonight."

Stefan whispered back, "After dress rehearsal. It might run very late."

"Dear God, I don't care if it runs until dawn!"

"I'll be there before the birds awake." He was reeling. And he figured he had probably better start looking at the score to make sure he stayed in the right aria.

Chapter 45—Second Breakfast

LISA AND STEFAN finished copying by early afternoon and parted with proper formality (others were in the house now) but with barely suppressed emotions that rattled them. Lisa took her carriage home, and Stefan walked to the theater to troubleshoot last minute details for Wolfgang. The dress rehearsal began at seven o'clock and was indeed long, finishing at midnight. Stefan tried his best to be all business but was barely aware of his surroundings.

Stefan got to the Nightingale Street house as fast as his tired legs would allow. As he approached the door, he thought he could see the dim light of a single candle illuminating the front hall. Sure enough, he did not have to knock—the door opened gently as he approached, and he was beckoned in by the waiting Georg. Silently closing the door, he said, "She is in the garden." He took the candle to light the way.

As in act four in *Figaro*, no light was needed in the garden; the moon was full and the sky clear. Georg opened the French doors; Stefan stepped into the moonlight and saw Lisa hurtling toward him. She left her feet as she threw herself into his arms.

"*Stefan, Stefan, Stefan…,*" she cried, almost in desperation, squeezing him with all her force. She began to sob softly into his shoulder. "Can you forgive me?"

He took her by her shoulders and pushed her away to look into her face. "There is not the slightest thing that needs forgiveness. I was asking something impossible. And I should have told you before we lay together. Things happened so fast."

"Then I think we might never have lain together. I should have taken you at your word."

"Mozart didn't." Stefan explained how it had finally taken his singing melodies to a work that Mozart had not yet committed to paper to convince him.

Her tears stopped and wonder took her face. "Then you know all the music he is going to write for the rest of his life?"

"Not everything, but the major works." She looked at him with new amazement, which prompted him to add, "Lisa, there are countless things that I wish to God I did not know. And almost all that I know I can't speak of. It could cause such unforeseen damage."

Lisa reflected silently on this, then said, "That must be a great burden."

They fell silent, then kissed gently and long.

"Mozart brought us together, again," said Stefan, and Lisa nodded. Then she took his face in her hands. "Please come to my bed."

"With joy."

They ascended the stairs. Lisa was already in her dressing gown, and Stefan took off his heavy woolen layers. Naked, they slid under the sheets and lay facing each other, looked long, eyes into eyes, then entwined completely. They kissed, tasted, stroked lightly, then more deeply until Lisa sang high notes of release. Then they slept, Lisa nestling her back to Stefan's chest, his forearm between her breasts. It was the first peaceful sleep for either of them in many weeks.

———

They broke their fast as they had on their first morning together, in the bedroom. As before, they giggled happily while feeding each other.

Lisa said, "I never imagined that a man would want to give a woman pleasure. I didn't know I could feel this. A sister once talked to me about relations, and it was all about what the man needed."

"Well, maybe we learned something in two hundred years."

Lisa gave a low, earthy laugh. She grew serious again. "We'll need to be careful. What do unmarried women and men who are together do in your time?"

"Sexual matters between people are much more open in my time."

"But if one of the lovers is in the aristocracy?"

"There is no aristocracy. There are massively wealthy families still in Austria, and some of the families are even descendants of nobility. But no titles. No monarchy."

Lisa seemed quite surprised but did not seek an explanation. "Well, we definitely have nobles and royalty now, and they have great power. We must be careful. I think you should come to me after dark and leave before full morning. I'll give you a key to the garden gate. You should still come for my 'lessons' as always, maybe every two weeks? There is no reason to give those up."

"What can the aristocracy do to you if we're discovered?"

"Well, a loud scandal that I care little about, but I don't want to inflict a scandal on Aunt Catherine. I don't have many friends, but she does, and they might abandon her. And who knows what might come your way."

Stefan took a breath. "I can defend myself, but I respect the difficulties for your aunt."

Lisa then flared and said hotly, "When I think of having to be discreet, I deeply resent it. Why should we have to please these geese, as you rightly called them? Those who would call scandal down on us don't have the morals of rabbits. If we should be discovered, I will apologize for nothing. I want to shout of my love for you from the top of St. Stephen's!"

Stefan shook his head in delight and awe. "I have fallen in love with a lion." Then he reached to give her a coffee-and-marmalade-tasting kiss.

Chapter 46 — Dark Passage

VIENNA'S RECEPTION TO the altered version of *Don Giovanni* was enthusiastic. The production went on to receive fifteen performances, several more than the Vienna *Figaro*.

Lisa and Stefan had animated discussions about the opera at her house, illustrating their points to each other by playing at the pianoforte. Stefan of course knew it cold from having conducted it so many times. Lisa had heard it but twice, in different versions, yet her memory of the opera was extensive.

Their assignations were not regular, but they met for their afternoon "lessons" as usual, two or so weeks apart. And with the exception of tender hellos and goodbyes, in these they stuck to music. They continued exploring Bach's keyboard music and added Handel organ concerti to their fare. They thus had enough material for many weeks. From time to time, Lisa would play some of her own solo piano music for Stefan, which always moved him anew. But she did not feel ready to show her music to Mozart yet.

For their nocturnal meetings, Lisa made Stefan an extra key to the wrought iron gate to the garden. A couple of times a week, he would come after dark, unlock the gate, and access the house through the back French doors, where Lisa was awaiting him. They would sometimes take a late supper together or read to each other before retiring to bed, and lovemaking. He would be awakened before sunup and slip out.

Their hunger for each other physically was as unceasing as their love for sharing music. Lisa slowly opened herself more to Stefan. She also became concerned for his pleasure. She was unsure of how to achieve that, so at her gentle prodding, Stefan showed her—and she was an eager student. When his climax was reached and he cried out in near delirium, she was overjoyed, kissing him repeatedly. "I feel your pleasure directly, exactly as you say you feel mine," she finally purred, her head on his chest. "It's as wonderful as playing the pianoforte…but much easier!"

He burst into a belly laugh, which she joined.

—

The Mozarts moved back to the Alsergrund suburb a second time in early June. This time Stefan knew that the move was a money-saving one, as Mozart had confided in him. The bite of the war economy and the shifting tastes of the fickle Viennese was taking a toll. Also Constanze and their infant daughter Theresia were ill with fevers and bad coughs, and a doctor's care for two was expensive.

The friends met at a *heuriger*. "It is dark in my soul, Stefano," spilled Wolfgang. "I never have enough money, even though I've been less of a spender than I was. I'm in debt to a fellow Mason, Puchberg. Sometimes I can pay him back on time, but other times I have to borrow money to pay him." He gathered himself and then revealed more. "There are days when everything seems so empty and cold, like a void; then the next day I can compose almost without a break the whole day. I'm working like a demon for a series of concerts at Phillip Otto's new casino. Three new symphonies and two piano trios. I need to do something to get the attention of the Viennese again. Otto says he will put the expenses up, and I will repay him," Mozart told Stefan as they sipped the light sweet wine. "These are all extraordinary works, like no symphonies ever written. I'm hoping to make a trip to London and perform them there."

Stefan hid his surprise. There were no modern historical records of any performances of these last three titanic symphonies in Mozart's lifetime, numbers Thirty-nine, Forty, and Forty-one. Perhaps this was because the record keeping at a casino was sloppy about such events.

Might he get to hear Mozart perform these peaks of the eighteenth-century symphonic form?

"What can I do to help, Wolfgang?"

"I've found a couple of good copyists, but this is a lot of music. Since you and Lady Grünewald are now on speaking terms again, can you both help with the primary copies? Tell her that I always pay my debts, including my promise of lessons for her."

"We're trying to avoid scandal by spending too much time together, but I suppose this is acceptable behavior, as it's for work."

Wolfgang's bearing brightened. "I suppose there is no scandal in having the two of you sitting side by side at a table writing down music."

"Only if the music is scandalous."

Wolfgang, now revived, waved his hand airily and smiled. "I write only scandalous music these days."

———

They decided that Lisa had the most room for the spread-out work of copying parts, so Mozart entrusted the precious score to Stefan. Lisa and Stefan were both happy for the increased opportunities to spend time together, but the day-time visits were all business.

Stefan took the score of the Thirty-ninth Symphony from Mozart's hands on June twenty-eighth. On June twenty-ninth, Theresia, the Mozarts' fourth child, died of the lung infection that she had shared with her mother. Constanze had recovered but not the child, who had come into the world pale and sickly. Being born in the eighteenth century was a death-defying act.

Baron van Swieten, an important supporter, sent a note to Stefan for Mozart.

30 June 1788

Dear Herr Radowitz,

Wolfgang asks me to write to you. He and Constanze lost their sickly little daughter, Theresia, yesterday. He knows that your impulse will be to drop everything to be with them, and he loves you for that.

But they are well attended by many friends. His wish is for you and la comtesse to continue your work. He says that this is of paramount importance and that these symphonies must succeed for his family's sake.

Yours faithfully,

Van Swieten

Stefan offered the note to Lisa to read. She sighed painfully and handed it back. "I cannot imagine such a catastrophe for anyone. Although it happens all too often."

Stefan's voice fell as he recalled the pain of losing a child when Hannah miscarried. "They have it endured it three times. Four children born, but only one has survived. Karl is about three and seems healthy."

"Such sorrow." Then she shot an inquiring look at him.

He answered her look. "Yes, Mozart did ask me about future children the last time. I told him only that he would have other children. Nothing else."

"Then I should know no more than he, of course."

She rang for Eva for coffee. "The best thing we can do is to help him with this concert. Let's get to work."

They began working at Lisa's dining room table, the score situated between them, and started on the woodwind parts. Once again Stefan worked faster and got to the end of each page quicker, whereupon he politely waited for her. She finally stopped and asked, with a slight edge, "Do you have this symphony memorized as well?"

"Well, most of it."

"Then I think you should take full advantage, as we are pressed for time."

"To the extent my memory holds up, I'll do that."

Lisa probed, "And you know the next two symphonies as well?"

He replied patiently, "I could play much of them at the pianoforte for you."

She slumped in her chair, sighed, and shook her head. "You haven't been born yet. But here you are. It still is a lot to grasp."

"My God, for me as well. I knew so much about Mozart when I met him. He brought me back here. I knew nothing of you. But I believe now that the greater reason I came back was to love you and to help you nurture your gift in whatever way I can."

Lisa's eyes welled at this. She neatly stowed her pen, then took Stefan's pen from him and put it away. She began to kiss him, slowly, then hungrily.

"Will we change history if we break off from Mozart for a few moments and love each other?"

Stefan said, "No, we will fulfill it." Once more completely swept away by her, he stood without another word and followed her upstairs, where they remained for more than a few moments.

The three concerts at the casino were modestly successful but did not give Mozart the lift he sought with the Viennese public. His music was forbiddingly complex to some, even as it was held in awe by those who could hear deeply enough.

Lisa had had an experience that Stefan envied—a first-time hearing of these transformational works that he had heard so many times. She marveled at Mozart's use of instrumental colors, like a great painter, something that Stefan almost took for granted after many years of experience. He was delighted to hear Lisa's fresh ears and brilliant mind marvel at what was there.

"Does he have any limits?" she asked in wonderment. "The G minor devastates the heart like nothing before. The C major affirms it, like nothing before. What else will he do with a symphony?"

Stefan was silent. Lisa looked searchingly at him, then understood. "This is his last symphony, isn't it?"

Stefan said nothing, and Lisa did not ask, afraid of what he knew.

Chapter 47—New Teacher

3 September 1788

WOLFGANG AND LISA had scheduled her first compo-
sition lesson, for which she was working on a new piano sonata movement. It was her first try at this most traditional three-part form, as
most of her compositions to date had been more free-form fantasias.
The sonata form had clear shapes and proportions: a first section with
two distinct motives in different keys, a second section that explored the
conflicts between the two, and a third that resolved these conflicts. Its
underlying idea was simple—set up a conflict and resolve it. Stefan had
suggested before that the discipline of working within stricter boundaries would be a good exercise for her.

Before her lesson with Mozart, Stefan and Lisa were having their
usual coffee in the garden after one of their lessons on a warm, clear fall
day. The September afternoon light in Vienna had started to take on a
burnished hue, and there were touches of color in the foliage. "Stefan,
I've studied a number of Mozart's and Haydn's sonatas. I can fit some
of my musical thoughts into these molds, but I want the proportions to
be bigger and the harmony more…"

"Adventurous?" he suggested. "Maybe shocking?" he added, half
joking.

"Well, not for the sake of being shocking. But my ear takes me to
harmonic moves that I find beautiful and thrilling but that don't appear
in music that I know. Will he just tell me I'm wrong?"

"I'd be surprised if he ever used that word. Remember what he did in the G minor symphony? Can you shock more than that?"

"God, I can't come near that! He is a sorcerer!"

She then said quietly, "Stefan, I have a favor to ask."

"Anything, you know that."

"I should like to be with Wolfgang alone. I want to focus only on what he says. Not on what you might be thinking of what he says."

"Oh, I completely agree. It's your lesson. You don't even have to tell me what he says. Doctor-patient privilege."

"Erm…what is that?"

He paused to gather a definition. "In my time no doctor can be forced, or is even allowed, to disclose to another party what passes between him or her and a patient during treatment. Not even to the police."

"Ahh, I see. That sounds like a good rule." She paused, then asked, "Her? A female doctor?"

"Yes. It is common in my century and has been for some time." Taking a breath, he continued, "A woman performed my heart surgery. And she was Jewish."

Lisa's mouth opened in surprise, then she looked away, shaking her head and shrugging. "Well, why should a woman or a Jew *not* be a physician?"

She looked back at Stefan, who answered the question. "There is no reason at all, except men being chicken-brained idiots." She found that uproariously funny.

—

Lisa was escorted by Mozart into his studio with exaggerated, courtly gestures that made her laugh, and which put her at ease. She caught her breath at Mozart's working space, exactly as Stefan once had done; the neat stacks of manuscripts on the table were almost certainly finished copies of masterpieces yet to be revealed.

She settled at the keyboard, and Mozart sat about ten feet away to her right. His tone became businesslike. "What would you like to play for me, Your Ladyship?"

"I have a sonata first movement I just finished."

"Please."

Lisa drew a deep breath and started. She had composed the sonata more or less along the standard three-part structure that came to be called *sonata form*. She thought it well made, with some interesting harmonic moves. She finished, put her hands in her lap, and awaited the verdict.

The verdict was not immediately forthcoming. Mozart had his head down, a fingertip on his mouth. It was several moments before he spoke.

Finally he looked up and said, "I have never had a student like you. Most of my other students are trying to sound like me or Haydn and seek for me to bestow that sound upon them somehow. I hear my voice in your music, but you seek another path altogether. I'm not sure you know where the path is exactly, but I would like to help you find it. It lies only in you. That in itself is a great gift."

Lisa's blood rushed to her face, then out again. Was Mozart really saying this to her?

He paused, looking for what to say next. Then he suddenly sat up. "What do you like about your movement?"

Lisa, not expecting such a question, pondered for a moment. Then she said, "I like the overall harmonic picture, and I like how the melodies begin and develop."

"And what do you wish were better?"

Lisa took the score and pointed briskly. "Here…here…and here…I can't do what I want to develop the melody more because the proportions of the sonata will be distorted. The structure makes me have to turn a corner before I'm ready."

Mozart replied, "My feelings exactly. You have to find a more expansive structure, but through your materials. Look here," said Mozart, indicating. "This is one place where your finger is caught in the door. Let's try…" Mozart made an insertion to the end of one of her melodies. Lisa gave a little gasp. As she later told Stefan, what he wrote on the spot did not sound like his music; it sounded like hers.

Mozart did this a couple more times. He had dazzling fluency with the notes, and Lisa started to despair. How could she match what he wrote? But then in her mind, little snippets of melody started forming, and she leaned forward, after he had played another problematic place, and put her own insert in.

"Yes, that's it!" cried Mozart. "That's your voice!" He then turned the page and pointed to a passage. "This transition is weak. Fix it," he said crisply. She looked and realized that a harmonic move was indeed weak. She thought for a moment and found a substitution, which she notated then played. "Yes, magnificent!" Mozart almost yelled.

"Now," he commanded. "You can take this home and make a fine piece. But I want you to improvise a new piece for me. A fantasia, so no worries about a structure."

She replied tentatively, "I have some fantasias at home..."

"No," he said sternly. "I want to hear what's in your soul at this moment."

Again Lisa was not expecting this, and it brought her to a momentary stop. After a few moments she began. She had only played seconds when Mozart stopped her. "You're still hearing my music, My Lady. Search and find yours."

Lisa sat perfectly still and tried to listen to what was inside her personal imagination. An interval came into her mind, and the inspiration came to her to sing it rather than play it. She sang the pitches, then more started appearing, and soon she was singing a long melody in her rich mezzo-soprano voice. Her hands, seeming of their own accord, came to the keys and started providing harmonic underpinning. After a while she brought it to a close. Mozart, who had his hands clasped in front of his face, gave three loud claps and a dazzling smile.

"You have a great gift, Lady Grünewald. I would be honored if I could assist you further. Take the thoughts you just expressed and see if you can mold it into the three-part form of a sonata movement. Be free with the dividing lines. They are just a guide, not fences. Contact me when you are done and come see me."

———

The next day when she had finished telling this all to Stefan, she said, "Stefan, he opened a door for me. I think I stepped through. I feel changed, heightened. I…hardly know what to say."

She stopped, exhausted from the excitement of reliving the meeting.

Stefan, his face locked in amazement, finally said, "Lisa, I'm at a loss myself. What you just told me is the most…mind-blowing account of a lesson of any kind that I have ever heard. And I know that it was a thrill for Wolfgang. The music gods have touched you, as they have him. I think he is glad for the company."

"*Mind-blowing?* Do explain this term."

Stefan burst out laughing at this anachronism. He did his best to explain the drug culture from which *mind-expanding* came and its mutation into *mind-blowing*.

Lisa had her eyebrows in disbelief position, raised and scrunched at the same time. "Your century has some odd riddles. Such as how an exploding head can possibly have anything to do with Mozart."

———

Over the next five months, Lisa saw Mozart six more times. Mostly he was enthusiastic and inspiring, but his energy could falter, and he could seem, if not despondent, certainly distracted. Stefan had already confided to her about Mozart's financial difficulties. Lisa paid him generously for his time with her; he always resisted, declaring that teaching someone like her was reward enough, and she, in her firmest manner (which Stefan was beginning to know quite well), always insisted and prevailed.

Stefan followed Lisa's journey with Mozart as closely as was comfortable; he did not want to hover over the work they did together, so he never pressed. Most of the time he did not have to, as she was eager to share. Reviewing aloud what they had covered, the little steps and big breakthroughs alike, helped solidify the work for her, she said.

What she did not reveal was that occasionally she would see a look in Mozart's eye of growing tenderness. And of course she had strong feelings about this man who had brought out so much in her as a composer. But not from the same place as his feelings for her.

When she played completed sections or works for him, Stefan thought that her musical narrative was becoming clearer and the destination points, big and small, easier to feel. He also thought that her rhythmic gestures were gaining more definition. All of these steps were indicative of a more disciplined approach, which allowed her powerful energies to have more impact. Yet it all sounded like her. Her music had Mozartian qualities of balance and clarity but never sounded like anyone except Elisabetta Grünewald.

Stefan found new heights of awe at Lisa's brilliance, and new depths of love for her. Yet, as always, he carried two unspoken undercurrents: his yearning for Katrina and his terrible dread of the approach of Mozart's death—and what it might mean for Lisa and him. For he knew the exact moment, almost to the minute.

1 7 8 9 - 1 7 9 0

Chapter 48 — An Admission

ON A WINTRY evening in January 1789, unpleasant with sleet building up on the streets, Lisa and Stefan were by the kitchen fire, having a late supper. They sipped a rich Tuscan wine with prosciutto and melon from Sicily. The empire's reach for obtaining delicacies was long for those with the means (although there were plenty of times when Stefan would have given a piece of his soul for a cheeseburger and fries, or enchiladas). He had only recently discovered the extent of her family wine cellar. "It was my father's. Charles inherited a big wine cellar but actually preferred beer and ale."

They spoke of their friend.

"He ended your lessons rather suddenly," said Stefan.

"Well, he didn't say *end*, he only said *pause*, and the reason seemed sound enough. He wants me to compose with less guidance. He did say he would be happy to meet again in the future when I have more to show him, although I was in the middle of a project he had set me. But yes, it was odd." After a moment she added, "I hope he didn't end them because he is falling in love with me."

Stefan's mouth fell open, then closed. "Did he give you a reason to think he might?"

"No, just a feeling…sometimes the way he looks into my eyes." Smiling she added, "Rather like you."

"I am the last man in the world to judge another's heart, but that would be an unfortunate complication." His painful memory of Hannah's pairing with his good friend came back. Was he to find himself in a love triangle with a genius? Hesitantly he asked, "Are you at all…drawn to him?"

She thought for a moment, and the pause made Stefan's heart skip a beat. "To the being of divine brilliance in him who creates such beauty, yes. To the man personally, no. Although it's sometimes hard to tell them apart."

Stefan was silent and quite relieved when she took his hand and said, "My heart has only one room, and it's taken."

Recovering from this minor shock, Stefan said, "I think you are one of his few bright lights now. He's withdrawn and sullen. His composition output is low. He complains about Constanze. Sometimes it seems he's looking at me when I speak, but I can tell he's somewhere else. I'm told that he'll see an acquaintance on the street, and instead of a normal greeting, he'll put his finger to his lips and say, '*shhhh*,' then keep going. As if he did not want to be disturbed. Just…eccentric. He'll see me anytime I ask, and it seems that I put him in a better mood, after a few glasses of wine. But he doesn't reach out to me anymore. The only music he regularly composes are the silly German dances and minuets for his fee for being a court composer. Minuets and contradances! Why don't they ask him for a grand mass?"

Lisa asked, "Could it be that his musical imagination is taking a rest, gathering force for a new outburst?"

"Let's hope," said Stefan, although he knew already that a renewal for Mozart would come. "He just moved again, to the Judenplatz. Why is it called that?" Stefan asked. "The Jewish quarter is in Leopoldstadt."

"Not always," said Lisa. "Until 1421 the Jews were in the Judenplatz, prosperous and well. Then a ruler of Vienna named Duke Albrecht decided to drive them out. Many were killed. Some burned alive."

"The Jews in the next century will call that a pogrom," said Stefan, shaking his head sadly.

"I thought in your time Jews were liberated to do things like become physicians!"

"Yes, but before then the pogroms were in Russia." He stopped there, unable to tell her about the Holocaust. "There are in my time flareups of anti-Jewish sentiment, but there are no more pogroms," he said with finality. To know ahead of time that one's species was destined to commit such a crime would be unbearable.

Lisa fell silent, relieved. Stefan decided to bring up a topic which had been pulling at his thoughts.

"Lisa, have you ever been to London?"

"Yes, I spent a year there when I was fourteen. That's where I learned English. And Shakespeare. I have wonderful memories of London! Why? Do you want to go there? Have you ever been?"

"In my time, I lived there. I know that London quite well. The London of 1789 I know not at all, as most of it has been replaced. And, yes, I wish to visit."

"So is your interest historical, to see the current city?"

"Well, in a sense historical. But about the future as well."

"I'm intrigued," she said, leaning on her hand and sitting forward.

Stefan then told Lisa more details of the letter that Stephen Storace had placed with the director of the British Museum, to be delivered to his daughter, Katrina, in the twenty-first century. "It just tells her where and when I am, that I'm alive and well, and working closely with Mozart."

Stefan had spoken rarely of his twenty-first-century family, and Lisa had been wary of pressing him about his origin. But she could not hide her amazement on hearing this. "A letter to your daughter, in two hundred years…Can you tell me what you told her?"

He paused, then said, "I tell her I will find a way get back to her." Looking up at her, he said, "This was before you. I need to tell her of you, and say that if I have a choice, I will live my life here. So another letter for her that I will write with a broken heart."

Lisa was visibly moved. "You would…give her up…for me?" Then she said *sotto voce*, "And you think you will have a choice…?"

Stefan answered heavily. "Since the moment I awakened on the ground in 1785 and met Wolfgang, I've felt a strange kind of bond with him. I can't explain or describe it. There's part of my mind that's always aware of him, even when we're parted. He says he feels it too. He actually brought it up first."

He continued slowly. "After the *Giovanni* premiere in Prague, that feeling took on another aspect, which I also can barely begin to describe. It's a premonition that a moment will come when I may go through a door, a passage back. Or maybe not. It's not clear to me. My intuition—and Wolfgang agrees with this—is that something will happen when he dies. Maybe whatever strange science this is will simply open up the rest of my life as my heart desires. The bond I feel with you is stronger than anything else in my whole life, and that must count for something. If I can, I will stand my ground and watch the door close."

Lisa seized both his hands. "Dear God, let it be so!" But she was too courageous not to speak aloud the other terrible possibility that they both were thinking.

Almost in a whisper, she said, "Might you not have a choice?"

Equally hushed, he answered, "That's what Wolfgang thinks will happen. He said I was not given a choice in coming here, so…"

They found themselves in an anxious embrace. Stefan pulled away and said firmly, "Nothing is going to happen tomorrow, or next month, or next year. If the worst happens, I'll find a way back here. Meanwhile, let's live our lives as fully and as lovingly as we can."

They stayed long holding each other, not moving.

———

It was late March, and Stefan sought Mozart out at home. He found him at work on his arrangement of Handel's *Messiah* that Baron van Swieten had commissioned. Stefan had never liked the arrangement and asked about the changes.

Mozart shrugged. "Swietan wants it to sound more modern, with more woodwinds and brass instead of just oboes and one trumpet. Times change and tastes with them. He is paying me well, so *voilá*. But even if he were not, I owe him much for the support he has given me in Vienna since I arrived."

They repaired to a nearby tavern and ordered wine and a light supper.

Mozart changed the subject. "And how is my brilliant and beautiful student? Is she composing like a flame?"

"Everyday! The music spills out of her at different rates. One day it seems that she fills pages. The next, she will work all day obsessing over a single line."

"Ah, she understands that composing is a craft as well as an art." He changed to a more matter of fact tone, "You know that pausing our meetings was at my suggestion, do you not? It seemed that we had reached a stopping point, and that she needs to be under her own guidance for a period. Besides, I am making a trip to Germany in April and will be gone at least a month, maybe two, with Prince Lichnowsky accompanying me and paying all expenses! When I get back, we can work together again." All of this information flowed out rather like a rehearsed speech, Stefan thought.

"What's in Germany?"

Mozart gave a little shrug. "Hopefully opportunity, which doesn't seem to be in Vienna. Maybe another opera commission from Prague, maybe an audience with the King of Prussia. I understand him to be an excellent cellist, so maybe I can write some string quartets for him. Maybe concerts in Leipzig." Then in a confidential tone, he said, "Stefano, I am in a desert right now. I feel dry, stale. I need to put more wine in the sauce and stir it. New scenery, away from Vienna. New…" He left the sentence unfinished but gave Stefan a look that said, *"You know what I mean."*

"New nighttime companions?" Stefan had heard the tales of his friend's appetite but had witnessed nothing beyond the unconsummated yearning for Nancy.

Mozart looked down. "I am not a pure man, Stefano. But it's so hard to maintain loving feelings toward a woman who…presses me so. Money, money, all the time. All my dalliances have been with women I knew but little, like chorus singers. I am not unfaithful in my heart…well, almost not. But a man…has a need."

His hero had just confirmed rumors that had been sounding through history. No, he was no saint. Stefan did not judge; he had been raised in a time when sexual morality was an ambiguous topic. But the subject raised another matter to mind that had gnawed at him. He hesitated, then, possibly against his better judgement, decided to ask.

"Wolfgang…are you drawn to Lisa?"

Mozart raised his eyebrows to their maximum elevation and gave Stefan a long and direct look.

He said, almost contemptuously, "Of course I am, you idiot! What sane man could spend as much time alone with her as I have and not fall in love with her? She is Apollo and Aphrodite in one."

It was not the answer Stefan was looking for and his regret at asking was hard and deep.

Mozart then smiled and placed his hand on the taller man's shoulder. "I am in love with her gift, Stefano. I hope there is a little room in her heart for me. But I am not a rival." Then he stepped back and said lightly, "Germany awaits, I have music to write. Au revoir, mon ami." He turned and strode to the door, leaving a speechless Stefan.

Stefan and Lisa did not see him for two months.

—

Spring arrived late that year, as the winds and moisture out of the north were persistent. Stefan arrived at Nightingale Street after lunch for their "lesson." They were still exploring the Handel organ concertos.

She was waiting for him in the parlor, her face in high anticipation.

"I have a present for you," she announced.

She presented him with a folder, which he opened. The score, in impeccable manuscript, was of a piano four-hands work. Across the top was the title:

Fantasia for S.R.
For Pianoforte Four Hands

Stefan, amazed, held it with the delicacy he would have used for a new-born child.

She took it back from him and laid it on the music desk of the pianoforte. "Silly, it won't break."

"No one has ever dedicated anything to me before."

"It's a first for both of us. Shall we see how I've done?"

"Oh my God, of course!" he said sitting down beside her. "Do I get to look through it first?" He had started trembling slightly.

"I don't think it will challenge you that much."

The fantasia started in the upper register, in Lisa's part. It was a rather long unaccompanied melody, mostly in traditional harmony, but one that kept coming back to a moment which seemed out of place. The third time that happened, Stefan brought in the chords below, which suddenly turned the odd moment into a revelation. Both sets of hands joined now in a seamless flow that used traditional harmonies but with startling side twists that brought Schubert to Stefan's mind, as before.

The melodic flow was searching forward with graceful upward reaches that reminded him of Mozart but kept extending in a way that Stefan thought looked forward again to Berlioz. She was not a composer but a seer. Her compositional voice sought to create longing beauty at every moment. It was a distant look at the coming Romantic wave.

After a few minutes, Stefan thought that he needed to halt and collect himself. They turned the page, and to his great surprise, the music stopped.

Stefan spoke unsteadily. "Lisa, I have no words. But will you finish the work?"

"Stefan, this is about my love for you. It doesn't end because I cannot conceive of my love ending, no matter what may happen. I'll keep composing it, but I'll never reach the end."

Stefan's eyes quickly welled, and Lisa responded in kind. "Look, you've made me cry *again!*" she said, laughing through her weeping. He seized her almost roughly, and they kissed hard. Suddenly Lisa jumped up, took Stefan by the hand, and said, "Upstairs. Now."

They had had plenty of practice disrobing the multilayered eighteenth-century dress, but if there had been a record time, they would have shattered it. Nothing was neatly folded over chairs; the floor was the resting place for every item.

Lisa grasped Stefan in both familiar ways and also new, leaving him gasping.

"I want you in me, Stefan. All of you."

She lay on her back and enveloped him completely with her limbs. When the moment came, she took him until he had no more to give, with no resistance. They both gave moans of astonishment, and their eyes locked and merged.

"Stefan, how I love you…"

"Oh God…my Lisa…"

And for the first time, the house rang with simultaneous cries.

Afterward all was still. They were side by side, breathing and heartbeats slowing. Lisa turned, then Stefan, and they each gazed at the other in amazement.

Finally he whispered, "How do you feel?"

"Complete, full," she whispered back. "And you?"

"Happy as I never dreamed. It's like music."

"It *is* music."

Chapter 49 — Road Trip

IN THE DAYS following, Stefan was in a cloud, as pure as those that decorated the ceiling paintings of the many grand baroque castles in the time. He felt like one of the little cherubs, the pink *putti*, that floated serenely in the heavens on tiny wings.

But because of the new freedom in their intimacy, Stefan's frustration at the limitations on their contact grew weekly. He did not press the matter with Lisa. He still believed, despite her protests that she did not care what her peers thought, that she had the most to lose in in any scandal.

On an April night in bed, he suggested the possibility of some extended time together at a location away from prying eyes.

"I know exactly where we should go!"

She sat up in bed and leaned forward. "I have a cousin, Charlotte, on my mother's side, with whom I used to play when we were little. We loved playing dress-up and talking about meeting our princes. The last time I saw her was at my wedding," said with a roll of her eyes.

"She and her husband live on her family estate, in a modest but beautiful castle, outside Wiener Neustadt. We would have no need to look over our shoulders; the estate is large, mostly pasture and woodland. There are so many beautiful places on the estate, and I would be so happy to see Charlotte and Gregory! Oh, and they have a big stable, with beautiful horses!"

Looks like I'll have to learn to ride, thought Stefan, swallowing hard.

Lisa's cousin lived, as she said, in a "modest" castle. "That's like saying a small elephant," cracked Stefan, eliciting a laugh and faux slap on the cheek from Lisa. They set off in mid-May, taking different carriages and meeting at the stop in Wiener Neustadt. From there they took a hired carriage to the castle and estate, which lay on a sweeping hillside, northwest of the village, with soaring views of the eastern Austrian Alps. The castle was seemingly carved out of the hillside.

Over the next two weeks, Lisa and Stefan reveled in their ability to be together without the slightest regard for the time of day or if they might be seen. To be with each other day and night was a gift.

Charlotte had been one of Lisa's closest friends since they were six and had watched in amazement her blazing growth as a pianist. Now she had a pianoforte in her parlor, and Lisa would practice and improvise some afternoons for a couple of hours. Charlotte, a decent amateur singer, would join her. Other days they would go riding. An old and precious friendship was reawakened after her darkness.

During some of these afternoons, Stefan would be with Gregory, learning the basics of horseback riding on a gentle mare. Gregory also introduced Stefan to fly fishing (something he had always wanted to do in his own time) in a nearby stream, and with beginner's luck, Stefan managed to catch part of that night's dinner. He also learned to ride well enough to keep up with Lisa—if she was being kind. Lisa was a superb horsewoman; Stefan had become used to Lisa being so much more accomplished in so many things than he was. The days were thus sweetly filled, and each evening they enjoyed a leisurely dinner of fish, pheasant, or veal with superb Moselle wines, followed by bed and love to the sound of a crackling fire, which held off the chilly air from the nearby mountains.

———

On the next to last day, Lisa and Stefan mounted horses to ride to a small forest pool that she remembered from childhood visits. It was too far to walk but an easy ride. They left after an early breakfast, packing a picnic lunch of fresh bread, cheese, smoked boar, apples, and the same delicious

Moselle. They were side by side in an easy trot, Stefan still on the sweet animal that had shown such patience.

The pool was hidden deep in a grove of ash trees that were about halfway to being fully leafed out. They walked up the narrow trail that accessed it. Once there, it seemed they had entered a green cathedral, and the door closed behind them. Dappled springtime sunlight lay on everything, and the sound of the small waterfall at the far end of the surprisingly big pool was pure music, as was the song from a pair of nightingales in the nearby trees. "*Nachtigall*; it's prettier in English, night-ingale," said Stefan.

"I've always wondered who gave my street the name," Lisa answered.

"A prediction that you would someday live there…you also have a beautiful song in you."

They spread a cloth and went with gusto at the lunch. After, Lisa gazed at him while he was still looking around at the setting, trying to take in its perfection. "Magic," he said dreamily.

Lisa drew a breath in a way that Stefan knew indicated she had something on her mind. "Stefan, I understand your reluctance to speak of the future you know. The information you carry in your mind could be dangerous."

"Well, yes, it could." He looked up and said, "But…?"

"You've spoken a little of Katrina, and the letter in London. Other than that, I know almost nothing of your family."

He had often considered telling her more fully of Hannah and Katrina and had started to several times, but it was never the right moment. He was reluctant to let her know about the one person that still made him want to return to the twenty-first century.

The moment was now. He nodded, drew his own long breath, and started. "My ex-wife's name is Hannah, and our daughter's name, as you know, is Katrina. Twenty-one years old." In speaking of Hannah, he was surprised that it still was not easy to talk of his failed marriage. He kept to the basics: how they met, careers, birth of Katrina, miscarriage, growing apart—she gasped in shock when he told her of Hannah's affair with a good friend—and finally divorce.

"Divorce?" Lisa said with real surprise. "How?"

"The Catholic Church notwithstanding, in my time it's much easier."

She paused to process this. Then she said tenderly, "Could you tell me more of Katrina?"

Her question made him misty for a few moments. He then spoke long of his daughter's growing up and did not neglect giving Hannah credit for taking the brunt of the duties while he was concertizing. A highlight of the story was the discovery by a school choral conductor that she had a beautiful voice, and then listening to her sing as soloist. He told of the thrill of hearing his daughter sing the same concert aria that Mozart had written for Storace, then hearing Mozart and Storace perform it.

"How well I remember," she said.

He related to Lisa how Kat helped with his convalescence from heart surgery. When he spoke of her education, Lisa was dumbfounded. "*University?* A woman?"

"Many women," Stefan nodded. "You would be so at home there, although few could keep up with you." Lisa shook her head in wonder.

"Is she more like you or her mother?"

Stefan thought for a moment and replied, "I like to think she has the best parts from both of us and none of the worst. Of course I'm blinded by love."

Lisa paused again, then said softly, "Forgive me, I have to ask. Do you think you will see her again?"

"My life is here, if it's allowed."

Lisa again was moved by the choice Stefan faced and the sacrifice he was ready to make for her. She lay her hand on one side of his slightly off-center face.

Her face glowed, then took a darker look. "You said before that you might not have a choice."

Stefan shook his head slowly. "Something will happen when Wolfgang dies. I know in my bones that I am here at least partly because of him. More, I hope, because of you."

She said, hushed, "And you know when that will be."

"I would give anything not to know." He suddenly railed angrily. "Maybe it would have been better for me to be a twenty-first-century doctor rather than a musician. Perhaps I could save him!" He looked at Lisa, who seemed shocked by the outburst. He softened. "But then I would not have met you and would have been lost myself." She reached for his hand and squeezed it painfully.

Stefan was not prepared for Lisa to reach so directly into his aching heart; he had always thought it was more his duty to attend to her emotional needs. He was so wrapped up in easing her trauma that he gave scant attention to his own need to be heard. That he could never be in the same universe with both of the loves of his life was cruel. Yet to feel her gentle touch on his wound was healing, and he felt less alone. His love for her felt close to unbearable.

—

They fell silent for many minutes, bathed in the perfect day. Stefan finally gave cautious voice to the matter that had been growing in his mind for the last week here in paradise.

"Back to Vienna Friday," he said, trying to sound offhand.

"Yes." Lisa looked down.

"I would stay here forever," he said with more feeling.

She looked up, smiling tenderly, took his hand and nodded.

He wanted to say that he did not want to spend another minute of his life parted from her. But he couldn't at that moment bring that kind of pressure to bear.

Thus the silence deepened, but Stefan broke it with a new inspiration. "My Lady, you play the pianoforte, you compose, you speak numerous languages, you ride, all brilliantly. Is there anything you *don't* do brilliantly?"

"Like what, please?"

"Swim."

She put her hands at her waist defiantly and said, "Like a trout!"

"Then let's race to the waterfall!"

She leapt to her feet and began removing her riding clothes. He did the same, but it was less complicated for him, and he was naked before she. "Not fair! You have fewer clothes! Wait for me!" She finished the task, and they both shrieked as they charged into the water. She was indeed a strong swimmer and reached the falls two hands before he did.

They were both laughing and breathless. When they finally caught their breath, they silently entwined and kissed. Next to the falling water, there was a rocky shelf that they took advantage of, and soon their cries joined that of the nightingales.

———

Stefan's heart hurt as Lisa's morning carriage to Vienna pulled away from him at the Wiener Neustadt stop. He had five hours to wait for the afternoon coach, then the two-hour ride. He had a lot of time to reflect. Reclining under a flowering pear tree, he took stock. The past two weeks were the most joyous he had known, and Lisa was life to him. He had no more doubts that here and now was where he belonged—with her, day and night, partners in love, in music, and alongside his dedication to bringing her genius to the world. Even without Katrina. He had known it for some time, but only now, after this two-week cocoon of quiet ecstasy with Lisa, could he finally give in to it. He would pound on the door and give it the strongest push he could. If needed, he would break it, and the consequences be damned.

He no longer had a choice.

Chapter 50 — Healing

STEFAN AND LISA arrived back in Vienna two days before Mozart's arrival from Germany on June fourth. He had written a note to Stefan, asking him to meet on the fifth. They greeted each other warmly, but Mozart seemed exhausted, uncharacteristically unkempt, and sagging physically.

"You look…" Stefan decided tact was not called for. "…like shit."

Mozart actually smiled, perhaps remembering another occasion when their states were reversed. "As long as I don't smell like it…"

Stefan said, "Your cologne is as lovely as ever." He leaned forward. "What happened?"

"I am glad to see you Stefano," he said, then paused as if considering where to start. "I've been telling everyone that I was highly successful, gave several concerts, have commissions for quartets. But…you are the one person I cannot lie to. It's like lying to myself."

Stefan made a gesture with his open hands, *well?*

"Well, there were indeed concerts…hastily arranged, poorly attended. There are indeed quartets being composed, but without the promise of money. And…" He looked up. "I had two amorous encounters, neither of which gave me any real pleasure. Just flesh and sweat. I was eager to return to Constanze, but she is barely speaking to me. Not that I blame her; I went a month without writing. And I am more in debt now. Prince

Lichnowsky was paying for everything, but he abandoned me and stopped paying. Made me borrow money from him to complete the trip alone!"

"Wolfgang...did you protect yourself from disease?"

Wolfgang gave him a withering look. "What kind of fool do you think I am? I read Casanova's memoirs and his discussion of how to use sheaths long ago. I wish neither to die from syphilis nor to leave little Mozarts scattered here and there."

Stefan thought about responding but could think of nothing that would not come out judgmentally. Nevertheless, he was shocked at the casual tone Mozart took. The waiter appeared with a pot of beef stew with potatoes, carrots, and peas and a side plate of spring asparagus. Large bowls were set and filled, and the roast meat fragrance engulfed the room. Stefan lifted his spoon.

They ate in silence for several minutes. Then Mozart asked, "Tell me of my beloved Lisa."

"Well, we recently spent two weeks together in the country, every minute, every day. I haven't seen her in three days, and I am going mad."

Wolfgang's aspect became brighter. "The loving is good?"

"Wolfgang, when we make love, it's like making another kind of music. We play four hands, then go upstairs, and there is something so strongly in common between the two."

Mozart gave him a level look. "Where do you think music comes from? We feel it in our loins first. Tension. *Release.* We don't hear music, it seduces us. You're just now realizing that?" The patronizing lecture stung slightly, but the wicked smile made it lighter. "So, Stefano, what next for you two?

"We're going to marry."

Wolfgang's eyes bulged. He put his hand over his mouth and was stock still. Then he reached for Stefan to grip his shoulders with his small but steely fingers. "I am this moment a happy man. Was she joyful?"

"She actually doesn't know yet. I'm asking her tonight."

Wolfgang enjoyed his first good laugh in weeks. "What brought on this new resolution?"

"I want the freedom for us to be together always. Like we were just recently."

Wolfgang's face grew serious again. "Stefano, do you know of the possible consequences for her if you marry?"

Stefan's stomach became icy. "You mean a marriage between noble and commoner would not be legal?"

"Well, not illegal, but by a very old set of laws called the Landrecht, she could lose her title. Women's titles are derived only from that of their husbands' titles."

Stefan was shaken at this news. "So she would have to give up her title to marry me."

"That's what the Landrecht says, I'm told."

"Who enforces it?"

"Some sort of tribunal. If they notice. It isn't as rigorous as it once was."

Stefan sank into a glum silence. After several moments passed, he slapped his hand on the table. "I'm still going to ask her. Together we will find a way. Maybe a well-placed bribe."

"That has been known to work wonders in today's Vienna." Wolfgang smiled wistfully, then his brow furrowed with an idea. "Tell me when you know the date, and I will provide something appropriate."

—

Stefan was annoyed at his pounding heart and electrified nerves while walking down Lisa's dark carriage way. *Christ, stop acting like you're returning home after war.* But there was no suppressing his mad joy.

He unlocked the gate and circled around to the French doors off the garden. Lisa was standing outside, waiting for him in the cool night. She uttered an incoherent happy squeak, then threw herself at him, squeaking once more.

They squeezed each other to the point of pain, then suddenly released. Neither spoke, but Stefan led her by the hand to the two cushioned wrought-iron chairs on which they had sat for many hours in the sunlight. The current moon was near full, and the garden was illuminated.

He still had her hand. "Lisa, there's something I have to say."

Lisa's green eyes were ablaze in the moonlight.

Coherent language fled his mind. He pressed his lips together and doubled his effort. It came tumbling out, in spurts. "After those two weeks…the pool…I know what I…what I…I've always wanted…"

Her face seemed like a second light source, and she waited patiently.

Finally gathering his thoughts, he said, "For a very long time after I found myself in St. Marx cemetery, it seemed that random chaos had been thrown at me. I've been ripped across more than two centuries in time, torn from my daughter, and landed on the doorstep of the composer whose music has been my life—all of it mad or impossible. Just to stay sane has been like lifting a mountain. Then I met you, and the chaos started to make sense. You're why all this happened, and I'll lift as many more mountains as it takes to be with you the rest of my days.

"Lisa, I know you may face consequences, and I will understand if the obstacles are too great. But I must still ask…Will you take me in marriage?"

Lisa let out another sound, this time from deep within. "Yes, Stefan. I will take you as my husband. For this century, for all centuries." She started both laughing and crying.

"But you may lose your title!" he said, barely believing.

"Exchanging a meaningless word in front of my name for a life with you is such an easy thing to do."

For the rest of the evening they were wordless, rising from the garden chairs, going upstairs, slowly undressing each other, and slipping under the covers.

—

Stefan stayed the whole next day. Aside from the Landrecht, there was also the issue of Aunt Catherine to discuss. Her actual permission was not needed, but her blessing was of great importance to Lisa. And Lisa was still dismissive about her possible loss of her title. "In important ways, not being a countess will be liberating; no one can tell me anymore that I can't perform because I'm an aristocrat. Besides, the High Chamberlain's

Office is not as tight as it was in the day of Maria Therese. The High Chamberlain's agents were everywhere, sniffing for moral decadence. I think her son, Joseph II, doesn't have the appetite for invading bedrooms that his mother had."

They were enjoying a breakfast of Eva's rolls, sausage, oranges, butter, and coffee. Stefan broached the subject that was hanging like a too-large chandelier in the room.

"So we should address how to approach your Aunt Catherine."

"Armed with a musket?" She was in a bubbly mood despite the seriousness of the subject.

After a hearty belly laugh, Stefan continued, "The question is, who asks her? Shouldn't I? I did make the proposal."

"Definitely not. You're very brave, *chevalier*, but she is more formidable than you could know. The ground must be prepared for you to see her. What you must understand is that she is convinced that you're working to get something from me. With Charles it was to have a decorative female toy. Aunt Catherine is still convinced that you want my money and are putting up a façade to get it. Her allowing us to have music lessons is one thing. But the idea of marriage would confirm all her worst fears about you. Nothing can persuade her otherwise."

"In the twentieth century, such a person is called a gold digger. It's usually applied to women."

"I think the only path is for me to appeal to her and to try to convince her that you are not a…gold digger." Lisa sighed. "I'm to see her tomorrow. I'll begin making the case." She took a breath and said, "She cannot stop me legally."

"Lisa, I want you as my wife with all that I am, but I know the responsibility you bear for her. We can wait."

She said simply, "I do love you so."

—

Lisa waited for Stefan the next evening in the garden. He exhaled and asked, "What news?"

Lisa shook her head sadly. "Not encouraging. She cut me off after a minute, said I needed not to let my heart run rampant, and that I could not risk my title. I said that this was the first time ever that my heart had been engaged, and that I trusted it. She then went on and on about the consequences should the marriage proceed. I pressed, insisted that you wanted only my heart. I said that my life was full with you, and that I had experienced the emptiness of times without you and would rather die than do so again. And that I cared not a whit about the title." She paused and said decisively, "And that I did not intend to live without you. She was shocked by that. But she ended the conversation by saying she would think on it and be in touch with me."

"That was bold."

"I meant it. I'm not losing you and wanted to let her know."

———

Lisa waited for the reply from her aunt. It did not come in a day, a week, or weeks. They kept their scattered schedule of time together, but they both longed to be furtive lovers no more. An anxious cloud developed between them. Was she going to have to defy her aunt's will? Lisa could not bring herself to break with the last member of her father's generation.

The days crept by. Lisa became more and more distraught, both by the frustration of not being able to start a new life and by the wall that had come up between her and her aunt. Stefan tried mightily not to add to the pressure rising in her, but he could not hide his own growing restlessness.

Lisa was finally resolving to make the painful break when word came one afternoon for her to come to her aunt immediately. The old lady had collapsed and was unable to speak.

Stefan waited on the couch in the library through the night, dozing intermittently. Finally at first light, he heard the carriage wheels approach. He opened the door and took Lisa into his arms. Her face was drawn and colorless.

"She had some kind of apoplexy." Her face winced and she put her hands to her forehead. "Have I caused this? Like my father?" she asked in anguish.

Stefan took her by the shoulders and bent to meet her at eye level. He said with soft intensity, "Your monster of a husband caused your father's death. And you did not cause this for your aunt. The older we all get, the more vulnerable we are to being stricken like this."

Lisa slowly nodded.

"You were with her through the night?"

""I dozed on top of the covers beside her."

Lisa lay her head on his chest, utterly drained. "Is she still asleep?" he asked.

"No, she awoke. And when she did, she had regained a little speech, but with difficulty." She raised her head and placed her hands on Stefan's chest. "I must sleep now, then go and be with her. And stay with her," she said.

Stefan took her hands in his and pressed his lips on her fingers. "You are *not* to concern yourself with me right now. I'll be here for you." He smoothed her hair back from her forehead and said softly, "I will pray for her recovery. She needs you and you need her. Now go and rest."

—

Lisa's stay extended into a third week as, much to everyone's surprise, Aunt Catherine did not die. Nor did she particularly improve, except for her speech. The whole left side of her body was stricken. Lisa was there for all the tasks: bathing, dressing, toilet, and meals, working alongside the servants.

Stefan and Lisa stayed in touch by messenger. When Lisa told him the old lady was becoming depressed, Stefan suggested moving a pianoforte into her bedroom so that Lisa could play for her. He wrote, "It will be found in my time that recovery from some serious ailments can be helped simply by a positive attitude. She does love music…and it might help you stay in better spirits as well."

The moving of the instrument from the ground floor took the better part of a day. Lisa began with an hour of Bach. It seemed to have little effect, but on the third day the baroness asked her to continue, and she played even more the next day. After a week Lisa wrote to Stefan that her aunt's spirits were rising.

On a day when the afternoon sun filled the room, Lisa finished a Haydn sonata that had just been published, and the baroness seemed more responsive. She called Lisa to her side and, with a nod, indicated her left hand. "Look what you're done for me." She slowly closed her fingers into almost a fist, then opened them again.

Lisa was joyous. "Aunt Catherine! That's too wonderful!" And she leaned forward for a half embrace.

Improvements were incremental but steady over the next days. The old lady even smiled, mostly with the right side of her mouth. One day she said, "You have not left me for weeks, dearest. What about the other people in your life?"

"You're speaking of Stefan, Aunt?"

The baroness nodded.

"I've not seen him in weeks, but we communicate daily. My playing for you was his idea."

The baroness's eyes brightened. "And he does not demand any of your time or attention?"

"He insisted I not be concerned for him. He is praying for your recovery."

The baroness's right eyebrow moved slightly higher, and she looked down thoughtfully. "He would seem to be an unusual man, even if not of noble blood."

"Most unusual, Aunt, of any blood."

After a long pause during which Lisa could see her aunt's thoughts churning, Catherine looked up at her and said softly, "Perhaps I have judged him too harshly." Lisa's hands came to her mouth. "Could you ask him to visit me?"

Lisa dropped her hands. "Oh, Aunt Catherine, I'll do better than that. We'll both play Mozart for you."

———

Stefan came the next day. He brought a chair to the bedside and sat silently for a moment, thinking the baroness would speak first, as would be proper in a meeting between their respective ranks. But she simply looked at Stefan, as if trying to penetrate this mysterious commoner.

Finally Stefan took the initiative and reached for the baroness's right hand. He kneeled and lightly kissed it, then still holding it, he said, "Your Ladyship, it would be my honor to bring the healing power of music to you."

The baroness then smiled, and it encompassed both sides of her face. She said in a dry tone, "Well, Herr Radowitz, as you and my niece will certainly marry after I am gone, I thought I should take advantage of the time remaining to me to meet my nephew-to-be."

Stefan and Lisa exchanged looks of shock and amazed joy. Breaking their locked gaze with difficulty, they sat and played a Mozart four-hands sonata. Afterward Aunt Catherine beckoned for them, reached for them with her right hand, and in the process of doing so, was able to slightly raise her left arm for the first time since her collapse. Lisa saw this and quickly circled to the other side of the bed to grasp that hand as well. They sat quietly for several moments on either side of her. The baroness looked at one, then the other, and simply said, "Blessings." She never mentioned Lisa's title again.

Chapter 51—New Life, New Opera

STEFAN AND LISA were married on the fifteenth of September at St. Michael's Church, one of the oldest in Vienna. It boasted a stunning interior, including a ceiling-to-floor sculpture behind the high altar, the *Fall of the Angels*, and a magnificent organ. The air was taking on the sweet and heavy end-of-summer smell, with the afternoon light becoming more gold than yellow. The attendance at the ceremony was small, by Lisa's choice; she said the only people she cared to see at her second wedding were ones she or Stefan cared about to begin with. She still had some friends from childhood, like Charlotte, and several of Stefan's and Wolfgang's musician friends were invited.

The highlight of the wedding was Mozart's presence, as Lisa and Stefan had asked him if he would escort the bride down the aisle and present her to the groom. He was delighted to, and as promised, he cooked up a surprise.

Just when Wolfgang and Lisa appeared at the back of the church, a number of musicians of all types filed into a transept next to the altar. Mixed in with them were singers in costume. At Mozart's signal from the back, they began to play. The music was the wedding march from the end of act three of *The Marriage of Figaro*. The orchestra played the rousing march, then two sopranos, looking no more than aged thirteen or fourteen, stepped forward and sang the exquisite little duet in which thanks is expressed to Count Almaviva for ending the hated right of the master to take any young bride's first night. The whole chorus then took up the call of praise for His Lordship. The music was brilliant and joyous, and the couple both dabbed their eyes as Mozart tenderly passed Lisa's arm to Stefan.

———

In the carriage bound for Baden after the ceremony, Mozart's actions were the first thing they talked about.

"We could not have been more graced if the Pope had attended," said Lisa.

"I think no one, not the pope, not the emperor, not the king of England, could have come close to matching the gift he gave us," Stefan responded.

"Wolfgang's greatest gift to me was bringing you here."

On a sudden impulse, Stefan said, "He is in love with you, you know."

Lisa, through a touch of a smile, said, "I know," and looked out the window. Stefan wisely said nothing.

———

They spent a week in Baden, and Stefan experienced his first hot mineral baths. They then returned to Charlotte and Gregory outside Wiener Neustadt, where they rode and hiked in the foothills of the Alps and paid a return visit to the forest pool (which Stefan greatly preferred to the mineral baths).

Upon their return Stefan moved his few belongings to the Nightingale Street house. By law he could not take the title of count, but the servants wondered if he should still be addressed as *my lord*, as master of the house. He consulted with Georg on the matter and decided that *Herr Radowitz* would continue to do just fine, as it always had.

He kept his small apartment, saying that it was still an ideal place for his pianoforte and voice students. He did not want to inflict the shock on his students of coming to a lavish house after his little studio, which he preferred for teaching anyway. He also wanted to stay as financially independent of Lisa as he could. That anyone would think his motivation was marrying into money was anathema to him, although he knew he could not prevent people, especially the Viennese audiences, from seeking the fun of scandal, real or manufactured.

When Stefan was not teaching or copying, he and Lisa spent days walking or riding into the fabled Vienna Woods to see the Austrian maples put on their autumn explosion of reds, oranges, and golds. Evenings they spent at the pianofortes or reading to each other, a pastime that Lisa came to love, especially being read to sleep.

They also attended performances at Emanuel Schickaneder's new Theater auf der Wieden. Schickaneder was mounting a series of fairy-tale operas that were very popular with the suburban audience where the theater was situated. They had merry postperformance outings with Schikaneder, who was riotously funny. Stefan, with difficulty, refrained from telling Lisa that in a little over a year, they would be sitting in that very theater marveling at Mozart's penultimate opera, itself a fairy tale, and perhaps the most beloved of all his works.

—

While Lisa and Stefan floated through marital bliss, Mozart's fortunes were in steep decline, with performances few and debts mounting. Tragedy struck for Constanze and Wolfgang when on the fifteenth of November a little girl, Anna Marie, died within hours of her birth. The moment they heard, Lisa and Stefan went to the Mozarts to stay with them. They rotated with other friends of Wolfgang and Constanza to make sure they were always attended in this terrible moment. On the first visit, Stefan found Wolfgang sitting alone in his study, pale, drawn, exhausted. Wolfgang saw him, and his face and whole body drew into a look of agonized query. Stefan did not wait.

"Wolfgang, you will have another son who will grow to adulthood." Wolfgang's face drew up tightly. Stefan stepped near and accepted the tight embrace around his waist. He wished that he had told Mozart earlier about this last child, but that would have burdened Wolfgang with the knowledge that a child in Constanze's womb was doomed.

———

In the aftermath of fiscal woes, loneliness, and the grief of burying yet one more child, Mozart created another masterpiece with Lorenzo da Ponte, the opera *Così fan tutte, ossia La scuola degli amanti (Thus do all women, or the School for Lovers.)* Stefan was heavily involved in the preparation for the January twenty-sixth premiere. Mozart and da Ponte worked at top speed because it was a royal commission, and because the emperor was home from the war front, gravely ill. If he died then Vienna would start a period of mourning, and rehearsals would be stopped. Stefan was again put to work in Wolfgang's service.

Stefan gave Lisa previews of the opera she was about to see, playing it at home and talking through the plot. She thought at first it was absurd: Pairs of lovers swapping partners in a farce initiated by the men, prodded by a cynical father figure and an equally cynical and worldly wise maid. The men playing dead, to be aroused by a magnet held by the maid disguised as a quack doctor! The women falling for it, but the men as well, realizing that they did not know their own hearts. When the ruse is revealed, all is forgiven, and all are wiser.

"Mozart and da Ponte chose *this?*" she asked incredulously, before hearing a note of the music. "Where is it from?"

"I understand the story is original with da Ponte," Stefan replied with a shrug.

"It's hard to see how such a silly tale can carry Mozart's music."

"A great writer in my time talked about the sublimated eroticism in Mozart's music," Stefan said, "but in *Così*, it's much more on the surface." Lisa raised her eyebrows at this and said, "I'm not exactly sure what that means, but knowing that you know of things to come is sometimes unnerving, my love."

———

They sat at the opening performance, and soon Mozart's new (to Lisa) waves of sensuality began to roll over them.

The opera begins in gay innocence, both the men together and the women declaring their unassailable constancy to their paramours, and vice-versa. However, the men accept a bet from an older friend that they, could, in disguise, seduce the other's beloved. Lisa was at first exasperated with this silliness. Then, as the men supposedly depart for war, some newly ravishing music emerged during the farcical farewells. Lisa took Stefan's hand as the two girls and the older friend pray for gentle winds, while the orchestra mimics waves lapping at a boat. Time stood still for this moment of sensuous beauty wrapped around human sorrow.

The end of the act sees a fierce refusal by the ladies of the advances made by the men in ridiculous disguise. At the intermission Lisa was still not sold. "It's beautiful and the finale is exciting, but where can this go? They've been rejected, the opera is over."

"Ha! Far from over, my love. Remember, they all have Mozart's music to sing to each other."

Act two sees the two women melt in the onslaught, one very quickly. The first seduction number, between the baritone and the mezzo soprano, begins with courtly innocence and a flirtatious game with a locket, but then it takes a turn toward a lush, darker palette in which the first sister loses herself. The play now turns serious. *"What Vesuvius erupts in my chest?"* she asks as the music throbs around her. The new lovers' voices then wrap around each other, obviously to be followed by entwining of another sort as they leave the stage.

Lisa's face flushed, and she whispered, smiling, "There must be a ban on music this…" She paused, looking for the right word. "…provocative."

"The word in my time is sexual."

Lisa smiled, "Yes. The notes do make love."

The other sister, a soprano, holds out far longer, and sings two dramatic arias in which she declares emphatically and heroically that she is going to do the right thing, no matter how drawn she feels to the stranger. She decides that she will, in disguise, join her beloved on the battlefield. But her pursuer finds her and stops her with a vocal line of such beguiling beauty that all her walls come down, and she sings her surrender. As the two sang their ecstatic lines, Lisa's hand was at her mouth again.

After the opera ended, Stefan said, "Now they know real passion and heartbreak, unlike what they have read in novels."

"He finds a musical voice for every minute shade of love. I think the sheer beauty of *Così* surpasses even *Figaro* and *Don Giovanni*." Her face glowing, Lisa turned to him and said, "When we get home, I want us to take a bath together. With bubbles and champagne."

———

Lisa had a large bathtub that they both fit into.

"Stefan, when did you first want me?" she asked, moving the sponge slowly across his back.

"Well, I first noticed you at the *Figaro* premiere when you cried at the end."

"You saw me then?!" she said, greatly surprised, pulling him around, water spilling onto the floor.

"I could see you from backstage. From that moment you haunted my thoughts. I began to want you when I met you at the Countess von Thun's salon. And when you played Mozart's sonata for me, I fell in love with you. Same question to you," he said as he turned back and leaned through the suds into her breasts.

"Well, I noticed you at the concert when Wolfgang played his concerto between the Dittersdorf pieces. You were following the music with your body and that made me think you knew it as well as Mozart. Makes perfect sense now."

"You were there?!"

"I noticed you to a much greater degree at the *Figaro* performance you conducted, when you looked at me, and then at the salon at Lady Thun's. I fell in love with you through our lessons. And during the two-piano concerto slow movement, I began to want you. Rather fiercely. I think for women, love comes before desire." She began to purr, "Mmm…but then…the desire rushes to catch up."

With this she reached to sponge him on his front, his chest, abdomen, and lower. He began to vocalize with low moans, which encouraged her to continue her duties. Stefan, unable to be a passive recipient any longer, rose to his knees, turned around, and lowered himself, sliding his feet under her thighs. He then put his hands on her hips to slide her forward over him. They had not done this before, but Lisa quickly grasped the intention and lowered herself onto him easily. They began their rhythm and accelerated quickly, causing major water spillage. Lisa's expression took on an astonishment that Stefan had not yet seen, and her cry in her climax was more sustained than any he had heard, almost a keening that finally diminished into soft sighs as she fell forward. Her grip on Stefan with her legs on his sides and hands on his shoulders stayed tight for several moments more. He was about to become concerned when Lisa raised her head and, smiling at him, said gently, "Let's get in bed."

———

She slid off him, and he stepped out of the tub and helped her up, wrapping her in a towel as she stood. They dried each other with care and slipped under the covers, drawing close.

Stefan heard Lisa draw a breath to speak. "That almost scared me. Did any of the other women you were with, you know…?

Stefan formed the sentence with care. "Not like you just now."

He could tell her brow was furrowed. "Is there something unnatural with me? I thought I might faint."

Stefan raised himself to look down on her. "*No.* Everything is ever so right with you, in so many ways."

"Well, I'm relieved that you think so." She then spoke in an urgent but confidential tone. "Stefan, I want you every day." She looked at him expectantly for a response.

"Lisa, I thank God that you want me as I want you. Yes, every day."

She drew herself close upon his breast. "Good. Because I will want you again at sunrise. Maybe before. With me on top."

"Your most humble and obedient servant, My Lady."

———

Così did fairly well at the box office, even with a five-month suspension of all performances in Vienna on the death on February twentieth of Joseph II. The ascension of Joseph's brother Leopold II strongly concerned the composer. Even though it seemed that Joseph had blown hot and cold toward him, Mozart knew his patronage was always there when badly needed. He had no knowledge of Leopold. He worried now about his post as court composer, which required court dance music of him. The salary alone was not enough to support the family, but without it, they would have been in desperate shape.

The year 1790 saw Mozart's lowest output since his arrival in Vienna. His debts continued to mount, as did his entreaties to friends for loans, all of which amounted to borrowing from Peter to pay Paul.

Stefan's marriage meant he saw much less of Mozart, and he worried that Mozart, in his current low state, would hold this against him. Although he knew the basic history of Mozart's ups and downs and knew that he would have a great triumph once more with *The Magic Flute*, he still was distressed for his friend's current state. He invited Mozart for lunch at an inn that they had frequented in the first year of their relationship, hoping that they could rekindle a bit of the old comradeship. But Mozart was in too black a mood on that day, and that gesture exploded in Stefan's face.

"Interesting that you invited me to this particular inn," Mozart said in a numb, bleak voice. "Are you trying to remind me of what we once shared but do so no longer? Not that I blame you. Who would choose to spend time with this wreck of a man over a beautiful contessa?"

Stefan was shocked at this outpouring of raw jealousy. The man was at rock bottom and was deeply lonely.

"Wolfgang, I know I've been absent from you with my new life. Let me pledge this: I can't work for you daily anymore, but if you need me to help with any project, I'll be there. Lisa will too, if asked."

Mozart looked at his hands clasped on the table, then looked up. "Stefano, forgive me for that burst of childish jealousy. I'm jealous of both of you because you have each other, and I love each of you. But I am also truly happy for you in your marriage and grateful that we are together right now. It's wrong for me to blame my state on your happy marriage." He paused, then added softly, "But I still miss you terribly."

Stefan's throat was totally constricted, and all he could do in answer was nod.

Wolfgang then looked back at the table. "I am dried up, Stefano. In more ways than one. No concerts. No commissions. No music. Only debt. Darkness."

Stefan, his heart breaking, violated his vow once more. "Your fires will be stoked again, Wolfgang." Mozart raised his eyebrows at Stefan, who affirmatively nodded, then he looked away. "Well, the wood for the fucking fire is taking its bloody time getting here."

As always, Stefan later fretted about these moments. Had he changed the timeline by this partial leak to Mozart of his immediate future? Or was his part in history already written in? But if so, why was his name not in any Mozart literature? And if he had not made that last promise of better times to Wolfgang then would the composer have been headed to self-destruction, thus robbing the world of the last masterpieces? And if he, Stefan, wasn't here to intercede with Mozart, who would have? And how, if not through knowledge of the future? Stefan tried to work through this endlessly, with no result but a headache.

But 1790 did see some of Mozart's existing music receiving performances. The great clarinet quintet and a string trio were performed at a private residence, and some of his recent string chamber music was finally published. In June he took the ailing and exhausted Constanze to Baden for a protracted stay, probably for his sake as well as his wife's.

———

In contrast Lisa's own compositional fires were burning brightly during this time. There was less time for walking and riding, but Stefan was delighted to see her working. Her mind was as agile and quick as almost any he had ever seen. She often needed to work things out on paper, then at the keyboard, a process that gave Stefan great joy in observing. He felt he was in possession of the world's greatest secret, which was satisfying to a point, but it was a secret he was also eager to share. He and Lisa talked about a salon in her home, to which would be invited some of the Viennese music elite. They set a date, February fourteenth, 1791.

The rest of 1790 rolled by and remained distressing for Mozart. But Lisa and Stefan were in the glow of discovering each other through both love and squabbles (the latter usually about Stefan's wardrobe or lack thereof).

At some point in late 1790, Mozart's musical heart began pumping again, as Stefan had predicted. He completed two of the most beloved of his late works, a D major string quintet and a B-flat major piano concerto—his last. The concerto was dated January fifth, 1791. Wolfgang Amadeus Mozart, writing works that were more refined and more moving at the same time, had eleven months to live.

The couple did not discuss Mozart often, but they shared the terrible knowledge of what approached—Stefan's from historical knowledge, Lisa's from reading her husband. Some days he was stooped, physically and emotionally, as if carrying a dark weight, and she knew why.

Chapter 52 — Another Salon

THE FIRST DECISION to be made for Lisa's salon was, of course, what repertory would be offered. Lisa had a broad knowledge of piano repertory of the day, beginning with almost everything of Mozart's and Haydn's that was published. Thanks to her sessions with Stefan, who had been able to gather most of J. S. Bach's published keyboard music, she probably knew more of that composer's music than any keyboardist in Vienna.

The difficult decision was whether to play her own compositions. Lisa had to tell Stefan about the disastrous salon at the Countess von Thun's five years earlier. Stefan listened closely. She got to the end of the tale, her running from the room in fear and panic.

"And you had a bad reaction when I asked you if I could hear your music," Stefan commented. "That was from the same event in your marriage, yes?"

Lisa nodded. She looked in Stefan's eyes. "So many of those ghosts have been banished through your doing, your love. Might that carry me through this?"

"Listen to me, you're a student of Mozart. You are not the same composer as when you played at Lady Thun's. You have something powerful and cogent to say."

She nodded again and came up smiling. "Yes, many things have changed." She paused, then said decisively. "I'll do it. But I want you seated where I can look up and see you."

Stefan laughed. "I married a countess; I can sit wherever I want."

———

The newlyweds had their first real rows while planning the salon concert. The topics were common enough, but they did have different ideas about significant issues: the time of the concert, the order of the program, the placement of the instrument, and naturally, the invitation list.

It was not so much the substance of the disagreements as the tone. Stefan had vast experience in planning concerts, Lisa none. He knew that she would have her own ideas, but surely, she would listen to his logic, gained from so much experience in this area. Lisa never knew the term *mansplaining*, but nevertheless she reacted badly to being patronized.

"But this is your concert. Why do you want to end with Mozart's music?"

"I want to thank my friends for listening to my music by giving them something I know they will love. And I want you to be part of that…my husband sitting by me playing a four-hands piece."

"Isn't the whole point of this to make an impact for your music? You have a great ending piece, your *adagio* and *allegro*. They will jump out of their chairs!"

"Then they can jump a little earlier," she said, becoming heated. "We are ending by saluting Wolfgang! We owe him everything!"

Stefan saw that pressing further here would be costly, and he deferred. Even more serious was the issue of the guest list.

"Lisa, I know you may not care for Salieri, but his influence is enormous. He can help your visibility."

"The man stole a wealthy pupil from Wolfgang soon after he reached Vienna. Lady Thun told me about it. This is my salon, as it was my wedding, and these will be *my* guests."

"But that bad blood was long ago, and they are now friendly. Rivals, yes, but friendly. Mozart has gained the advantage over him on occasion as well."

"Is it not enough that I just don't want him? Must I do everything for an advantage?"

"Not everything, but given the opportunity…"

"Stefan," she said, her voice now quiet and steely. "I know that I am not in the history books in your time, and you want to place me there. Is that not so?"

The question brought him up short. He replied quietly, "Well, yes, perhaps I am trying to change the history books and set to rights a wrong that has been done to one woman. And by extension, all women."

Her voice and face softened, "Stefan, you have already changed history, certainly *my* history. Perhaps my music will become known to more listeners; I'd like that. But I am content for now to allow that to develop on its own. Maybe now. Maybe two centuries from now. But I wish for this outing not to bear such weight."

Stefan was moved by this. *Once again, she is my teacher.*

"Sometimes I am…a know-it-all," he spoke the term in English. "A conductor's curse. Forgive me. It is indeed your concert, and in your house. I am at your service, my love."

"And do forgive my unkind and childish outburst toward Salieri. He would be a distinguished guest. Let's invite him."

Later one thing she had said began to haunt Stefan: *"Maybe now. Maybe two centuries from now."*

———

The performance was February fourteenth. The program was a C major sonata by Haydn, Lisa's single movement *adagio* and *allegro*, an improvisation on an aria from *Così*, a longer fantasia of hers, and the Mozart F major four-hands sonata played with Stefan. This was the work that had broken through to Aunt Catherine, and the indomitable baroness was attending.

Her salon accommodated around fifty people. The crowd included a few friends, including Charlotte and Gregory; a number of members of the musical community, including Baron van Swieten and Niklaus von Jacquin, both important supporters of Mozart; Josef Luetgeb, dedicatee of a number of Mozart's horn concerti; and of course, the Mozarts. Salieri did accept the invitation, slipping in late after Lisa had begun. He stood quietly in the back.

When Lisa came to her own music, Stefan caught her eye and nodded slightly. She started tentatively, and Stefan had a momentary surge of panic as her tone became faltering. But he saw her set her jaw, take hold of herself, and plunge ahead in a fiery manner that actually drew a couple of gasps. Stefan noted to himself that a young virtuoso named Beethoven would draw similar reactions from the Viennese in just a few years.

The reception was enthusiastic. Lisa's music—and her performance of it—was warmly applauded, although it left some of its listeners puzzled. This was not true of three attendees: Stefan, Wolfgang, and Antonio Salieri. The latter waited until the crush of well-wishers had died down, then he quietly approached her and introduced himself.

"Your Ladyship, thank you so much for your invitation. I had advance warning both of your playing and the unusual but beautiful qualities of your music."

"Where on earth might you have heard such a thing?" asked Lisa in astonishment.

Salieri motioned his head toward Wolfgang. "He is an ardent admirer of yours. He suggested that I might possess a useful pair of ears for your music." Handing Lisa a card from his waistcoat pocket, he said, "I am at your service, gracious lady." With this he deftly took her hand, lightly kissed it, turned, and departed.

Stefan and Wolfgang took in the exchange and, both broadly smiling, glided up to Lisa, whose mouth was still open.

"I see you met my friend Antonio," said Wolfgang.

"Conspirators. I love you both, you scoundrels," said Lisa, shaking her head.

1 7 9 1

Chapter 53—Three Minutes

ON MARCH FOURTH, 1791, Mozart performed his last piano concerto in a small venue, Jahn's Hall, his last performance as a pianist. A month later, Antonio Salieri conducted what Stefan considered a masterful performance of Mozart's Fortieth Symphony and an aria sung by Caterina Cavallieri. It was a triumph for Wolfgang, and all adjourned to Salieri's spacious home near the center of the city, where fine wines and cheeses awaited them.

A circle developed with Wolfgang, Constanze, Aloysia, Lisa, Stefan, the hornist Luetgeb, and Salieri.

"Mozart, I performed other of your symphonies in Paris, you know—I carry copies in my valise—but never before in Vienna. This G minor symphony is sublime. From the gods, but difficult as the devil to play!" Salieri laughed. "And your new concerto last month was divine. Vienna waited too long for a new concerto from you." All present nodded in agreement.

Mozart was exuberant. "It was a wonderful night, friend Salieri, thanks to you. You know, I feel my fortunes are turning a bit. I received a letter from the soprano Josepha Duschek about a concert she sponsored in Prague at which she sang two of my arias, and a young Czech pianist played my D minor concerto. And," lowering his voice to a conspiratorial tone, "another opera may be aborning."

"The best news is that a new generation is discovering your music. May that happen for all of us!" said Salieri.

Stefan thought about how Salieri's wish would come true for Mozart but not for himself—Salieri's music would all but disappear from performances, even before his death. Salieri then bowed and excused himself to attend to patrons.

"You won't believe how that man is treated by history," Stefan whispered to Lisa. "What I just saw is a revelation."

"It's wonderful how Wolfgang's news is finally good. I understand his debt burden is also now lessened."

"How would you know that?" Stefan asked.

Lisa looked at her husband, smiled, sipped her wine, and said nothing. It was only a moment later that Stefan made the link with one of the questions historians had pondered—how it was that Mozart's considerable debts were lightened in 1791.

—

Another assistant had appeared in Mozart's circle in 1790, a young man named Franz Xaver Süssmayr. His arrival took a great burden from Stefan's shoulders, who felt that someone had arrived that could help Mozart in the ways that he, Stefan, had. Süssmayr also became Mozart's composition pupil.

Stefan took an immediate liking to the young Austrian. He had a nimble mind, a positive spirit, and was utterly dedicated to Mozart. Stefan knew of the contribution the assistant would make in finishing Mozart's last work, the monumental Requiem. Stefan invited the composer to lunch in early summer.

Süssmayr was in awe of the man who had been with Mozart for some of his greatest creations and plied him for war stories. He did have some news of his own for Stefan. "Herr Mozart said to tell you that he and Herr Emanuel Schickaneder are spending much time together," said Süssmayr excitedly over potato noodles and gravy. "Herr Schickaneder has a libretto, a story of a magic flute, that Herr Mozart loves. It will be produced at Schickaneder's Theater auf der Wieden." Stefan smiled, and also shuddered. Each historical event was one more step to the last event. Each day was part of a heavy tread toward darkness.

———

In June Constanze was again taking the water cure in Baden, while Mozart traveled back and forth from Vienna. Stefan recalled the circumstances of the premiere of what he felt to be one of Mozart's greatest miracles, a choral work of only three minutes, "Ave verum corpus." There were rapidly diminishing chances to share the premiere of a work dear to his heart with Lisa. Stefan knew the work was composed and premiered in Baden, so he arranged for a spa visit there to coincide with the historical record of that date.

Stefan shared with Lisa what he thought they might hear. "You know the text of the old Eucharist hymn 'Ave verum corpus'?" he asked.

"What good Catholic child doesn't?" she said. "It used to scare me with the talk of Christ's side being pierced and flowing with water, and the test of death. Now I think it's beautiful. The promise of rising to heaven by remembering the mortal body of Christ."

"It's Wolfgang's setting of it that I want you to hear. He'll write it for the local choirmaster for Corpus Christi feast day. Very simple, for a country church choir. Three minutes long."

"We're going to Baden to hear a new *three-minute work?*"

"Trust me."

She smiled and did a small curtsy.

———

They sat in the diminutive church with its small choir on the feast day. The strings and organ began the gently murmuring two-measure introduction. The choir entered with simple, sweet harmony, the strings undulating and caressing: *"Hail, true body, born of the Virgin Mary."* Mozart had found a sublime musical expression of Christ's suffering, which was the key to final release in heaven. The music was angelic and consoling. The most painfully exquisite harmonies of all lay under the line: *"Be for us a foretaste of heaven in the pain of death."* The short string choir epilogue was full of loving tenderness.

Stefan, his throat constricted, looked at Lisa, whose eyes were closed, cheeks moist. After the service they sought out a secluded park bench.

Lisa spoke first, dabbing her eyes. "His pain, then our redemption. The essence of Christ. In three minutes," she said, her voice breaking. "So beautiful that it hurts my heart…oh, Wolfgang…"

"A writer in my time called it 'the voice of God, a whisper in your ear, a breath.'"

"How could any but a divine being create that?" Lisa asked.

No, he thought, *he is not divine but mortal and will die in pain before the year is out.* The combination of the serene rapture of the music they just had heard and the approaching tragedy crashed on Stefan. He fell into heaving sobs. Lisa took him in her arms and gripped him.

Chapter 54—Last Premiere

BY MIDSUMMER 1791 Mozart and the impresario/singer/ librettist Emanuel Schickaneder were engrossed in creating *The Magic Flute* for the latter's Theater auf der Wieden. Mozart had to squeeze in a premiere in Prague of *The Clemency of Titus,* and they had to wait until he returned just weeks before the September thirtieth premiere of *Flute* to finish it. A healthy son was born to the Mozarts on July twenty-sixth; 1791 seemed full of rich promise for the family.

Another significant event for the Radowitz family was Lisa's commissioning of portraits of both of them from Constanze's brother-in-law, Joseph Lange. Stefan knew him to be the painter of a well-known unfinished portrait of Mozart. To someone of Lisa's station, it was a perfectly normal thing to do. Stefan found the hours of sitting boring and frustrating—he had real work to do. He grumbled to Lisa, "An improvement in my time is something called a camera, which can make an accurate image of anything instantly."

Lisa was unimpressed. "Where is the artistry in that?"

———

It was September thirtieth, and Stefan and Lisa shifted uncomfortably in the rough seating of Schickaneder's suburban theater for the opening of *The Magic Flute.* The suburban audience was of a different make-up than the social elites at the Burgtheater. Commonfolk--tradespeople, people in service, clerks--were mixed among the musical sophisticates. They were there for the fantastical entertainment that Schickaneder invariably gave them. But to have an opera by Mozart was special, as his legend was widespread. The air was electric.

Mozart entered to cheers such as in modern times would have been given to a star athlete. A brilliant overture, then a *dragon!* Howls of delight! The act unfolded with its effortless combination of the silliness of Papageno, the fearlessness of both the romantic Prince Tamino and his destined partner Pamina, and the majesty of the Temple of Wisdom and its priests.

Stefan waited for his wife's reaction to the act. She simply observed, "Sarastro's priests and their Temple of Wisdom…they sound like Freemasons."

"The opera is full of Freemason symbols."

"So Wolfgang is a Freemason?"

"Yes, he is."

"And Sarastro is inviting Prince Tamino to become a Freemason?"

"Well, he's inviting him to take the trials to see if he is worthy of Pamina. But basically, yes to your question."

She nodded, then said with wonder, "Wolfgang's music seems to get simpler yet also more beautiful."

Act two, Pamina and Tamino are allowed to reunite briefly, but because he has taken a vow of silence that she knows nothing about, he cannot speak to her. She thinks he has abandoned her and sings a heart-stopping aria of sorrow and longing for death. A heart-stopping aria of another sort comes with the appearance of Pamina's mother, the Queen of the Night, a force of evil. She flattens her daughter, and the audience, with a vengeance aria using previously unheard pyrotechnics in the stratosphere of the voice.

The evil queen and her minions are finally dispatched, with the opera ending in a blaze of Enlightenment glory. Wild, cheering, stamping applause ensued, especially when Mozart stepped out.

Lisa said, "At the end both Pamina and Tamino are in the priests' robes, so she has been admitted to the Order with Tamino." Her expression became pointed. "Are women admitted to the Masons?"

"No, I'm quite sure they aren't."

"Then I believe Wolfgang is making a rather radical argument about including women."

Stefan cocked his head in surprise, then smiled. "That had not occurred to me."

Lisa then said, "I hope the censors don't notice and shut it down. Because the whole world will fall in love with this opera."

"Yes, it will, beginning tonight. It'll run long here and soon will be produced all over Europe." He paused, considering how much more to say. "In my time, it's given dozens of productions around the world every year."

A few days later, Mozart happily related to Stefan and Lisa how Salieri had reacted to his new opera. "I sat with him and Caterina. He stood and cheered, 'Bravo!' after every number! He called it an *operone*, a grand opera!" He was in an enthusiastic state; things had not gone his way so consistently for a couple of years.

"And what is next, dear Wolfgang?" asked Lisa.

"Some weeks ago I received a very strange anonymous commission delivered by a messenger. For a requiem, can you imagine? Whoever is it for? Well, it's a very dramatic text, so it will be like writing another opera."

The sudden severe knot in his viscera made Stefan turn away.

In the carriage home, Lisa noted Stefan's distress. "What did Wolfgang say that upset you? Something about his requiem commission?"

Stefan closed his eyes then exhaled loudly. "I've been dreading hearing him tell us this."

"The requiem?"

Stefan looked at her with eyes stricken with grief. "It will be his last work. He won't finish it."

Lisa went white, her face pinched with pain. "Soon then."

"Soon."

Chapter 55—Lacrimosa

STEFAN'S DREAD WAS almost as great as if he were facing his own end. In his century Mozart's death at thirty-five was accepted by history as a tragedy, but it brought forth no feelings of personal grief over two hundred years later, even among those most dedicated to his music. But in 1791 Stefan felt both the intense dedication from a lifetime of study of Mozart's music, plus a personal knowledge and love of the man. His whole body felt painfully knotted as the tragedy drew nearer.

And what about the connection? What consequences would Wolfgang's death bring for Lisa and him? To his relief he felt no change in this strange, almost physical bond to the composer and began to think that if Wolfgang already had a terminal illness, and Stefan did not feel it, then perhaps Wolfgang's passing would not affect him.

He and Lisa were now rarely apart, and the stress of the pending loss made them snappish. Lisa wanted lovemaking, often and fierce. Stefan thought perhaps this was for her a bulwark against his being snatched away. If she could possess him completely enough…

Mozart had wild mood swings and began to speak of being poisoned. Constanze battled valiantly to keep him cheerful. He had become deeply morose about the imagined implications of composing a requiem for the dead—he sometimes speculated that it was for him—and Constanze tried to distract him by getting him to concentrate on a smaller work, a

Masonic cantata for a local lodge. This did brighten him up, as did the success of the new cantata on November seventeenth.

But two days later on November nineteenth, he was in bed, feverish and in sudden severe pain with swelling all through his body. He had been weak but still functional, then the bottom dropped out.

On the next day, the twentieth, Stefan felt several waves of heavy weariness in the afternoon. Lisa was out and returned at dinner time. Sitting down at the dinner table was their first contact since breakfast, and Stefan told Lisa of his experience. "The weariness is gone now. I think perhaps it's nothing"

Lisa's brow was still dark. "Is it connected to Wolfgang?"

"I'll go tomorrow and see him."

They spoke little through the meal. Afterward, they retired to bed, although they were far from sleepy. The November night was rampant with a bitter north wind, and they could hear sleet pelting on the window. They clung to each other as if in a small cocoon.

—

The next morning, Stefan went to the Mozart home. An obviously strained Constanze answered the door with her infant son in her arms and said, "Stefan, he is not well. His joints and stomach are swollen, and he is in pain. Franz is with him. He is insisting on composing his damned requiem!"

All was unfolding exactly as Stefan knew it would. The hot knife of sorrow pushed deeper and deeper.

"May…I stick my head in?"

"Yes, but don't tell others I let you in. He needs rest, and many have asked to visit."

Even though he knew in advance something of what awaited him, Stefan was shocked on seeing his friend on the bed. Wolfgang's facial features and joints were swollen, his countenance gray and lined. But on seeing Stefan he lit up. "Stefano!" he croaked. "I feel better already!"

Süssmayr was sitting near the foot of the bed with a lap desk and a table next to him covered with writing implements. Also in the room was

Sophie, Constanze's younger sister. Stefan did not look at Mozart, as he was suddenly seized by an empathic connection with Wolfgang's pain. It hummed for a few seconds through his entire body, then released. He stumbled, and Franz jumped up as quickly as he could to steady him.

"Sir, are you all right?" Franz asked as the spasm released.

"I'm all right, it passed." Steadying himself, he turned to Wolfgang and forced a bantering tone. "Well, I think you've had better days, from the look of you." Wolfgang waved him off, still smiling. "Can I bring you anything? Wine, schnitzel, a billiards partner who doesn't know you?"

"Stefano, I'm fine. My wonderful Franz is helping me with my requiem, as my hands are too swollen to hold a quill." He held his hands up; the fingers were swollen so much that bending a digit was not possible. "I must finish in time to conduct it at my own funeral!" This crushed Stefan anew.

"I'll let you two get back to your work. I just wanted to make sure that you're drinking enough wine."

"I am well cared for, Stefano, but please come back. If the swelling goes down and I look presentable again, please bring your beautiful Lisa. But not until I tell you!"

He did actually look far better when Stefan left than he did prior to the visit. Stefan resolved to come often before the terrible date. But when he was back on the street, he felt a bigger wave of exhaustion. He made his way home slowly, and by the time he arrived he felt normal again.

———

Lisa was sipping coffee in the breakfast room. Stefan came in and leaned against the door jamb. The anxiety on her face grew graver as she looked at him.

"What did you find?" she finally asked.

Stefan cleared his throat noisily, then said, "He's very ill. It's as described in the history books. Swelling all through his body."

"And you?"

She saw that he was carefully measuring his words. "I had a stab of pain throughout my body when I saw him. It passed quickly. I had a wave of weakness on leaving the house, and it passed as well. I feel normal now, although I am a bit shaky."

Lisa's face was grave. She summoned what steadiness she could muster. "What do you think will happen?"

"He's very ill, and I feel his illness. When he dies, I hope the connection will simply be broken with no other effects. Life may continue for us as it always has."

Both spoke with faltering voices.

"And your door back, and the choice?"

"There is no choice. *I belong with you*," he said, suddenly firm.

Lisa burst out frantically, "Stefan, tell me the date! Not knowing is killing me! How can I prepare?"

He paused, then said softly, "Just before one in the morning on December fifth."

"Please, keep nothing back from me about how you feel. *Nothing!*"

He took her up to hold close. "Never," he said softly into her hair.

—

The next week and a half went by without alarming setbacks for Stefan, while Mozart's decline was slow yet steady. Stefan visited several times, came away heartbroken, but physically feeling no worse. He began to think that he might escape the worst and that the bond might simply evaporate.

Stefan got a note from Süssmayr on December first, saying that Wolfgang felt better and was hoping to get a visit from both Lisa and Stefan the next day to sing through some of the requiem.

They were joined by Franz Gerl, who sang Sarastro in *The Magic Flute*. Braving the sickroom stench, Constanze, Gerl, Lisa, Stefan, and Franz crowded around the bed that held the almost unrecognizable man. They sang as much as he had written, up to the opening of the "Lacrimosa." Lisa told Wolfgang that it surpassed anything she had ever heard, from any hand. The sick man smiled lovingly at her, his hand over his heart, and Lisa gently kissed him. Wolfgang then began weeping. "I have failed my family."

"No, no, no, dearest, we are doing better now," insisted Constanze.

Mozart turned to Süssmayr and said, "You will finish the requiem as I have instructed you, yes? You must, for my family." Stefan knew that Süssmayr's version of a finished requiem would be the standard for two centuries.

"I will, upon my life, Maestro," he said, his voice filled with absolute truth.

———

Lisa quietly wept all the way home. Not soon after they arrived back, Stefan suffered a wave of dizziness and had to sit at the breakfast-room table. A shaking hand brought a cup of steaming coffee to his lips. He almost dropped the cup when Lisa emitted a short scream.

"Stefan! Your hand! Look!"

Putting the cup down but still holding it, he saw what caused the scream. His right hand had become semitransparent, and he could dimly make out the lines of the cup that should have been covered by his fingers. The vision receded as the hand filled back in.

He stared fiercely at his hand. He inspected it, flexing it, wiggling his fingers. All of it worked.

Her face frozen, Lisa asked, shaking, *"What just happened?"*

Frigid horror gripped him. "I…I started…to fade."

"Like Wolfgang is fading."

Stefan looked at her silently, then slowly nodded his head.

"And when Wolfgang fades from this world on the fifth of December, so will you."

He nodded again, but then said, gathering strength, "The difference is that I *will not die.*"

"Stefan!" she burst with a cry as she rose. He jumped up to meet her, and they embraced in near fury, Lisa pounding his back with her fists in anger.

"You *must* come back, *you must!*" she said repeatedly through heaving breaths.

"I will come back through a thousand hells," he said.

She pulled away from him. Her sobs ceased but her voice shook. "Stefan, I made you promise to let me know whatever your body was feeling. I owe the same to you"

"Yes?"

She wiped her cheeks and said, "While I was married to Charles, Eva's grandmother, who is known as a healer among the Roma, got for me some herbs from which I would make a tea. It was to keep me from conceiving a child. Charles knew nothing about it. It also had a soothing effect. And as you and I had not discussed…children, I kept taking it after we met."

"Yes?" Stefan had not known any of this.

"I stopped taking it in early fall. And I became even more ravenous for you." She looked up again. "My flows…are late this month. Two weeks. Forgive me for not telling you of all this. I was so used to being secretive about it."

The dawning implication was thawing his puzzled expression. He asked carefully, "Is this unusual for you?"

"I am never late. I was waiting…for this all to resolve somehow; I kept telling myself it was nothing, caused by all of our anxiety. But," she said, putting her hands on her belly, "somehow I know now." She locked her eyes to his. "Stefan, I'm carrying our child."

Speechless, he took her face in both hands. How could anyone grasp this new joy in the face of such disaster without rupturing? They were holding each other up but barely, both sets of knees faltering. "Oh, my love!"

"May God smile upon the three of us."

Without another word they retreated to the bedroom and climbed under the coverlet, still clothed. They held each other close, not speaking, and a rare, peaceful sleep was granted to them, as if bestowed by a beneficent presence.

———

After that initial shock, the couple realized they had preparations to make and not much time.

If Stefan disappeared, then an explanation had to be found. "I think we need the brains and strength of Georg," said Lisa.

"We'll have to tell him about me."

Lisa managed a smile. "He's known for some time. He, like others, could tell that you're just…different. One night, out of concern, he closely examined me about you. So finally I told him."

"And he believed you just like that?"

"Yes, he did. I told him of Wolfgang. And I've never told him anything but the truth."

—

The plan the three worked out was that Lisa would tell everyone in a few days that Stefan had left on a concert tour of France. A long one. His failure to reappear—if he did not reappear—would be attributed to unknown foul play, but Lisa would not give up hope. She would have to put on her bravest face.

There was not as much discussion of how Stefan would return. Lisa asked, "You came through a connection with a great composer whom you love. Are there any more like that?"

Stefan said, "Yes. Ludwig van Beethoven, a young man living in Bonn. He will become a titan like Mozart, but different. Mozart has made the world more beautiful. Beethoven will upend it. He'll be in Vienna in a year. I'll wait in my time until you've had a chance to contact him, then I'll try to reach him as I did Mozart. At his grave. He is second only to Wolfgang in my heart."

He added, "You must make contact with him. He has to be told that if he dreams of me, he must try to make contact in the dream."

Lisa thought for a few moments, then asked, "But how will you know when I've contacted him? I'll have been dead for many years in your time."

Stefan wrestled with this new conundrum. If they were in the same continuum, the contact would already have been made when he arrived back. But what if the two times were structured differently, parallel universes running in tandem but independently? That might mean that

Stefan would have to time his actions so as not to move before Lisa had made contact with Beethoven. How would he know?

Katrina suddenly came to his mind, and the letter he wrote and left for her at the British Museum. "Leave me a letter, like I did for Katrina. In it you can tell me of our child and when you see Beethoven." Stefan balled up a fist and lightly pounded his forehead. "Where is there safe keeping for a document for over two hundred years? All the massive museums and government buildings I know of won't be built until the nineteenth century."

She considered this, then asked, "Do you think my house will last?"

Stefan knew that central Vienna had been bombed repeatedly in World War II and many buildings were destroyed or heavily damaged, including the State Opera. He could only hope that Lisa's home was far enough from the center. "It's as safe as any place I can think of. In my time many grand homes from this period are still around."

"Then follow me." She took him by the hand and led him to the back of the garden, to a far corner. "I have a bronze storage box. It should resist the elements well." She tapped her foot in a corner. "I will write to you and bury the box here, maybe half a foot deep. Come find it." She looked at him, her eyes burning and urgent. *"Find it,"* she said fiercely, gripping his hand hard. He looked at her and simply nodded.

———

On December fourth they laid the plans with Georg and spent the day literally side by side, as if attached. Lisa kept looking to see if the transparency effect made an appearance. She did not see it, but Stefan did while shaving that morning, as the razor handle shone through his hand.

At six o'clock in the afternoon, Stefan said, "I must go say goodbye."

She whirled and said, "No! What if he dies while you're there?"

"He doesn't go until after midnight. I'll be back."

———

Stefan entered the sick room. Constanze's younger sister, Sophie, sat on the bed. She rose when Stefan entered. Wolfgang's swelling was worse; he was unrecognizable. Stefan's legs almost gave out under him.

Settling gently next to him, Stefan whispered "Wolfgang…"

Wolfgang was unable to speak but formed with his lips "Stefano" and made a fleeting hint of a smile.

Stefan bent close to whisper. "I am going to break my vow once more and reveal to you two future events. The first is that your family will be well cared for. Your new opera will make much money, and Constanze will become a brilliant money manager. Your sons, Karl and Franz, will grow to be fine men, both, under her care.

"The second is to tell you that in my time, your name will be honored around the globe as the greatest of all composers. Not just well known. Revered, worshipped. To say the name Mozart will be the same as saying the word music. That is what brought me back to you, and to Lisa."

Wolfgang was listening with his eyes closed but opened them at Lisa's name. He gave Stefan a tender glance, then closed them again.

Stefan bent closer and said, "I love you, Wolfgang Amadeus Mozart," and gently kissed his hot forehead. There was another thin smile and a trickle of a tear.

———

At Nightingale Street, Lisa awaited his return. Each tick of the clock was a stroke of calamity.

Stefan was in a weakened state and struggled to make the journey back. When he arrived, Georg greeted him at the door. "She is in the bedroom."

Stefan entered to find her standing by her dressing table. She was wearing the same gray velvet nightgown she had worn the first time they made love. She turned to him.

"If I am to lose you soon, then I want as much of you as I can have now." She dropped the gown off her shoulders to reveal her simple nakedness. "Love me, Stefan."

He disrobed, and they made furious love, Stefan roused once more by Lisa's undying passion. It was all they had left against the fear and loss. They entwined and merged, crying out painfully at the finish.

Done, they spoke, still locked together, one last time. A whisper, "You complete me, Stefan."

Stefan whispered in answer, "You are the universe holding me, Lisa."

"Come back to us."

"I will find you both."

Then there were just moments left. They stood, Stefan dressed, and they embraced. *Never let go!* Both wept on each other's shoulders.

Stefan drew a stabbing breath that he knew was Wolfgang's last breath. A strong shock took him. Before Lisa slipped into darkness, he heard her roar of anguish.

"STEFAN!!!"

Like Tamino with Pamina, he could not answer. The door opened, and he was ripped through it, powerless. Then all was black.

Lisa's grip on his solidness started to soften, as if he were becoming like dough. His final fading away was quicker than an eye closing. She felt the howl of grief exploding from her, then all was mercifully black for her as well.

2 0 1 8

Chapter 56—Home and Home

THE FIRST SENSE that made its way through Stefan's blackness was smell. Or rather a stench, of some foul thing burning.

He was not yet able to think, as his nervous system was still firing spasmodically. The first thought that rose was, *That hurt way more than last time.* The next thought was the identification of the smell. The old Vienna boasted a bevy of foul smells, all organic, but not this one—fumes from internal combustion engines. He had accepted this smell as natural once. Now it was nauseatingly strong.

Then he noticed the light—early morning. But it was after midnight…He struggled to his hands and knees and looked. *Grass?* But he was in the bedroom…*Lisa!!* He looked to his left. The Mozart memorial, the sad angel. *Wolfgang!!* He was in St. Marx Cemetery, his starting place more than six years earlier. The moisture of her tears and her smell was still on his jacket.

The completeness of the dual catastrophe hit him, and he let out a long wail of despair. That spurred a coughing fit such as he had experienced after the transition back to 1785. It was violent and painful, as if trying to expel something. It finally ended, along with the impulse to scream.

As devastated as he felt, he grasped that now was not the moment to vent his grief. The dreaded thing had happened, and it was not unexpected. He needed to find out to when he had returned. The year, by his reckoning, was 2024, having started the journey in 2018. What was the world like? He looked at his garb and remembered that he had put on his six-year-old suit, the one that he had borrowed from the State Opera costume shop for the benefit concert with Julya. He had an idle, crazy thought that he should return it, though many years late. It looked in decent shape. No. He would need it again.

Would he have to walk the three miles to Vienna once again? Then he remembered that he had stashed his wallet and mobile in a deep crack in the old wall. They would have deteriorated, but perhaps some of the euros might be salvageable.

He found the stash with no trouble and pulled the items out onto the grass. They were astoundingly well-preserved, not a blemish or water stain. A couple of hundred crisp euros were nestled in the wallet, and his credit cards and driving license seemed not to have aged.

This was startling. Cautiously he picked up the smart phone, so familiar and yet so foreign, and out of habit pressed the home button. Katrina's laughing face popped onto the screen, giving him a start. How was there still a charge?

Then the time on the display:

06:21.

And date:

1 November 2018.

Stefan's mind went to neutral, then started looking for explanations. The phone's processor had frozen, of course. He stared at the screen, trying to will this into being true.

Then a digit advanced:

06:22.

OK, it wasn't frozen right now but had been. Something he had done taking it out had…unfrozen it. Try the internet, some news website. Try…bbc.com.

The BBC website popped up with the lead story having to do with a row between the mayor of London and the imbecilic US president, a story he was aware of. He looked at other stories, found some that had been current in 2018…and seemed to still be so. The smart phone was in perfect working order and fully charged. With that, bewilderment descended on Stefan, growing into fear for his sanity.

He had six years of the most extraordinary memories but could technically account for only six hours of it. He felt weak, on the verge of fainting—the same feeling as the first time he entered Mozart's house.

This is not happening. This is not happening.

He had to get somehow back to Vienna and away from the cemetery. He looked at the app on his mobile and ordered an Uber. Just like old times.

———

He entered the lobby of the hotel dressed exactly as he had left it the previous evening. He did not have his room card but the clerk remembered him, and with a brisk smile, provided another. Opening his door, he picked up the light disinfectant scent, then went to the closet and saw his hanging shirts and trousers. On the second bed was his suitcase. His mind and heart were screaming, and he wondered how long he could hold off screaming for real.

Hallucination? Six years' worth of fantasy that happened between the time he blacked out and the time he woke at dawn? Did a maddened mind really invent the myriad detail, the tapestries of soaring emotion, the music, the heartbreak, the love? The six years he had experienced were every bit as real as his shirts hanging in the closet. *Yet, why is it not 2024?* Stefan felt as though his soul was being ripped in half.

He took the coat off, thinking to change and get himself back to London and Katrina, whom he had seen a month ago, or six years ago, as quickly as he could. Even if she concluded that he was insane, she would not judge him, just love him.

Pulling his arm out of a sleeve, he heard the crinkle of a piece of paper. He retrieved it and saw a folded note of beautiful, thick, textured paper. He opened it, expecting some new assault on his senses.

It was Mozart's note of introduction to the Countess von Thun for Stefan for the salon where he'd finally met Lisa. Mozart's signature was unmistakable. And the paper was not brittle with age.

It happened. *It happened!* The explanation might never be known, but the only thing that mattered was that the last six years were real, not spent on a ventilator in a hospital room. Somehow he had swapped six hours for six years, and now he had to give them back.

Stefan's first reaction was immense relief that he had not lost his mind. Before long, that was replaced with holes of bottomless grief, for Wolfgang and Lisa, blasting into his soul. His tears trickled, then flowed, then poured. Stefan wept long, like a small boy. And midway through this tempest, the one bright spot in his circumstances blossomed and buoyed him—he would see his beloved Katrina, whom he had been resigned to never see again.

Chapter 57—Search Engine

AS SOON AS he could gather himself, he forced some food down. The hotel coffee was a pale shadow of Eva's, but caffeine was caffeine. The lift was welcome and was amplified by thoughts of Katrina.

He would call her, but he had to prepare so as not to cause alarm. She would not be expecting a call, but he yearned to hear her voice. In this time, they had spoken recently. How could he disguise his blasted state from a person who knew him completely?

Keep it short. If her questions became too sharp, put her off. He knew he would go to London, so the tough questions could wait.

Her bouncy greeting made his whole spirit leap. "Da! Kind of early in the day, hey?"

God, her voice! "Oh, I'm sorry! Did I wake you?"

"I meant early for you. I'm always up by now."

"Well, maybe the old dog is learning new tricks." He was making an effort to keep his voice at his normal low pitch.

"Concert go well? Did you have a nice suit?"

"Concert fine, suit splendid." *It has lasted for six years of daily wear.*

She lowered her voice conspiratorially. "Did you take the opportunity to visit Mozart?"

He had forgotten that he had shared this ritual with her and waited a little too long to answer. "Oh, well, I did…I'm coming home soon, will fill you in on Mozart." He could feel his voice starting break at the thought of his friend.

She spotted it. "Da, are you OK?" *Her radar is always perfect.*

Denial was useless. "Well, it has been a strange experience. But not on the phone."

"When are you coming to London?"

"Give me a week. I need to sort some things out."

"Dad, sort *what* out? Is your ticker OK?" Her stubbornness called Lisa to mind.

"Kat, my heart is fine, really. I'll tell you the story when I see you. I promise."

Her voice now heavy with concern, she said, "OK...Call if you need me. I love you, my pop."

He was swept by a love whose expression had been long denied.

"Kat, I love you so much," he said, his voice quavering.

OK. That could have gone better, he thought, sagging into the chair, sleep finally taking him.

———

Upon arising he took his first hot shower in twelve hours or 227 years, depending on the perspective. He felt only marginally stronger, but he had to set about his prime mission: the letter box buried at twelve Nightingale Street—if the house had escaped American bombs.

He took a cab to the address. If anything, the whole street looked grander, with mature trees lining it. When he saw number twelve, his heart squeezed hard. It had not only survived, but it had also changed little. And the garden gate to the side was the same.

Stefan's strategy was to be direct and try to talk his way in—knock on the door and explain that he was a descendant of a resident of centuries back and that there was family lore about something buried in the garden. Might he have a look? He had bought a simple metal detector at an electrical supply shop, which he carried in a black case, hoping it would not cause suspicion.

He half expected Georg to open the door, but there was no response to his knock. He had tucked the garden gate key into his waistcoat pocket when they'd hatched the letter plan, and there was no one about now. Should he come back at night? No, if someone saw him slipping in at night, it would be highly suspicious. He was there, and things were quiet; he would summon his most confident bearing. Unlock the gate as if he owned the place.

Amazingly, the lock had been oiled and maintained, and it still worked, and the noisy tumbler clacked. *How many times did I do this in the dark?* he thought.

The architecture of the garden was completely different, for which Stefan was grateful; he did not think he could bear walking in the same patterns as Lisa had designed. He strode quickly to the back corner and located the spot she had indicated with her foot.

The soil was soft, and he swept the detector over a wide area. The bronze box was not there.

—

Stefan retreated to his hotel room. He despaired at the missing letter box, but he had faith it had been there once. The only path left was to go directly to the current owner. He started looking through city tax records on the Vienna municipal website.

The structure of the website was Byzantine. Terminology was unclear, and not a few links were broken. But he finally found the records for Nightingale Street. And the owner and resident was a Rheinhardt Radowitz, architect, aged forty as of 2017. The house was still amazingly in the family, under his family's name. Which meant that the child Lisa carried in 1791 was a son. And he had grown to adulthood and had had male offspring to carry the name. This was thrilling news. Rheinhardt was the family name of Lisa's father. And this Rheinhardt was his great-grand-son times…four, five?

Stefan googled Rheinhardt Radowitz, found the name of his architecture firm, and sent him an email at his business address, introducing himself as a distant relative who would like to call on him. He immediately received an away-from-my-email reply, giving a return date three days hence.

Stefan spent three lonely days wandering aimlessly about Central Vienna, desperate for the comfort of his daughter's voice, but knowing that the next time they spoke, he would have to unload his tale. And he wanted to do that in person.

Finally the email popped up. Apologies, the family had been on holiday. Yes, please call at home two days hence, at ten o'clock in the morning, for coffee.

—

Not Georg, but a tall and strikingly handsome man with dark hair opened the door. He took Stefan in with a top to bottom glance, then had an odd, fleeting look of recognition, which passed. The man extended his hand, and both his strong grip and his facial structure reminded Stefan achingly of Lisa. He stepped into the house, so familiar and loved but now so strange, and held on tight.

"A great pleasure to meet you, Cousin," said Rheinhardt warmly.

"And you, Cousin Rheinhardt," Stefan responded, trying not to get swept away as he stepped inside.

"Would you like a quick tour of the family castle?" Rheinhardt offered. Stefan wanted very much to see the house but also dreaded it.

"Yes, of course," he said, with all the phony energy he had.

The library was a shock. Shelves, books, all gone. In the corner was a small Bösendorfer piano, a chair, and music stand, set for performance. The room had been turned into a music practice and listening studio, with an elaborate audio system on the opposite wall. Plush chairs that swiveled were placed in the middle for listening to whichever end of the room was producing sound. "The library was here, but the books have been moved to an upstairs study." Stefan was relieved that they still were in the family.

They walked through the house at leisure, with his host giving Stefan a brief history of each room, some of which he already knew. The house had all new furnishings. It was an echo of the Secession period at the turn of the twentieth century, simple and utilitarian but elegant. But it both gladdened and pierced Stefan's heart to see Lisa's old pianoforte lovingly set in a corner of the parlor.

"Is the pianoforte still played?"

"Oh yes, my grandfather was an ardent amateur pianist and had it painstakingly restored. I play a little, and our children both take lessons. It's not gathering dust."

"Do they prefer the modern or the period instrument?"

"They do have a special love for the pianoforte, I think, just because it's a treasured family friend. The stories it could tell!"

I could tell you many of those stories, Stefan thought.

They ended up seated in the breakfast room next to a beautifully appointed modern kitchen. Gone, of course, was the large open fireplace and the wood burning stove on which Eva had long ago created such miracles. The drastic change of the kitchen hurt Stefan, as it was one of his favorite haunts with Lisa for late night snacks.

They sipped a good Viennese roast that Rheinhardt brewed, as Eva had done scores of times in that very room for Lisa and him. He was hanging on by a thread.

Rheinhardt spread his large hands. "I am so glad you contacted me. Tell me, how did you find my name?"

Stefan was ready for this. "A friend of mine in London is thinking of relocating to Vienna. He knew I would be here, and he asked me to research some neighborhoods and architects. Your name was oddly familiar when I saw it," he said with a short laugh.

"And do you know how we are related?" Rheinhardt asked.

Stefan was ready for this too. "My daughter is an amateur genealogist and said that we have a common great grandfather times five. Our DNA should be a match."

"Then we were meant to find each other! What brings you to Vienna?"

"I'm a musician and had a concert at Schönbrunn Castle a few nights ago. My engagements often bring me to Vienna. I love the city, so I come as much as I can."

Rheinhardt's face lit up at this. "Ahh, amazing! I've started doing some family genealogical work, and there were several musicians among my forebearers, and yours. There was a female ancestor who lived here, a countess who was said to have played with Mozart. Maybe in this house, on our instrument."

Stefan tried with all his might not to show how shaken he was at these words. It did not work. He was weak and dizzy, and his heart was skipping beats.

"Stefan, you've gone quite pale! Are you ill? Do you need a doctor?"

Stefan gathered a breath. "Thank you for the concern. I recently had a difficult trip, possibly with an episode of food poisoning. I'm fine, though."

Still, Rheinhardt regarded him with worry. "Well, you will let me know if you need anything. Honestly, you look exhausted. Why not rest here? Stay for the night and meet some other relatives."

Rheinhardt's kindness touched Stefan. He tried to focus, but he had close to nothing left in him. He needed to get to the point of the visit and back to the neutrality of his hotel room.

"Nothing would give me greater pleasure, but I have a pressing errand, then I must go. The errand is with you, actually. It's very, very odd."

His host leaned forward, eyebrows raised. "Whatever I can do."

"Rheinhardt, do you know if any of your ancestors ever made reference to a small bronze box buried in the back corner of the garden? It contained letters."

Now it was Rheinhardt's turn to lose color. He was perfectly still, but his face showed a sudden disturbance. "Stefan, I must ask you to excuse me for a moment," he said, his voice betraying some shock. Stefan heard him walking up the stairs, then back down. He was holding a sturdy plastic shopping bag, and he was clearly rattled.

He spoke slowly, carefully. "Four years ago, we were having drainage problems in the back of the garden. We called a landscaper, who did some excavation to reroute the water flow.

"We did indeed find a corroded bronze box. There were two letters enclosed, very old, both with the remains of wax seals. The lettering was indecipherable, faded from all the years of moisture."

Stefan wrenched anew at this.

Rheinhardt noted Stefan's reaction and quickly added, "That's not the end. I have a friend in the archaeology department at the university who has access to various types of scanners. He was able to read the script.

"The letters are dated 1792 and 1793 by my great-grandmother times five. Elisabetta, the musician, who called herself Lisa. They are addressed to Stefan, her husband. They are beautiful letters, full of love and sorrow. Why they were hidden the way they were was a mystery to me, but my scientist wife, Josephine, conjectured that they were meant to be read by someone in the far distant future from when they were written. Time travel is alluded to in the letters. Outrageous, I thought. Our argument was heated!

"My reaction has been, for a long time, that this was a hoax. Someone in the landscaper's office, perhaps an amateur genealogist, found out about my ancestor and made this elaborate physical evidence. Pointless, perhaps, but maybe there are types of practical jokers who like to keep the joke to a small circle.

"But Josephine is a physicist whose field is string theory, and she refused to dismiss their authenticity out of hand. She has done work on the nature of time. She thinks traveling backward in time unlikely, but a maxim for her is that the universe is far stranger than we can even dream. She also believes that any differences we perceive about past, present, and future are mental constructions, and that there is no difference between them. Much like the early Buddhists said. She insists we cannot dismiss any possibilities.

"She even wondered if someone named Stefan would one day knock on the front door and ask for the box." Stefan found his hand going to his open mouth, much as Lisa did with high emotion. Rheinhardt opened the bag and unwrapped the package from layers of bubble wrap. It was a six-inch square bronze box with a latched top, pitted and corroded.

There was also a plain manila envelope, presumably the transcriptions. "Until now, I have always been skeptical of the implications. But no one else knows about this, and you have the right name." He held it out to Stefan and said solemnly, "I think this belongs to you."

Stefan's hands shook noticeably as he took it. The latch was long gone, but the hinges still worked, and he creaked it open. The original paper was there. He then started to open the clasp on the modern envelope, but Rheinhardt put his hand out to stop him. "Stefan, you will want to read these in private."

Stefan meekly obeyed and closed the clasp. His tears were starting to spill, and Rheinhardt offered a box of tissues.

Rheinhardt said, "I cannot wrap my mind around even a fraction of what your experience has been. You were...are...Elisabetta's husband. And you knew Mozart."

"I lost them both the same day," Stefan choked out.

A new realization showed in Rheinhardt's face. "My God, Stefan," he said, "You lived *here!*"

"From 1789 to 1791."

"This is your house as much as mine."

"It was Elisabetta's...Lisa's when I lived here."

Rheinhardt allowed a small smile. "I should address you as a count."

The smile was returned. "I didn't even let the servants call me that."

Rheinhardt became serious again. "Stefan, how long have you been back?"

"About a week."

His host was aghast. "You must be overwhelmed."

Stefan's face winced. "I fully intend to return to Lisa."

"Dare I asked how this happened?"

"Of course, and I will tell you...but just not at this moment. I don't have the stamina now to relive it."

The two men sat in silence, both stunned. Rheinhardt finally spoke. "I have one more thing to show you. First, a question. Did you and your wife ever have your portraits done?"

"I did, in Spring of 1791. Lisa's sitting was scheduled, but then Mozart's illness...my departure..."

Rheinhardt's eyes widened. "Who was the artist?"

"Joseph Lange...He was Mozart's brother-in-law and did the famous unfinished portrait of him."

"Could you follow me?"

He led Stefan out of the breakfast room, into the hall, and through the doors into the formal dining room. Stefan was surprised and delighted to see that the sturdy table and chairs were the same set he had known. They were a contrast to the rest of the newer furnishings.

Rheinhardt gestured to a portrait on one wall near the head of the table. "Does he look familiar?"

It was Stefan in his performance pinstripes, trying to make a stern eighteenth-century expression. "Oh my God..." The artist's name and date were clear in the corner.

Rheinhardt said, "I decided earlier not to believe what my eyes told me at the door. But I think I must apologize to my wife for doubting."

He touched Stefan and turned him around to the opposite wall. "Brace yourself."

There was Lisa's portrait. Her hair partly up with combs and partly down, in the arrangement that Stefan loved. A garland of small blossoms formed a tiara, which she often wore. Her look, down and to one side as was Mozart's portrait, was gently pleasant, but Lange had caught the sadness in her eyes.

Stefan emitted a cry, and fell into Rheinhardt, who was expecting it and held him up. Stefan reached toward the portrait but did not touch the surface. "Lisa...," he gasped. The younger man slipped a chair under him.

Her green eyes were like the tidal waves of music that had washed through him so many times. He did his best not to explode yet again in tears.

"Is it dated?" Stefan asked as he looked closer. "Yes. 1792. I was pulled back in 1791, when Mozart died."

"Why don't you take her with you, on your mobile?" Stefan gratefully acknowledged the suggestion and took a set of photos. "She was a great beauty," said Rheinhardt.

"She still is," said Stefan, emphatically. "And she is one of history's great musicians. She's still there, across time. Right now. No matter what it takes, I will return to her." He held up the bronze box as if in affirmation.

Rheinhardt asked, "When will I know the whole story? And Josephine must hear it. She was an early believer."

Stefan replied, "You deserve nothing less." He paused. "I'm not sure what I'm going to do or when. I need to get to London to see my daughter. Then I'll come back to Vienna, to make the return to…" He gestured to the portrait. "I hope to have Katrina with me, and we can call on you. I'll tell you all there is to know. And I'm eager for her to meet you.

"But for now, Rheinhardt, I must get back to my hotel. You're right. I am terribly drained."

Rheinhardt called an Uber, then said, "It has been wonderful to meet you. *Please* stay with us when you return. We would so love to meet Katrina." They shared a brief but hard embrace. Rheinhardt pulled away, took Stefan by his upper arms, and squeezed so hard it hurt. "This is your home for all time, dear great-great-great-great-great—is that enough?—grandfather Stefan."

Stefan turned to go out. Looking back, he held up the box with a smile, "I must go read my mail."

Chapter 58 — Mail

STEFAN SHOWERED BEFORE opening the box. He was terrified and tried steadying himself with some Irish whiskey from the minibar.

He first inspected the letters themselves and with difficulty made out the shadows of a few strokes. Thank God for forensic science.

Stefan opened his phone to one of the photos of Lisa's portrait and propped it up. He then pulled out the transcripts. Even on plain office paper with a standard font, the words rolled over him like a great cadence in Mahler.

Vienna
7 November 1792

My most beloved Stefan,

Almost a year has gone by since that terrible night that we parted. I wanted to let enough time pass so that I could report more completely to you things other than just a chaotic outpouring of sorrow. It seemed that any delay on my part could not be noticed immediately by you, 230 years in the future.

It is my greatest joy to tell you that we have the sweet blessing of twins! A strong and beautiful son whose name is Stefan Wolfgang Amadeus Mozart and an exquisite daughter named Amelie Maria Antonia. Born the fourteenth of July. I wish now I had one of those marvelous devices from your time (that I disdained) that can make an instant image on paper. They look more like you than me, but I'm told that they have my eyes. Little Stefan smiles and laughs frequently, while Amelie is a little quieter and more thoughtful, but also with a beautiful smile.

Our babes have been my anchor to this world. After you were taken, I spoke often to you with my hands on my growing belly. It was all I had of you. Since they were born, I talk to them—and you—all the time. They, and through them, you, are my all. Our lives are quiet and uneventful. We spend each day rarely separated, and they both seem to enjoy my practicing (although Amelie listens more patiently). Playing the pianoforte also calls your presence to me, of course.

Oh Stefan, the depth of my grief sometimes is bottomless, but our beautiful children help to pull me back. As does this act, finally, of putting pen to paper for you to read. That we are somehow communicating, I in this moment, you in your moment. Who is to say what the true measure of time is? Who is to say that I am not writing this at the exact moment you are reading it? That in writing it, am I not touching you, here, in this eternal now? Are we ever really parted?

Are you finding that you missed things there while you were here? I remember some of the medical miracles you told me about, and I pray that you don't need them. Please, do not be in one of those fast carriages you spoke of. They sound terribly dangerous!

I went to Mozart's memorial service a week after his death. They performed as much of the Requiem as he finished, which wasn't much. I'm told that that lovely man Süssmayr is finishing it.

Of course now that Wolfgang is gone, Vienna is paying all manner of homage to him. It seems that Constanze has a gift for business and is realizing several new sources of income. Salieri has been kind to the family.

Young Beethoven will be here soon, according to your history. I will wait before contacting him. I think he will need time to find his footing here before I reach out. An addled contessa asking about his dreams may not be received well in the midst of the chaos of moving. I will be patient.

Yes, my heart, I will be patient. I will wait for you for as many lifetimes as it might take. But not too many lifetimes…Please, come back to us. Come back to us.

Always, always, until time ceases.

Lisa

The second letter was briefer.

1 July 1793

Stefan, my love,

Just a quick note before this goes underground. Beethoven is coming to see me tomorrow! I asked him to my salon, and he graciously accepted. He will be a little surprised that he is playing for an audience of one, but I want him to myself.

Stefan, I do not know if time flows parallel or at the same speed in our separate times, but please, my love, try to make the transition through him as soon as you can, as soon as you read this. God grant that this makes it to you!

We will be together again in God's good time. I know it.

My heart, your heart, our heart.

Lisa

New grief tore through him at these words from his long-dead wife. Yet he had only recently been with her, and he knew now that neither life nor death was absolute. She was somewhere, fully alive, and he would reach her.

He found Lufthansa's website and made a reservation to London for the next day. He then texted Katrina to tell her that he would be coming home. A clear path seemed to emerge from the dark haze; but he knew he needed Katrina's help in walking it.

Epilogue

May 1793

LISA WAS AWARE of almost the exact moment that Beethoven arrived in Vienna in November 1792, less than a year after Mozart's death and Stefan's disappearance. She tried, through friends like Lady Thun, to keep tabs on him. He began to build a reputation as a virtuoso pianist and gained access to aristocratic salons. The city began to buzz about him being the new Mozart.

Lisa held in check her impulse to make contact with him, thinking that he needed some time to become established before she approached him with something that might well be considered bizarre. She also had little to do in Stefan's absence, save receive condolences, and she was very much a hands-on mother, reluctant to consign the baby to servants' care. As she had written to Stefan, the little boy, just now learning to walk, was what kept her from an abyss of despair.

But after six months, time enough surely, she penned him a note asking him to visit the Countess Elisabetta Radowitz in her salon. She would be pleased to hear him play a composition of his, if that were possible.

Beethoven made his way to the beautiful Nightingale Street, striding with purpose as he always did. He knocked and was admitted by a polite but stern-faced Georg. He was dressed fashionably in a well-cut suit. Nevertheless, his presence was slightly unsettling. He wore no wig, and his dark hair was bushy and curly. His face was wide, and everything about it was strong, with no delicate features—an expansive forehead, large expressive eyes that were slightly scowling, a wide sensuous mouth, and an intimidating square jaw that was articulated by a pronounced dimple in his chin. Lisa had heard from friends about how he radiated a sense of power.

The countess had come to the front hallway to greet her guest. Beethoven's look lightened as Lisa approached with her hand extended.

"So good of you to come, Herr Beethoven! I have long anticipated meeting you." Her poise, beauty, and grace disarmed him instantly, and he displayed a warm smile that portraits of him never caught. He took the proffered hand and touched it delicately with his lips. He noticed that her hands were large and strong, a match for his own muscular grip and steely fingers.

Retiring to the salon, she offered a coffee service and effortlessly led him though small talk and supremely delicate pastries. She noticed him looking to see if anyone else was in attendance; he seemed quite surprised to see that she was alone.

"Are you settled comfortably in Vienna, Herr Beethoven?"

"I am lodging with Prince Lichnowsky. He and his wife are most generous."

"Excellent! They were very close to Mozart, as you probably know." She smiled briefly. "They were at my wedding. And do you have everything you need?"

Beethoven said in a suddenly gruff and annoyed tone, "The only difficulty has been to procure a quality instrument, as the rental pianofortes in Vienna are usually *abominations*. To rent a good instrument is expensive, but I finally found one that I can almost afford. Such a difficult city."

She had seen him cast a discerning eye at her very fine instrument made by Anton Walter. She also noted the confirmation of what she had heard—that he could be brusque and was not one to mince words.

The chat continued and then seemed to have run its course. "I would love to hear you play this instrument, Herr Beethoven," she said, indicating with a gesture.

He stood and bowed formally. "It would be my honor, Your Ladyship."

He sat self-consciously at the pianoforte and tossed off some scales and other figurations at dazzling speed, taking the measure of the tone and touch of the instrument. He cast a quick glance toward her with a smile that acknowledged its high order of craftsmanship. Taking a deep breath he announced, "This is the first movement of a sonata that is unfinished. There will be a set of three. This one is in F minor."

Beethoven began the brisk first movement of a sonata. Lisa was immediately caught up. The fast arpeggio that opened was not a traditional, shapely melodic gesture; with lightning speed it became a building block in a quickly moving trajectory. The bass line was a powerful part of the restless unfolding, and the left hand was the absolute equal of the right, sometimes downright adversarial with its stabbing accents. As light and transparent as the texture was, there was a surging energy overall, an impatience to keep moving—Haydn and Mozart's language, but with a sweeping drive that was new.

Not long before the end, Lisa's hand had gone to her open mouth, as she often did when moved. The music had lifted her, and she felt she was running beside some powerful animal. The sudden end shocked her. She remembered vividly Stefan's description of this young man as one who would "upend the world." She had now had a glimmer of that potential.

Beethoven looked up at her and smiled. "Is this too coarse for you? I get that criticism. I am asked, 'Where is Mozart's beauty? Haydn's charm?'"

After a breath she said, "This is neither. But it is Beethoven's drama."

After a longer pause, Beethoven said, "Frau Mozart tells me that you compose. Would you do me the honor of allowing me to hear some of your music?"

Deeply blushing, Lisa shook her head no, but then he began to insist.

She had not played for anyone else since Stefan's departure and felt shy, but she knew that it was somehow right that she reveal this side of herself to this man, especially after hearing his boundary-pushing music.

Reaching into a leather folder on the pianoforte, she pulled out a manuscript. "It's...a fantasia. Like most of my works."

Beethoven smiled amiably. "That sounds lovely."

Lisa's hands trembled slightly as she spread the manuscript pages on the desk. She sat then played the first music she had composed after Stefan's departure back to his own time.

The low, rumbling bass notes in fifths that slowly began to move and enrich harmonically raised Beethoven's eyebrows. Then out of the moving harmony rose a single tendril of a few intervals that transformed itself into a sweet and yearning melody that coaxed the low rumble into a tender accompaniment. Lisa heard a quick intake of air from her guest. And a soft vocalization.

Lisa plunged into the tale of the musical fantasy, with its pulsations, sudden contrasts, and harmonic drops that Stefan had loved so. She had her own piano technique in mind when she had composed it, and her technique was formidable. When, after several turns through light and dark, she brought the work to its gentle close, she looked at her guest, who was open mouthed and wide-eyed in astonishment.

Lisa was suddenly choked with emotion. Beethoven leaned forward, about to speak, but Lisa held up her hand.

"That was the premiere performance. It's the first full composition I've finished since my husband's departure."

"I know of your loss, My Lady. I offer heartfelt condolences."

After a pause she asked, "Do you have any comments to make?"

Beethoven snapped into professional mode, jumped up, and abruptly seized the manuscript, thumbing through it until he found what he was looking for. He spoke bluntly. "Your transition here is ill-timed." He turned more pages. "Maybe here as well, I'd have to hear it again." He added ruminatively, "Transitions are the hardest. I've been studying Mozart's for years. He made it seem so easy.

"But *here*..." He pointed emphatically. "I was sure you had written yourself into a corner. Yet you resolved it so unexpectedly with the sudden *pianissimo* and the drop of a third in the bass. It was not a transition. It was a revelation."

After a pause he added, "There is great feeling here. I hear your loss, but there is also hope."

"Yes," she answered quietly. "It's all there."

"Your level of craft is already high. And just as important, you are composing from the heart, and to the heart. That is our highest aspiration as artists."

Beethoven replaced the manuscript on the desk and sat back down.

"With whom have you studied?" he asked.

"I had counterpoint lessons as a child with Herr Fux and pianoforte with Herr Steffan. I was fortunate enough to have compositions lessons with Maestro Mozart. Now I see Maestro Haydn for composition."

Beethoven burst out, "As do I! Have you shown him your fantasia?"

"Goodness, no! He would disown me. I show him short works that are more like his."

"But you played it for me?" he asked, more gently.

"I…thought you might be more open to it."

Beethoven paused, a finger resting on the big chin. Then he sat up and looked directly at Lisa.

"My Lady, you are an artist. Your music is a bridge to…somewhere new, something full of wonder, exactly where or what I can't tell. I would be honored to look at more of your music and try to help you."

Lisa was as flabbergasted as she was on hearing that Mozart would teach her. She stammered, "Herr Beethoven, I…yes, yes." That was all she could manage.

He raised an index finger. "One stipulation."

Her heart pounding, Lisa said softly, "Yes?" What could this possibly be?

"I will do it if I can in turn play for you *my* music and hear your comments to me as a composer. Haydn barely looks at my exercises and constantly tells me what not to do. Your ear may help open new paths for me."

Lisa managed to get out, "It would be my honor."

Beethoven pulled out a pocket watch and, after a glance, said, "I am afraid Prince Lichnowsky has plans for me later today, and I must go and prepare. Shall we meet again, say in one week at the same time, and hear more of each other's music?"

Lisa was trying to calm down and catch her breath. She thought of Stefan's first visit, when he was too shy to suggest another meeting. No shyness in this young man! "Yes, I would very much like that."

On their way to the door of the salon, Lisa put her hand on Beethoven's arm. "There is one thing more...silly, fantastical, maybe."

"Your Ladyship, anything."

"My husband, Stefan, knew of you when you were coming up in Bonn. Please don't think me an addled fool but..." She stopped and turned to face him. "I have reason to believe that he may come to you in a dream. If he does, please...try to make contact with him. I know it sounds utterly mad, but...if you could indulge me in this promise, then I would be most grateful."

Beethoven raised an extraordinary eyebrow, then lowered it and smiled gently.

"Do you have a likeness of your late husband?"

"In the front hall. A portrait done two years ago." She indicated where it hung. Beethoven walked up to inspect the portrait, then froze, his face falling. He stared intensely at the image.

"Herr Beethoven, what is it?"

Beethoven turned to Lisa and said in a secretive voice, "My Lady, I dreamt of this man three nights ago. It was him, I am certain. He was trying to make contact with me, but he faded before we could touch."

Lisa Radowitz went pale, her eyes rolling into her head, and Beethoven caught her as she slumped, unconscious.

Finis Part One

Appendix—List of Works

In order not to run afoul of possible copyrights of videos, the works appendix lists only the names of the works with the page number from the text. A simple internet search using these titles will reveal numerous recordings of each these well-known works, usually on YouTube.

———

The designation of "K." represents the work of Ludwig Ritter von Köchel, a chronological listing of Mozart's works, finished in 1862.

———

All works by Mozart unless otherwise indicated.

———

Printed in the USA
CPSIA information can be obtained
at www.ICGtesting.com
LVHW050606051223
765725LV00033B/395

9 798822 913646